M. WILLIAM PHELPS

THE GIRL LEFT BEHIND

A *Linda Kane* Thriller

SUSPENSE PUBLISHING

THE GIRL LEFT BEHIND
by
M. William Phelps

PAPERBACK EDITION
* * * * *
PUBLISHED BY:
Suspense Publishing

Copyright
2020 M. William Phelps

PUBLISHING HISTORY:
Suspense Publishing, Paperback and Digital Copy, September 2020

Cover Design: Shannon Raab
Cover Photographer: Shutterstock.com/ Aleksandra H. Kossowska
Cover Photographer: Shutterstock.com/ Arlo Magicman

ISBN: 978-0-578-74255-7

SENSITIVITY WARNING

This book contains elements of racism and violence.

ACKNOWLEDGMENTS

This novel is the culmination of four years of writing and editing—20 years of being involved in true crime. Stephanie Finnegan helped me shape this book into the final version you are about to read. Along the way, Stephanie was instrumental in pushing me to write the best book I had in me. I appreciate her dedication to the craft of writing and editing.

Shannon and John Raab at Suspense Publishing were excited after reading the manuscript and I could not be happier to have the book land at Suspense—a publisher that still cares about writing and, most importantly, the enjoyment of reading.

I could fill pages with those in my life who have supported me. They know who they are. Readers continue to support my nonfiction, and I am in awe of each person who spends hard-earned money to buy one of my books. It's humbling. I am very grateful.

Lastly, there are moments in life when what might seem like a momentary decision to go east or west, instead of your normal north/south routine, occurs and your life changes instantly. One of those moments occurred for me during the Covid summer of 2020. I went east, walked into a building and knew, upon walking out, that my life would never be same. Regardless where this unanticipated direction takes me, I am grateful for that day, meeting L.A., and will be for the rest of my life.

PRAISE FOR M. WILLIAM PHELPS

"M. William Phelps dares to tread where few others will: into the mind of a killer."
—*TV Rage*

"Phelps is the Harlan Coben of real-life thrillers."
—Allison Brennan on **TOO YOUNG TO KILL**

"A chilling crime…award-winning author Phelps goes into lustrous and painstaking detail, bringing all the players vividly to life."
—*Crime Magazine* on **NEVER SEE THEM AGAIN**

"Phelps gets into the blood and guts of the story."
—Gregg Olsen, *New York Times* bestselling author of *Fear Collector* on **KILL FOR ME**

"Phelps expertly reminds us that when the darkest form of evil invades the quiet and safe outposts of rural America, the tragedy is greatly magnified. Get ready for some sleepless nights."
—Carlton Stowers on **MURDER IN THE HEARTLAND**

"M. William Phelps is the rising star of the nonfiction crime genre, and his true tales of murder are scary-as-hell thrill rides into the dark heart of the inhuman condition."
—Douglas Clegg on **EVERY MOVE YOU MAKE**

"Readers will be rewarded with shocking television-worthy twists in a story with inherent drama."
—*Publishers Weekly* on **OBSESSED**

THE GIRL LEFT BEHIND

M. WILLIAM PHELPS

PROLOGUE

EXCEPT FOR MAYBE THE previous day being Halloween, there was nothing different about the night the girl went missing. November 1 was, traditionally, the unofficial end of the autumn season in New England. The rain was coming. The last of the bronze, orange, and red leaves would soon fall from the trees and stick to the ground like wet newspaper, collecting a scummy film, slippery and slimy, leaving branches stripped bare. Then the kind of cold air that seeps in through windowpanes and underneath drafty doors would settle in—and with it, a gray, gloomy send-off to the holidays.

Darkness and seclusion: the bottom of the ocean.

Leading up to that night, Cassandra had felt invisible for months. In that respect, she didn't need to be among the missing. If you asked Cassie, her world had become a bubble of teenage mediocrity no one else could possibly, like, understand. Okay, perhaps she'd brought it on herself. Or she was overreacting. Regardless, Cassie's life had spiraled into an abyss, where a lack of hope seemed more painful than death. Anyone who truly knew her would have agreed with that.

When the eleven o'clock hour passed and she had not yet returned home, initially, there was no need to panic. Cassie was forever late and unreliable, anyway. Like the time she'd promised her mother she'd make it to her sister's recital.

Didn't happen.

Or when she said she'd escort Katherine, nervous and not wanting to go, to that kiddie birthday party up the street while Mom worked a double.

Again, a no-show.

That was Cassie's modus operandi: make promises you never had any intention whatsoever of, like, keeping. Typical fifteen-year-old. Her life was more important than everyone else's.

Cassie's world revolved around, well…Cassie.

<h1 style="text-align:center">1.</h1>

AS LINDA KANE UNHOLSTERED her weapon, she crouched down and got a good bead on where the suspect stood. She understood that a split-second decision had the potential to change the course of a life.

Not always for the better.

The detective was positioned alongside a rack of potato chips, gluten-free corn poppers, wheat crackers, and various salsas sitting price-tag-out on a metal rack. The pharmacy counter was to her right. A blood pressure station you sit down in, with the short tube to stick your arm through, sat to her left.

There were no customers nearby.

Kane viewed the world much in the same way she did her own life: on the defensive. Lined up at the end of the barrel of her Glock 23, her right palm on the grip, left eye squinted, her index finger was poised to drop the unlucky son of a bitch.

She did not flinch. Linda took a quiet breath in through her nose. Slowly exhaled through her mouth.

"You'd be wise to put the weapon down, son," Linda said. "Then lie face down on the floor, arms behind your back. This can all end peacefully, without anyone getting hurt."

As soon as the words left her mouth, Linda knew they sounded TV-cop-like. These situations never went that way.

He looked toward the cop. Back at the pharmacist.

At the cop.

At the man in the white lab coat with his hands up.

"We can talk this through," Linda said.

He pointed his weapon at the detective, then at the pharmacist. Rubbed his mouth on the back of his wrist. His right leg twitched. He took deep breaths. In and out. In and out.

He needed that dope. It was a matter of necessity. A desperate man would do anything. Linda had seen it too many times.

Rexel's Drug had put up a sign months ago that the pharmacy did not stock OxyContin any longer. Yet, it did not stop the tweakers and dopers, who seemed to hit the place up every few months, thinking that maybe the sign was nothing more than a ruse to keep them away.

The detective peeked around a display of reading glasses on a carousel in front of her. This doper, Linda guessed, was in his late twenties. He epitomized the new drug addict in town. He could have easily passed for one of those Ivy League college kids, suburban-white, clean-cut, same as you might see on the news standing in court, nose in the air, a scowl born of family money, facing a judge on rape charges. A lacrosse or soccer standout. Blond hair. Blue eyes. Clear skin. Docker pants. Collared shirt. Boat shoes. If he wasn't holding a .38 snub-nose pistol, the serial number surely filed off, Detective Linda Kane would have believed he was in the drugstore to buy Altoids and a pack of menthols. Dude belonged at a Tiesto concert taking Ecstasy with other white kids, drinking gallons of water, dancing under laser and strobe lights all night long. Not in the crosshairs of a detective, flanked by several blues, ready to take him out with one shot.

"Open the safe and take out the Oxy," he said. His voice phlegmy and hoarse, shaky. "Sudafed too…I want all of it."

The pharmacist stared at the cop. She was on bended knee, low, her back up against a row of Ensure, adult diapers, boxes of denture cleaner, and Alka-Seltzer. Linda Kane had her Glock pointed at Ivy League's head; she could drop him any moment she chose. Only Linda did not want to end her day with a senseless death that could be avoided.

So she waited.

"We don't keep those drugs here anymore," the pharmacist tried to sell. "The Sudafed, yes. OxyContin, no."

Ivy League's eyes darted back and forth. Then, without warning, he made his move toward the counter, rushing the pharmacist.

"Open the safe and take out the drugs. Now!" The barrel of his weapon shook just a few yards from the pharmacist's face. The counter separated the two men.

Linda Kane could see that the back of Ivy League's shirt was drenched with sweat. *Nerves and the DTs.* She stayed close to the ground, scooted to an aisle across from where she had been stationed. Here, she had a better view. Once positioned, Linda motioned with her eyes for two blues to sneak in behind the counter, surprise the dude if they could. It was clear she was going to approach him from behind.

Before Linda could train her eyes back on Ivy League and make her move, the shot cut through the stale and dry, filtered air of the drugstore.

Three customers in front of the store screamed and ran out.

Chaos erupted.

The pharmacist, grazed by a bullet, fell back into a rack behind the register, knocking the thing over, pill bottles flying everywhere.

One of the blues ran toward him.

The guy was alive. A streak of blood across his forehead. He'd turned away just in time to miss the impact of the bullet, but it sliced a gash near his left temple.

"You are one lucky bastard," the cop said, standing over him.

The other blue pointed his weapon at Ivy League, but stopped himself from taking the shot.

Linda Kane had lurched toward Ivy League, but could only watch as he bolted out the side EMERGENCY EXIT door just after firing his weapon.

She made chase.

Two blues outside the door were startled, bowled over by the door flinging open, the suspect running out and past them.

Linda kicked the door open, ran toward the back of the building, by the Dumpster, where she saw Ivy League heading over a wooden fence. It was past eight o'clock. A spotlight shone down and cut a cone-shaped, golden hue over the area.

"Go around, back me up from the side street, a cul-de-sac there. I got this!" Linda shouted. "Hurry…right now. Move."

She jumped up on top of the Dumpster, hopped the fence, landed on both feet, looked left and right, weapon drawn in front of her body. It was dark back here. Save for a streetlight about twenty yards north, it was hard to see much of anything.

The detective crept carefully, knowing Ivy League couldn't have gone far. She stood in a wooded area at about the noon-hour hand of a cul-de-sac. The area was covered densely by brush. Secluded, the closest residence was a few blocks away.

"Let's do this peacefully and get you some help, son," Linda Kane said, her Glock trained in front of her, guiding the way.

There was an electric company utility shed about ten feet away. A small light on a pole brightening the area around it. She could almost feel him standing behind the corner of the shed, trembling, thinking that suicide by cop was going to be better than jonesing and seeing spiders that weren't there, sweating and itching and being a slave to a drug you could never get enough of.

As Linda Kane walked around the corner, stepping on a branch that cracked under her feet, Ivy League popped out. Then jumped toward her, thrashing Linda in the head with the butt end of his weapon, sending her to the ground.

Linda's Glock went flying into the grass out of arm's reach.

She felt a warm stream of blood trickle down the left side of her face. A burning wound, open and stinging.

Linda lurched and grabbed him by the neck in a headlock. She wrestled Ivy League down to the ground, but somehow within the entanglement—him being much bigger than she had anticipated— she wound up underneath him.

Pinned.

Now Ivy League straddled the detective, his knees holding her down, his .38 pointed in her face, the barrel just inches away from her eyes. Linda could see the weapon trembling. He was crying. Snot ran down his upper lip.

Linda stared at him.

Silence.

A cruiser pulled up. She knew her men would proceed with caution, position themselves and shoot Ivy League in the head first chance they got.

She did not want to see this addict die today.

Without a second thought, Linda swatted the weapon away and, in one quick move, traded places with Ivy League. She was now on top, her forearm across his neck, pushing down as hard as she could, that .38 in the leaves ten feet to her right.

"It's over" was all she said. "You're going to be okay."

The blues rushed in and took over from there.

2.

TRUDI CALDWELL ARRIVED HOME from work at 11:15 p.m. Her legs throbbed from yet another double shift at Marty's. Having grounded her daughter for the trouble she'd gotten into two nights ago—when Trudi realized Cassandra had disobeyed her, left the house, anyway, and had not come home—she didn't feel the least bit alarmed. Upset that Cassie had not listened, yes. But worried? Not a chance. There was *no need* for concern. Cassie was simply being Cassie again.

In another hour, Trudi presumed, her daughter would barge through the door, drop her backpack, and stomp her way up to her room, mumbling things teenagers often mumbled. When she calmed down, she would tell another story, give another excuse.

Cassie.

Funny what ran through your mind in moments like these. After sitting on the couch, absorbed in silence, massaging each of her calves, Trudi walked upstairs. Standing in Cassie's doorway, one hand on the knob, the other on the jamb, staring at her daughter's empty, still-made bed: *That damn girl. Fifteen going on thirty.*

How much there was that Trudi Caldwell did not know about her daughter.

The following morning, somewhere around four o'clock, the tone changed in the Caldwell house. It was then when the blood drained from Trudi's core and she felt a chill. Trudi had gone back downstairs to make some green tea after visiting Cassie's room. Turning on the TV, she fell asleep on the couch to a rerun of *The Jeffersons* as her tea went cold on the coffee table. When she opened her eyes and realized how late it was—Cassie still not home—Trudi felt flushed, a sudden pull, and then that knotty twist in her stomach. A maternal instinct that only mothers with troubled daughters can speak of. It was in that moment a coiled knot of dread tightened. A sinking reality presented itself: Cassie and her sassy adult attitude—*"You'll never understand me, Mother"*—forever blaming Trudi for destroying their lives, were gone for good.

Something was wrong.

Something was indeed very much out of whack.

A mother knows.

Trudi tried to ignore the feeling. She stood, a breath of dust and lint from the couch cushion puffing into the air behind her. She found the remote, shut off the TV. Walked into the kitchen.

It was 5:45 A.M. now. Outside, the aubergine night sky gave way to the amber yellow of early morning.

"Where's Cassie?" Katherine asked, after getting up for school and making her way downstairs. Cassie's younger sister sat on a stool at the breakfast bar next to her mother. Trudi's longtime boyfriend, Vinnie, was upstairs sleeping. Overlooking the two of them was a tacky doodad on the wall: a rooster, actually, red and white, orange beak, its fat belly a clock, ticking away the moments until this world of theirs ignited and, *kaboom*, burst. Cassie had completed the "rooster project," as she so cutely named it, in sixth-grade shop class, giving it to Trudi for Mother's Day that year.

That seemed so damn long ago.

Katherine, a wistful look about her, rubbed her eyes. "Mom, what's wrong?"

The words didn't register with the mother. Staring at an empty napkin holder on the counter, Trudi fell into a black hole of memories from the previous week—trying to figure out what it was Cassie had wanted to say. Why hadn't she listened? Why had she never told Cassie she'd make time for her and they could talk like they used to? Why had the last few months been nothing but friction, arguments, the two of them at odds all the time?

"Mom, are you hearing me?" Katherine poured a bowl of Fruity Pebbles. Covered the cereal with soy milk. Lactose, once a cold, comforting rite of youthful passage, was now the dreaded enemy. The Pebbles made crispy, crackling noises.

"Mommy?"

Trudi had caught Cassie rummaging through her dresser. *"What are you doing?"* Trudi had asked. *"Nothing, Mother,"* Cassie had snapped back, startled, closing the drawer. She walked out of the room, left the house. They saw each other the next day and avoided any discussion about it. Because both were busy and both were, well, uninterested in what the other had to say anymore.

"Katherine to Mother…are you in there?" Katherine pushed her glasses up the bridge of her nose, chewed slowly, the cereal gumming up in her braces.

Why hadn't she said something: *Cassie, talk to me, what's going on with you?* Why not embrace the child? Be the mother. Just because your mother was not there for you, didn't mean you had to continue the cycle.

Five minutes into the memory, Trudi dialed back in and watched as Katherine sprinkled a spoonful of sugar over her cereal, having realized it was as stale and tasteless as Styrofoam.

"Cassie left the lid of the box open *again*," Katherine complained. "Mom? Are you awake?"

Trudi sat stoic, blank. Staring.

"Mother," she heard Cassie say, *"you* never *hear me."*

"Mom! Hey?"

She's gone, Trudi knew. *Never coming back.* That connection between mother and daughter had been severed.

Forever.

Trudi stood. Katherine looked on. Trudi said nothing more. She picked up her cell phone. It had been the deep thrust of that one word: *Mother. "Nothing, Mother."* Trudi called the police to report her daughter missing. Cassie had never used the word in that context. All that pressure of being a teenager in today's world reduced to a word. Trudi knew it. For a long time now, Cassie had been in over her head, unable to open up, unable to share with her

what was going on.
    Mother.

3.

THE INTERESTING THING ABOUT a municipality building funded by the great taxpayers of a small town is that, if the representatives themselves don't work inside the facility, you had better forget about any money being allocated to upkeep and new equipment.

When cops walked into the squad room of the Royal Oaks PD—the tile floors a gaudy, seventies, puke-green color, alternating checkerboard white, any wax worn off long ago, dust bunnies like small tumbleweeds in every corner, under every desk—the officers understood not to complain. Old equipment. *Ha!* A cop banging on the side of the copier, trying to get the thing to work. Toilet tissue as thin and sharp as newspaper. Always a faucet or two not working. The heat in winter an every-other-day occurrence; air-conditioning in summer equaled a small fan on your desk. It was all part of civic duty. As long as you were a scrub, a non-tie-wearing government servant with a badge and a gun, you put up with it because the alternative was to be labeled a crybaby.

On the afternoon after Cassandra Caldwell had been reported missing, Detective Linda Kane rode the elevator up to the second floor Royal Oaks squad room. She held her head. The throbbing was intense. Linda's brain pounded, her temples beating to the rhythm of her heartbeat. It felt like a hangover, but Linda hadn't drunk alcohol in weeks. She'd spent hours in the hospital after the drugstore chase and capture the previous night. She'd be okay. The cut on her head from the doper needed only a few stitches. Ivy League was in the psych ward of the hospital. He'd end up in prison, Linda knew, and come out as a worse addict than when he went in. What could she do? No matter where you lived, who you were, this was the cycle of life now.

Cam Van Zandt sat at his desk waiting for his boss to come in. Linda was Cam's superior—yes, he her protégé—but Linda was no paper-pusher or task-designator. She was a cop who got her hands dirty same as everyone else—a verve and street toughness to go along with a strict assertiveness when she wanted things done. The detective was tall for a woman at five feet nine. Solid, too. Not a chick you wanted to mess with. They called her "Lin" for obvious reasons. Though she did not like it, Linda Kane allowed the cognomen because she knew it forged comradery.

"Well, look at you," Cam said as he spied Linda walking toward his desk. "Rough evening, I hear."

Linda just stared.

Cam and Linda were up next. The squad allocated cases much like parking attendants: the order the cars came in, the grunts parked them. Cam had been awake for twenty-six hours straight already, running down a robbery suspect. He'd heard, of course, what had happened to Linda.

With hands the size of oven mitts, Cam stood six feet four inches tall. A chiseled 225 pounds from all the working out, protein shakes, and flag football on Sundays with the boys from the fire department. Black hair. A solid patch on top swept back straight and fine as a new paintbrush, buzz cut along the sides; the perfect sideburns, cut close and narrow, running along his square jawline in the shape of Florida. Cam completed the *GQ* look with a faultless amount of stubble, a secret grooming technique he would not share with anyone. On the right side of his neck, that curve where the shoulder begins, the big man had one tat: an Asian symbol of some sort that looked like a pagoda.

"Cam, I tell you, I have no idea why I continue to do this work. There has to be an easier way. Jesus."

"Because it's in your blood," Cam said. He laughed. He knew

that was a bullshit line.

Linda liked Cam. She'd never shared it with anyone, but there was something there between them. She hoped he felt the same way. She had always hesitated to act on her feelings because of her position, the age difference, and all the baggage she brought into a relationship. None of it changed how she felt, though.

Cam had once dreamed of fighting in the Olympics. Judo. He saw gold. That changed after a student twisted Cam's knee once during a workout and the instructor heard a pop and winced. *Shit.* Any thought of standing on the podium mouthing "The Star-Spangled Banner" was replaced with whispers about the agony of defeat. Yet, Cam sucked it up. Became a teacher of the sport and joined the police academy. Never left Royal Oaks.

Here he was.

"Good work out there last night, Lin," Cam said. His voice took on a serious tone. Linda considered Cam a nexus of loyalty, honesty, and dignity. "Why not take the day off, though? Take it easy."

Linda furrowed her eyebrows and stared at her partner. Cam knew the gaze. Then: "Tylenol. Find me two Tylenol if you want to be helpful, Cameron."

The detective stood by her desk and sifted through several pink messages the previous shift had left. All of them calls. All of them having to do with that same subject: The opioid epidemic had taken up more of Linda's and Cam's time these days than anything else. Not only your sore-faced tweakers, but suburbanites like Ivy League, strung out after a back injury and a prescription from Dr. Feelgood. Royal Oaks was a "quintessential New England town in northern Connecticut," the brochures and website with the town seal promoted, a white gazebo dotting the center green, the church spire poking through the tops of trees like a witch's hat. Yet, it was not immune to the pill popper turned heroin addict when the prescription ran out. Narcan was the EpiPen of the day. Every cop carried the revenant agent like a Bic in his or her top pocket. And every cop had administered the resurrecter.

"You look like you got a pretty good-sized wallop there on the forehead, Lin. Just go home for the rest of the day, come on." That voice of Cam's, all testosterone, a deep baritone, thundered in

Linda's ears. The blood had drained from her face. She'd just come in and was exhausted already. "Here," he said, handing Linda two red-and-white capsules and a paper cup of water.

"Thanks, Cam." Linda tossed the pink messages on her desk. Swallowed the pills, downed the water, crumbled the paper cup, tossed it, sat down.

Cam found his chair and leaned back. Their desks faced each other. He knew Linda. She was not taking the day off: "Listen, Lin. I have this missing kid. Came in early this morning. I'm betting it's a runaway…almost certain, actually. But the mom is pretty batshit about it. Insists it's more than that. Name is…let me…Cassandra. 'Cassie,' they call her. Cassandra Caldwell."

Linda stared at her man. She was thinking of the other problems she had besides all the drugs flowing into her town. It had been another long week of trying to mend fences with her daughter, Jenna. Linda had missed yet another weekend of volleyball tournament games and Jenna was upset. Asking why, then breaking into that same daughter/cop-mother conversation detectives become resistant to after years on the job. Linda did what she could. It was bad enough Jenna had demanded to live with her father, Teddy Boy, the accountant ex-husband scrub who'd married the hottie from his office. "*Stability,*" sixteen-year-old Jenna had said, with Ted standing behind her, nodding his head in agreement. "*I need a home to feel comfortable in as I think about college.*" Linda had willed herself to stay calm and not respond in kind as a coldness seeped under her skin, sucking up this parental slight.

"Where, when?" Linda asked Cam, zeroing back into the conversation. She wanted details about said 'missing child.' She felt a bit of reflux burn up her throat from the coffee she'd just finished. Choked it down. Linda Kane had seen her share of missing kids throughout the years: toddlers swiped during bitter divorce proceedings, and then AMBER Alerts issued, teenage runaways, plain old-fashioned stranger-danger, sicko pedophile abductions, and most everything in between.

Cam flipped open his notebook. Put his hands between his thighs, leaned up in his chair and searched through what he'd written down. "Um, let's see. Grant Street, apparently, was the last time anyone saw her, about eight o'clock last night. She left a friend's house and has not been seen or heard from since. She's fifteen. Bit of a handful. Doesn't get along with her mom or sister. Stepfather lives in Texas."

"Biological father?" Linda asked. She stared at her desk. In front of her were a pile of vanilla folders fanned out—a case she'd been working on—a roll of yellow police tape, and, for reasons no one in the office understood, an old-school computer monitor the size of a microwave that Linda would not part with, now smudged filthy with dust. It had been left on from her previous shift. Those familiar screen-saver windows bounced from side to side. Linda followed them with her eyes.

"Dead, apparently. Some sort of work-related accident when the girl was very young."

"What makes Mom so sure she's not run away?" Linda asked, looking up at Cam, holding on to his eyes.

"Unlike her to be gone this long. Nobody's seen her. Unless her friends are lying. I told the mother it's early for us to get involved. Give it the day. But she's adamant. I was just about to call the mother's boyfriend. He wasn't home last night. He lives there. Works a lot, she said. He was at work. Mom was working, too. Waitress up at Marty's. Little sister is pretty freaked out. She was the only one home last night."

Linda ran her hands through her red hair, took a deep breath. "Make sure you run down some of the friends, too."

"*Me?*" Cam snapped, pointing at himself. "I know you've had a rough night, but this would have to be your case for now, boss. I'm going home. Been up all night. Unlike you, I need my beauty sleep. I can catch up with you later on."

Something didn't feel right. Something was off. Linda didn't like this. It was dangerous territory, however, and Linda knew it. Cam knew it. The entire squad knew it. Hell, Teddy Boy knew it better than all of them. In fact, anyone close to the detective knew that missing teenagers for Linda Kane was emotional kryptonite.

Long story.

"Give me that," Linda said, reaching over her desk and grabbing the Cassandra Caldwell file from Cam's hand. "Go get some sleep.

I'll take a look."

4.

THE MISSING GIRL'S MOTHER, Trudi Caldwell, dumped scoops of ground coffee into a shopping-bag-brown, V-shaped paper filter. She poured the water into the chamber. Hit the button. The percolator popped and hissed.

That's what moms do when their kids go missing. They fold their arms, hug themselves, and pace. They listen to people calling the house and talking to them about unimportant things, not hearing any of it. They stare out the window through the blinds at nothing, everything. They make pots of coffee they'll pour down the drain. They accept food from strangers that will collect mold in the fridge. They question the past, everything about it. How many times they could have said *I love you*, but, against the advice of the Oprahs of the world, they chose not to.

Who does, anyway?

Trudi knew Cassie should have come home by now. This late in the day. Gone all night. No one had seen her. She'd missed school. She'd never taken it this far before.

"What time did you get home?" Trudi asked Katherine. A guy with a cocker spaniel on a leash walked by the house. Trudi had locked her eyes on them before turning from the window and addressing her youngest child in the kitchen.

"I got home about seven-thirty. I was at the library. Cassie called at eight or so. She was at Teresa's. She asked if you were home yet and said she was on her way."

"Why didn't she use her cell phone or text?"

"'Cause you took it away from her."

Trudi saw that conversation play out inside her head: screaming at Cassie, saying she was a troublemaker. Immature. Yelling that she was a little bitch who didn't deserve a phone. After what Cassie and her friends had pulled on Cabbage Night—that *Purge*-like bender of mischief the day before Halloween, which older kids, not trick-or-treating age anymore, embark on—Cassie was lucky the phone wasn't taken away for good. Cassie called Trudi a pathetic excuse for a mother. Katherine stood nearby as the argument got heated, saying, *"Stop it…. Stop it. Both of you."* Katherine held both hands over her ears, she started to shake. Trudi, finally fed up, grabbed a wooden spoon on the counter, smacked Cassie across the leg. Cassie held her thigh, teared up, ran out of the house, saying something about going to live with her stepfather, never coming back.

"She was supposed to be grounded," Trudi said.

"I know," Katherine said. She dropped her head. "I cover for her sometimes when you ground her, Mother. I'm sorry."

"Call your father again," Trudi told Katherine. "Tell him there's no more time for holding out if Cassie is on her way there. Ask him if she called. He needs to fess up. Cops are involved now. She's been officially reported missing."

It was funny to Trudi how as she spoke, the words felt shallow and worthless as they came out of her mouth, as if nothing she said mattered. As if the police could check everywhere, call every friend, drive by every place where Cassie had hung out. None of it was going to make a difference, though. The child was gone. Despite what anyone did, Cassie Caldwell was never coming back.

A mother knows.

5.

AS DETECTIVE LINDA KANE walked out of the office, hit the elevator button, Carmen came running out, calling for Linda to hold up a minute, don't leave. Carmen—a full-figured, in a sexy, curvaceous way, Puerto Rican mother of four, grandmother of two—kept the squad in check. She made sure everyone did what they were supposed to do: completed paperwork, kept appointments, made it to trial on time to testify, answered calls, took messages. Truly the heart and pulse of the squad. Without Carmen, the detective squad could not function.

"You have a call, Lin. Says it's 'important.'" Carmen cleared her throat. "Sounds urgent, actually, not necessarily important."

Two uniformed officers, talking and laughing, walked between them. Didn't say, excuse me. Linda noticed how Carmen shot them a look, seemed as if she was about to toss a shoe, scold them. Then she focused back on the detective.

"Say what it's about?" Linda asked. Behind her, the elevator doors beeped. They would close soon enough if she didn't step in. "I'm heading to see the mom of the missing kid."

"A note. Something about this girl and a note."

"You're kidding me? How does anyone even know we're looking into this case? Is it even a case, for shit's sake? Christ."

Just then, Cam walked out of the squad room and stole Linda's elevator. He smiled. Had a backpack over his shoulder. Cam was heading to the gym, then home to get some rest.

"Good luck, Lin…" Cam said, raising his eyebrows. "Bub-bye. Probably another psychic with some solid intel for you. Oh, and I spoke to a few of her friends. Nada. Haven't seen or heard from the girl." Cam smiled and waved as the elevator doors closed.

"Have a good workout, huh." Linda half-smiled. Turned and headed back into the office.

She took the phone. Never sat down. This was going to be quick. She didn't need some quack with yet another vision of Sherri, Linda's missing childhood friend, buried in the woods. She'd heard it most her life: Dig out by the old wooden bridge. You'll find her there just underneath the railroad ties by the river. That last "tip" was too much. Had everyone running crazy for days. The fact that when these types of calls came in, the squad had to run them down, regardless of how stupid and baseless they knew they were, wasted time and caused frustration.

Impatient, Linda stared at the ceiling tiles above Carmen's desk. One tile was spotted with water stains that looked like brown clouds.

"Yes," she said. That cut on her head burned. "Detective Linda Kane."

The caller was male. Fiftyish, Linda guessed. He had that phlegmy gurgle to his voice that comes with decades of yelling. He also sounded African-American, a slight Caribbean accent Linda picked up on. She knew this from working vice. You spend a year on the wire inside a fart-filled van listening to people's lives and you learn to pick off ethnicity.

He said he didn't want to give his name.

Shocking, Linda thought. *Let's see: You've had this dream about a girl that has gone missing and you want to report…*but as Linda began to mock the guy inside her head, "Check the kid's dresser, look for a note," the man said.

"Sir, what kid? What are you referring to?" Linda was all business. She didn't need this now. They were probably talking about a damn runaway. Such a wayward flock, the teens in this town. They do nothing more than take up important cop time with their entitled attitudes, demands of attention, and narcissistic personality disorders.

Fucking social media. Thanks a lot.

"You know who and what I'm referring to, Detective. The girl. The girl who is missing. Cassandra. Read the note."

Dial-tone.

Linda held the phone out in front of her. Stared at it. Then cradled the receiver back where it belonged, said nothing to Carmen, walked back to the elevators.

As SHE DROVE TOWARD the missing girl's house, Linda Kane called her daughter. She needed to make things right with Jenna. Linda knew she would not sleep on this night if she didn't at least get an *It's okay, Mom* out of Jenna. *Don't worry, I understand* was probably asking too much. But a little bit of compassion from an Honor Society student with colleges beating the door down was warranted, Linda felt.

"Just hear me out," Linda pleaded.

Jenna wasn't having any of it. She threatened to hang up.

"Please, sweetie, just give me two minutes."

"I need to study for this physics test, Mom. I can't do this with you right now."

"Jenna, listen to me. I need to work. I'm sorry I'm not at every game, at every science fair…band concert…."

"Mom! Speak factually, okay? You haven't made *one* game or *one* tournament since last season. That's months ago, if we're speaking in truths." Linda did not realize kids kept score. They knew and spoke in absolutes. They never under- or overestimated anything. It was always straight up—especially with Jenna. When she sat first-chair clarinet during her junior year for the closing spring concert, as the designated tuning student stood and made sure with an A-flat note that the band was in key, Jenna looked out, as the kids often do, studying the crowd. She took in each face. When she saw that her mother had blown off yet another school function, Jenna put a check in that "enough is enough" box. At least that was the way Ted had described it to Linda during an argument.

"I'm sorry, honey. It's… You know that it's hard for me with your father and that woman." Linda looked up at the roof of the car and realized the words were nothing but a cheap, manufactured excuse.

"Get over it, Mom. They've been married, what, geez, like, four years now? End of story." Jenna knew it wasn't about Dad and his new wife. It was about Linda the cop and her missing childhood friend. The job and the past consumed Linda Kane. Ate her up inside like a cancer. Everyone around her paid the price.

Linda didn't respond. She was at a stoplight. Two blocks from where Cassandra Caldwell went missing. She stared at the light. She saw nothing but the past. How she'd been walking with Sherri. How they were talking about school and boys and how great that summer was going to be. How there were dozens of people around, men and women with their kids, grounds crew cutting the lawn, lifeguards, townies. And how Linda said something to Sherri, heard someone call out her name, a man's voice, turned around for a moment, and then Sherri, as if she had turned to dust, disappeared.

Gone.

Linda Kane's childhood was over in that moment.

A car beeped.

"Mom! Mom? You there?" Jenna said.

Linda was back. "Yes. I have to go, Jenna. We'll discuss this later. I'll call you this weekend and take you out for lunch."

"Typical," Jenna said, and hung up.

Linda realized she was close to the house where Cassie Caldwell went missing. She pulled over, turned around, drove up the road, and parked alongside the town green, just across the street from the last house Cassie had been reported leaving.

There was a Gothic-looking Episcopal church across the street from the green on the corner. A row of Colonial houses lined the block, those wooden signs tacked by the doors indicating the historic date of the dwelling. Two of the houses, side by side, had been converted into businesses—one a funeral home, the other a flower shop.

The corner house, a brown clapboard Victorian, weathered and very much New Englandesque, had a three-foot-tall statue of Mary praying in the front yard, Mary's blue robe dulled from the elements, weeds overtaking the thing. This was the house Cassie had walked out off and had not been seen since. Or at least, that was the information Cam had been able to gather before handing Linda the case. Providing the info had been Cassie's BFF, Teresa Noble, who lived in the house. Her older brother and mother backed it up: "Yes, she walked out the door about eight o'clock," the mother had said to Cam over the phone. "I offered her a ride home, but she said it wasn't a problem. She liked walking. She seemed fine. Cassie was—how shall I put it—filled with resentment. She and her mother were often at odds."

Is this even a case? Linda asked herself as she got out of her car, looked both ways, crossed the double yellow lines in the center of the road. She stepped over the curb and onto the grass. Then walked up the concrete steps, by that statue of Mary, and up to the door. Why was she so wrapped up in a girl missing for, what, fewer than twenty-four hours?

Because this was what Linda Kane did: obsessed over missing teenagers.

1871, BARTON ANDERSON HOUSE was painted on a wooden white sign to the right of the front door. The porch wrapped all the way around the corner of the house. There was a hammock and a rocking chair. Leaves from an elm in the front yard had fallen and collected in the corner. Several wooden-slat porch boards were rotted and crumbling apart. As Linda stepped, the wood underneath her feet squeaked.

She knocked.

A small man, bald except for a patch of black hair circling his head, black socks, navy blue slacks, white wife-beater, quite the stomach, answered. He seemed angry at something that happened just before he'd opened the door.

Linda grabbed her gold badge clipped on her belt, held it up. "You Teresa's father?"

Bald Man laughed. "Are you kidding me? That piece of shit is dead. Doper. Od'd. I'm the boyfriend. Come on in."

Linda walked through a cloud of old-man cologne Bald Man left in his wake, which tickled the back of her throat. She stood in the foyer inside the house. It reeked of cabbage cooked hours before; a horrible smell. Linda had expected a dirty place, but it was well kept.

"Teresa is out. Her mother is out. I have no idea where or when they'll be back."

"Are they together?"

"Nope."

"Sir, were you here last night, say, eightish?" Linda looked around, taking in what she could.

Bald Man sat down at the kitchen table, a napkin dispenser in front of him, next to salt-and-pepper shakers in the shape of lighthouses. He had a glass of what looked to be cola or wine, Linda couldn't tell, in front of him, the sports page spread out on the table.

Linda stayed in the foyer. Hands on her hips. Up at the top of the stairs in front of where she stood, a kid, maybe twenty, poked his head out of a room. Linda looked up; he quickly closed the door. Loud music fired up. It sounded muffled and heavy on the bass. Death metal. *Thumping. Thumping. Thumping.* The glasses inside the china hutch to the left of Linda shook and clanked.

"That kid and his fucking music. Shit's sake. What's this about, anyway? I'm not sure I like it," Bald Man said, never looking up from the newspaper.

"A missing child."

"That friend of Teresa's?"

"Yes, sir. Cassandra Caldwell."

"I was gone. Working, actually. I'm a machinist at the foundry in downtown Rockville. I work second shift. I have no idea what the hell goes on here when I'm not around. That idiot upstairs. Lazy bastard. Doesn't want to work. Just plays video games, eats Cheetos, and listens to that Devil music all day."

"How'd you know I was speaking about Miss Caldwell?"

"Is it really a shock to anyone that that girl has run away?"

"Your name, sir?"

"Al Carsen." He rattled off his Social Security number and date of birth. "I got nothing to hide." He looked at Linda, who stared at him. "Why aren't you writing this down?"

"I will."

She didn't want to explain, but Linda Kane had an impeccable memory. She didn't need to write things of this nature down. In junior high, after she had been tested, the team called it "photographic reconstruction memory." Linda disliked that description. It sounded nerdy and unrealistic. Another team of so-called experts in high school called it a gift, sort of a *Rain Man* thing, only on a much smaller scale. Linda had never been diagnosed as autistic, but had this one singularly exceptional talent that only a few they'd tested had: the ability to perfectly recall a certain amount of numbers and words.

Remembering details about what happened on the day her friend went missing, however, was a different matter.

Linda flipped a business card out of her back pocket, walked over, placed it on the table. She tapped her index finger on the number with one hand, held her palm on her Glock with the other. "Have the kid and her mother call me when they return—you got it, Mr. Carsen?"

Bald Man picked up the card and squinted, holding it far out in front of himself. "Sure, Detective…um…" He was having trouble seeing the name.

Linda finished for him: "Kane."

"You betcha, Detective *Kane*."

"I'll see myself out."

As Linda walked down the steps and toward her vehicle, she looked to her right at the funeral home next-door to the Noble house. The entrance was elaborate, a canvas canopy covering the walkway up to the front door. It reminded Linda of the entrance into a Manhattan steak house where she'd once had a meal. There were green shrubs, knee high, groomed in the shape of cones along the funeral home's pathway.

What grabbed Linda's interest was something she spied in the driveway, above the garage. Facing the walkway where Cassie would have walked out of Teresa Noble's house, a security camera pointed directly at the road.

Linda stopped and stared at it.

She then stepped back, looked toward the Noble house and back down the street. There was no doubt the camera had one of those wide-angle lenses. Why else have the thing? And if that was the case, the camera would have caught Cassie walking out of the Noble house, down the pathway, onto the sidewalk running perpendicular to the street, and at least part of the way down the block. It would prove—or disprove—what Teresa and her mother had said. Maybe more important, put a direct time stamp on when Cassie actually left and which way she went.

Linda got to her car and called Carmen. Told her to get hold of the funeral home—WALDEN SCOTT FUNERAL SERVICES, the awning said—and ask them not to erase the video. Most businesses, if nothing happened, recorded over the day before with the new day. Linda told Carmen to then rustle up Cam if the funeral home balked and have him get busy on the paperwork so they could get hold of it as soon as possible.

As Linda pulled away from the neighborhood, a nagging memory in the back of her brain went to work.

Sherri.

Her BFF.

How ordinary life could be torn apart at any moment by some sort of unexpected, random event you never saw coming. Evil, truly, lie around every damn corner of the world. And there was nothing, not a god damn thing you could do to stop evil if it had you in its sights.

The ghost that had snatched Sherri off the face of the earth right in front of her, Linda had to wonder, was it back?

6.

KATHERINE CALDWELL SAT IN her room with the door closed. Her entire bedroom was color coordinated, just as Katherine had to have it. The pink walls complemented the white carpet, which went well with the light pink bedspread and pillowcases. Katherine had everything in its place and made sure there was a place for everything. This was how the missing girl's sister lived.

The thirteen-year-old tried to study, because she believed that's what would be expected of her. But considering what was going on, Katherine could not retain much information. Every time she looked down at the words, she thought of Cassie.

What was Mother thinking at this moment? How much pain was Mother in? What would happen when Katherine went back to school? Would they point at her? Would they be friendlier? Would the bullies leave her alone while she was still the sister of the missing girl? Would they bully her more than they already had? Would the faculty treat her differently?

The teachers barely paid any attention to Katherine as it was, knowing that she did not need help in any subject. She was breezing through school and could have moved on to high school by the time she was twelve—college probably by next year, if she wanted.

She'd know the answers to some of those questions tomorrow, because that was when Katherine decided she was going back to school. One day off was enough. She couldn't fall behind. Plus, there was that social media-invented condition she knew she had suffered from the moment she saw the meme: FOMO—fear of missing out. The anxiety Katherine felt was too much to bear sometimes. She had to know what was happening in school. When the unease gripped and overwhelmed her, she'd head off into her closet when no one was around and scream into a pillow. Maybe slap herself on the head several times, hard, crying. She had no idea what made her this way.

Then there was Cassandra. Here it was, Cassie not even around, missing, the police out looking for her, and she was *still* causing Katherine discomfort and problems. Could Katherine ever step out from underneath the swarm of attention Cassie had sucked out of this family? Was it ever going to end? But then, the idea of never seeing her sister again. It was gut-wrenching. Katherine wanted to curl up into a ball and hug herself until everything was better and Cassie was back and the three of them loved each other without any pain.

There was a knock on Katherine's bedroom door.

"They're here," Trudi said. "They need to speak with us, Katherine. Let's go. Downstairs. Right now. Put the books away. And remember what I told you about this."

Katherine did not speak. She did what she was told.

Always.

It was well after six o'clock. Twenty-two hours since Cassie went missing. Not a word from her. Not a sighting. Nothing from a friend indicating he or she had seen or heard from her. Not one text. Most cases of missing kids need a solid twenty-four to forty-eight hours before cops kick into high gear and call out the troops. But Trudi seemed to think Cassie was not coming home. The Royal Oaks PD, Trudi had been told, believed she had run away because Cassandra Caldwell checked every box in the runaway category. Fort Worth police had checked in with the girls' father after Linda made a call. He had not seen or heard from the kids— Katherine or Cassie—in weeks. Cops there did a welfare check of his house and found nothing. All the train and bus depots had been contacted. Airlines too. Only way Cassandra could have used public transportation to get out of state or even out of town was if she'd had fake identification made and planned the entire event.

And so, while many believed Cassie had likely run away, being a typical troubled teenager looking for some attention, there were others who whispered about possible harm having come to the girl.

7.

DETECTIVE LINDA KANE STOOD in Trudi Caldwell's living room, waiting for Katherine and Trudi to come from upstairs and join her. It had been about an hour since she'd asked Carmen to check on that funeral home security video. Linda stood as Trudi and Katherine entered the room. She nodded to both as her iPhone *dinged.* Then looked down.

A text from Carmen.

VIDEO ALL SET. YOU CAN PICK UP DISC ANYTIME.

Carmen liked to text in CAPS.

Interesting to Linda, magnifying a feeling of loss, was the lack of any photos of Trudi and the kids anywhere inside the home. The living room was, as Linda dredged up a word her late mother might have chosen, nondescript. The house wasn't dirty or clean. Like most, it had its own smell. Yet, it was kind of empty. No soul to it. A stopover for Trudi, the boyfriend, and kids. Linda could see them all passing one another, but never taking the time to stop and interact. Not eating dinner together. They lived separate lives. All the trappings of a family beset by dysfunction.

Linda Kane could *so* relate to that.

"Here's her phone," Trudi said, handing Cassie's iPhone to Linda. "You're going to want that, I assume."

"So she didn't have it with her, then. Why not?"

"I took it away the other night."

Trudi appeared hopeless. Linda saw shame, sadness, and a furtive desperation. There was a hardness about Trudi, too, Linda felt. Something crudely confrontational. The mother bowed her head. Came back up and looked pale. Her lack of color was more from being tired than scared or worried. Maybe a combination of all three. Sleep for Trudi, Linda knew, was going to be something she should forget about for the next few days. Or until they brought her daughter home.

"We are not on good terms," Trudi explained. "You'll hear that from whoever you talk to. It is a constant struggle to keep her in line. I'm not sure why Cassie is so abrasive, what turned for her, but that is my daughter." Trudi threw up her hands. "She went from sleepovers at friends, the two of us binging on Disney DVDs, us shopping at the mall and talking like mothers and daughters should, to a scorned teen who hated being part of this family and was invisible whenever she was here."

Katherine had her arm around her mother and would not let go. She placed her head in the crook of Trudi's armpit.

Linda noted to herself that Trudi was referring to Cassie in the present tense. A positive sign.

"Drugs?" Linda asked.

"I could never be certain, but I don't think that was the issue. I've checked her room in the past. Never found anything."

"Boys?"

"The norm, from what I understand. A few boyfriends here and there at school, but nothing steady."

"We'll need a list of any boyfriend, however long ago, however serious."

"I can do that."

"Have you gone through her room?"

"Just glancing around. Haven't touched anything."

"For right now, don't, okay?"

"Okay…"

Katherine let go of her mother and stood behind her. She crossed one ankle over the other. She picked up a bag of gluten-free kale chips from the table and started eating them. The way she held herself, her distant gaze, the way she followed Trudi wherever she went, Linda felt, spoke of a much younger girl. The braces didn't help. The fact that she didn't speak much and seemed to fidget with her hands like a toddler made Linda think Katherine was much younger than thirteen.

"Well, look, right now we're thinking she took off somewhere," Linda explained that simple, canned narrative all cops give to parents in this situation early on. "That seems to be the case ninety-nine times out of a hundred. We're looking at it from that angle until we have something that tells us different. Can I see her room?"

Another *ding*. This time, a text from Cam.

There's something U need 2 see. I LFT it on UR desk. Give me 3 hours sleep and I will be back in.

Mr. Mystery. Why can't he just explain within the text? Why shroud the damn information in suspense?
Cam—the Constant Dramateer.

Upon entering Cassie's room, Linda went straight for the dresser. Around her was a typical teenager's quarters: posters of her favorite musicians, a puppy calendar with nothing written on it, a beanbag chair in the corner, with a small tear in the top, a handful of books in a case, including some type of astrology nonsense and a book of Emerson's poems, a closet full of the modern clothes any girl Cassie's age would have. There was nothing, Linda felt, setting off alarm bells of any type that this kid was into things that might have led to her being in any kind of serious trouble. Nothing goth. Or emo, as they say today. Nothing Slender Man–like. Nothing screaming out, *Help me, I'm lost.* Linda had been in those rooms. Seen things that told her the kid was in deep, strung out on dope or off the rails into an Internet world way over the child's head.

Not the case with Cassie.

"You say you looked around in here?" Linda asked. Trudi stood in the hallway with Katherine, not wanting to broach the detective's investigative space.

"I have, but rushed through, not knowing what to look for

and, to be honest, somewhat out of my mind. I also didn't want to disturb anything. I've searched this room before, as I said. Trying to stay on top of things."

"'Things,' ma'am?"

"Teenager stuff. What she's into. What she's up to. I work so much. I'm not home a lot." Trudi kept one hand in her right pocket, a nervous tic, an observation Linda had registered by now. She rubbed her head and face with the other hand when she needed to take a moment and work out the stress of what was going on.

"What is she into?" Linda asked. She snapped on a pair of blue latex gloves. Each one made a popping, slapping noise plastic makes when pulled back and released. As she did this, Linda glanced into the hall and could tell it made both Katherine and Trudi nervous. Like things had just taken a more serious turn.

Linda saw a piece of paper on top of the dresser, the reason for the gloves. It was folded in half. She picked it up. Opened it. Read.

It was a note presumably written by Cassie, just as the caller had said. Short, but very much to the point. It was addressed to "Mother." Cassie wanted Trudi to understand that she was in love with a boy, an older kid from a nearby town. They were talking about running away together. Yet, the note ended abruptly, midsentence, as if Cassie had never finished it. Which was why, Linda thought, it was folded up on her dresser and not left on the kitchen counter as a sort of good-bye note. Cassie was in the process of composing it, figuring out what she wanted to say.

Linda took a plastic evidence bag out of her coat pocket and dropped the note inside. Why hadn't Trudi discovered it? If she'd gone through Cassie's room, even hastily, how had she missed this note?

"What's that?" Trudi asked.

"Did she have a laptop?"

"No."

Kid without a laptop?

Strange.

"Can you tell me about any boys she might have been dating?"

Trudi said, again, she had no idea. She considered Cassie to be a typical girl in that respect. She dated boys, nothing too serious.

How much the parents don't know.

"Benjie," Katherine said, speaking for the first time.

Linda looked at Katherine, then back at Trudi: "What about your boyfriend, ma'am, when will he be home?"

"Vinnie works all the time. First *and* second shift sometimes. Not sure where he is right now. He might have stopped for a few drinks. He hangs out at the bar I work at, Marty's."

"He lives here, correct?"

"Yes. We've been together ten years. He's lived here eight. The kids like him."

"They don't love him, ma'am?"

"You'll have to ask them."

Katherine spoke up. "Vinnie is satisfactory. Always been good to me."

"Please tell your boyfriend we need a statement and he needs to contact the office," Linda said. "Also, I know this is a tough time, but I need you and Katherine to come into the station and sit down and give us a statement too. It's important we have all the facts in front of us as soon as possible." Linda paused. She looked at Katherine: "Benjie? Can you tell me more about him?"

"Name's Benjie. I heard Cassie tell her friend one day she loved him."

Linda felt she wasn't going to get much more out of the kid.

Trudi said no problem—to coming in and providing statements, that is.

"Last name?" Linda asked Katherine.

"Not sure," the child said.

Linda walked over to Trudi and showed her the note through the plastic. "Is that your daughter's handwriting?"

Trudi read the note. "Yes. Yes, it is." She rolled her eyes. Breathed almost a sigh of relief. Cassie had run away. That's what Linda believed Trudi felt in that moment. As if she'd expected this course of action long ago.

Staring at Trudi up close, Linda noticed the bags under her eyes, saggy skin, a bit of a lift around her jawline and eyes. Weird, a suburban mom, a waitress, going to the expense of having work done. Closing in on fifty and no crow's-feet for Trudi? A waitress all her life, she was in good shape, but came across as being a bit distant. Her light brown hair was pulled back in what was a perpetual ponytail, graying in silvery strands along her ear line and forehead. Her black roots showed. Her eyeliner was rough, flaking. She used pancake makeup, like TV talk show hosts. Putty to hide all of life's bumps.

Trudi had not had an easy life. These kids had worn her down. The past ten years or so had not been kind. Now this. Linda knew her type. Felt indifferent about these women. In most cases, they had tried their best to make a life out of the shit hand they'd been dealt. Men, mostly, had let them down. They were constantly struggling to breathe, treading water. Once in a while, a crisis came up and knocked them so far under, it either made them stronger, providing it did not involve their children, or broke them when it did.

As they made their way back downstairs, Linda felt sorry for Katherine. She was a smart girl—that much was so obviously clear. But quiet and passive. Those tin braces. Her glasses, thick as Plexiglas, a bit of tape on the frame. Out-of-trend clothes that were not in style with the times but what her mom could afford. Katherine didn't have to work hard at being smart. She was one of those kids for whom schoolwork came easy. But her home life, Linda measured, was another story. She had basically raised herself. Her social skills, Linda seized on, were not what the thirteen-year-olds Linda interacted with should be. She spent a lot of time, it was clear, with her head pointed down at screens and books.

"Let's just take it hour by hour. We're not jumping to any conclusions here. I need to get back to the station. Later tonight or tomorrow, I'll take a look at some things. I'll be in touch. You two can come in tomorrow; that is, if your daughter doesn't come home tonight. My guess, ma'am, is that you'll hear from your daughter soon enough."

Linda had been in a rush to get alone. She'd heard her phone *ding* several times while up in Cassie's room and wondered what was up. Nobody ever texted Linda Kane that much; they knew better. Anyway, Linda hardly ever answered texts.

It was probably Cam. Mr. Drama setting up some sort of puzzle for Linda to solve because Carmen woke him up and made him get to work.

Linda laughed at the thought.

Cam.

Sitting in her car, staring down at her phone, the texts were about Jenna, however. Ted wanted to know if Jenna was with Linda. Their daughter had left volleyball practice early, at four p.m. for some reason, and had not returned home. She wasn't answering her phone and not responding to texts. Ted was worried. This was not how Jenna generally acted.

Call me, Lin.

Linda felt the acids in her stomach churn, bubble, set a fire inside. She recalled how she hadn't eaten anything all day. Nothing tonight. Just coffee.

The worst thing for reflux.

That wound on her head throbbed. She could feel the stitches tighten.

Jenna.

Still, Linda wasn't going to fall victim to her demons. Cassie missing, a runaway. A history with her best friend, Sherri, never seen again, alive or dead. Linda wasn't going to put her daughter anywhere inside that same box. Not a chance. Jenna was out. She'd probably told Ted she was going somewhere days ago, not to worry, and he forgot. There was no need to get all stressed out over this.

No need to concern herself.

No need to drive around looking for her daughter.

No need to think your kid was now among the missing.

8.

TWO EIGHTEEN-YEAR-OLD dropouts sat in front of a campfire in the woods behind Royal Oaks High School. One had spiked hair, loops of silver bracelets an inch up his left wrist, fingers of rings; one, a large skull. He wore a Sid and Nancy T-shirt, studded belt, ripped jeans, black Harley boots, leather jacket. Although he was too young to know the reference, he was a Joe Strummer punk, Clash throwback from the eighties. The other kid was more of a tattooed-from-head-to-toe, shaved-head, plain-white-tee, jeans-and-denim-jacket, chain-wallet-connected-to-a-loop-on-his-pants, a-scar-across-his-right-cheek-from-a-knife-fight type. The follower, for sure.

"Shit town we live in, huh?" one of them said.

"Ain't that the truth."

They smoked weed and passed back and forth a forty-ounce malt liquor, with a gold label, wiping their mouths on the back of their wrists after each sip. The fire warmed their front side, while the cold snap of fall chilled their backs. The juxtaposition of the two extremes was profound. When weed smoke wasn't coming out of their mouths, they could see their breath. The grass around the fire was damp. It was the first night since last winter that frost would cover everything in Royal Oaks.

Spiked Hair stood up from the log they sat on and announced that he had to take a whiz. He took a glug from the bottle of beer.

Finished it. Then glanced at the backwash in the bottom for a moment before tossing the bottle into the fire, smashing it to bits.

"Open the other bottle," he told Shaved Head. "I need to take a piss."

As he walked into the woods about twenty yards away from the fire, into a densely forested area, unzipped, and began his business, Spiked Hair sang a tune out loud that Shaved Head was trying to figure out. As he butchered the song, Spiked Hair noticed something in front of him. The pulsing light from the fire illuminated the object in strobe-like flashes. At first, he thought he was just high. Maybe seeing things. The object looked surreal. Like a mannequin. A female mannequin, at that. Young, maybe fifteen or twenty, on the ground, sleeping, arms folded over her belly like a body in a casket. Spiked Hair thought maybe the weed had been laced with embalming fluid—"the poor man's angel dust," Shaved Head called it. Was he hallucinating? Because a female on her back, fully clothed, eyes wide open, as if staring into the sky, was about as strange a sight as Spiked Hair could have imagined seeing while standing and urinating all over his boots.

"Yo, Benjie, come here," Spiked Hair yelled, shaking his junk, zipping up with one leg off the ground.

"Man. I don't wanna see yo shit, dog!" Shaved Head Benjie yelled.

"No, man, come here. Look at this shit, yo. Come on. Serious here. You have to see this."

Spiked Hair slid up his iPhone flashlight icon, hit the button, and shone it toward the mannequin. As he did this, he heard Shaved Head walking through the woods toward him, breaking branches and snapping twigs underneath his feet.

"What is it, man? Come on. You're ruining my high."

They both moved in for a closer look, the iPhone flashlight guiding the way.

Fully illuminated now, the girl startled them.

They jumped back.

"Shit, yo," Shaved Head Benjie said. "Holy M-effing shit! She's dead, yo. Her eyes are open."

"Take some photos, man. Take some pics of her."

Spiked Hair didn't like that idea.

"You pussy," Shaved Head said. Then walked over and snapped about twenty photos of the girl from various angles, before they grabbed their weed, backpacks and beer, and got the hell out of there.

9.

LINDA WENT HOME. SHE needed a break. It was well after nine p.m. Nothing would come of her driving around town searching for Cassie.

Or Jenna.

Her head throbbed. The wound was more tender now than it had been after the stitching. She needed Tylenol and sleep.

Linda's apartment was more or less a stopover. A place to crash. No TV. Very few photos or paintings. No knickknacks. No Pier 1 Imports table ornaments and seasonal table settings. There were a few citations and awards for her work with troubled teens at the YMCA and the heroic rescue of a girl who'd jumped into the river during a suicide attempt. But those sat in a box inside the closet. Linda kept one magazine on the coffee table, *Travelscape*. She liked to read about the places she would never visit. Not that she couldn't afford it or take the time off, but Linda Kane had no desire. It was Sherri. That unfinished business of her teenage BFF. Like a familiar song you've heard half of before shutting off the car, you find yourself singing it inside your head all day long. That's your brain wanting to hear the end of the song. As opposed to what victims' family members had told Linda after a case was over—that catching and jailing their son's or daughter's killer could never be closure— for Linda Kane, finding Sherri's body, knowing what happened to her, would be. She could close that chapter. Move on. Take that trip. Hear the end of the song. She could pull Sherri's spirit from whatever orbit it was floating in and give it a place of rest. It wasn't even so much anymore about finding out what happened, who took Sherri, what some sicko did to her. It was about bringing the girl back home to her family. To the community. And Linda finding the relief of knowing Sherri wasn't out in the world, alone anymore.

After washing her face, Linda had a long look at herself in the mirror. She had learned to embrace her shoulder-length, red hair. As a kid, she hated it. Teased, she wished she'd been born blonde, just to give her that easier edge in life those girls seemed to take for granted. Yet, she'd come to figure out that redheads, and she despised the proverbial "Red" nickname, as research had shown, just might be genetically superior. She laughed at the "study" at first, but then accepted there could be some truth to it. And the blue eyes: What was with redheads having bluer eyes than any other human being? Linda didn't care. One of the rarest combinations in genetics, it did not matter. She put that one in the "win" column. Along with not having the pale-white skin most reddies were born with, on top of freckles all over their bodies; her skin was far more subtle, almost a soft vanilla, like book pages. She was grateful for that hereditary dice roll in her favor.

As she thought about it, Linda couldn't recall the last time she actually had a man in her bed. It was hard to find her equal, which was why Cam seemed so perfect. And if he wasn't, she could sculpt him into what she needed, anyway.

She'd put the job before everything else in life, including her own happiness. Why couldn't it just be booze? Rehab. The clichéd cop with the clichéd drunken excuse. No. For Linda Kane, it was the past that had her in chains, drove her every move. She was chasing a ghost. A ghost that had just made another appearance in the form of a missing girl who, Linda decided, had *not* run away.

She walked toward her bedroom. Fluffed the pillow. Changed into her sleeping garb: an old, knee-length Boston Red Sox T-shirt, no panties.

Staring at the ceiling, Linda told herself that Cassandra Caldwell was gone. She had fallen into that same hole Sherri had been swallowed up by long ago. There was an apparition in this damn town, one that swooped in when you turned your back, or let your guard down, it scooped up teenage girls. Within a four-town area, three additional girls had gone missing over the past forty-five years. Linda had gone over it and over it: There had been no common profile among them. They all looked different. Dressed different. They came from different backgrounds. Different hair color. Different ethnicities. There was no victim link. The FBI had once looked at the earlier cases, including Sherri's. Agents decided the girls had been abducted by a serial offender, taken somewhere, raped and murdered, their bodies disposed of. That was easy to say. Linda despised those types of classroom sleuths, learning a trade from an instructor and then sent out to crime scenes to guess. No practical, street experience.

Trained soldiers.

They knew nothing.

"What do you think about it all, Cam?" she had asked her man one day months ago when they got to talking after work. She loved that little secretive gesture: *My man.* Even though Cam was obviously not.

They'd met for a drink. Linda was all in the mood that night to finally say something. She'd suspected a shimmer in his eyes for weeks. A sense he might feel the same. But after a few drinks, she opted out of being honest.

"What do *I* think?" he had said. "I think there are psychopaths in this world. We have not a clue as to what they are thinking or, more important, *how* they think. We need to understand these minds better, if we are ever to get a jump on them in a case like Sherri's or those other girls."

Then there was Jenna? *Damn Jenna.* Linda was back in the moment, trying to focus on falling asleep. Why would Jenna take off and not contact anyone? Where in the hell was she? Ted had called and said not to worry. Jenna was okay. She'd be home. He had not heard from her, but a friend said she had never left the high school after practice. Instead, she'd hung out with some girls in the ball field out back by the woods. Where was she now? Ted asked, predicting Linda's next question. Probably at a girlfriend's house. She wasn't texting or calling because her phone had died. She wasn't using a friend's phone because that's not what girls her age did. It was Jenna's way of "cutting the cord," Ted concluded.

A phrase that made Linda sick.

Linda was fighting an urge not to call out every available blue to search a few hot spots in town for her daughter. She did not want to ring that bell. Jenna would just hate her more. You could only cry wolf so many times. She'd done it obsessively after the divorce, by now no one would believe her, anyway. And doing such a thing always ran the risk of her superiors thinking she was unfit for duty. There was a careful balance between her anxiety, what she wanted to do, what she knew, and the professional action she took. Linda had to be cautious if she wanted to keep her job.

"You call me the minute she walks through that door, Teddy!" Linda told her ex-husband. It was close to ten p.m.

Linda Kane hung up and fell asleep.

10.

THE PHONE WAS RINGING. Well, buzzing, actually. It was not a nightmare this time. Linda wasn't standing by the edge of a cliff, trying to talk Sherri Lafontaine from jumping. She wasn't going to wake up sweating, breathing heavily, her chest cavity tight, and her jaw aching from clenching her teeth in her sleep.

Linda Kane opened her eyes. She was in bed.

Yes.

Sleeping.

Yes.

Something had awoken her.

Indeed.

What?

The phone. Shit. Someone's calling!

Jenna?

She turned her head toward the noise. The phone was rattling its way across her bedside table.

Rolling over, Linda looked at the alarm clock with the little red LCD numbers: *3:19.* She could not recall the last time she got a full night's sleep.

Jenna!

Linda threw her legs over the side of the bed, elbows on her knees, bowed her head, flipped her mane of fire up and over her head, let it fall down her shoulders, picked up the phone.

Her next thought was that Ted had not done what he'd said and called when Jenna got home.

Because she never made it home. That's why.

Jenna.

Linda Kane stood. The sudden indication that her daughter was among the missing sobered the detective.

She looked at the screen.

Cam.

Not good.

"Yeah, Cam?"

"Royal Oaks High. Get out here, in the back, soon as you can."

"What is it, Cam?"

"We got a body. Young girl, Lin."

Linda hung up and broke speed records as she dressed, left the house and hit the accelerator, siren off, the one blue light on top of her Crown Vic above the driver's side flashing for the three-mile trip from her apartment to the high school.

Jenna.

She called Ted. It rang once.

No answer. Straight to voice mail.

Same with Jenna's phone.

Shit. No. God. Please...

There was no way, Linda figured, Cam would call and tell her he had ID'd Jenna as the dead girl. He would summon her to the scene, stop her before she could see it herself. Or would he knock on her door? Walk in. Break the news gently. Cam would never tell a fellow cop—especially Linda—that her daughter had been murdered and left in the woods behind the high school, found by two punk-ass kids who'd phoned it in without giving their names. That was rookie cop stuff, even by the standards of a grown man who played Pokémon GO on his iPhone.

Linda drove through every light heading down Highland Park Road, into the parking lot of the school, straight toward the back ball fields. The Crown Vic went airborne as Linda didn't bother to stop for a curb—hitting the gas, instead, soaring down a short embankment. Then, seeing the gathering out back on the north side of the soccer field, the big spotlights set up and illuminating everything. She hit the brakes, turned the wheel a dogleg left, and came to a sliding sideways stop near the parked cars in the woods. The front tires sprayed grass; the back kicked up debris.

By now, CSU had the scene cordoned off. Blues were milling about, setting up a perimeter, blocking anyone who didn't belong from coming to the scene. Cam's car was parked to the right side of a cop huddle, all of whom wore latex gloves, had badges hanging around their necks, black windbreakers. Cam was speaking to a blue, Linda could see, bending down to hear him, his little notebook opened in his hand. Linda ran straight toward him.

"Cam," she screamed. "Cam!"

"Not her—not Cassandra Caldwell," Cam said, holding up two hands, palms out, hoping his boss would slow down. "Relax, Lin."

"It's Jenna."

"What? No. Shit no, Lin."

Linda fell to the ground in front of Cam. Clenched both fists.

"What do you mean, Jenna? Lin, we've got a young woman, maybe twenty, murdered, left out there, posed like some life-sized doll."

Linda looked up. Cam stood over her.

"What?" she said, collecting herself, realizing what was going on.

Linda had shown her cards. She needed a way out.

The detective stood.

"What in the hell, Lin? What are you talking about?"

"Cam, listen, it's Jenna. She didn't come home last night, hasn't been answering texts. Ted hasn't called me…long story. What do we have here?"

Cam looked at her. "You all right?" He put a hand on Linda's shoulder, squeezed gently, stared into the vacuum of her eyes. "You need a minute? What are you talking about? …Jenna's probably just pissed at you again. She'll get over it."

"Nothing. Nothing. I had a fight with her, you're right. What. Do. You. Have. Get to it." Linda was breathing easier. The rhythm of her pulse slowing down: her adrenaline registering back to the bottom of the thermometer. All of that pent-up and coiled frustration and anger, Linda pushed down into a place she'd learned long ago to manage. You placed it there, knowing you could revisit anytime you wanted.

Cam walked Linda to the body, filling her in on the facts they knew so far.

Kneeling, looking at the girl, Linda could tell it was not Cassie. Cam was right. Certainly not Jenna. That was the silver lining here. No…actually, there could be no upside to this tragedy. How people could compare bad things, weighing them, Linda Kane never understood. The dead girl was a fact, Linda concluded. One family would soon breathe easier, knowing Cassie still had a chance, while another was about to be forever changed. They'd hold their breath for the rest of their lives. Stuck in this moment. This one moment of their daughter, sister, wife, whoever she was, out here, alone and dead in the woods. A cop knocking on their door. The relaying of the news Joe Friday-like, with the proverbial, scripted *"I'm sorry"* salutation.

How could any of that be okay?

This girl was not twenty, not fifteen. Just about eighteen, Linda figured. Brown hair, shoulder-length. She wore blue jeans, the shiny type. Expensive sweater, cashmere or something similar; maybe camel hair. As the sun came up and the natural light of the morning shone on her, Linda guessed she was either Arab or Indian. "Muslim," someone said, as if it were a race of some kind, and Linda shot him a steely gaze.

None of the missing girls in the area over the years fit any description even close to this girl. She was from another town, far away. Soon enough, e-mails and faxes would go out with a photo of her lifeless face and they'd have a positive ID. A family would arrive at the morgue, destroyed, crying and shaking, unable to speak or stand. Identify her. Shake their heads: *"Yes, it's her…. My God, who could have done this to our baby?"* But none of that did Linda any good right now. She had a body that fit within a profile of a group of missing teenagers, including Cassie and Sherri. Why here? Why did this girl wind up in Royal Oaks, in back of the high school? Why have the others not been found?

It did not add up.

"And the caller wouldn't give a name?" Linda asked Cam. They walked toward the county coroner's black station wagon. It was parked on the edge of the soccer field by a row of player benches. They watched an empty white body bag being unzipped. As they came upon the back bumper, stood and talked, two coroner's office employees preparing the bag discussed a football game they had watched the previous night.

Another day on the job.

"No," Cam said. "Some punk kid. That much dispatch said she could tell by the Eminem tone and choice of, let's just say, urban vernacular."

"We have to find that kid, Cam. How do we know he didn't compromise the scene? What did he see?" Linda knew the kid wasn't involved; otherwise, he would have never called it in.

"Yeah, we're working on that. We had a custodian here last night at the school. Said he saw a couple kids walk out back here, so he came to the door, got a solid look at the two of them. He's sitting, going through photos now."

They discussed how she might have died.

"Dr. Epstein says strangulation with ligature," Cam explained, referring back to his notes. Epstein, the coroner, had come and gone already. "He was here earlier. But he can't be certain, of course, until he…"

Linda's mind veered. She knew it didn't matter how the girl died. Not now, anyway. What mattered was her connection, if any, to Cassie or the others. The entire feel of the scene spoke of something different. Something dark and ominous. Linda felt a change in the course of the case direction. She wasn't about to share her instinct with anyone now, but her gut, that tense twisting, told her that this murder was not going to help them with the other cases.

"When will he have the autopsy done?" Linda asked.

"They're bringing her to the morgue in about an hour." Cam looked at the two coroner's office employees, raised his voice: "If they ever get their asses in gear." Then back at Linda: "Epstein claims by end of day today he'll have some news for you."

"Send someone to watch the autopsy. Have them text us if anything strange turns up. Also, find any connection you can, once we get an ID, to Cassie. Did our gal here know Cassie? They hang out? Same circles? That sort of thing. I'm not sure you're going to find anything, but double check." Linda started to walk away, stopped, turned: "And you know what," she added, staring at the ground, "the more I think about it, you had better get the state boys out here before they remove her so they can have a look. Let them make the call to release her to the coroner. You with me on that, Cam?"

"Good call. Yes. Got it." Cam then texted Carmen, regarding sending a detective to the autopsy.

She responded immediately: DONE.

"I want a grid search of the entire grounds here, evidence, and, shit, we have to make sure she's the only vic out here. There could be more bodies." Linda looked toward where the girl had been found. She got lost in the idea of it being some sort of killer's burial ground. "If you can get a few dogs, I'd appreciate that. See if Somerville PD can spare a few—they owe us. Ask for Officer Hillary. Tell him he needs to pony up on our bet."

Cam nodded. Wrote it all down.

There was a commotion over at the police line blocking off the area. This startled Linda and Cam. They looked in that direction.

It was a woman. Linda walked toward her.

Trudi. Screaming for her baby. She'd heard something on the early-morning news, drove over.

When Linda got close, she grabbed hold of Trudi, cradled her, nestled Trudi under the yellow police tape as a blue held it over their heads.

"It's not Cassie, ma'am. Calm down. Please. We need to get you out of here."

The crowd was now a throng. Word had spread once it hit the morning's radio news. Neighbors walking their dogs, teachers heading into work, school children. All of them collecting on the other side of the yellow police tape as if waiting to get into a concert.

Linda could feel Trudi's body tremble. She wailed; screamed: "Why, why, why…"

"Ma'am, look at me," Linda said, grabbing Trudi by the face. They stood near midfield, <40 written in white paint underneath their feet on the grass of the football field. Linda took hold of Trudi and forced her to look into her eyes. "Focus on me, ma'am. That body out there—please hear me—is *not* your daughter. Cassie is *not* the deceased girl we have located here. Do you understand me?"

Trudi fell to the ground. Pounded her fists into the grass. Collapsed into herself. All hope had left the mother in that moment. She was no longer on Team Cassie, the runaway. Trudi Caldwell felt her daughter was gone for good.

Linda motioned for a female blue to come over. "Make sure she gets home okay. Please take care of her." Addressing Trudi: "Ma'am, please take care of yourself. I will be in touch by the end of the day. I'm going to find your daughter." Linda stared Trudi in the eyes again, paused, then got right up close. In this moment, the two of them understood each other. Each had demons from her past to reconcile. "Ma'am, listen to me. I *will* find your daughter and bring her home to you. That is my promise."

Cam walked over and looked on.

Trudi had a blank stare. A single tear streamed down her face. She didn't say anything.

Linda heard her cell ding.

Jenna is fine. Got home late is all. Didn't want to wake you.

Ted…asshole.

Looking behind her at the gathering crowd, Linda saw something she'd feared ever since Cassie had been reported missing: the story trickling out into the mainstream media. She'd tried as best she could to keep the case quiet and out of the murder-porn industry. This little town of Royal Oaks did not need the attention. Linda did not need some exploitative crime network looking for a nonexistent connection between Sherri's and Cassie's cases. But with news of this body hitting the wires this morning, it was not going to happen. The satellite truck was hard to miss, suffice it to say, with its round and scalloped cone dish on the roof pointed into the sky, a metal lollipop in the center beaming out images and audio to a studio somewhere in Gotham. TCN was plastered across the sides of the truck, on its doors, the hood, and every piece of equipment. Not hard to tell that the network had sent its top loudmouth true-crime pundit and exploiter of white middle-class tragedy to the scene: Iris Starr.

As if that was her real name.

Iris Starr had actually taken on the namesake of the Greek goddess of the rainbow and messenger of the gods, she freely, patronizingly, admitted whenever asked.

The nerve.

The reporter wore only black leather skirts. Tight-fitting blouses with black buttons, and always a shade of dark red, heavy lipstick to complete the look. Her thick mane of brunette hair with platinum highlights ran down her back, silky and smooth and always salon ready. She'd spent money on that hair. Lots of it. Her breasts were worth maybe just south of $35,000—large, round, perfect, and plump. Gravity had zero effect on this woman. Any story Iris covered focused on the controversial, most despotic aspects of it. She had the audacity to call herself an investigative journalist when all she did was set pieces for that murder/porn–watching crowd that had made the True Crime Network—"TCN" to the "addicts"—all anyone in television talked about these days. *Scene of the Crime, with Iris Starr* was not the highest-rated series on the network, but it brought people into their living rooms and onto their streaming gadgets, nonetheless.

"Shit," Linda said as she spied the TCN correspondent. "Here we go."

This was the first time Linda would have to deal with the likes of someone like Iris Starr and her trashy network. She knew from forensic conferences, talking to cops around the country, that once Iris dug in, the woman was relentless. She never let up. If you didn't help her, she trashed you all day long on TCN and any guest appearances she made on the cable news channels. For Linda, she'd done a good job of avoiding all the media hype throughout the years, on anniversaries and other times when Sherri's story had been pimped for ratings.

Not anymore.

Still, Linda welcomed the fight. She could not have cared less what anyone, especially a woman as brash and shallow as Iris, thought about her, or how she went about investigating her cases.

"Don't let her anywhere near this line, Officer," Linda told one of the blues standing by the yellow taped-off area behind the high school. "Get your men to put some sheets up there by the body and block it all off. I don't want that girl's body bag being lifted onto a gurney on television tonight. I hear about that, I personally blame you."

"Detective?" Iris shouted. She had one of those long microphones in her hand, a square box at the top underneath the spongy black ball, the TCN logo on all four sides. Her high heels dug into the grass and she had a hard time walking. "Can I speak with you for a minute?"

Linda ignored Iris and walked back down toward the scene, after making sure Trudi was on her way home. As she approached the edge of the woods, Linda didn't turn, but she could feel Iris's eyes burning into her back. This wouldn't be, Linda knew, the last time she and Iris Starr ran into each other.

There was nothing left for Linda to do here. Her time was better spent in town, talking to people, learning what she could about Cassie's lifestyle and, at the same time, working to identify the deceased.

Plus, Linda Kane had a little score to settle with her ex.

11.

THERE WAS A STACK of mail on the counter. A few bills, several religious packets of rosaries and crosses for donations. Coupons from local car dealers and restaurants. A supermarket circular announcing the weekly buy-one-get-two-free deals. A bottle of Benadryl next to that. A set of car keys. A newspaper, the headline of the morning mentioning how a "teenager's body" had been found in back of the high school. The superintendent quoted in the story said he was closing school for a day, maybe two.

On the way back to the station, Linda stopped at Ted's, who was just then getting ready to leave for work. She needed to talk about what had transpired the previous night with Jenna—leaving practice early, going out with friends, not telling anyone. Ted not calling to let her know their daughter had actually come home at eleven and, not feeling well, went straight to bed. It was unacceptable. She wasn't going to be treated this way.

Ted let Linda in and offered his ex-wife a cup of coffee after saying he had a few minutes to chat before taking off for work. His wife, who'd left already, had just made a fresh pot.

"It would have been nice," Ted noted, "you two seeing each other this morning." He laughed out of the corner of his mouth, fastened a button on his wrist, looking down at it, then up at Linda.

"Too bad," Linda said, snapping her fingers. "And that's a negative there on the coffee, Ted. But thanks."

"You own any other set of clothes, Linda? That is all I ever see you in." Linda's ex paused to take a sip of his coffee. He noticed a piece of lint on his black trousers and picked it off. "What *happened* to you?"

Linda wore khaki slacks, not too tight, not loose, either. The perfect fit, her pants displayed a shape referred to today as "the modern woman." Cam called Linda thick, which he had to explain was a major compliment.

She also routinely wore a white button-down dress shirt. Linda left it untucked because of the slight little pouch she had trouble getting rid of after having Jenna. Black boots. A black windbreaker, like an FBI agent. Her Glock 23 was inside a strapped shoulder holster, allowing Linda to draw the weapon with her right hand from the opposite side. Her gold badge was always clipped to her hip. She lived in this getup. Rarely ever wore anything else. And for Linda Kane, this was okay.

"I'm a cop, Teddy. What do you want from me? This is it." She threw out her arms, crucifix-like, spun around, fashion model-style, then abruptly stopped. "Wait, I know. I am supposed to wear those tight black yoga pants or sweats with 'Pink!' scrawled across my ass like your little size-two wife, right?"

"Funny, Lin. Real fucking funny."

"Look, love to trade barbs, but I need your focus on bigger issues, Teddy."

Ted wagged his finger, then slapped his hand on the counter. Took a deep breath. Ted Schultz had the look of what he did for a living: accountant. The businessman haircut, runner's frame, not tall, not short, but average. He shaved every day, didn't like the dudes who wore the stubble. He favored sheer suits with a skinny "power" tie, always dark in color (red was his absolute, hands-down favorite), against a white shirt.

This bothered him, the way Linda spoke, and she knew it. "No, Lin…not gonna happen here." Ted added, "You don't get to do that in my house." Ted had always disliked it when she called him Teddy. Same feeling as when a mother scolded her child by using his first and middle name after finding out he'd done something bad: *"Teddy Joseph, you get your ass in here this minute."*

"Come on, Teddy, lighten up."

"Stop it, Lin. Don't do it."

Funny how people present a button to push, then get mad when people keep pushing it.

A car drove by out front, interrupting the moment. The tailpipe had one of those sporty mufflers that made it sound like a super loud kazoo.

Teenagers.

"Where was our daughter last night, and why didn't you call me when I asked you to?" Linda had this thing where she'd angle and turn her head a little to the left when she was serious and angry.

"She was out shopping with friends, Lin."

"That can *never* happen again, what she did. What *you* did. Not with what is going on out there."

"Besides the fact that you do not get to tell me how to parent, what *is* going on? That body. That what you're referring to?" Ted walked over to the fridge and put the coffee creamer back inside. He closed the door and, waiting for an answer, didn't turn immediately around.

"Just keep tabs on her, always," Linda said. She had not moved from where she stood. This was an old-school cop trick when interrogating people without them realizing it. "Let her know that she needs to check in with one of us. Next year, when she goes off to college, fine, she's on her own. She can come and go and do whatever the hell she wants. But right now, Ted, I need to know where she is at all times. She's not going to listen to me if I tell her. I'm serious about this. This shit going on, it's dangerous. I can feel it."

"Ah, yes…I get it now…imminent threat, huh?" Ted said as he turned. Then walked toward his briefcase on the counter.

"Make terrorism jokes, Ted, that's fine. Just make sure she is aware that this little town we live in, right now, is unpredictable. There's something going on."

"Shit, *that's* what this is. About Sherri, Lin." Ted knew better than most the toll that case had taken on his ex-wife. He also knew that pulling out that card was grounds for serious battle. Linda grew nervous whenever the subject came up between them. She didn't even realize her hands balled into fists whenever Ted mentioned it. "Unresolved feelings of guilt and shame and everything that has held you back?" Ted continued as he opened his briefcase to a double *pop*, tossed in a brown paper bag—his lunch—and closed it. "This is why Jenna doesn't live with you, Lin." Now he looked at his ex, holding his briefcase by his side. The entire movement, Linda observed, was Ted trying to act superior, like some politician holding the nuclear codes, following the president around. It made Ted feel important. Like what he said still mattered to her. "This is why you find it so hard to get close to her," Ted added, walking up to Linda, standing in her personal space. "Can't you let Sherri go after all these years, for fuck's sake? Is that what all this is about? I thought you'd gone and talked to someone about that."

The fact that Linda had not resolved the past had not been the death knell to the marriage—as many of their friends and family might have assumed. Still, the "Sherri Incident," as Linda had termed it to her therapist back in the day, had played a role. The night sweats. Closing up and not talking to anyone. Depression. Not eating. Not being there for Jenna the way she should have. The way in which Linda saw Ted as the enemy, not someone she could have ever leaned on for support. Then the office bimbo coming around and the opportunity for Ted presenting itself, somebody giving him the little bit of attention his ego craved. It was all for the best, anyway, Linda had surmised long ago. Save for Jenna and how that played out, she was glad to be rid of Ted. She needed to be alone.

Linda turned and walked toward the door. With her hand on the knob, she thought of saying something that would ruin his day. Maybe mention the size of his…but, instead, she opened the door and walked out without speaking.

While starting her vehicle, Linda decided to put a blue on Jenna when she knew the department could spare one. A cop she could trust not to say anything. She considered that they were past all the petty insults and Ted attacking her mental instabilities. It was never about one-upping the guy or having the edge in a fight. For Linda, it was isolation and fear. That was how Ted made her feel. Like a doe in the woods, roaming around by herself. Putting the cop on Jenna from here out, maybe just a drive by of the house once in a while, or a look in when Jenna was at the mall or on her way home from practice, was the assurance Linda needed to get on with the work of finding Cassie and keeping her promise to Trudi. The tail couldn't be too obvious. Just a shadow when Linda felt separation creep up and that apparition back in the air. Jenna could never find out. She'd have a conniption fit. Get angry and nasty and go running home telling her father Mom was up to it again, paranoid and losing her mind. Ted would call. Threaten. It would get ugly. Then Linda's superiors would find out and begin asking questions, sending her back to the shrink.

She did not need any of that now.

The stakes outweighed whatever fear she wrestled with this time, though. There was a killer in the midst of it all, on top of a ghost, Linda was certain, out there snatching kids. Yes, she was sure the two cases were not connected, Cassie and the dead girl behind the high school.

But, hell: One could never be too careful or overprotective when lives were in the balance.

12.

SHAVED HEAD AND SPIKED Hair sat in the basement of Shaved Head's house, thrash metal playing in the background. They'd lost interest in playing Warcraft. Neither was much good at the game, anyway.

Scottie Mathers—a.k.a. Spiked Hair—walked over to where Benjie—Shaved Head—sat on the floor in front of the television. He showed Shaved Head the screen of his iPhone.

"Hit send, yo," Shaved Head said. "Do it, man. Stop obsessing over it and just send that fucking photo."

Scottie had one of the photos of the dead girl cropped enough so you could tell what it was without giving away the entire package. He'd placed the photo in a text message to Iris Starr after seeing a dispatch she'd reported from the high school parking lot, which had aired live on TCN just before they started playing Warcraft.

"I'm tellin' you, yo, she'll pay us for those photos. I know her type."

"You don't know any *type*, Benjie—what the *hell* are you talking about…*type*. Shit, man."

Shaved Head stood and got into his friend's face. He screamed over the music, more to be heard than out of anger: "Fuck off, man. You see that fine piece I've been hitting lately? Look, just send the photo. We can make some serious money, yo."

Scottie stared at his buddy. He looked down at the screen. Back up at Benjie.

Then he hit send and—*whoosh*—off the photo went.

They waited.

No response.

Ten minutes went by.

Nothing.

"Turn that game back on," Scottie said. "I told you, she's a reporter. She'd never buy that shit. Now what? She probably turned it over to the police. We're fucked!"

Benjie said, "I told you not to do it. You stupid son of a bitch. Why do I let you get me involved in things you have no idea what in the fuck you are doing!"

Ding.

A text message.

Scottie looked down. Then started jumping up and down as if a girl he liked had sexted him.

"It's her, man—that Iris chick. She wants to fucking play ball here. Holy shit!"

Benjie pumped his fist toward the ground. "I knew it, yo."

Scottie looked at his friend. Then got to work negotiating where to meet, texting Iris that he was finished sending any photos via phone or through online channels. If she wanted to see the goods, she'd have to bring cash and meet them somewhere.

How much?

"What do I say?" Scottie uttered, looking up at the ceiling, biting his lip, thinking. "Shit…how much?"

Benjie blurted out "$200."

"I don't know, man. That's an awful lot of money."

Come on, how much?

Scottie tapped out a text. Then deleted it. He sat down, pulled out a cigarette, lit the thing, took a pull while it hung from his lips, his thumbs moving up and down—tapping once again, like two tarantula spider legs.

BEHIND DELI. BRING CASH. $100.

Whoosh.

Ding.

One hr. Bring all photos U have.

SEE YOU THEN.

One more question: Do you know anyone you can put me in contact with who might know the missing girl, Cassandra Caldwell? More $$ if you can.

Benjie walked over. "What is it?"

Scottie showed him the text.

"Don't you fucking tell her, man. Don't. You. Do. It."

MY FRIEND, BENJIE HERE, HE'S HIT THAT A FEW TIMES.

Whoosh.

13.

CAM AND LINDA STARED at Linda's computer monitor, watching the security surveillance video from the funeral home next door to Teresa Noble's house. This would be documentation, if it panned out, of Cassie leaving her friend's house on the night she went missing.

They sipped coffees from 7-Eleven. Cam liked the blueberry flavor, a subtle little aspect of his metrosexual side he took grief for around the office. That, and getting a *man*icure once in a while.

"See that picture of the Fat Boy Harley-Davidson taped to my computer," Cam said, leaning back. "Saving my pennies for that chrome horse right there, Lin. Someday, some fine day, it's gonna be all mine."

If she was only a few years younger and didn't work with him, Linda would try to convince herself in moments like these that Cam was her perfect counterpart. They'd do well together. She'd tried for years to push away the feelings, but there he was, always making the argument tougher. Only he didn't know it.

"Could you see *me* on a Harley?" Linda asked.

Cam started coughing in a mocking fashion. "What? You? Sure, Lin. Sure thing. You on a Roadster, hauling ass down one of the farming roads, pissing off all the farmers. Me behind you, laughing my ass off. Now *that* I could see."

Linda smiled.

"Save some pennies and buy me one, too, then. We'll ride off into the sunset together."

"Funny. Hey. I got a new one for you."

Linda did a slight eye roll. "Okay, Cam. Let's have it."

"You know what the 'zacklies' are?"

"Cam…come on. We gotta get to this video here."

"Yeah, Lin, well, the zacklies are when your breath smells 'zackly' like your ass. Means you got a case of the zacklies." Cam stood and mimicked a mic drop. Clapped his hands together. Laughed.

"Sit down, you. Let's do this."

Linda was focused on nailing down a timeline for Cassie to see if it matched what everyone had claimed. She stared at the screen, a pen between her teeth. Her hands in a praying formation in front of her, tucked underneath her chin.

Pure, utter focus.

In her mind, Linda Kane knew this video would hold answers. Maybe she had been looking at Cassie's disappearance entirely wrong from the get-go?

They'd found out from speaking to Katherine and Trudi that Cassie, though grounded, had walked to Teresa's house about four that afternoon and planned on leaving in time to make it home before Trudi or her boyfriend got back to the house from work. This way, it would appear as though she'd never left the house. Katherine had agreed to cover for Cassie. Teresa's house was a seventeen-minute walk from Trudi's, Linda had been told by the blue she sent out to trace the girl's steps. If you were Cassie, you left Teresa's, walked east down the block into downtown, by Town Hall and a convenience store, along with a few local retail shops. The green Linda had parked near when she visited Teresa's was on one corner, that church on the other side of the street, a small walk-in medical clinic across the street from the church. From there, Cassie would have walked south if she was headed home, down Union Street, which intersected with West Street, and finally the road that Trudi, the kids, and Vinnie the boyfriend lived on, Regan Circle.

"Cassie made the trip maybe fifty times without an issue," Teresa had told Linda during a phone call earlier that day. "I have no idea where she could have gone."

The black-and-white video was surprisingly clear. Cars drove by. Cam and Linda could make out the model, light or dark color, even the person driving: female or male; black, white, Hispanic. Each license tag moving in and out of the shot was discernible. Linda felt a sudden ease when she realized this.

"If someone picked Cassie up," she said to Cam, "we'll likely be able to get a tag number."

Cam kept his eyes on the monitor.

As the timer in the bottom right corner of the shot wound down toward the eight o'clock hour, about the moment Cassie was said to have left Teresa's, they both paid close attention.

"Son of a bitch, there she is," Cam said.

Cassie walked out of the house, down the pathway, onto the sidewalk, took a right, and headed toward the direction she should have gone to head home. It was such a perfect shot, as though the camera had been trained on the girl.

Linda sat up straight the moment Cassie walked into the frame.

"She looks serious," Linda observed. "Like she's thinking about something important."

In her memory, Linda photocopied that Cassie wore a jean jacket with studs along the front breast region, light-colored pants—which Katherine had said she remembered her sister putting on before she left the house. Cassie walked slowly, looking straight ahead as she made her way across the computer screen.

"She never hesitates about which direction she's heading," Cam added.

This was part of the reason why Linda became a cop: the exhilarating feeling of being actively involved in solving a case and providing answers to families. Her first idea of a career—business management—was such a damn dead-end, soulless life, Linda was grateful for the law enforcement bug that bit after troopers visited her high school and explained how civic duty, regardless of how you were viewed in the world, was rewarding. The recompense, she figured in the days that followed, was going to be finding her friend Sherri and bringing her home. She signed up for the academy the day after she turned eighteen.

As Cassie made it to the center of the shot, between the funeral home and Teresa Noble's house, she looked up.

"It's as if someone off-screen is calling out her name in front of her," Linda said, thinking out loud. "Up until that moment, she's kept her head down—it even seems as though Cassie is curious."

"She was playing that superstitious game kids play by not stepping on any of the sidewalk cracks," Cam added. "Am I right?"

"Yeah."

Just before walking directly in front of the funeral home, Cassie stopped. Then, suddenly, she looked behind, over her shoulder, as if startled. Then up in the air, in frustration, like she knew the person who called out to her.

"Or maybe beeped a horn," Linda noted to Cam. "Clearly, she didn't want to deal with this person who'd called out to her from behind."

"It's not an alarmed look, though," Cam added.

Linda agreed: "Right. No. More of, *'Oh, it's you…great.'*"

Looking straight ahead again, Cassie took off running in the direction she had been looking toward first, away from whoever had called out to her in back.

After she disappeared from the screenshot, a light-colored pickup truck drove in the same direction, following where Cassie had headed. An African-American guy, between forty and fifty, Cam and Linda guessed, was behind the wheel, his head close to the windshield, as if he was struggling to see out. The truck drove slowly, then sped up past the funeral home and was soon out of the shot.

Cam and Linda looked at each other.

Just then, quite vaguely, Linda thought she could see a person running through the park across the street. But it was too far away to make out clearly.

"Could be a dog," Cam said.

"Yeah…you're right."

Cam froze the frame there.

"It's too grainy, Lin. Our guys will never be able to blow it up."

"Likely nothing to do with Cassie, anyway."

Cam hit the ESCAPE key and the video stopped. "That's about it. What do you think?"

"For one," Linda said, "the phone call I took about the note—that dude was definitely black. Our guy here in the truck is black. Might just be a coincidence, but we gotta run it down."

Cam made a note.

"There are no other cameras anywhere along that street that might have caught her?" Linda asked, leaning back in her swivel office chair, staring at the monitor, screen-saver bubbles bouncing around. "What about Town Hall? It's a block away on the same side of that street."

Cam stood, grabbed a map of the area from a nearby table, and rolled it out on top of the files and other odds and ends cluttering up Linda's desk.

"There are," Cam said, pointing them out on the map, "but none captured her. And the one that could have"—he tapped on where it was located—"well, wouldn't you know, that has been erased. We got to it too late. I left a report for you on your desk and texted you about it."

"What about the truck?"

"Yes. You can see that same truck stop at the light here. He takes a right, and then vanishes from the shot. Can't see who's inside of it, though. We're assuming it's the same black dude."

"You run the plate?"

Cam tossed a file on Linda's desk. "It's all there. Let's go talk to him."

Linda opened the file. There was no photo of the guy, but he lived in town. No priors except for a trespassing charge when he was eighteen. He'd moved to the area within the past six months.

As Linda read, Cam said, "Hey, that DB in back of the high school, the state police are taking it over, I'm told. They found a few things out at the scene indicating it could be connected to a case from Hartford they've been working on for years."

Linda looked up. Then back down at the report.

She flipped the page: "Cam!"

"Yeah?" Cam was back at his desk. Sitting, reading something. He looked up.

"You didn't see this?" Linda stood. Walked over. Folded the report to the page she was on and threw it on Cam's desk.

The paper landed with a subtle *thud*. Cam looked at Linda, then down at the paper.

Linda stood over his shoulder. She presented a certain amount of intensity, giving a feeling for how serious she thought the information was.

"How long have you had this report, Cam?"

"I don't know…five, six hours."

"You read through it?"

"Kind of scanned it. Been busy, Lin. Come on. We got other things going on. The state police are here now. Captain's talking to them. You hear me? They're taking over lead on that DB."

Linda looked toward the captain's office.

Good riddance.

She didn't care about the political nonsense associated with cases. Whereas some other small-town police forces might balk and not allow their egos to accept the help, Linda welcomed it. Anytime cops wanted to step in and offer a hand, Linda knew, you never refused. Especially with a savage murder like the one behind the high school.

"Doesn't our guy here live in the opposite direction from where he's seen driving down that road toward Cassie?" She paused a moment. "Doesn't he live *just* around the corner from the Teresa Noble residence? Isn't that a one-way road he is driving down in the wrong direction?"

Cam bounced his fingertips on the desk, thinking.

"Yeah, you're right," he said.

"Read *that*." Linda pointed to the top of the page.

Cam put his index finger on the sentence and followed the words across the page with his eyes, reading to himself.

Linda got a whiff of P Diddy's—err, Sean John's—cologne wafting up from Cam's neck into her space. It made her tingle inside. She caught herself and went back to being the boss.

"Shit," Cam said, stopping where the black guy was employed.

"Yeah, exactly."

Linda turned and walked out of the office.

14.

"HEY, LIN, PEDRO HERE. Listen. We been following that reporter, like you wanted, Iris…whatever. And we see her meet with a couple of punks and exchange some money earlier today."

"Where, Officer Rodriquez?" Linda had not even made it to her car when she took the call.

"You know that deli behind Evergreen Printing?"

"Yup. Where'd they go from there?"

"We lost the reporter, followed the kids," Rodriquez said, explaining how one of them, the one with the Spiked Hair, was a fireman's son who'd been out of the house for about a year, on his own, living with a friend in a nearby town. "Name's…um…Scottie Mathers. Troublemaker. The other kid, he has a shaved head. His name is Benjie Britton. He's from a good family, far as we can see. Just kind of recently fell in with an older crowd of tough kids."

"Benjie" was all Linda heard.

"Where are they now?"

"Hanging out in back of the pool hall. They bought some weed with the money they got from the reporter."

"Thanks, Officer Rodriquez. Hey, excellent work."

"You want us to find that reporter?"

"Nope. She'll emerge. I know where she lives."

Linda went back upstairs into the squad room and grabbed Cam by the lapel. They tore off and out of the driveway, heading for the pool hall. It was an area of town on the fringes, essentially; a village about four miles away, unassociated with Royal Oaks, a rough part of the general county called Rockville. This was where all the kids went to find their dope. Welfare housing. Cheap rent, WIC, and state assistance. Dollar stores and bodegas.

"You come from the left. I'll drop you off by the Chinese food restaurant, you go through the kitchen with your badge out, wait by the back door into that area behind the building where they are. I'll be coming out of the pool hall, back-door exit."

"Got it," Cam said, concentrating. Linda was schooling Cam and he loved it. Even though Cam had been involved in countless takedowns, nobody in the department had the reputation that Linda Kane had for this sort of thing. Linda went about it in a different manner than most. It was never run and gun for Linda, kick in doors, wave badges around and flash your muscle. Linda used her intellect. She always took the smart, safe route.

They knew the boys were still there, in back of the pool hall, because as Linda drove down the road toward the strip mall where all these businesses were, she spied two people out back and pointed it out to Cam.

Wasn't hard to make out a kid with spiked hair and another with a shaved head from a distance.

"Wait for my text, though, Cam. And look, we don't know what's going on in their minds here, so hand on weapon, but keep it holstered, okay? Let's not get carried away. We want whatever information they have. Getting that will depend on how we treat them on first impression. Especially Benjie."

Cam shook his head. "Got it."

They exited the car.

Cam walked into the Chinese restaurant, flashed his gold badge; everyone stepped aside. He found the back door with the bar set halfway across the center to push and exit. Stood, iPhone in hand, waited.

Linda turned all eyes inside the pool hall when she entered. She explained to the manager that she needed to use the back-door exit and that nobody was to leave the pool hall until she came back in and gave the word. If she needed to card everyone in the establishment who was drinking, well, she could get a few blues over here right away to do that.

The manager said, "Anything you need, Officer. Nobody leaves. Got it."

Linda stood by the exit. She texted Cam to walk out the door exactly when their iPhones hit 2:50 p.m.

Two minutes and counting.

The time came, they popped out each door, both arriving on each side of the two boys, who sat on a pile of old wooden skids.

Shaved Head Benjie Britton froze.

Spiked Hair stared at Cam, then at Linda, and took off running. Linda chased him.

Cam told Shaved Head to get on his knees, hands behind his head. "Don't fucking move a muscle."

"Yes, sir."

Confident he'd just scared Shaved Head into submission, Cam ran after Linda and Spiked Hair, who had gone around the other side of the building, out of sight.

As Cam reached the corner, he stopped, drew his weapon, inched his way toward the edge, just in case a surprise waited for him.

Linda was two feet in front of Spiked Hair. He had a switchblade brandished out in front of his midsection, its blade reflecting in the afternoon sun, pointed at Linda.

"Shit," Cam said to himself.

Cam took a breath. Studied the scene to figure out how he could sneak up on the kid, maintain control without him knowing until it was too late. He could walk around the corner with his weapon drawn, huffing and puffing all that cop nonsense.

"Too dangerous," he whispered.

Linda would not want him to do that, anyway.

Linda had not gone for her weapon because she never saw Spiked Hair take out the knife as he ran. But now the scene was straight out of *West Side Story* and Linda Kane knew there was no way she was going to introduce a gun into the situation. He was just a kid. Eighteen. She could talk him off the ledge here, where several years in prison waited at the bottom of the cliff. There was no need to scare him any more than he was already. A gun always made matters worse.

Cam backed away from the corner and disappeared.

Linda said, "Let's not take this into an entirely different place, okay? We can get you out of this. You need to trust me here. It's Scottie, right? That your name, son? We just want to talk to you."

Spiked Hair waved the knife in front of Linda. One wrong move that spooked him, she knew, and he might slash her face before she had a chance to react.

"Fuck off, cop."

"Come on now…Scottie. I need you to trust that I just want to talk to you."

"We had nothing to do with that dead girl. Fuck off, I said." He stabbed the knife into the air.

They circled, facing each other, still that two feet buffer zone separating the space between a peaceful conclusion and bloody violence. Linda took on a Sumo wrestling stance, hands out in front of her, knees bent a little, her head crouched down a bit. She was considering going for her weapon because she did not like the look on Scottie's face as the situation grew in intensity. He was high and his eyes were darting back and forth. None of that was good. Linda wished like hell she could at least get her jacket off and wrap it around one arm and hand, and use it to protect herself. But that wasn't going to happen, either.

Scottie flipped the knife between both hands, to show he knew what he was doing and could handle it. He lunged short swipes into the air in front of Linda, just inches from her face.

"You scared yet, cop? Am I scaring you? You wanna get cut today?"

"Scottie, you won't win. You might hurt me, but you will ultimately lose this fight. My partner is nearby. You see the size of him?"

"Fuck off," Scottie said, stabbing into the air again. "I'll shank him like I'll shank you."

Linda could sense a bead of sweat developing on the back of her neck. Her muscles tightened. Her heart raced.

Scottie took another stab into the air, this one closer to Linda's face, and she jumped back and out of its way.

"Huh! Scared you, cop. Didn't I?"

Linda could see Scottie was breathing heavier and faster. Bad sign. Inside he was talking himself into what to do next, she knew. Psyching himself up for whatever he had in mind.

Cam was ready. Linda didn't see him—that's how stealthily Cam had found a spot and positioned himself to take Spiked Hair out. Plus, Linda was focused. Her eyes never leaving the subject in front of her.

Linda Kane was the target.

As Spiked Hair went to say something, a man the size of a bear flew off the roof above and onto Spiked Hair's back and head, flattening Scottie to the ground before he ever knew what had toppled him. The knife in his hand went sliding across the pavement. Cam had a hand on Scottie's neck, whispered in his right ear, "Don't fucking move. I'll squeeze the life out of you."

Cam had found an iron pull-down roof ladder, climbed the thing, crept along the roof over to the edge where Scottie and Linda were doing their little circle-dance, then waited for the right moment. When it appeared, he leapt about fifteen feet through the air onto Scottie.

Linda had backed away once she saw Cam flying through the air, like a WWE wrestler coming off the corner of the ring.

"You're fucked now" was all Cam said as Scottie tried to catch his breath, which Cam had knocked out of both his lungs as they hit the tar.

On the ground, Scottie's neck in one hand, his body covering the boy, Cam looked up at Linda: "You okay, Lin?"

She sensed the intensity in Cam's voice. The emotion. He wasn't just asking.

15.

TRUDI NEEDED TO GET back to work. If not for the money, for the ritual and monotony that serving drinks and food offered. It had been two days. Not a peep from Cassie. A friend of Cassie's called and said he might have seen her the day before at an area lake; but by the time he made it to the girl, she had run off. He wasn't about to tell police, he said, and would deny it if ever asked.

"Sorry, Ms. Caldwell," he had said, "but it would open me up to sharing what I was doing at the lake, and who I was with. If that girl's mother *ever* found out, I'm screwed."

"Was it *her*?" Trudi asked. "Tell me if it was her, goddamn it all."

"I think it might have been."

She hung up.

Vinnie was at the bar when Trudi walked in for a shift she'd called and demanded from her boss, who insisted that she stay home. He'd even sent over a tin of macaroni and cheese, with a note that said to "keep it in the fridge and force yourself to eat."

Walking into the bar section of the restaurant, Trudi went over and stood next to Vinnie. He'd gotten out early and worked only first shift.

"This is how you help?"

"Trudi, come on, what can *I* do?"

"Make some flyers or something. Get together a search team and look around. Anything other than sitting here, drinking, watching sports on TV. My daughter is missing, Vinnie."

Vinnie Costello usually worked fourteen-hour days at the paper mill in Rockville. All those hours in a warehouse on your feet consumed any life you had left. When he was done, Vin wanted only to sit at the bar, sip his Budweiser in the longneck, dark bottle, head outside and smoke when the urge came on. Then, with a good glow on, head home. Collect his check on Fridays. Do it all over again the next week. He and Trudi had a nominal relationship. Habitual. They helped each other pay bills. They had sex when they both felt like it; the sex rather plain, missionary, and planned. They took care of Trudi's kids best they knew how. A fat man with large fingers and a bulging belly, Vinnie was an old-school Italian from Queens, who happened to have run into Trudi one night when he stopped at the bar for a cold one. They hooked up. He moved in two years later and, here they were, now ten years strong: strangers and roommates.

"You know I love the girls, Trudi. What can I do? I need to keep working. We need to pay the bills."

Trudi walked away, stopped, turned around. "I'm working all night. Go home, Vin. Be *there*, at least, in case someone calls or comes to the house."

"I can do that, Trudi."

Vin paid his tab by leaving a twenty on the bar under his Bud bottle, kissed his girlfriend on the cheek, hugged her.

"It's gonna be okay," he said before walking out of the bar.

In the kitchen by the time clock, Trudi searched for her card in the rack. As she came to a name that vaguely reminded her of Cassie, a sudden feeling of loss consumed her. She fell back against the wall, sliding down, landing on the dusty floor. Trudi was crying, her entire body pulsating. She couldn't do this. Work. No way. Her baby. Cassie. Little Cassandra—with the skull of brown hair and flaky, red skin upon birth, smiling first thing out of the womb, not giving her mother any sort of trouble in the first ten years, sleeping through the night after only two months—was gone. Where in the hell was she? Had Cassie ever been away from home this long without calling, saying she was sorry, returning, begging for forgiveness? Never. The most time she'd ever taken off without anyone knowing was overnight. Then she was home early the next morning, looking for a meal and her warm bed, telling her mother she'd never do it again. No matter how much they fought, no matter how many obscene vulgarities they hurled at each other, no matter how many times they'd scream one was never talking to the other again, Cassie and her mother called a truce the only way they knew how.

Forgetting about it all.

"Hey, what are you doing?" he said, walking over, helping Trudi by the elbow off the floor, hoisting her up onto her feet. There was a comforting tone to his voice. "Come on. Let me help you up." The man then yelled into the bar: "Get me a glass of water, Charlie. Bring it here now."

The bartender did what he was told.

"Thanks."

The man sat Trudi down in a booth out in the dining area, away from a full crowd in the bar laughing at a rerun of *Two and a Half Men*. He sat next to her, made Trudi drink the water in short sips.

"Thanks, Freddie," Trudi said.

Freddie was looking around, seeing who, if anyone, was watching them. This bar and restaurant, the people that frequented the place, were pretty straight. They didn't much care for butting into people's business. You put their drink in front of them, put the Keno and sports on the television above the bar, and they kept to themselves.

"Trudi, you have *got* to hold strong here. What are you doing at work? You should be home. I told you *not* to come in."

Freddie Banks was an African American from Jamaica, New York, who had moved to Royal Oaks months ago and started working at Marty's Restaurant & Bar. He'd graduated from Hofstra, a degree in restaurant management, and held jobs at some of the swanky Manhattan hotels, but claimed to have wanted a change from city life. He coached a local youth soccer team. Volunteered in town at the food bank. He was the manager of the restaurant and was thinking about buying it. Freddie had one of those chiseled, soccer player bodies you'd see on a South American World Cup athlete. His skin shiny, more bronze than black. He stood about six feet. He had a full head of short-cropped, kinky Velcro hair. Born on one of the islands, he spoke with a slight Caribbean accent. Patrons and employees of the bar loved Freddie. He always had something generous and positive to say. He never came across as facetious or phony. The guy seemed sincere to the core. Trudi liked him because he smelled of coconuts and palm trees, she'd often joke during happier times.

Freddie and Trudi had been sleeping together for about eight weeks. They'd meet up before and after a shift, sometimes share a bottle of merlot. Or just talk and have sex. Other times they'd screw inside Freddie's apartment, a one-bedroom carved out of an old Colonial about four blocks behind Teresa Noble's house in the west end of town.

Trudi had just recently broken it off with Freddie after Cassie caught them behind the restaurant in Freddie's truck, talking, making out. Cassie had just happened to stop by the restaurant looking for some money to borrow so she could hang out at the mall and go to a movie.

"Great…will you look at this," Cassie had said, walking up to the window of Freddie's truck. "One black guy in town and you gotta get with him. You disgust me, Mom. You really do."

"Cassie, wait," Trudi said. "Let me explain."

"Explain? You think you can explain this away like you have my father and what you did to *him*? Trudi Caldwell, the local waitress sleeping with her boss. How clichéd can you be, Mom? Jesus. Get a fucking life."

Days later, Trudi told Freddie that Cassie demanded she end it, or Cassie was going to tell Vinnie. Trudi didn't need the trouble. So she ended the relationship with Freddie, acted as though it never happened, and went back to her shitty life with Vinnie.

"Vin will never know, Freddie," Trudi explained. "He'll never figure it out, either. He's just not that smart."

Freddie didn't take it so well. He pleaded with Trudi.

"You should not allow your children to control your life! I love you, Trudi. Vinnie will understand and get over it."

Trudi said that was not what she wanted to hear.

"It's over, Freddie. Accept that. Move on."

"Have you told them about us?" Freddie whispered. He kept looking into the bar to see if anyone was staring. "Come on, Trudi, take a sip of that water. Just get the fluid in you."

Trudi gazed at the glass, twirling it in circles, her fit of mourning over for the moment. Dried tears on her face, mascara smudged and all over her right cheek. The woman was a mess. Her life in free fall. She'd been debating whether to tell Linda about Freddie. "I haven't. But I should, Freddie. I need to be honest. This Linda Kane cop is good people. She needs the facts so she can find my baby."

That one word—*baby*—turned the tears on again.

"No, you don't. It'll only cause you problems. If you bring us into this, it'll disrupt any momentum they have in locating her right now. They'll make their investigation about *us*." Freddie looked toward the bar. Then back at Trudi: "About *me*. And hey, look, Cassandra will be back in a day or two more, so there's no need to say anything."

Trudi looked at Freddie. He put his hand on hers. She didn't see it, because she was entrenched in the sadness of a missing child, but Freddie Banks had a scratch along the backside of his palm, near his knuckles. The scratch went across his entire hand, about the thickness of a pen. It looked fresh. Still, as Trudi took a sip from the glass of water, with Freddie saying, "Good, good, drink, drink, Trudi," she made the decision to tell Linda Kane about Freddie Banks. About their affair. About the arguments she'd had with Cassie over Freddie. About the night the three of them got together to try to work it out. About how Cassie stood and told Freddie there was no way she could accept her mother living with one man, sleeping with another—and how Freddie became enraged that Trudi was allowing a fifteen-year-old to control her life.

Linda, Trudi decided, would soon hear about it all.

16.

CAM HAD TWO BLUES with him. All three cops had hands on their weapons pointed out in front of themselves as they waded through the thick brush, thorny pricker bushes, tall weeds, and muddy terrain. The north end of Shenipsit Lake—"the Snip" to Royal Oakers—ran along the edge of town. A 522-acre body of water, one hundred feet deep in sections, the Snip was a popular place for kids to hang, have sex in cars, drink a few brews, have an occasional keg party, maybe smoke a little ganja, sit around a bonfire, and come of age. Linda and the boys left them alone up here. As long as the kids played by the rules, stayed away from the hard-core stuff, and didn't bother anyone, they were fine.

Trudi had called earlier that day, before heading out to work, and told Cam about the boy who said he'd seen Cassie; or, rather, *thought* he'd seen Cassie up in the woods behind the old Appleseed Farm. There was a log cabin out there the kids used as a party house. It was deep in the woods, off the beaten path, not visible from the dirt road snaking along the edge of the lake. Cam had texted Linda to let her know he was heading out with a couple of uniforms to check out the lead. After realizing it was going to be too long a text, he left a voice mail, concluding, "We think somebody saw Cassie."

Linda was busy running down information about Benjie, that alleged boyfriend of Cassie's. She wanted to dig deep into the boy's background. When she listened to Cam's message while sitting in her Crown Vic parked in front of the squad building, for the first time in as long as she could recall, a smile forced itself on Linda Kane.

A potential Cassie sighting. Finally, something to grasp onto.

The previous day, as Cam and Linda were walking into the department together, they had discussed Benjie.

"I'm thinking that with Benjie, Cassie's supposed boyfriend, we need to get him to talk, Cam. Any word from his lawyer? Is there anything we can force his hand with?"

"Working on it, Chief."

"We also need to be careful, though…" Linda trailed off.

"How so?"

She stared at the farm fence across the field to the right of the PD's entrance, a red barn in the distance. Acres and acres of corn clipped about eight inches from ground-level, the stems sticking out in perfect rows, like marching soldiers, separated the two. It was a tranquil scene when the sun hovered over the field in late winter. Something Linda looked forward to every year.

"You take a suspect, Cam, and you need to treat him—or her—as if they're innocent. That's what we're told. But it's not that simple, is it? We go with our instinct. Benjie's feeling guilty right now, whether he is or not."

"Right."

They walked toward the door into the building.

"This Benjie kid, he has answers, certainly, but we make a wrong move with him, put him on the defensive, and we've lost not only him but potentially important information for our case. I was always told to treat a suspect like a human being, they'll give you what they have. Keep them at arm's length, yes. But appeal to their emotion and needs and, to be honest, their version of truth, whatever it is. Do that, and you'll make a connection. A lot of times, they just want to hear themselves talk it through."

"That's good advice, Lin. You ever want to talk about Sherri and that whole thing, you say the word."

Linda looked up at Cam quickly. She hadn't realized how well he knew her. Everything she loved seemed to disappear or die or was out of her reach. She didn't want that to happen to Cam, too.

She needed to fight off the feelings.

"Just get that Benjie talking. You hear me, Cam?"

They stepped into the elevator, silent for the ride upstairs.

AFTER TRUDI HAD CALLED it in, Cam sent a cop out to check on the cabin. "Stay back, don't be seen," Cam warned. "Watch the cabin and report back to me what you find out."

That cop radioed in an hour later. He'd spotted someone walking in and out of the cabin. Could be a female. He needed a closer look.

Cam and the two blues had staked out the cabin most of the afternoon, Cam using binoculars to monitor if anyone was hanging around. Sure enough, out of the rickety door came a young female, her hair appearing to be crudely dyed goth-black, wearing what could be considered, bearing in mind Cam had seen it on the video, Cassie's jean jacket. The girl even fit a description of Cassie, though Cam was not convinced it was her.

As they made their way closer to the cabin, about maybe fifty yards away, one of the blues cracked a branch. With the mountainside to their right, a canyon to the left, the noise echoed.

The door of the cabin sprang open.

The girl walked out. Looked in all directions.

Cam yelled, "Don't move!"

She took off in the opposite direction they were facing, running like an antelope, as if she knew these woods better than any native creature.

"Shit" was all Cam said as he took off after her.

One blue double-backed around to the north side of the mountain, the other to the south. She was cornered. No way out.

"Come on," Cam yelled, his hands cupped on both sides of his mouth. "We just want to talk to you."

Famous last words.

As Cam bent down and underneath branches, squashing bulbs of fiddleheads and stepping on skunk cabbage, sending up wafts of the potent odor, one of his blues called out, his voice reverberating throughout the canyon.

"I got her."

They all met back at the cabin.

Inside was a makeshift bed with a grungy blanket, likely infested with lice and tics. A pot to boil water. A few unopened bags of Ramen noodles, a pack of cigarettes, several beer bottles on the floor—one of them half empty, the others full. A wooden table made from an old spool of cable wire, on top of which was a square of tinfoil, charred black on the bottom, a long glass tube, a lighter, and a spoon.

"Partying it up, I see," Cam said, picking up the glass tube.

Cam photographed everything with his iPhone, texted the images to Linda, along with a photo of the kid.

She was not Cassandra Caldwell.

Her jacket, however, Cam pointed out in an accompanying text, bore a striking resemblance to the one Cassie was wearing on the night she went missing.

"Take that off," Cam told the girl, who refused to speak.

Staring at her knotted hair, nearly dreadlocked, dirty face, bruises on her arms, Cam wondered about her life and where she was from. How had she wound up in this cabin smoking crack cocaine? She could not have been older than twenty. Still, she seemed to be well fed and able to fend for herself out here in the middle of nowhere. Where had it all gone wrong for this girl? Where was her damn family?

She refused to do anything she was told.

"Collins," Cam said, "strip that jacket off of her and put it in an evidence bag when you get back to your cruiser. Bring her in." To the girl: "Where did you get that jacket?"

Nothing.

They all walked back to the road. The girl, handcuffed, being pulled along by the crook of her arm, had a look of disdain and defeat on her face.

Cam checked his phone. Linda had responded. She said to clean the girl up, get forensics to process the jacket and anything else they pulled out of the cabin. Feed the girl, hydrate her, put her in a cell, and do not talk to her. Offer her cigarettes and plenty of sweets. No one was to talk down to her or say anything more than necessary.

Got it, Cam texted back.

Linda wanted the girl to stew a bit. Think about her situation. It always worked. Lock someone up. Feed and clean them. Provide a bit of empathy in the form of compassion, and if they have anything to say, you'll get it out of them soon enough.

Most human beings were so goddamn predictable.

17.

A YOUNG MAN OUTSIDE the bar stood underneath a light hanging over the blinking neon sign—LOUNGE—at the entrance to the building. His back against the cinder-block wall, a damp hoodie warming his head and torso, he had one leg up against the brick, that knee sticking out to form a triangle. He exhaled blue smoke into the cold November night air and scrolled through several messages on his iPhone.

Linda Kane parked in front of him. The lights of her Crown Vic illuminated the guy's blue jeans and white sneakers, a lightning bolt of glare darting off his silver watchband. He turned when the bright lights of the cop's car shone on him.

Before getting out of her vehicle, Linda went through a mental checklist. She'd followed up with Cam about Benjie, Scottie Mathers, and the girl living in the cabin. Scottie was in a cell and would be arraigned in the morning. He knew nothing about Cassie, as far as Cam could get out of him, besides Benjie having sex with her a few times. The rest would have to come from Benjie. The girl in the woods was sitting, beginning to warm up. She had been fed. Allowed to smoke.

"What can we do about Benjie?" Linda asked.

"Different story. He lawyered-up and we're waiting to hear from Daddy when we can speak with him."

"Great."

"Exactly. But, hey, I got them both to admit they sold some photos to that reporter."

"Photos?" Linda asked.

"The crime scene in back of the school. It was those two clowns who called it in."

"You think our boy knows anything about Cassie? What's your gut on that, Cameron?"

"Not sure, Lin. He's scared shitless, that kid. Knows he's in way over his head. Let him calm down, get a taste of reality, talk to his lawyer. Daddy is barking in his ear, too. He'll come around." Cam went back to an earlier subject: "You want us to haul in the reporter and see about those photos?"

"No. She'll come to us soon enough. She might be able to help us without knowing a damn thing. Lead us somewhere, like she did with Scottie and Benjie."

"Right."

Linda needed to get into the bar and finish what she had set out to do when that call about Scottie and Benjie had come in, sending her and Cam out behind the pool hall.

Here she was.

Linda nodded to the dude under the light; then she pulled the door open and walked up to the bar.

She asked the bartender where she could find Mr. Freddie Banks.

"He'd be in back, in the office, about now. Doing the night's receipts."

It was just after eleven p.m. Another long day. Linda had not eaten since breakfast, a stale corn muffin that'd crumbled all over her lap. The lounge smelled of tangy buffalo chicken wings, which a man bellied up to the bar was munching on, smeared sauce all over his face. There was also a raw aroma of sour beer spilled on carpet. A bar sign, advertising an Icelandic vodka, Reyka, buzzed on the wall to Linda's left. It was distracting and sounded dangerous, like an electrical fire could start up at any moment. Linda took a quick look, then asked the bartender to show her to the back room. She held up her badge.

"This about Cassie?" the bartender asked.

Linda didn't answer.

They walked through a set of swinging waiter doors into the kitchen, by a series of long metal tables where food was prepared; a walk-in cooler the size of a shed sat to Linda's right, its tiny square window frosted over.

When they came upon a door into Freddie Banks's office, the bartender, a short man of about sixty, a full shock of thinning gray hair, holding a wet and smelly dishrag in one hand, peeked through the window and knocked.

Freddie Banks looked over his shoulder, stood, opened the door.

"Mr. Banks," Linda said, nodding. "Royal Oaks PD. You have a minute?"

The bartender did not move. "Thanks, Charlie," Freddie said to him, beckoning with his head in the direction of the bar. "You can begin closing out your register. Flick the lights, last call, too. Let's close up for the night."

"It's only eleven-o-five," Charlie said, looking at his watch.

"Thirty minutes, Charlie. Please."

Linda sized up the bartender. He could feel her presence. Linda had a certain look when she meant business. Her eyes teemed with concentration, focus, in between slits and squinting. Her facial muscles relaxed; the subtle, starfish-shaped lines near her eyes were beginning to show with age. She stood straight, right hand in her right pocket, left hand on her side. She made sure to fold out the right side of her jacket so the Glock in her holster was visible. She gave the impression that at any time she was fully capable of taking care of any contingency that came with the job.

"Come on in, Officer," Freddie said. He spoke in a low, soft voice.

"Detective," Linda corrected. "But, anyway, you know why I am here, I assume."

"Yes. Yes. I presume Trudi told you about us. You know, the affair—such an ugly word. I told her not to. It would only hamper the investigation and make you focus on things that have no bearing on anything having to do with Cassie gone missing. I warned her. It would become about us. And, well, here we are. You looking at me with that glare of guilt."

Linda took it all down, imprinting the surprising information into her brain. She thought about what to say to keep Freddie talking. She had not yet decided on his guilt or innocence, and this bothered Linda. Cops immediately judged. Didn't matter what pundits and chiefs standing at lecterns at press conferences said: You work the job long enough and you know when you're standing in the presence of evil. You might not have all the answers, but there is a sensor inside of every good cop that flickers. Linda's was not working for some reason on this night. She couldn't understand why.

"I'll need a statement from you, sir. A formal statement of where you were, what times, anyone that can back you up, an alibi, if you want to call it such. That sort of thing. Can you do that for me? Can you come down to the station and do that for me, Mr. Banks? It would save us some time, hassle, and help Cassie's mother out."

Linda saw the scratch on Freddie's hand and her radar sounded. She did not want to mention that it was Freddie in the surveillance video. Linda needed him to either admit or omit that information in a statement. His answers would say a lot about Freddie Banks.

"I can. When were you thinking?"

"Anytime you want to—*now*, if you can?"

"Well, no, that's not going to work. It's late. I have responsibilities here right at the moment and I won't allow this to overrun any of that. You understand, Officer, don't you?"

"I do. And let me say for the record"—she put up some two-finger bar quotes—"that Trudi did not alert us to your affair, as you call it, but thanks for that info."

"Oh, is that so?" Freddie said. He stopped short of saying something else.

Linda knew he was contemplating asking why she was there, but held off.

"If you want to sit and talk for a few minutes," Freddie then suggested, "I can give you some information." Freddie grabbed the back side of a chair next to his desk, pulled it out, and faced it toward Linda. "Have a seat."

The office was small, just enough room for the two of them, a three-drawer desk, two chairs, and stacks of paper plates and time cards bundled in plastic, along with white Styrofoam coffee cups, samples of coasters and other bar accessories. Freddie kept his office a mess, Linda made note, and this told her something important about the man.

Disorganization.

Not a check in a box that cops liked to see.

"I'll stand, thanks," Linda said. "But please continue, sir." She wasn't about to refuse an invitation to listen to Freddie talk.

"What can I help you with?" Freddie asked, pivoting the topic.

Focusing on a suspect, trying to build a case around circumstantial evidence, however visual and sketchy that evidence might be, to the elimination of others, was a tactic Linda had told her squad to avoid at all costs. More than that, add race into the mix and the line in the sand became thicker and longer. Royal Oaks was, mostly, a liberal, white, middle-class farming community of about five thousand, with the county around the town adding another forty thousand or more. There was no corporate pharmacy on one corner, its competitor down the block, a series of chain restaurants and fuel stations across from that. This was small-town life, unaffected by the outside corporate capitalism of most other towns, with their strip malls and gas stations-slash-grocery stores offering fatty, high-calorie, cheap foods under heat lamps, that all look the same. "More cows than people" was the common, however untrue, slight that outsiders often remarked about Royal Oaks. Freddie was one of the few blacks in the town. They made up only about 3 percent of the population.

"Maybe a little background on yourself?" Linda said.

Linda would have to tread carefully. She did not need the NAACP and the Al Sharptons of the world getting wind of any pressure placed on an African-American suspect in the case of a missing white girl. The last thing she needed was an activist or agitator crawling up her ass to play the race card. Once that happened, Freddie was as good as a free man. She wouldn't get anything more out of him or anyone connected to him.

"I just should tell you, Officer, I know my rights. I'm not saying this to be abrasive or make you think I am hiding something. But I do feel like you are treating me as a suspect, not someone who can help your investigation." Freddie used his hands to emphasize the points he wanted to make. "I am a well-educated black man, and in this country, being black—with cops the way they are—you are smart to know your rights."

There it was: the race card. Flipped over and stuck directly in Linda's face.

"This is voluntary," Linda said. "At least, right now. Everyone we speak to, I guess, could be considered a suspect, Mr. Banks. I won't be reading you your rights here tonight. I come as a cop looking for some answers to questions in an investigation. You should be clear that evidence led me here." She lowered her voice, tilted her head to the right. "I am searching for a teenage girl, Mr. Banks. A girl you know. A girl whose mother you've been in a relationship with. Anything at all you can offer to help me find that girl would be greatly appreciated."

"I understand." Freddie shook his head. But he still seemed standoffish.

Freddie wore a pink shirt, with the sleeves rolled up. Blue jeans—the shiny, wet-look, expensive kind you bought in the mall at a specialty shop. His black shoes were caked with a film of grease from the kitchen. He smelled of sweat and aftershave. His Caribbean cadence was not forced or overblown, and Linda thought it was genuine. He wasn't playing it up for any advantage. Having the accent made him pronounce words more slowly and clearly. Linda could tell the guy was intelligent by the way he articulated himself and the words he chose. Some dudes, you begin to question them and they speak like they have sand in the back of their throats. They twitch and shake their heads. Skip words. Jump around. Doesn't mean they're guilty of anything; it means they're nervous. Freddie displayed none of this. He was calm in a manner that spoke of showing complete confidence.

"You left New York, Mr. Banks, to come here, to our small town of Nothing Going On?" It seemed Linda was saying Freddie was running from something. She also had an issue, though she was holding on to it at the moment, with Freddie calling into the station to report that letter in Cassie's room. She recognized the voice the moment he opened his mouth. Sure, he could have seen it one day while at Trudi's. But how could he know about it and not Trudi?

"They call this 'country living,' right? Isn't that what city slickers call your way of life out here, Officer? I wanted my piece of it. You grow up and live in the big city long enough, the car exhaust alone is reason to leave."

Absent of any guile whatsoever, Freddie's face told a story. He'd been pulled over and harassed, Linda knew. The cultural differences and his skin color had been something of a weight this man was forced to carry because of being born. That was the way the world worked today. Linda had dated a black man in college for several weeks and she knew from him that to be black and male in America was to subject yourself to pat-downs and stop-and-frisk whenever some ignorant cop wanted to flex his ego and massage his bigoted values. The deck was stacked against you the moment you walked out of your home every single morning. You were a color; a target.

"My bet is it's more than that," Linda said about Freddie leaving.

"Well, let's just say, Officer, you cannot fight the system for too long or it will consume your soul. You'll be bitter and jaded and not trust human beings to ever be legitimate or genuine. It will, as you seem to know, take over your life. So one is better off taking oneself *out* of the situation."

"You were born where?" Linda knew from his file that Freddie had emigrated to the United States as a fifteen-year-old from Saint Lucia.

"One of the islands. We believed that America offered opportunity, like so many millions of others. My mum, she lived her life for her seven children. 'Miss Conch,' they called her in my neighborhood back in New York. She cooked conch better than anybody on the block. She's gone now. But, man, swimming in the river during summer, playing in the park, rushing to the house for Mum's home-cooked meals, all of us sitting around, talking, eating, laughing, that was life."

Linda noticed that Freddie's voice and overall demeanor was devoid of any arrogance. She appreciated this. When a cop went to question a suspect or witness, they often became defensive, guilty or not. The idea that Freddie was taking this in stride after telling Linda he felt as if he was being viewed guiltily became neither alarming nor comforting the more they spoke. It told Linda that the guy could comport himself under pressure. But he held his morality, she seemed to recognize, close to the vest. Freddie knew what to say, when to say it. Plus, he still hadn't mentioned several key pieces of information she knew he had knowledge of.

They were speaking in circles, each sizing the other up. Not much being said about Cassie or Trudi. Nothing more than small talk.

So Linda made a move. She backed away from the door and now stood outside of the office. Freddie appeared to be writing something: figures on a spreadsheet. He held up one finger, as though in the middle of a thought, asking for a minute to finish before continuing the conversation.

"I am a black man," Freddie said, standing up, walking out of the office toward Linda. "I will be viewed as such during this process. You cannot tell me any different, Officer."

"That is true," Linda said, perhaps to Freddie's surprise. "I won't lie to you. But I can tell you that I am going to treat you fair. I follow evidence—not public opinion. I follow leads—not biases. You be straight with me, Mr. Banks, we'll get through this. You try to lie—for whatever reason—and we'll be wrestling with paperwork and warrants and all sorts of legalese. You'll become your own worst enemy."

"I think I believe you, Officer. And, for some odd reason, I also trust you."

"Help me to understand this relationship between you and Trudi, and, honestly, you and Cassandra. You must have known both of Trudi's girls. You must have spent some time with them. Or were you and Trudi able to hide the affair from everyone?"

Freddie turned, walked back into the office. He settled into his chair again. It squeaked as he sat down. He rubbed his face with his hands and took in a deep breath through his nose.

He was irritated, Linda guessed, that she'd gone there. She knew in this moment that the crease between her eyes was pronounced; it was a definitive tell that Linda Kane was curious and, at the same time, questioning something about her subject.

"Are you and Trudi still together?" Linda asked after she realized Freddie was not fond of answering her last question.

Freddie stood once again and walked toward the cop; Linda backed up a few steps. She felt the urge to reach for her weapon and scolded herself for reacting in such a manner.

"Why don't I come down tomorrow afternoon, after lunch, and we go through it all, yeah?" Freddie suggested.

"You can't answer a few questions right now, Mr. Banks? I find that to be guarded and mysterious. Did you know both of Trudi's girls?"

"Only the one—the one missing. Never met Katherine, though we talked a lot about both. Now, I will answer all of your inquiries tomorrow when I come in."

Linda thought about it. She decided to risk alienating her suspect. "The note in Cassie's room, Mr. Banks, how did you know about it? And why did you call us? Has Trudi seen the note?"

He darted a look at her. "I saw it on Cassie's dresser one day while I was at the house…" Freddie said, then stopped himself. "I didn't tell Trudi because I did not want to worry her. I figured I'd speak to Cassie about it…"

"And?"

Linda saw Freddie lawyering up tonight or tomorrow morning and never coming into the station. But she was caught here: She could not force him to do anything at this point. She might press a judge to sign a warrant based on the video, but that was going to take time. Hell, they hadn't even found a body or any indication that Cassie had met with foul play of any sort. Just a gut feeling that the girl was not coming home. You couldn't start making arrests and reading Miranda based on instinct.

"Listen, I'll come by tomorrow and explain everything."

She considered they had reached an impasse.

"I'll pencil you in for two," Linda said, giving in to not questioning Freddie Banks any further. "You'll keep that appointment, Mr. Banks, won't you?"

"I give you my word, Officer."

18.

ANOTHER NIGHT WENT BY and Cassandra was still missing. They might have her jacket and a witness to question. They might have Benjie prepared to talk at some point. But Cassie remained among those girls who'd left home one day and faded into dust.

Linda slept well after leaving Freddie Banks at the restaurant, calling in to put a tail on him for the next twenty-four hours. She was at it again first thing the next morning. Driving into the station, Linda took in the perfectly straight rows of pines and spruces growing on each side of the main driveway. A red brick building erected in 1920, the building had a character unto itself that Linda appreciated. The large, adult-sized windows, with the cross section of white wooden grids sectioning off each pane, were inviting, mirroring reflections of the open fields in front of the entrance by the flagpole and gold-lettered Royal Oaks PD sign. Most of the cops bitched about building maintenance, paint chips flaking onto the floors and the absence of new carpeting, but it was a homey place to come to work every day. After a few twenty-four hours like the ones that she and Cam had just spent, walking in and saying hello to Officer Brown behind the desk, the same face you'd seen for the past fifteen years, was about as comforting as the apple cider doughnuts, gourds, and squash sold up the road at the farm stand.

This was Linda Kane's life. She desired little else.

As she got out of the car, Linda looked up. The sky was a light, robin egg blue. A flock of geese above, like a school of minnows, squawked and kazoo'ed their way south.

She shut the car door, producing a metal-on-metal *thump*.

Once inside the office, Linda stood next to the photocopier, the flashing light blinking with each missing person's flyer spit out the side. The heat from the machine warmed her thighs. She held a flyer out in front of herself and studied it for typos. The most important part of any BOLO teletype sent out to area police departments, or on those flyers hung on telephone poles—cops referred to as 'paper ghosts'—inside Laundromats, on supermarket corkboards, and posted online and given out around town, was the photo. The missing person's photo had to be as up-to-date as possible. Linda had pulled a selfie from Cassie's phone dated just two days before she went missing. Cassie wasn't making a duck face or smiling puckered lips or hamming it up in any way for some silly Instagram post; it was stripped-down Cassie Caldwell, doing her best to look into the camera lens—no smile, no frown—just the sad, sullen face of a lost teen. Her porcelain skin, perfect in every way, Cassie was a girl who had never had to deal with acne. Her light brown hair, big and long coils, curled down the side of her face. Her blue eyes shone like island ocean water. Her long eyelashes were dark and natural-looking. Her mouth filled with teeth straight as a fashion model, white as paper. Cassie looked like one of those girls, Linda considered while staring at the flyer, on a billboard with MISSING etched eerily above her head, an 800 number scrolled along the bottom. So wholesome and innocent-looking, she fit the mold of a milk carton kid. It was as if Cassandra Caldwell's face belonged there.

Along the bottom of the flyer, Linda traced the phone number to the squad room with her eyes, felt someone looking over her shoulder.

"You want me to get a stack of those to the family?" Carmen asked.

"Yes."

"Spread about the town, too?"

"Yes." Linda now focused on Cassie's eyes.

"What about the county?"

"Everywhere you can get volunteers to hang them."

"Any luck with her cell phone?" Carmen asked. Linda had spent hours the night before going through Cassie's phone for the contacts she'd recently texted and who had contacted her. E-mail, Facebook, and Twitter posts. Anything she could find.

"Not a thing," Linda said. "As if she hardly used the phone."

"Or someone washed it—wiped it clean."

Linda felt indifferent for not spending the entire night out looking for Cassie, mounting search parties and conducting grids along the freeway leading into town, the fields around the high school. She believed now more than ever that it wouldn't have made a difference, anyway. That first forty-eight thing all TV cops promote, how every second early on counts more than any other, was bullshit, Linda knew from experience.

"We can go through the motions here, as textbook as we can, flyers and interviews and tracking down leads," Linda said to herself more than Carmen. "But after days of questioning people, posting flyers, conducting grid searches the family is now pushing, even after conversations with other law enforcement agencies outside the county, Cassie won't be found."

Carmen stood, listened. This was her job: sounding board. "What makes you so certain, Lin?"

"If she chose to leave, Cassie was long gone," Linda stacked the flyers. "A preplanned, carefully thought-out exit from life was hard to backtrack and figure out, even if a teen had scripted it. If Cassie had been grabbed, well, it wasn't by our high-school-girl killer. Otherwise, she would have been lying somewhere next to the girl found."

Carmen searched a file in her hand. Took out a piece of paper. "It's Ariana Olahu, actually, Lin. Just got the name from the state boys. She turned out to be Hawaiian, not Arab or Indian."

"Thanks, Carm. Leave me that report."

Linda looked up. Cam walked into the squad room, Trudi and Katherine behind him. He made it over to Linda's desk, where she was now waiting, expecting them.

Linda beckoned Katherine, Trudi, and Cam to follow her into the conference room on the outer edge of the office space.

"Anything on that Benjie character?" Trudi asked as they walked.

"Working on that currently," Linda said.

"And the lake story that other boy told me—you looked into that, too?" Trudi wondered.

"We're going to discuss that with you shortly," Cam explained.

"Katherine, can you sit outside here for a time so I can talk to your mother alone for a bit?" Linda said to the young girl when they reached the conference room. Katherine wore baggy brown corduroys, non-brand white sneakers, and a green turtleneck. Her brown hair was pulled up in a butterfly clip. "Cam will sit with you, honey."

"Certainly," Katherine said. "Miss Linda?"

"Yes, Katherine?"

"Do you know when they're going to open the schools again?"

"Tomorrow, for certain. We're all done out there. Wait, though, the middle school was closed, too?"

Cam nodded. Shrugged his shoulders. "Go figure, huh." Then, after Trudi and Katherine were out of earshot: "The super wanted to be certain there wasn't some sort of, how did he put it, 'pattern.'"

"Everyone's a detective, eh. I guess that's about right, though," Linda said.

Linda explained to Cam that she wanted him to sit outside the room with Katherine; keep her company. Trudi was a bit intimidated by Cam, Linda added. This had to be a woman to woman thing for right now. She didn't need Trudi feeling pressured or uncomfortable in any way.

He nodded his head in agreement.

Trudi walked into the conference room ahead of the detective and took a seat at a large, oval-shaped table so shiny you could see your reflection. On the wall opposite the table was a fifty-five-inch monitor. Beside it was one of those whiteboards, with red, blue, and black markers in the slot below. In the middle of the table was a star-shaped phone. Linda had a file she dropped with a slap on the table in front of her as she pulled out a chair and sat across from Trudi. To their left was a cassette recorder. Beyond that was a large, brown paper shopping bag with red tape and black lettering marked—EVIDENCE—across the front. The date was written in

Sharpie on the bag, Cassie's last name next to a number with two letters at the end.

Carmen came by and opened the door. "Looks like I don't have to send these over to the house," she said, directing her attention toward Linda, holding a stack of flyers. "I'll leave them out here in the hallway."

Linda said she'd explain the situation to Trudi.

"You're going to be recording our conversation?" Trudi asked, looking at the cassette recorder. She hugged herself, as if cold, rubbing her shoulders with the palms of her hands. She seemed worried about something, Linda picked up on. Trudi had usually projected the mannerisms of being on the verge of saying and doing the wrong thing, forever making the wrong decisions. It was almost some sort of self-fulfilling punishment she clutched onto, banishing herself to an island of bad parents, blaming this mess she found herself and her daughter in on the poor choices she'd made in life.

If only…the battle cry of the single parent.

"I'm trying to figure you out," Trudi said to Linda.

"Excuse me, ma'am?"

"Whose side you're on, you know. Sometimes I think you want to find my daughter and other times I feel like you are looking at me judgmentally for not taking good enough care of her; or, honestly, as if I had something to do with this."

"Trudi, I'm sorry you feel that way. We're here to find your child. I made you the promise that I was going to bring her home. What you do—what you've done, rather—has no bearing on me, as long as it doesn't affect my investigation or anything having to do with your missing child. That's on you. My entire focus is on finding your daughter."

Trudi rolled her eyes.

"Now," Linda continued, a touch of contempt in her tone, "you wanna tell me why you never mentioned Freddie Banks?"

Trudi looked away. Outside the window, two landscapers raked leaves away from the side of the building. They had earbuds and bounced their heads to the beat. Trudi stood, walked over to the window, stared at one of them. Her back to Linda, she said, "Because, oh, that's been over for a while. I didn't see the significance in mucking up what you're doing. I did plan on telling you. Apparently, though, someone else beat me to it."

"Can we start from the beginning, with the caveat that I need to be the judge here of what is significant and what is not? I cannot be of use to you or your daughter without having all of the information. I need all the facts, Trudi. Every detail matters right now."

Trudi came across overwhelmed and beaten down, as if on a losing team. She turned and looked at Linda. "I am so sorry. I don't know how to do this, Detective. There's no playbook for having a missing child. It's like we are walking in water, trying to trudge through our days, forcing food down our throats, forcing ourselves to even get out of bed. It is all-consuming. I'm going to make some bad choices here because, shit, I have no idea how to respond to any of this."

Linda felt she had reached Trudi. There was a certain wince behind presenting yourself as tough, as someone who could withstand any sucker punch that life threw. Trudi seemed, in this instance alone, to be not an emotionally strong-enough woman to deal with the pressure of lying or holding back. Linda had seen the type. Had broken many witnesses by simply making them see that she could help only as much as they helped her.

"Tell me about him. Freddie Banks." So far, Linda had not shared with Trudi any of the information she'd learned on her own about Freddie, about him driving the wrong way toward Cassie that night. His attitude. The fact that he called in about the note.

Trudi sighed. She sat back down and stared at her reflection on the table, drawing circles with a finger. She twisted her head a bit to one side and took a moment to think about her answer.

"We do not live in a community with a lot of interracial relationships," she began. Then laughed. "I have not seen one, actually. We had to be not only mindful of that, but also of Vinnie. Not that he would actually give a shit about me sleeping with another man, but, God forbid—and I am going to use the language he would—a *'nigger'*? If Vin ever found *that* out, he'd get his buddies together from work and give Freddie a good solid whooping, for sure. Plus, Freddie is my boss. I would go to the park. Meet Freddie there on some days. He would stop by when he knew Vin and the kids were gone. It was nice when we started. You know, that euphoric high of a new relationship, the unexpected sex, the roses and cards, all that nonsense. Freddie did all of that. But he went and fell in love. That scared me. Then, I thought, it'll keep me busy and from thinking about my life. Sooner or later, I'd kick Vinnie out, and Freddie and I could maybe take the next step—"

Linda interrupted, "So Vin, let me get this straight, he doesn't know about you two?"

"No way. If he did, Freddie would have been put in the hospital."

"But you and Vin, you're not close anymore? You're saying that you're a couple on paper only?"

"Yes, that's what I am saying." Trudi stood and walked over to the window again, her back to Linda. She stared at the men raking leaves and listening to music. "There's something comforting about doing manual labor, like weeding or raking, isn't there? You do the same thing over and over and it puts you in a trance."

"Ma'am, I'm going to need you to sit down so the microphone can pick up what you're saying. Sorry 'bout that, but it is protocol. I need you to sit here across from me, if you will."

Trudi turned and walked back to her seat. The leather made a familiar squeaking noise as she sat down.

Linda added: "Please continue."

"After Cassie found out—"

Linda stopped her: "Explain how she found out, please."

"Well, Freddie thought she found out one night when she showed up at the restaurant and caught us in his car. But she knew from almost the first week. I think she saw us one day at the park, but I really don't know how she found out. This was another one of Cassie's 'secrets.' Still, we had lots of conversations about it after that. She did not like the idea."

"What idea?"

"That he is black and we live in a town where she had to deal with it among friends and classmates whose attitudes are, let's say, from the old-world way of thinking. If they ever found out, she always warned me, they'd disown her. That was her word. *Disown.* These kids today, the pressures of the past they live with. Incredible."

"So there was friction between you two about this?"

"Look, I'm not gonna lie to you. Friction might be too strong a word, but, did we discuss Freddie many, many times? Yes. Cassie insisted I end it. She would get heated sometimes when I told her I was trying to. Get right up in my face."

Linda turned and looked out at Katherine, who was busy with her head buried in a book. Cam sat nearby, reading a magazine, one leg crossed over the other like he was in the doctor's office waiting to be seen. Every once in a while, Cam looked up at the child and smiled.

"What about Katherine? Does she know?"

"I am not sure. It's never come up between us. Katherine is, you have to understand, my chance to get it right. She's going to college. She's never been in trouble. She has very few friends. She is focused on goals."

"I understand."

"That friction, as you put it, began to intrude on the relationship. Plus, I was so worried that Vin would find out and beat Freddie senseless. So I told Freddie about the problems I was having with Cassie and her disappointment in the relationship, and how she demanded I end it."

"You say 'demanded.' What does that mean to you? Explain how she communicated this."

Linda was trying to burrow deep down into the core feelings of the relationship—if there was any animosity there between the two that could have morphed into an altercation. She'd seen this: Family members argue; resentment builds. Words they don't mean are said. A slap one day turns into unexpected rage and terrible violence the next.

"She told me flat out that I could not be carrying on some affair with a black guy. It was not going to happen. If I continued, Cassie said she was going to spread it around town. Which would eventually get back to Vin, which would eventually get Freddie fired, which would eventually destroy everything."

"What was Freddie's response when you told him?"

Trudi looked away. Her senses had been assaulted, Linda felt. There was so much to be said for the look on her face and what was behind it. Linda knew she wasn't going to get the entire story from Trudi here, on this day.

For the time being, that was okay.

"He would sit me down, almost on a weekly basis," Trudi explained, "and he would tell me everything that was wrong with my kids. Both of them. He berated Katherine to me for the way she acted, you know, sometimes like a small child—withdrawn, unemotional. I'd be upset and explain to him what was going on with Katherine, and, not knowing her, never having met her, he'd judge her. You see, Freddie has this sort of undue need for structure and planning and everything having its place in the world. It's what makes him a great restaurant manager." Trudi stopped herself. Teared up. "But it was not good for us, for how he dealt with me and talked about my kids."

Linda disagreed with that. Freddie appeared to be disorganized. But she didn't mention this.

"What is it?" Linda asked.

Trudi took short breaths, as if she was starting to hyperventilate.

"Ma'am, are you okay?"

Trudi nodded her head and held up a hand. "Just give me a minute."

Linda waited. Then: "Help me out here, Trudi." Linda got up. Walked over to where Trudi sat. Bent down. Took Trudi's hand in hers. Whispered: "It's just you and me here, hon. You're safe here."

"Cassie did not like Freddie. Freddie did not like Cassie." Tears streamed down her face now. "Freddie grew very angry one day when I told him I was leaving him. He screamed at me in the restaurant kitchen, threw a pan across the room. Broke a window. It's not like we had a hostile relationship; or that he scared me. But on this day, he said, 'That bitch daughter of yours, she'll never break us apart. I love you. No one will stop me from loving you.'"

Linda looked toward Cam. He was monitoring the situation. Linda nodded for Cam to escort Katherine away from the area.

19.

WHEN AT HOME, IRIS Starr worked in her soft cotton jammies. She'd pop on her pair of thick black-framed glasses she did not want anyone to see her wearing. Put on a pair of furry white, bunny-hair slippers. Sit with her legs tucked underneath her butt on a dining room chair. On this particular morning, while Trudi and Linda were at the Royal Oaks PD talking about Freddie Banks, Iris was at her desk inside her Greenwich town house ninety minutes south of Royal Oaks. She stared at an e-mail to Linda Kane she'd just composed.

> We need to talk. I have something you need to see. I don't want to run with it. I would rather get your opinion about it first. Please call me. Let's say, oh, within an hour. But no longer than that.
>
> —Iris Starr

The television host hesitated. Maybe she needed to run the e-mail by one of the corporate lawyers at TCN before sending. Was it a threat? Unethical? Rude?

Perhaps all three.

Then again, was it enough to get Linda Kane to bite?

Just might be.

Iris popped a K-cup into her coffee maker.

Coffee in hand, she sat back down at her computer and hit the SEND button.

Screw it.

Inside Iris's apartment was plush gray carpeting, smooth to the touch, the texture of elephant skin. Expensive stuff. Her furniture was Swedish and had all the sharply cut edges and wavy designs the Swedes loved to sell to Americans as being authentically Scandinavian. Each end table had one matching lamp—a long silver arm, curved and contemporary, covering an LED bulb inside a tulip-shaped glass shade. There were matching wooden bowls on the coffee table, a pile of strange wicker balls the size of oranges in each. The entire room spoke of no one ever using it. Iris liked to work at the dining table on her laptop.

As she began searching online for any new updates in the case of the dead girl found behind the high school, her cell phone buzzed.

That was quick.

It was Sidney Richton—or, rather, Detective Sid Richton. Not Linda Kane.

"Damn it all," Iris snapped, looking at the screen.

Sidney was a small guy, with biceps the size of ham hocks, a full head of dark hair, six-pack abs, thighs bursting with hormones, like frozen chickens. He'd been a wrestler in high school and college, maintained that muscular physique, and developed a crush on Iris the moment he saw her on TCN. Since then, for maybe two years and change, Sidney had fed Iris stories and given her leads when other reporters were left in the dark. For that reason, and the fact that Iris slept with Sid from time to time, he was a loyal member of Team Starr. He always called, no matter how she treated him, with tips about crimes she was interested in. It had something to do with men not being able to say no to Iris.

"What do you have, Sid?"

"Well, how are you, too? Nice to hear your voice."

"Look, Sid, get on with it. I'm *really* busy here. Lots of things going on."

"How's that husband of yours? He getting along okay? You fully supplied with Viagra and Metamucil for the old fuck?"

"Sid, don't do this. Please. Please don't do this. Why are you calling me?"

"Well, when are you going to be in town again?"

The bartering had begun.

Sidney worked out of Troop N of the Connecticut State Police, the lead investigators on the dead girl behind the high school. Royal Oaks was still involved, conducting certain (small) investigatory tasks, but they had their hands full with the missing teenager and the war on Oxy.

"I'm heading back, hopefully, real soon, Sid. Trying to set up a meeting with that Detective Linda person now. Why? What do you have?"

"How 'bout dinner?"

Iris dropped her head. "Sid, *not* now. I'm in this thing all the way. I'll be in and out of town a lot for the next few weeks, maybe months. We'll get together, promise you. Now tell me."

"Looks like the girl behind the school, Ariana Olahu is her name, might be part of that dude they're looking at in Hartford for killing those girls and dumping them behind the strip mall. All those bones found last year, do you remember that case?"

Hartford, the capital city, had open murder cases on several girls, mostly transient types, prostitutes and drug addicts, murdered and left in the woods behind a popular shopping plaza. A homeless man had stumbled upon one body, which led to three more in various stages of decomposition. Cops were chasing a psychopath who had been seen with all of the women at one time or another. Sid explained that the suspect had ties back to Royal Oaks. Last anyone had heard, the guy was in Florida. Hartford Police, along with Troop N investigators, were tracking him at the moment.

"I do remember, Sid. But how are they connected?"

"DNA looks good on it all. His blood found on Ms. Olahu's jeans."

"Confirmed?"

"Nearly. But this is not public yet. Look, don't report it until I give the word." Iris rolled her eyes. "She was raped, by the way, despite what those hokey Royal Oaks cops said. Apparently, the sick son of a bitch raped her and put her pants back *on*. Her vag was torn apart."

"Connected to this missing-girl case they're looking into out there—the Cassandra Caldwell girl?" Iris asked. As she spoke, Iris typed notes. The sound went straight into her phone, which sat on a speaker next to her keyboard. Sidney heard the clacking. Every so often, Iris looked up at her e-mail in-box to see if Linda Kane had sent a reply.

Nothing yet.

"I am not so sure about that. Right now, no one thinks there's any connection. In fact, the consensus here is that the missing Caldwell girl will turn up sooner or later—that she's alive and well and smoking dope in some abandoned building, holed up with an older kid. I'm told there was a note involved in the case. Like she left a good-bye note to her mom."

If you were a true-crime fan, and you paid even the slightest bit of attention to popular culture, you knew the legendary Iris Starr, former newscaster for the highest-rated cable news channel turned TCN celebrity investigator. The ad the network liked to run for her series included a shot of Iris holding a cell phone to her ear, wearing sunglasses, looking coy and secret agent-like into the camera. The shot was taken as if she had just turned around and been surprised by the camera. *Who…little old me?* It was utter nonsense. Staged branding promo to make her look as though Iris was out in the field and knew what she was doing.

On the other hand, if you were not a TCN fan, and you shopped, you knew of Iris from the tabloids. She had become constant fodder for the best rags in the supermarket lines after having married a wealthy Fifth Avenue hedge fund manager who ended up bilking seniors out of millions and going to prison for twenty years. Many thought Iris, who left Manhattan in shame after the trial and moved to Greenwich, Connecticut, got all the cash in the divorce that followed. Not one to be alone, she'd hooked up with a Realtor in Greenwich who sold no homes under $5 million. They had a nice, fake life together to attend functions and parties. There was even a rumor—again, tabloid silage—that her new husband was gay and she was being paid to be his front.

"I have work to do, Sid. Gotta go now."

"Wait, wait, wait…"

"What?"

"Us? What about *us*? When are we having dinner again?"

That was code for: *When am I going to get to bang you?*

"I'll be in touch."

Click.

Iris looked down at her phone. A text: CALL ME. NOW!

All caps. Iris's boss was pissed.

Iris texted back: What?

Her phone buzzed.

Iris looked up at the ceiling in frustration.

"Yes?" she said, answering. "I'm really busy."

"You wanna tell me about this e-mail you sent a detective in Royal Fucking Oaks, Bum Fuck Egypt Farm Country, who is right now all the way up my ass asking for you to be taken off this story?"

"I am busy, Jimmy, working a lead. We can discuss this later."

Iris hung up. She knew from experience there were more ways than one to skin a detective. She'd have to approach Linda Kane from another direction.

20.

THEY WERE BACK TALKING after a break. Linda had walked over to her desk to check e-mail, text messages, and voice mail. And that was when she saw the e-mail from Iris Starr, which she forwarded to her boss with a note: Keep Lois Lane off my ass.

Sitting at her desk, Linda watched Trudi, who stood near the watercooler, drinking from one of those flimsy, V-shaped paper cups. Katherine had her arms coiled around her mother's waist, frowning, hugging her, trying to get whatever amount of love Trudi was willing to part with in that moment. The two of them seemed like strangers, as if Cassie's departure had put a wedge between them. Linda thought she saw fear on Trudi's face.

What Trudi couldn't hide was a look of despair. She held the cup of water with two hands in front of her face, intermittently sipping from it, staring into the liquid. Linda felt Trudi was searching for answers she was never going to find. Linda knew that space, the pain that resided there. She could empathize with Trudi in that respect. She'd been wading in the same sewage herself for about thirty years.

Sherri.

It was time to get Trudi back into the conference room, sitting, relaxed, calm, so Linda could show her that jacket. See if she recognized it as her daughter's. Linda didn't think it was Cassie's, but she needed to write off the lead or pursue it. Afterward, she and Cam could question the girl Cam had brought in. Take things a step at a time—one of Linda's core investigative philosophies. Freddie Banks and his role in all of this pecked away at the back of Linda's mind, but she knew dealing with guys like Freddie took patience, prowess, and skill. Lots of thinking about your next move.

There was that problem of Freddie's anger, however. The way Trudi described it, the guy had some rage buried deep and it erupted at certain times. There was one piece of information Trudi passed on as they were wrapping up earlier that Linda could not shake: *Freddie did not like Cassie…. He blamed her for the end of their relationship.*

Play that to a grand jury, see what they come back with?

"You ready?" Cam said. He stood over Linda.

"Oh, yeah…was just thinking about some things, Cam."

Had Freddie confronted Cassie to try and talk her into accepting the relationship? Had he picked her up, driven her somewhere, initiated an argument? Then that volcanic rage, which Trudi insisted she had witnessed firsthand, came out of him? Linda had seen it happen. Hell, she'd even sided with some women who'd snapped after being beaten by their man for one day too many.

It happened.

All of this was a possibility Linda Kane had to consider. Until, that is, she could rule it out.

Linda got up from behind her desk and walked toward the conference room.

"The jacket?" Cam said. "My bet is…it's hers."

"Not sure, Cam."

"Oh, boy…"

"Exactlies." Linda cracked a half-smile.

"Something during lunch I noticed, boss." Cam and Katherine and Trudi had lunch together during the break.

"What was that? You ate with Katherine, right?"

"I did. Katherine had to have her food; like none of the food on the plate could touch."

"An OCD-type symptom, I guess," Linda said.

"I think so, too. How you holding up here with all this? How's that cut? How's the noggin?"

"I'm good, Cam." Linda stopped walking. She stared at Cam. "Thanks for asking. I mean that. And the other day, with Scottie, that was incredible work."

"We take care of each other, boss."

After a time, when all of the leads had been chased down and Cassie was still missing, back home, or buried, Linda would return to her life of scurrying around town, rustling up Oxy and heroin addicts for shoplifting and petty crimes. She was resigned to think that her squad couldn't handle the dead girl found in back of the high school and was content with the state police going nails to the wall with it. While, at the same time, following her around the office like an intern, not to mention at home and when she was alone inside her Crown Vic, was Sherri's ghost. Sherri was dead. Linda was not going to be naïve about it.

Cassie, too, damn it all.

She couldn't explain how she knew, but over the past day, Linda had never been more certain.

"What are you thinking in your gut, Cam, about Cassie?" They approached the conference room.

"Um…I…I'm working on a few things. I'm not ready to commit to anything right now."

Linda believed Sherri was a set of bones settled in the woods somewhere, crumbling into dust a little bit more each day. There was no way, after thirty years, Sherri would remain gone. Someone had grabbed her that day. Grabbed her and put her in a van. Zip-tied her hands together. Gagged her. Raped her. Killed her. It was the same image Linda saw whenever she went back to the moment—a part of it all that Ted and the others could never understand. They only looked at Linda's reaction throughout the years, never at how the loss and guilt had eaten her up inside. How she'd let go of her friend's hand, turned around that day and looked because somebody had called out her name, and Sherri was gone.

Cam gets it, though. He understands.

How does a person live with such a loss? How does someone go on with life, trudge through the motions and emotions, knowing that your best friend had vaporized in front of your eyes and blew away with the wind? And, as a cop, all these years later, you hadn't one fucking clue as to what might have happened.

"You okay, Lin?" Cam asked as they stood in front of the

conference room door, where Trudi and Katherine waited.

Linda looked at him. "I'm cool, Cam. Thanks. I got this."

"Okay," he said. "You nod if you need me."

With no body—and everyone, including Sherri's family, having stopped talking to Linda years ago because of all the questions Linda started asking—it was mere speculation. No one knew for certain. Which offered that false sense of hope, like a sure bet. And for Linda Kane to assume that Sherri wasn't being kept somewhere in Nevada or Idaho in a man-made dungeon, or some nutbag's bunker, or in a backyard tent, impregnated and made to care for her abductor, like that Jaycee Dugard girl, was appalling. Sherri's father had said so the last time they had spoken. *"How dare you? You call yourself a cop? Don't you ever come around here again, Linda. It's because of you that my daughter is gone, to begin with."*

Door slam.

At times, Linda found herself—especially now, with Cassie missing—driving by the schools in town at different intervals of the day, the street corners downtown, walking through supermarkets and malls, even various places outside the county. She would study each person's face. Try to see if one of the moms picking up their zit-faced suburban kids, with perfect teeth and designer clothes, was Sherri. Maybe she'd *wanted* to disappear. Maybe she didn't know who she was. So many people. Nothing more than faces in the crowd.

"Lin? Lin?" Cam said. He snapped his fingers in front of her face. She'd drifted off. "You all right?"

Linda came back. She looked into the conference room where Trudi waited.

"Let's do this."

Cam put a hand on the door. "You better get that head checked out, Lin. You might have a concussion."

21.

AS LINDA ENTERED THE conference room, she had the file with Freddie's life in her hand. Cam had walked her into the room and then taken off to the state police barracks, after Linda asked him to get a personal case update on the dead girl behind the school. "Katherine will be fine with Carmen."

Olahu had been strangled, apparently. Now they were claiming she had been raped or sexually assaulted with an object of some sort, a stick or the handle of a hammer, perhaps some other tool. But the strangest thing: The medical examiner, Dr. Bernard Valentine, said the girl had consumed massive amounts of mushrooms, the psychedelic type. Like beatnik, 1960s, Allen Ginsberg stuff. Magic 'shrooms.

"You ready to get started again, Trudi?"

Trudi nodded. She was quiet, her head bowed.

"You okay, ma'am?" Linda asked.

"Let's get this over with, Detective."

Looking at a photo of Freddie Banks, which Linda had since gotten from Trudi and placed in the file, the detective thought for sure Freddie might hold a key to finding out what happened to Cassie. There was a strong possibility Freddie picked her up and gave her a ride—that much was clear from the video. Perhaps he hurt or harmed Cassie by mistake? Or maybe he could tell them which way she went, where she was headed, where she had asked to be dropped off? What person was she waving at, whom they couldn't see out of screenshot, in front of her? Who was it that yelled to Cassie behind her, just before Freddie drove into the picture? Was that, in fact, Freddie beeping his horn?

"Katherine, I need to speak with your mother again. Is that okay?" Linda asked, bending over, staring into the young girl's eyes. "Do you mind waiting outside the door again? Carmen will get you whatever you need."

Katherine collected her things and left the room.

Trudi's youngest daughter had a shyness about her that ten-year-olds sometimes displayed. But Linda considered that the girl was also introspective. They'd diagnosed the child with a mild form of Asperger's at one time, Trudi explained.

"But I stopped taking Katherine to the doctor because of an issue with insurance. Since then, I've done my own Internet research and decided my daughter is fine. A bit eccentric, maybe. A bit nerdy and quiet, but otherwise a healthy teenager, chugging her way through school, straight A's to prove she is not sick in any way. Socially inept, maybe awkward, doesn't talk much, but a good, solid kid."

"She seems to be," Linda said. Then she looked out at Katherine, who stared back for a brief moment, before directing her eyes back down to the drawing she was working on. She sat on the carpet just outside the door.

There was no delicate way to do this. Linda reached out and slid that brown paper bag toward her. She then hit PLAY/RECORD on the recording apparatus to her right and made an announcement into the device as she picked up the bag: "Opening evidence bag number 4-4-6-2-1-6-6…um…dash *A-K-Z*. Removing one black jean jacket with silver studs."

The crunching of the paper bag made a noise and Trudi winced as Linda opened it.

Wearing latex gloves, removing the jacket from the bag, Linda unfolded it in front of Trudi. She stood up quickly, put her hands over her mouth, and took a dramatic breath in.

"Oh, God…oh, God…oh, God…" Trudi said as she stood and backed against the window, the chair underneath her falling over.

"Ma'am, please sit back down if you can. Please, Trudi." Linda got up and dashed around the table. "I need you to sit back down at the table."

Trudi's legs gave out and she crumpled to the floor. Eyes closed, she pounded a fist on the carpet. Katherine looked in through the glass door, saw what was going on, and darted into the room.

"Mother?"

"Trudi, please," Linda said, grabbing her by the arm.

Carmen walked into the room and asked Katherine if she could step back out into the hallway with her.

"Mother…"

"Trudi?" Linda said.

"That's my sister's jacket," Katherine said. Stoic and matter-of-fact, the comment felt chilling to Linda and the blue.

Linda waved off Carmen to leave; to wait outside the room. Katherine could stay.

"I'll need you both to sit down." Linda helped Trudi up off the floor.

She had a hard time speaking. All Trudi could manage were tears and mumbling: "My girl…my baby girl."

"Do not touch the jacket, please," Linda said as Trudi grabbed and held it close to her chest and face, her eyes closed, her nose buried into the collar.

"I can still smell her," Trudi whispered through tears.

Linda and Katherine looked at each other.

After ten minutes, Linda calmed Trudi down, but knew their conversation for the day was over. The jacket had destroyed the mother. If there was ever the slightest bit of hope inside Trudi that Cassie was still alive, seeing that jacket had erased it.

Two female officers escorted Trudi and Katherine home. Linda said she'd be by at some point soon to talk and check in on them.

Carmen grabbed hold of Linda as the detective walked back to her desk.

"Benjie's lawyer called. They want to talk."

Linda dialed Cam.

"Pulling into the parking lot now," he said. "Be up in five. What's up?"

Linda told Cam to meet her outside.

22.

BENJIE DIDN'T WANT TO meet inside the PD. Or at his house. Not even his lawyer's office.

That was okay, Linda had told his father over the phone. "We can meet wherever your son feels comfortable and wants to, sir."

"The high school parking lot, out in back," the father said. "And don't bring that Frankenstein cop with you."

"Got it," Linda said.

Cam.

She smiled.

Outside, in the PD parking lot, Linda explained to Cam that she had to go it alone to the high school. Benjie only wanted to speak with her.

"No worries, Lin."

"Set up Tiffany Barnes in the box so when I get back we can get into it with her."

Tiffany—the girl from the cabin in the woods—had found Cassie's jacket.

"You sure I shouldn't come along and hang behind—I mean, you trust these people? The high school, Lin? Where they found the body? That kid is strange, don't you think? He wants to go back out *there* to talk? Why not the lawyer's office or his house?"

"I know, right. But at this point, let's allow them to drive this thing, until we know what he knows." The fact that Cam was worried about her, more than cop-to-cop, Linda felt, was comforting.

"I ever tell you about that girl I was engaged to, remember her? Lauren? Well…her father. This guy here, Benjie's dad, reminds me of the guy. No sense of right, wrong, what's good for the kid, what's not. Just a real tool."

"You loved her, though, Cam. You'd have done anything for that girl." Was funny to Linda how she detected a smidgen of jealousy as she'd said it.

"I did. Yet, I must say, coming off a double shift after a hostage situation to find her banging the dude next door, ah, that kind of puts a little damper on the love thing, you know."

They both laughed.

"You're smart to poke fun at it. That's the way around those nasty emotions. Does you no good to be Mr. Tough Guy who can take a punch like that. You laugh in the face of it. Been there myself, as you know."

Cam told Linda to stay safe. He walked toward the door back into the PD. Before stepping into the building, he turned and gave Linda a smile he reserved only for her; then she took off.

The lacrosse team was practicing on the field in front of the woods where Scottie and Benjie had found Ariana Olahu. Indeed, it was strange, Linda thought as she pulled up, that the boy would want to return to this place, but what the hell. To each his own. He must have some connection to the place.

Linda shook the father's hand, nodded to the lawyer, who looked at his watch, and said, "You've got ten minutes with my client, Detective. Then we are out of here."

"Hey," Linda said, snapping her fingers, "haven't I seen your photo and your ads on the side of the big city buses? You're that smiling guy, pointing your finger at the camera, with the pinky ring, looking to represent anyone with a credit card and over a thousand-dollar limit, am I right?"

"You want five minutes?"

Linda could not resist.

"Benjie, do you know where Cassandra Caldwell is?" Linda said, a more serious tone taking over the conversation.

He shook his head no. Stared at the ground, both hands in his pockets. Mouth closed.

"We got a weed charge here pending, Benjie…do you understand? And that, I should say, is only the beginning."

"Be careful, Detective."

"As I was saying," Linda continued, ignoring the lawyer, "we've got you pretty solid, despite what you're being told here by Mr. Infomercial. Plus, selling those photos to the reporter—I'll find a charge in there, too. Being part of a crime scene. Which leads me to you perhaps knowing what happened to our gal here out in those woods…."

"That's enough. Really, Detective? You wanna go there with this and mess with me?" The lawyer used his right finger, pointing to each one of them.

Benjie was holding back. He watched them go back and forth, listening.

"I'm speaking in facts here, fellas. Cold, hard facts. You want to face them, fine. You wanna waste my time, I'm coming after this kid, who, by the way, is an adult at eighteen years of age last time I checked. So stop treating him and this situation as if he's a child. And one other thing: I need your phone, Benjie."

"Just tell her…" the dad said. "Go on, Ben. Tell the woman what you told me."

The woman? Linda laughed to herself. *Sexist prick.*

Benjie was uncomfortable. He looked toward the woods. He seemed agitated and tried cracking his neck, to no avail. He stared at his father. Then at the lawyer. Then back down into the woods. Never into Linda's eyes.

The man put his arm around his boy's shoulder. "Go ahead. It's okay, Ben." The father looked up at Linda: "His phone, Detective, by the way, is at home. I wouldn't let him bring it here."

"I waited for Cassie down the street from her friend's house the other night. I called out to her as she came out of the house and she walked by a funeral home next door to her friend's. We met up on the sidewalk just down the road from there. She started crying. She said she didn't want to ever see me again."

"That it?"

"About, yeah."

"'About,' Benjie? I have *about* a year in a men's prison waiting for you… I have *about* this much"—Linda put her index finger and thumb close together and stuck it in the kid's face—"patience left with you right now, Benjie. I will walk away if I don't get it all out of you. This here, this shit is serious business. I have a missing kid, a dead girl, you in the middle of it all, and you're playing games with me?"

"Okay, okay," the dad said. "He gets it. Go ahead, Benjie. *Tell her.*"

Benjie looked up into the air. He ran a hand over his shaved head, rubbing it in a circle pattern. Kept the other hand in his pocket. Breathed in through his nose.

"Cassie told me that she was having problems with her mother. That Vinnie douchebag, too. The boyfriend. That she wanted to run away and was planning it out. She said her mother was sleeping with some black dude. I didn't care about that. She said there was something else, too, but she never said what; I had a feeling it had to do with me. She then turned and took off. A truck drove by, I remember, and she took off toward it, as if she recognized the guy driving, but I'm not sure if she did. I got really pissed and ran into the park. I turned. Yelled something. Then said to forget it and booked. Haven't seen or heard from her since."

Linda noticed that Benjie's right knuckle had a bruise. She didn't mention it. She also figured that the person she and Cam thought they spotted in the park was probably him.

"You sleep with Cassie, Benjie? You have sex with that underage girl?" He answered by nodding his head affirmatively—admitting, in effect, to a felony.

"That's enough," the lawyer said. "That's all he has, anyway, Detective. There's nothing else. I can verify as much. Now you need to drop those charges, and you need to do that immediately. You've got what you want."

Linda looked at Benjie. He had more, she was certain of it. To the lawyer: "Fuck off. Keep quiet."

Linda turned and started walking away. "You call me, Benjie, when you're ready to remember what else it is you know. Do we understand each other? In the meantime, I'll process the DNA and work up a warrant."

Linda walked over to her car.

Before getting in, her hands hanging over the top of the door frame, she said, "About those charges? Let me work on that for you. Tell you what: I'll get your number off the city bus and call you as soon as I have some info for you." She turned to Benjie: "You drop your phone off at the PD tomorrow—we'll want to verify that information you just gave me and have a look inside. You holding out on me and I am coming for you, kid."

Linda Kane hopped into her vehicle and took off.

23.

THEY'D CLEANED THE GIRL up. Under Linda's direction, they'd fed and clothed her with fresh Walmart-bought togs, and a bag of McDonald's food she said she'd been craving for weeks. She was actually a good-looking kid, Linda considered as she entered the interrogation room, Cam behind her.

Linda held a yellow legal pad for show in one hand, a cold can of soda for the girl in the other. Tiffany Barnes was eighteen. Had left her home in Massachusetts months ago and bounced from one friend's house to another. Why?

"My dad, he was, well…he," she picked at her fingernail, "he would sneak into my room at night."

"How long?" Linda asked.

"Years." Tiffany stared at the table.

A typical story Linda had heard so often that she felt there was an epidemic of child sexual abuse in suburban white America and nothing was being done to stop it.

Tiffany had blonde hair and a light complexion; for a drug addict living in the woods, she had kept herself in fairly decent shape. Once she got to talking, Tiffany explained that she'd just started smoking crack and was able to manage her habit fairly well. That's why she wasn't shaking and withdrawing, scratching at her shins. She insisted she wasn't some street whore junkie, selling her body to support a habit growing out of control.

"I party once in a while and shit."

Linda opened the soda to a *crack, pop, fizz*. Handed it to the girl. "Thanks," she said.

Just then, Cam sat down with a *thud*, sporting his interrogation poker face: flat, no emotion. He made sure his one tattoo was visible on his neck, giving him that tough, ex-con look. He had his arms folded in front of himself, head tilted right—an orchestrated way to set an authoritative tone.

Linda steepled her hands in front of herself, tapped her fingers together. After a moment, she placed her hands up to her lips, took a breath, then stared at Tiffany. "Okay, we need to know where you got that jacket, Tiffany. This is *very* important to us. And so very important for your future."

Cam met Tiffany's eyes. She was calm, willing to help. This was a far different person from the timid and defiant girl he'd met in the woods. There was even a genuine grin on the girl's face. A total change had come over her, just as Linda had predicted, simply by them showing her a bit of empathy. As Linda had instilled in Cam, treating a suspect like a human being, not a criminal, told them you were not there to fuck their lives up. But that you actually gave a shit.

"I can tell you," the girl began.

Linda spied a look on Tiffany that gave her pause.

"Go for it," Cam intoned.

"Yes, Tiffany, please enlighten us."

Tiffany said she had been living in those woods for about two weeks. She'd hitchhiked and walked from Massachusetts just over the Connecticut border, which they knew to be about a ten-mile trip from Royal Oaks, north up the freeway, just outside the county line.

"I'd been staying with friends at this point, but overstayed my welcome and had to move on."

"Go on," Cam said.

Tiffany had chosen those woods and the lake area after she'd met a kid on an app called Hook-Up.

"Some dude who sent me dick pics and seemed like someone to party with for a while until I could figure out my next move. But the shitbag blew me off and never showed his face once I got into town."

Linda shook her head, indicating she was listening.

"So I was left alone in fucking Farming Town USA and I started walking home and shit. It began to rain. Then pour. I mean that hard, slanted rain and shit, sideways. The kind of cold rain that stings when it hits the skin…."

"We get it," Cam noted. "Continue, please."

"So I ran into those woods and wandered upon the cabin. It was shelter for the night. Kept me dry."

"And the jacket was inside the cabin when you got there?" Cam asked. Linda met his eyes, glaring at him to back off a little and let Tiffany explain it on her own terms.

"No."

"No?" Cam said.

Linda kicked him underneath the table.

"No. I found the jacket in this water well back in the woods, about a ten-minute walk east, I guess it would be"—and she used her hands to try and figure out which way she had walked, turning in her chair, trying to get a sense of the direction. Then she took a pull from her soda, spilled some on her chin, and wiped it with her wrists. "Thanks for the soda, by the way," she said, saluting Linda with the can. "I appreciate it."

"So when you say 'water well,'" Linda asked, "what does that mean to you, exactly?"

"Like a 'short well'—my uncle calls them back home. A square lot of land about the size of a small garage, about five feet deep, like boards and shit on the sides to hold the dirt up. Nothing anyone would use today, but the old farmers, so says my uncle"—she rolled her eyes—"would use them for irrigation. They'd fill up with rainwater."

"And shit," Cam added.

Linda dropped her head and looked at Cam: "And this jacket was just sitting there?" she asked Tiffany.

"It was actually inside one of those plastic shopping grocery bags that get caught in whale spouts and on dolphin noses—look, I've seen the Greenpeace YouTube videos and thought about joining." She stopped, looked at Cam, twisted her head to one side: "And shit!" Then back to Linda. "You know, the bags grocery stores put each item separately in and waste. It was tied up at the top, like a knot. That's why I took the jacket, because it was in such great shape. It was dry and seemed almost brand new."

"Did you notice anything else in that well?"

"No. Didn't go looking for anything, either." She sipped the soda again, this time loudly slurping it.

"Where is the bag you found the jacket in?" Linda asked.

"I tossed it in the lake."

Cam tapped the button end of his pen on the table. Then clicked the button on and off with his thumb.

"Did you search the jacket, find anything inside the pockets?"

"I did go through them, of course. But found nothing."

A text came in from the lab as they sat talking to Tiffany. Linda held up a finger in Tiffany's face, and said, "Hold that thought for a moment," while she read the text.

Found along the collar of the jacket, forensics reported, was blood soaked down into the cotton liner and about halfway down into the back area. A lot of blood had been spilled on the jacket. The head bleeds like no other part of the body, Linda knew, so that didn't mean the blood was an indication that Cassandra Caldwell was dead.

Still, things didn't look good for Cassie.

Linda excused herself to Tiffany and Cam and texted back, asking forensics to send the blood for DNA testing. Trudi had already given a sample, so they had something to test it against.

Fast-track it. Linda typed with her forefinger, one letter at a time.

The reply from the scientist was immediate: LOL!

Back to questioning Tiffany, Linda asked if the girl wanted to go home or be released in town. She was eighteen. She could make up her own mind. They were going to overlook the drug charge. Still, Linda noted, "If I see you again and you're high, or you have dope, I'm going to run you in and overcharge you. Do you understand me, Tiffany?"

"Yes. Thank you."

"And we need a DNA sample from you, too—you good with that?"

"Yes."

The girl said she'd be fine. She'd like to go stay with family in a neighboring town. Get her life back on track. Find work. Look into community college.

"And one last thing," Linda said, "providing you don't have anything else to share."

"I don't."

"Okay. You wanna press charges against that piece-of-shit father of yours?" Linda asked, knowing what the answer was going to be. "I will make a call to your local PD. They'll pick him up tonight."

"Not right now, but I will consider it."

"Leave contact info in case we need you," Linda said as she stood. "Family. Friends." She tapped a finger on the table. "I want several numbers and addresses; e-mails, too. Understand?"

Cam motioned with his hand for a blue to come in and take the girl away.

Before the door closed behind her, Tiffany stopped and turned. "What's up with this jacket?"

Linda said, "I can't really get into that with you, Tiffany, I apologize. I realize you are probably wondering. But please understand that you have tremendously helped us out with the information you provided."

Tiffany left the room. The door closed behind her. Linda turned to Cam and spoke. "I need you to get a sample of Freddie's DNA. Can you do that for me without him knowing?"

Cam smiled. "That's a specialty of mine, Detective. But, hey: Why are you so quick to think that Tiffany the doper didn't have anything to do with Cassie disappearing? Or that she doesn't know anything more? Shit, she could be friends with Cassie. Maybe they met online? Who the hell knows?"

Linda knew Cam was a solid investigator and would be a great detective one day, with more experience. So she was not averse to schooling Cam when the situation called for it.

"She look like a killer to you?"

"Well, who does…?"

"No, listen to me, Cam. If she had anything to do with Cassie disappearing, taking off, hiding her out somewhere, or her demise, we would have cracked her within two minutes. You see how open she was once she got a taste of her old life back? And, do you not think for one minute"—Linda stood and started to walk out of the room—"that I am not going to put a tail on her for the next week to see where she goes, who she interacts with? If she knows where Cassie is, she'll lead us right to her. That's why we offer to drive her where she wants to go."

Cam nodded. "Understood," he said.

Linda made her way out of the box, stopping by the door. "I need you to get a team together, head out and find that well. Tell CSU to meet you there as soon as possible." She walked back over to Cam, who was still sitting, stewing, a little disappointed in himself. Linda put her hand on Cam's massive arm. "You call me, Cameron, as *soon* as you find anything. Okay?"

"I'm on it."

They shared silence and one of those glances that scared Linda.

"And get me that DNA sample from our guy there, Freddie Banks."

"You bet."

24.

THE RED-AND-WHITE covered bridge went over the Kibbe River just outside downtown Royal Oaks. Iris Starr closed her eyes as her cameraman laughed, watching his reporter cringe and wince as they made their way across.

"Oh, my God. Always had a fear of crossing bridges," Iris said. She grabbed the cameraman by the arm. "Childhood thing, Roger."

Roger laughed so hard his shoulders bounced up and down.

"You think there's a Starbucks in this town?"

Roger looked at Iris, twisted his head. *Come on*, he said to himself. *You that stupid?*

"So, apparently," Iris explained, "this maniac they were looking for in Florida, the guy who supposedly killed all those girls found out behind the strip mall in Hartford, turns out he was under their noses the entire time. He's been spotted back in Connecticut. They haven't found him yet, but my source tells me they have a good lead they're running down now."

"What are we doing here, then?"

"I want to do a stand-up about the dead girl, Olahu, out at the high school. Then I need to go see our detective, Miss Linda Hardass."

"We get a permit to shoot there at the high school?"

Iris gave Roger that look.

Please.

"Your call, Iris. I'm just the grunt behind the viewfinder."

Royal Oaks High School was your typical small-town, redbrick, one-floor, L-shaped building with lots of glass, same as you might expect to find in any farming community. The staff managed about four hundred students, give or take. The dropout rate, Iris had found out with a Yahoo! search, was about 6 percent. Kids here in Royal Oaks graduated. A majority might go on to spend their lives sitting behind the wheel of a John Deere tractor, teaching, or being a homemaker, but this was a good life, anyone in town would agree.

Roger pulled the van back behind the school and drove out to an access road toward the edge of the woods where Ariana Olahu had been found. The yellow tape was gone. Only remnants that an investigation had occurred out here were tire tracks and footprints in the mud and soft grass.

"We have to be quick, Roger. Once the school realizes what we're doing here, they're going to shut us down."

"Roger that." He laughed. Loved saying his name as an affirmative.

Iris rolled her eyes.

The school was closed for the day, but teachers and custodians had reported.

Roger parked the van. He'd loaded his camera with a card beforehand, hit the ON button. He walked into the back from inside and made sure he had the right lens for the shot. Iris sat and went through her notes, talking to herself out loud, warming up her vocal cords for the piece.

"I'm all set," Roger indicated. He popped open the back doors of the van. He and Iris got out.

They made their way down a slight embankment, into the brush, found the path and worn-down area of the woods where campfire remnants had been left behind by Shaved Head and Spiked Hair. They stopped there.

"Get me some B-roll of that space, Roger. The campfire. Then pan across into the woods, there, where she was found." Iris looked at her phone for a moment. Those photos. Then back up where they stood. "You see the brush all stamped down—right over there— that's the spot."

Roger shouldered his camera and went to work.

Iris walked in between the campfire and dump site, stood, then checked her face and hair in a little mirror attached to the lid of her pancake makeup compact.

Roger walked over. Pointed the camera at Iris and gave her the sign to go.

Iris held a microphone in her right hand and let it rip.

"I'm standing here between a campfire and the area of woods where she was found. My sources were sitting around the fire, drinking, sharing a bong, when one of them decided he needed to use nature's restroom. He walked over here." Iris pointed and Roger panned slowly to the area where the girl had been found. "As he was doing his business, there she was, like a life-sized doll, sleeping. These photos I am about to share with you are exclusive. I've tried to crop out the goriest details"—she actually hadn't—"but you, my trusted viewers, and the people of this close-knit farming community, *you* need to see the brutality of this crime. This was a young girl. She had a full life ahead of her." Iris walked into the dump site. "Her life cut down in an instant by a psychopath."

They stopped. Roger and Iris had worked together so long they knew each other's rhythms and didn't need to communicate when it was time to change the shot.

Iris moved over to where the girl's body had been located. She stood over the space.

"Go," Roger said.

"Right here. In this spot, among the bugs and sticks and brush, lay the body of a young girl. A dancer and honor student, I'm told by family, who wanted to become a chemist." Iris paused. She tried the best she could to show some emotion. She knelt and patted the ground with her right hand. "Right here," she whispered.

"Her life didn't end here, however," Iris continued, now standing, looking into the camera. "I'm told via law enforcement sources that she was murdered in another location and dumped here." She paused for great effect. Then: "I'm also told who it is that law enforcement is in search of, as we speak, to question for this savage murder."

They moved to the embankment. The shot Roger set up was

Iris walking over the crest of a short hill, delivering what Iris had claimed on the way was going to be her "money line."

"Ready when you are," Roger yelled from his place. Iris couldn't see him from below the hill line. She began walking and talking.

"The question I have is this," Iris said, stepping into Roger's viewfinder, delivering her lines down the barrel of the camera. "Are two contemporary cases connected to a cold case? The missing girl, Cassandra Caldwell, and this dead girl, Ariana Olahu, found just behind me, a name you are hearing here for the first time." Iris pointed over her shoulder. She blinked several times. "Are these two cases part of some twisted, diabolical killer's plot? And *this* is probably the most delicate and sensitive part of my investigation." Iris looked down at the ground, then back up and into the lens. Roger zoomed in on her face. "Does the cold case of a missing teen some thirty years ago, Sherri Lafontaine, have any connection to what we have here in this small farming community known as Royal Oaks—and the detective, Linda Kane, at the center of *both* these cases?"

"Got it," Roger said. He held his thumb up. "Great work, Iris. I'm telling you, *Dateline* and *20/20* are coming after you when this one is all done. Mark my words—"

"Roger!" Iris said. "Turn around."

There was a man, waving his arms in the air, trying to get their attention, walking across the soccer field toward them.

25.

DETECTIVE CAM VAN ZANDT and his team parked along the edge of the woods by Shenipsit Lake and huddled together near a Royal Oaks Police cruiser. There were ten uniforms and three CSU techs. Cam ran the show.

"It's got to be somewhere over there," the big man instructed. "East. Stay in one line. Five of you have radios. Hit me when you come upon it. Don't touch anything until I get there."

Cam loved this work. He was never going to win Cop of the Year, but that did not drive this large man who looked up to Linda Kane as a mentor. Cam was thirty-six. Single, with plenty of women chasing after him, he dedicated his life outside work to the boys at the YMCA. He taught old-school ground fighting—"grappling" was what they called it before the boys with the hard knuckles and mushroomed ears came in and turned it into mixed martial arts. They made cage fighting and blood-spraying more the sport than the Brazilians who founded the style had ever wanted. The kids looked up to Cam, like the Big Brother he'd been for the past ten years. This was Cam's passion: helping inner-city kids realize their full potential.

"Anything yet?" Cam said into the radio.

Nothing.

As they trekked through the woods, Cam and his team came upon a steep cliff, a ledge of bedrock that dropped straight down.

On the top of the cliff was a dirt road snaking around the lake. There was about twenty feet between the ledge and the road. Aluminum guardrails protected cars from sliding out in the dirt and heading over the ledge to certain death.

Two officers stood down below the 150-foot drop and seemed to have found something.

Cam's radio sounded, a static mishmash of muffled words.

"Got it," Cam said after keying the radio. To his guys: "They found it. Down there. Bottom of this ledge."

As Cam walked around the cliff to the other side, so they could make their way down the mountain and survey the well where Tiffany had found the jacket, he texted Linda:

Found well. Heading into it now.

26.

TRUDI SWALLOWED A XANAX with a gulp of water. Her doctor had prescribed only five pills the previous day. Last thing Trudi needed now was to get herself strung out on narcotics. But taking the edge off of seeing the jacket was what she needed to make it through this day and maybe several more.

Katherine took care of her mother. She held a damp cloth over Trudi's forehead as Trudi lay down on the couch and fell asleep. They didn't speak much after getting back from Royal Oaks PD. What was there left to say?

After about thirty minutes, Vinnie walked in.

"What are you doing home?" Trudi asked, just opening her eyes. "It's four o'clock."

"Yeah, listen, well, I…I need to talk to you, Trudi. I've been meaning to say something, but it cannot wait any longer." There was a soft edge to Vin's voice. Something kicking up in the back of his throat. He seemed unlike himself. Fidgety and anxious. "Not the best time for you, I realize, but this thing…what we have here"—Vin looked around the living room, as if referring to the house—"now with Cassie gone, God knows what else is gonna happen, it is not gonna get any better between us, with me here and you looking at me like I had something to do with it all. Or I'm not doing enough. Or I'm just one more knickknack on the mantel. Or I'm invisible. A cash machine for you to pay bills. A babysitter…"

Trudi did not speak.

Vinnie walked over, sat on the edge of the couch. He looked at the wall in front of him.

"I know that we are not a thing anymore," he said. "Haven't been for quite a while."

"Vin," Trudi said, "my feelings for you are based more out of habit at this point, you're right." Trudi surprised herself by sounding clear-minded.

"Yup. Yup. I…I…so there is no sense in you and me, *us*, going through the motions here. Playing this game. You need to focus only on Katherine. If you need me to watch Katherine, call me, be glad to, when time permits. I will give you money until you can figure out what to do on your own."

"Where are you going?"

"I'm gonna stay with Tony, from work. He and his wife are good people. They have a room in their basement. It's close to work. It gets me out of your hair. I'm sorry, Trudi."

Something told Trudi that Vinnie was leaving out of guilt. Maybe not from having done something to her daughter, but Trudi noticed that he never mentioned being there for Cassie, too, not just Katherine. As she thought about it, he also seemed agitated, nervous. Trudi was glad he was leaving, but it suddenly occurred to her that the timing of it was suspicious.

Cassie had become the great distraction. With her now gone, the entire focus of Trudi's world was on that one situation. Vinnie saw a way out and was taking advantage of it. If that was the case, it was cowardly, Trudi considered as she stared at him, but it didn't matter. He was going to be gone. And she liked that idea.

"If that is what you need to do," Trudi said, "I won't try to stop you."

"And I appreciate that. You need my help for *anything*, you call me."

Vinnie stood. He walked upstairs, packed a bag, came back down, but then stopped by the door before leaving.

Katherine stood in the kitchen. She'd listened to the conversation. She did not have any sort of look on her face that would indicate how she felt. It was as though Katherine was unresponsive to everything.

One hand on the doorknob, Vinnie stopped, looked toward the ceiling. He wanted to say something else.

"What is it?" Trudi asked. She had sat up, the washcloth, hot to the touch from her body heat, fell down onto her lap. "Spit it out, Vin. I know you. Come on."

Vinnie turned around. "I know," he said. "I've known all along, Trudi. I need you to understand that."

Trudi looked at the floor.

Vinnie walked out.

Trudi made her way into the kitchen, her head throbbing like a thousand miseries.

"What did he mean, Mother?"

"Who knows, honey…who knows? I am so sorry about all of this."

Katherine said nothing. She leaned in, hugged her mother.

It had gotten dark out by the time Trudi was ready to go upstairs and lie down. The sky like a brushstroke of sharkskin-gray, backlit by the brightness of a full moon. Having the bed to herself from now on seemed comforting in thought alone. Just as well that Vinnie Costello left. Although she'd told Linda different, Trudi had considered that Vinnie knew about Freddie after the first few weeks. But she always wondered why he hadn't ever confronted Freddie. Or her. The idea that Vinnie hated blacks was something Trudi had fed Linda, hoping she might take a closer look at him. If it backfired, she'd blame stress. Make something else up.

Trudi stared at Katherine.

Vin was gone. No warning. No epilogue. Just a short speech, a packed bag, a closed door. The timing was a plot twist in Trudi's life; the entire situation, she had begun to think, was awfully strange.

27.

LINDA HAD WAITED AT the office until three o'clock that afternoon to call Freddie Banks at the restaurant. She'd given him the benefit of the doubt, but now she wanted to ask Freddie where he was, why hadn't he shown up at two, per his promise from the previous night?

There was still that conversation she needed to have with Freddie about him driving down the one-way toward Cassie.

The tail she'd put on Freddie had not happened. Two blues Linda sent out radioed in that they couldn't find him. Wasn't at work. Wasn't home. She put one blue at each location, waiting.

"You call me as soon as you locate him."

Cam and the boys were busy excavating the water well. Linda wouldn't be any help out there, busting on them to get it done her way. She knew that. Plus, Freddie Banks was Linda's priority. She understood he wasn't going to hold up his end of the bargain they'd made. Here it was, hours past the time Freddie said he'd be down to the station, and there was no sign of him.

Liar.

IDLE TIME WAS NOT something Linda looked forward to. Her mind wandered in moments such as these. As she sat, thinking, Linda reckoned her life had little spice, save for that one weakness she had shared with no one, which, to her, was very much well-deserved.

146

She had been thinking lately it was time to head out and do it; something she knew to be unhealthy and probably wrong in some ways. Yet, Linda was happy to permit herself such whimsies. She would defend the behavior as a stress reliever she forever chased and continue it, no matter what anyone said.

She'd been waiting for the right time to share it with Cam. A few weeks back, she'd approached him: "Let's have a drink after work."

"Sure, what's up?"

"Just meet me at Friday's in Vernon, Cam."

A different town. Interesting.

Linda showed up an hour before and had a few whiskies to lighten her mood, dredge up the old liquid courage. She wanted to acknowledge that she was having feelings for Cam. Didn't matter nearly ten years separated the two or that they worked together. She'd wanted to tell him how she felt and what she had been doing—that *stress reliever*, she called it to herself. Maybe they could hook up once in a while? You know, a "friends with benefits" type of thing. See where it went.

"Hey, boss," Cam had said, walking in, ordering a beer.

"Cameron! How the freak are you?"

"Oh, my…I can see you got here earlier than me," he'd said.

After he sat, took a pull from his beer, Cam said, "My mother's brother, my uncle, we just found out he's stage-four liver cancer. Shit, Lin. It's terrible. He won't make six weeks."

"Oh, geez, Cam. Sorry to hear that."

"Yeah, you know how close we are. This family."

She nodded. "The Fucking *Waltons*," Linda said.

"Right." Cam cracked a slight smile. "Gonna be tough on everyone."

"Well, listen, I'm here if you need me." She placed her arm around his shoulder. "Let me know what I can do."

"That's sweet, Lin. Appreciate it. Now, what's up? What's with the drink here tonight?"

There was no way Linda could share her secret now. Bad timing. He'd be shocked to hear about it. *"Linda Kane likes to do what?"* she could hear him say. She figured he viewed her as a by-the-book type. It was going to make her happy to let him in. Reveal this private side of herself. Just so happened that tonight wasn't going to be that night. Nor was it the best time to float such a stupid idea as Linda and Cam hooking up.

The next morning, feeling the whiskies throb, Linda sat in bed and scolded herself for almost allowing her feelings to be known. She'd have to watch that.

As she dialed the phone, Linda refocused, returning back to the moment, now thinking about what she could do to entice Freddie to talk once she found him. What did he want to hear from her? What promises could Linda make? What lies could she tell? Freddie was scared. Linda knew this. Being black, he faced a white wall of what he presumed to be ignorance and bigotry. He was a black man in a white town being looked at as a possible suspect in the disappearance of his white ex-girlfriend's daughter. Why *wouldn't* he be afraid to say anything more than he had already? Why *wouldn't* he lawyer up and not show up for an interview with cops?

"Not here," that bartender from the night before said. "Have not seen or heard from him since last night."

"Thanks," Linda said, and hung up.

Standing, Linda could feel the stress of it all constrict her body like a pulled muscle; her chest a ball of tangled wires, her mind the only part of herself unaffected. That was the odd thing about stress on the job, she'd learned years ago. Your body reacts without you recognizing it. Sitting, not realizing your fists were clenched. Waking up in the morning with a sore jaw from grinding your teeth all night. Some mild discomfort in the stomach out of nowhere turns into unpleasant trips to the restroom. The body had its own chemistry and balance. A few dizzy spells here and there, some vertigo. Linda hadn't told anyone about it, especially the doctors. She decided she needed to keep an eye on it, instead.

28.

GOING TO BED AT 6:30 p.m. wasn't any part of a normal routine for Trudi Caldwell. But all normalcy had left the Caldwell house on the morning after Cassie failed to come home. Any sort of familiar rhythm was long gone. The only foot firmly planted in the ground here, Trudi felt, was Katherine's. The child was always so minimal and impassive. Steady and true. Like there was an invisible wall up around her, a force field. Trudi's gut told her it *was* a mild form of Asperger's, just as they had all tried to convince her years ago. She just couldn't deal with it. Not then or now. The kid was fine. Sure, she had no close friends; teachers hated when she corrected them; she kept to herself. But how bad was all that, actually, in the scope of life today running at one hundred miles per hour, the entire world staring down into their iThings? Then you turn around one day and, *poof*, everything was blown to bits. Was it actually so bad that Katherine could tune out the world and live comfortably inside her own little emotional biodome?

Trudi put her bathrobe on, which felt like a chore. Heavy. Same as everything else. Walking felt as though she was trudging through mud. Thinking was like having a perpetual headache and trying to do math equations.

Cassandra.

The mother sat down on the edge of her bed to a squeak of the box spring. Then took a deep breath. Sighed.

She didn't even feel like wiping off her makeup or brushing her teeth.

What the hell happened? Where have I gone wrong in all of this?

A noise came from the walk-in closet in front of Trudi. She looked up. It stopped. She thought maybe she was hearing things.

Then another bump.

Then some rustling.

This time, it startled her.

Subtle, it sounded as if somebody had moved.

Trudi stood.

That same squeak of the bedspring again.

She put her hand on the closet doorknob. She hesitated before opening it. As she began to turn the knob, however, the door burst open thunderously and knocked Trudi back.

She fell onto the bed, scared and confused.

"Don't say anything," Freddie Banks said in a loud whisper. He'd leapt from the closet and was now on top of Trudi, straddling her. He placed one hand over her mouth so she couldn't talk, the other on her shoulder to hold her body in place.

Trudi was in pain. Freddie's grip was powerful. She could feel his anger.

"When I let go, don't scream…*don't* say a word. I will tell you when to speak, okay?"

Trudi blinked.

Freddie let go of Trudi's mouth. As he did, a noticeable red blotch appeared on her skin around her lips in the shape of Freddie's hand.

Trudi did not utter a word.

Freddie stepped off his ex-girlfriend. He walked over and closed the bedroom door with his foot. He then turned and stood above Trudi, over the bed, staring down at her.

Trudi was frozen. Couldn't move a muscle.

"I need to explain something to you. I need you to *listen.* Do not talk over me." Freddie paced. He had one hand by his side. Every once in a while he stopped, raised a forefinger, as if giving a warning, then lowered his voice into an even softer, yet angrier, whisper. "I am going to be accused of things I did *not* do and you need to hear from me *exactly* what happened." He stopped. Stared at the carpet. Then back up into Trudi's eyes. "Look what I have to do to explain myself! I have to fucking break into somebody's house and I have to hide in the closet. And I have to surprise that person and plead with that person to believe me. And this is supposed to be a person who had feelings for me? Do you know why, Trudi?"

She didn't respond. It was not a question.

"Because I'm a black man in a white world. And it doesn't matter if you or anyone else thinks what you feel *isn't* racist. What matters, is that it *is* racist. The fact you don't realize it is the problem."

Trudi's stomach tightened. What was Freddie trying to tell her? *Oh, God.* What a mistake she'd made not telling Linda about him sooner. About the affair. About his rage. How he'd once grabbed her by the arm so tight that it left a black-and-blue bruise. How he'd once snuck into her house while she was asleep, stood over her bed like he was now, knowing that Vinnie was working late, and she awoke to Freddie staring at her in the dark. How, out of a mild fear, she'd had sex with him on that night.

Freddie said: "I saw Cassie the night they say she went missing. I went to speak to her. I saw her go into her friend's house around the block from my apartment. I waited down the street. I beeped and then caught up to her as she walked home. I asked her to step inside my vehicle. I drove out to the lake. I wanted to speak with her, Trudi, about us. You and me. I needed to reach her." He turned toward the wall. Balled up a fist and tapped it against his lips. Then back toward Trudi: "I needed her to understand that she cannot make life choices for you. That we love each other."

Trudi's eyes darted, like watching tennis, back and forth. Tears now forming in the ducts. She was paralyzed by the terror of this man being alone with her daughter inside his truck up at the lake. *Had she actually gotten into his vehicle? Cassie hated Freddie.*

Arms at her sides. Legs stiff as boards. Trudi's gut stirred. She could think of nothing else but Freddie Banks strangling her daughter until she was dead, tossing her body into the lake.

My baby. You killed my baby….

"I told her she was being a selfish little bitch for demanding we not see each other and it wasn't fair. She screamed at me and pounded on the dashboard of my truck. She told me to fuck off. She said she was going to claim I had tried to rape her. That's why she got into my truck! If I didn't leave you alone and forget about the relationship, she was going to the cops to tell them I had touched her and she had sex with me because she was scared. I believed her, Trudi."

Freddie paced. Stopped. Looked at Trudi.

"Did you kill my daughter, Freddie?" Trudi said without moving. She had no idea where the words came from.

"No!" Freddie yelled through clenched teeth. He tried to keep his voice down. "It was not like that."

Trudi looked at him. Freddie paced more.

It was not like that?

Trudi watched as the sweat, in bead-like condensation, rolled down Freddie's forehead. He stopped and patted his brow every so often. The guy's mind was running a million miles per hour.

"Did you hurt my Cassie, Freddie?"

"I said *no*, Trudi. She was screaming and yelling these things about sexual assault and how she knew my 'type' and how I should have never taken advantage of you as my employee, and how you were going to sue the company and…well…I, I told her to get out of my truck. I even reached over and opened the door."

Freddie put a finger up to his lips. Tapped it there a moment and breathed in fast and heavy.

Trudi did not take her eyes off him.

It was not like that.

"She would not get out. So I drove away from the lake. Got onto Meadowbrook Road. I sped down the block until we got about two houses from here. Down there near that…that empty lot. She said she would jump out of the truck if I didn't stop the vehicle. So I slammed the brakes and her head hit the dashboard. Knocked her backward. She was fine. She turned to me and said, 'You are fucked now. I am going to make sure you are sent back to whatever jungle you came from.' I punched the dash, cut my hand. She jumped out. I peeled off. Went home and drank a glass of scotch. I sat through the night staring at the phone, drinking, trying like hell to dredge up the nerve to call you and tell you what happened." He paused.

"Look, Trudi, would you have believed me? *I'm black.* That's all I hear in this shit town."

Freddie had tears in his eyes.

"Can I get up?"

"Yes, of course, Trudi." Freddie walked over. Took Trudi's hand. "I'm sorry to scare you like this, but I knew you wanted nothing to do with me after I saw you walk into the PD this morning. They asked about me, right?"

"You followed me?"

"Trudi, are you *not hearing* me? They are going to blame me for Cassie's disappearance. I'm the guy. I'm the scapegoat here. I'm their way out of this. I was with her. I have no idea where she went, or why she hasn't come back yet."

Freddie had a vein like a small worm that appeared down the side of his forehead whenever he got himself going. Trudi knew this from staring at his face as they made love. Now the thought of him being inside her, of Freddie ejaculating and that vein becoming more pronounced, made Trudi Caldwell sick to her stomach. All she could fathom in this moment was Freddie Banks killing her daughter. Punching and punching Cassie until she was dead.

It was not like that.

"Get out of my house, Freddie."

"You don't believe me? You think I hurt your kid." Freddie threw his hands up. He wiped the tears from his eyes with the back of his hand, collected himself. "You think like the rest of them." He stared into Trudi's eyes. "What about all that bedroom talk? How many times have we fucked in this bed right here"—Freddie got up in Trudi's face, and she could feel his hot breath and the spittle wetting her skin—"while your boyfriend was at work? While your kids were in school! How you whispered to me that who I am, what I am, doesn't matter to you. You see, now it does, right? I'm just a black-boy nigger to you now. Same as the rest of them. That is all you see." He calmed himself. Spoke slower. "I'm nothing but some African with anger issues who…" He stopped himself from finishing the thought. "You're just like everyone else in the end. You want to shoulder all of your wrath, all of your inhibitions, all of your fear and hatred on me—the black man. I'm your way out of the shit life you have given your children. I'm easy to blame for the mistakes you and your fucking daughter have made. You cannot even get your child the help she needs for a condition she was born with—and you call yourself…" He stopped.

Just then, Katherine pushed the bedroom door open. She stood in the hallway. She had her mother's cell phone in her hand, the screen pointed out at Freddie. It was on speaker. Freddie could hear it ringing.

"Nine-one-one," the dispatcher said.

Katherine walked over and hugged her mother. Gripped her hard as she could.

"Get out of my house right now, Freddie," Trudi said.

Freddie said nothing more. He looked at the two of them; a tear streamed down his right cheek. His temples throbbed to his heartbeat. He had a look of defeat on his face. Trudi could feel it. Before Trudi could explain to the operator what was going on, Freddie Banks had run down the stairs and out of the house.

29.

CAM AND LINDA MET in the parking lot outside the Royal Oaks PD building. It was pitch dark, the sky above them a sheet of black velvet adorned with little diamonds sparkling throughout. A raw smell of cow manure permeated the air; the farmers had spread their fall fertilizer earlier that afternoon in the cornfields across the street and the wind had carried the potent smell across the meadow. Amazing what human beings could get used to. Neither Cam nor Linda could smell it much anymore. It was only the newbie cops from out of town, just out of the academy, who complained.

"That search of the water well produced nothing more than an old shoe, likely not Cassie's, several beer bottles, a tire, and some old cordwood that looked to have been tossed off the cliff, down into the ravine where the well is located," Cam explained. "We sent it all in for DNA, but don't expect anything back."

Linda seemed rushed. "What are you thinking, Cam?"

"Well, that was how the jacket got down there, too," Cam said. "Somebody bagged it up and tossed it off the cliff above."

"Sounds like you guys did a thorough job."

"Those CSUs conducted a freakin' archaeological dig, Lin. I was impressed. Didn't think our boys had it in them. So quick and efficient, too. Wow."

"Okay, we need to forget about that for now," Linda said. "Prioritize and focus."

Linda explained the call she'd taken earlier from a very shaken-up Trudi Caldwell, who was scared for her and her daughter after Freddie Banks had somehow slipped into the house before them, hid in her closet, and jumped out at her. Blues were at the house now. There was no sign of Freddie anywhere, but cops were out looking for him.

"He somehow knew that Vinnie was not going to be around," Linda said.

"He's our guy. Gotta be."

Trudi had repeated Freddie's soliloquies best she could remember under duress. Whatever she couldn't recall, however, Katherine got on the phone and repeated, word for word, saying she sat outside the room in the hallway after hearing a commotion, waited for the right time to step in. The girl's memory, it appeared, was better than Linda's.

"The kid doesn't talk much," Cam mentioned, adding how he'd tried to get Katherine to open up when they'd had lunch that day, but all she did was stare at some drawing she was working on. Every once in a while, Cam added, she'd stop what she was doing and, without a word, walk over and hug him.

"It's a symptom—same as that memory of hers," Linda said.

"Of what?"

"Her condition."

"The OCD?"

"Asperger's, actually. I spoke to one of Cassie's teachers. She mentioned how they'd tried to get Trudi to take Katherine in for tests after Cassie complained about it in school. Cassie had arguments with her mother about it, apparently. But Trudi just wasn't interested. There's social isolation, too. It's mild, though, with Katherine, I'm sure of that. So be easy on her, Cam. Have some patience with the girl."

"Of course. Well, at least we know the official, clinical cause of her issues." Cam paused. Then changed the subject: "So you never spoke to Freddie today, like you two planned?"

"I was wondering why Freddie never called and came in—and there you go. He answered that question for us. He was figuring out how to break into his girlfriend's home and scare the shit out of them."

Linda put a hand on her revolver. A tic she'd catch herself doing several times a day.

Cam was now in favor of Freddie's guilt. More than having seen Freddie's truck on the video and hearing about the conversation Linda had had with him at the restaurant. Freddie had to be their man. Cam didn't need much more convincing than the story Trudi had just told. Freddie and Cassie out at the lake. The jacket and the blood. The argument. Well, Freddie had more than some explaining to do. Cam told Linda how, if he had to bet, Freddie made up all that about driving Cassie away from the lake. That was extra. He killed her there. That's why her jacket was in the woods. He murdered the girl, tossed her body into the lake, and tried to throw off the scent with the jacket in the well.

"Should we begin to think about getting a few divers to head into the water at first light?"

"I made the call already."

Linda said she was sure she had enough for an indictment, but wanted to wait. She'd typed up an arrest warrant on breaking and entering, as well as kidnapping charges, to be safe. It was with a judge now. She was just waiting for a signature and they could call out the troops, hopefully find Freddie, and bring him in.

"Wherever the hell he might have gone," Cam said. He took out a round tin, the size and shape of a hockey puck; chewing tobacco from his back pocket. He twisted the cardboard lid off, grabbed a pinch of the snuff, and placed it between his right cheek and gum. After a moment, Cam spit.

Linda watched. Waited for him to finish.

Cam smiled, little bits of tobacco stuck in his teeth like coffee grounds.

"I want a search of the woods around the lake tomorrow. Dogs. All the volunteers and off-duty cops you can rustle up. We start there. I need to wrestle with some bureaucratic nonsense first, before I can get the divers. Fucking budgets! Incredible. It'll happen, but I need some time and a few favors called in."

Cam nodded. "Sounds like a plan." He spit again.

"I'm thinking Freddie is across town," Linda said. "He has an employee who lives by Riley Brothers Tree Service in an apartment building fashioned out of an old Victorian house. He thinks we don't know this. But I found out from talking to a waitress, a young girl a few years older than Cassie, who said she recalled Freddie once hitting on her, making a pass, which she wrote off and forgot about. Nothing too strong, just a look, a question about dating. Probably in her mind that Freddie wanted her, but who knows now? She also told me he stays with another guy from the restaurant once in a while when they are busy because the dude's apartment is closer to work. They watch soccer together, too, I guess."

"You're thinking he's there, hiding?"

"Yeah."

Cam spit again.

"Why not New York? Lin, why wouldn't Freddie go home?"

They walked toward Linda's Crown Vic, talking under the amber light of the parking lot lamps. When they arrived at the car, Linda opened the trunk. She spoke with one hand on the raised trunk, the other by her side.

"New York is too obvious. He wants people to believe he didn't have anything to do with this. He'll stay here to defend himself and fight for his lies. Typical narcissist. Plus, from what Trudi says, he's a man of 'great integrity' when it comes to being right and him being blamed for things he claims he didn't do. She admitted to me why he actually left New York. A kid down there on a youth soccer team he coached accused him of inappropriate behavior in the locker room. I'm trying to nail down what happened, waiting on New York to e-mail a report. But it seems that Freddie has a history—and this would not have come out unless Trudi told us, which is important, Cam—of problems with youths. He filed a civil suit against the school once the kid rescinded, Trudi seemed to think he told her. That's why there are reports about it—and even a deposition of his testimony I am trying to get my hands on. But still, he told me in general terms that he moved here because he felt jaded by racism and was tired of the City life. Big difference. Why lie about any of it?"

Cam spit again and Linda told him to stop spitting around her. It was disgusting and she didn't want to come in the next morning and see tobacco spit all over the ground.

"When the hell did you start chewing that shit, anyway?" She closed her eyes and shooed her hands. "Forget it. I don't care. Just swallow your spit if you wanna chew that nasty shit in front of me."

Cam smiled. "Stakeouts and take-downs is when I chew. Gets the blood pumping."

Digging inside the trunk of her Crown Vic, Linda picked up a Kevlar vest and shoved it into Cam's chest. "Put that on." Then took one for herself.

"What's up with the terrorist garb?"

"Trudi claimed Freddie kept a gun at the restaurant behind the bar. She said he seemed 'fixated' with it sometimes. He'd get a few drinks in him and wave it around."

"Never be too safe, right, boss?"

"Just put the thing on and get in the car, Cameron."

Linda's phone *dinged*.

You're all set.

The text was from the local prosecutor. He'd just gotten off the phone with the judge, who'd signed off on the warrant.

Linda sat in the Crown Vic a moment before starting it. She looked over at Cam. He was fastening the vest around his stomach.

Finished, Cam looked at her. "What is it?"

"Be careful tonight, Cam, okay?"

They shared a silent stare.

"You, too," Cam said.

"You ready?"

The big man nodded.

Linda reached down and grabbed hold of the microphone on her two-way: "All units with me tonight, we're good to go. Warrant is signed. Please do as you've been instructed. Wait for my lead. Meet us at the rendezvous point and wait for me there."

Linda Kane hit the accelerator and peeled rubber as the back tires kicked up stones and the Crown Vic hightailed it out of the driveway.

No lights. No siren.

Complete stealth.

Linda explained to Cam along the way that this was a mission of sneaking up on the house, checking things out, then doubling back and bringing the rest of the crew in to serve the warrant, old-school style, surrounding the house. "If he's even there!"

Linda, Cam, and two other blues chosen by the captain were going in under the cloak of night to survey the property. The goal of the first part of the mission was to get a peek inside a window or two. See what was going on.

According to a neighbor, a guy one of the two blues had known from a bowling league, he saw a "black dude with a white dude" enter the property at about 10:45 p.m. They had not left, the neighbor said, because when he took his dog out for a walk around the neighborhood later on, maybe around 11:45 p.m., he saw the same car they had both arrived in parked in the driveway. "Unless that black dude walked home, he should still be inside."

"So we're not going in blind," Cam said, rolling down the window.

"You're going to spit out my window, are you?"

Rolling it back up, "Of course not."

"Right. We have a witness sighting. He's there, Cam. No doubt about it. And listen, when we take him down, I want to show him who's in charge here. He's had his chance to come in and talk this through, if he's not done anything to the girl. He's had a chance to be honest about seeing Cassie that night. Instead, he decided to lie to us and break into Trudi's house. We're going at him like he's done something."

"Right." Cam swallowed a mouthful of spit, gagged a bit.

"Oh, for shit's sake, just spit out the window already. But don't ever chew that nasty stuff inside this car again."

Cam rolled the window down and let go a solid mouthful.

"Here's the thing," Linda said. "I mean, if you haven't committed a crime, why lie to the cops? Doesn't make any sense."

"I can easily show Freddie Banks who's the boss here in this situ, Lin." Cam gave her a look of total control. Linda felt her desires justified in that moment.

"Just be careful, Cameron. Follow your training here. Remember, we have no idea what he is going to do or how he will react."

"Understood."

"Consider him armed."

"Got it."

Linda parked two blocks away from the house where they suspected Freddie Banks was hiding out. It was well after midnight. No streetlights out here at this end of town. Total darkness.

The way Linda wanted it.

"I mean it, Cam," she said before they got out of the car. "Eyes and mind on what we're doing at all times. I need you to be…" She began to stumble over her words. "I need you to be at the top of your game." It was not what Linda Kane truly wanted to say.

Cam looked at Linda, who saw zero fear in his eyes.

He nodded. "Game on, boss."

30.

THE TWO BLUES WERE waiting when Cam and Linda arrived. One had binoculars. He was staring through them down the block.

Cam knew both cops from the locker room and roll call.

"What's up?" Cam said.

The men bumped opposite shoulders, shook hands like basketball players meeting on the court when lineups are announced, patted each other on the back. Brad Clarkston and Dave Michaelson. "Good dudes, as far as I know," Cam had told Linda on the way. "Straight-up cops." The kind you want watching your back. Cam had heard that they'd conducted countless meth and Oxy raids and were accustomed to this type of police work. Robots. You give Brad and Dave orders. They deliver.

"Been looking down there," Dave said in a low voice. "I don't see anything."

"No movement whatsoever?" Linda asked.

"Nope."

"Lights on?"

"Just two. Front porch and one inside." He dropped the binoculars from his eyes, focused on Linda: "Looks to be a living room light on and someone moving around."

They all wore black leather gloves with the fingertips cut out. They looked like part of a SWAT team. Linda got a rush out of these moments. But as she thought more about the potential danger involved, she hoped with this team that all would go well.

You just never know.

"Cam, boys, I need you to be careful here. Look, he doesn't strike me as the violent type, but he did break into his ex-girlfriend's home and scare the shit out of her and her child. He seems to have anger issues. But I don't know. Something is off about all this. So please take every precaution you're trained for. Let's use our heads, too. It'll go smooth. Just be smart. Ready?"

They nodded.

The four of them stayed low and hustled down the block, making it to the front lawn of the house without being seen or heard. The building was an old home, split into two apartments, two doors in front, side by side. Freddie's friend's door was to the right, a small light in the shape of a question mark hanging above it. The left door entered the other apartment.

The plan was to first make sure Freddie Banks was inside, then call in six other blues nearby and surround the place. Linda and Cam would knock on the door and ask Freddie to step out. Hands behind his head. Move slowly.

All that trained-cop protocol nonsense.

The silence of the night was deafening. Crickets and cicadas. A dog off in the far distance barked every once in a while, but the town was asleep.

They managed to make it behind the one vehicle in the driveway, a large white van, a bit of brown rust over each fender wall. As Cam and Linda prepared to creep up to a side window from there, the sound of a door opening was the first contingency about to throw this entire plan into a very dangerous direction.

All four knelt farther down behind the van, their backs up against the driver's side of the vehicle.

"Shit," Linda whispered to herself.

Linda held her right hand up to her lips to shush everyone.

Don't move. Wait this out.

With two hands, they held their weapons to the right of their waistlines.

Linda shimmied her body up and turned. She had a clear view of the porch through the driver's-side window and windshield.

She watched Freddie Banks walk out the door, look left and right, straight ahead, nervously, and then turn around to close the door with his back to them.

Opportunity.

"Let's move in on three," Linda whispered. "Spread out, flank the front door. Block that porch off. Let me do all the talking."

She counted it down.

They jumped out and surrounded the front porch in one swift motion, surprising Freddie. On all sides, Freddie was covered. He wasn't going anywhere without running into four weapons trained on him.

Freddie did not move. Frozen, he kept his back to them, his front facing the door. His right hand was on the doorknob, as if he was getting ready to lock it. He must have realized what the noise was in back of him.

"Mr. Banks," Linda said with a touch of military firmness, "do not move. We—four of us—have our weapons pointed at you. I have a warrant. You need to lie down on the ground, arms behind your head. Do this now, please."

Freddie did not do as he was told. In fact, Freddie Banks did not move at all.

"Mr. Banks, please immediately do as you are instructed." Linda motioned with head nods for Cam to move in closer toward the subject; Dave and Brad to follow him. They stood about twenty feet in back of Freddie. It was dark. Hard to see. Freddie had turned off the front porch light before walking out of the apartment.

Linda breathed slowly. Deep in, deep out, through her nose, just as she had been trained. She could feel her pulse ratchet up several notches, sweat bead down her back. Her Kevlar vest felt tighter around her midsection and breasts.

Dave took one more step forward than the others. He cocked his neck a bit to his right, like he was having trouble seeing something.

Linda looked at him. Noticed Dave squinting.

Freddie, so Dave would later say, reached around his waist without turning his body. Then put his hand—again, according to Dave—close to the small of his back.

The exact point where everything went to hell.

Linda felt her heart explode. She looked at Freddie, then at Dave.

Freddie.

Dave.

Freddie.

Dave.

No!

But it was too late.

A crack shot, without a word of warning, Dave put a bullet through the back of Freddie Banks's head, spattering tissue and blood and brain matter all over the front door.

Cam turned to his right and screamed.

For a moment, Freddie didn't flinch. Then his entire body, in one motion, as if his bones dissolved, crumbled onto the porch.

Brad ran toward Freddie and trained his weapon on him.

The shot had instantly killed Freddie Banks.

Cam walked up. Stared down at Freddie. Then looked up at Linda, who rushed toward them.

Standing over his corpse, staring at the hole in the back of his head, Linda realized Freddie Banks had his wallet in his hand.

31.

SEVERAL DAYS PASSED. IT had been a week since Cassie went missing. It was now officially puffer jacket, see-your-breath weather. A sudden snap of cold had pushed down from Canada and settled in over New England. Time for woodstoves and hot chocolate. Apple-picking season was over. The thrill of fall, those fiery colors bursting everywhere, were mere memories—fallen to the ground and rotting.

After the "event," as Linda's boss would come to call it, Linda found herself buried in paperwork; Cam, too. They'd been questioned by the Internal Affairs Bureau and gave detailed statements. Dave had been sent out of town to an "undisclosed location." Brad was taken off the job, put on desk duty. Linda had gone over it in her head a thousand times. A split-second question every cop faces: *What do you do?* Well, she had her weapon trained on Freddie, too, and not once did Linda Kane ever think he was reaching for a weapon at the small of his back, like Dave had claimed. It was about judgment. Simple deduction. Careful reasoning.

What type of person are you?

Since the news broke, several women had come forward and accused Dave of using the *n*-word in their presence on occasion. He'd also belittled a black girl behind the counter of the local 7-Eleven, which a social-media user behind him in line, who'd recorded it, had since uploaded onto Twitter.

Dave was, it was being said around the squad room, fucked.

As well as it should be.

The entire office, most of the time bursting with energy and life, had a pall of gray over it. Linda went through a series of emotions: from fury and anger to complete and utter depression. This was not the type of police department that handled scandal and high-profile attention well. It was going to destroy people. Careers. But more than that, take the focus off of Linda and Cam finding Cassandra Caldwell.

As she sat, Linda's gaze had concrete in it. She stood and walked over to the window, resisting the urge to scream. Being on the second floor of the building gave the viewpoint of looking out onto the parking lot, down the long driveway leading up to the circle turnabout at the front entrance, where the flagpole stood in the middle.

The blinds had been closed. Another form of seclusion and hiding since the event.

Outside, the press gathered. In Hartford, a chapter of Black Lives Matter was gearing up to stage a protest on the street in front of the building. They'd managed to employ some sort of Al Sharpton wannabe, a local pastor by the name of Rufus Smalls—a fat man with gray dreads down his back, a bullhorn, and an attitude toward all cops. Smalls, himself, had done time for burglary and assault years ago. But that did not make any difference now. He was the voice of his people. And the people wanted not only to be heard, but were tired of being treated like second-class citizens. They wanted justice in any form they could get it.

The only thing that had given Linda a moment of respite was the fact that there was no damn video of the murder. *Yes*, she thought, standing by the window, watching the crowd swell, it was the appropriate word to describe the event.

Murder.

Dave had committed a homicide.

There were no two ways about it. Which made Linda half-smile, hearing in her head a saying her dad used to utter all the time: *"No two ways about it, Linny."*

"The DA is going after Dave," Cam said, walking up behind

Linda.

"Does he have any choice?"

"I guess not."

Linda did not look at Cam.

"From all I know, Lin, Dave is a good guy."

This made Linda spin around. She gave Cam a pained look. Then: "No, Cam, Dave is *not* a good guy. Not for nothing, but we all had the same choice Dave had, and three of us did *not* commit a homicide."

Silence.

Cam stared at the carpet. He didn't like where this conversation was headed.

"You think you know a guy," Cam finally said.

Linda was speechless. She walked to her desk.

"He was reaching for his weapon," Dave had said right after taking the shot, walking up, looking over Freddie Banks's dead body. *"Tell me, all of you, he was reaching for a weapon, right?"*

His wallet. Freddie Banks had his wallet in his hand as he fell to the ground, dead before hitting the cement.

"His right hand was on its way up, wasn't it, Lin?" Cam said, standing by Linda's desk, Linda sitting down. "He was going to put his arms up."

"That's what I saw, Cam. Mike, too."

"I worked out with Dave a few times. We had beers here and there. But you're right, I didn't know him. Not personally, anyway."

"Cam, listen." Linda turned toward her man and stood. Cam stood tall over Linda, but they were equals. Always. That was the energy Linda exuded. That was part of what attracted Linda. She knew they were going to get through this. It was a shit show and would be for a while, but it would end. Whatever happened to Dave from here, whatever the "movement" did, however they wanted to address the situation in the media and within the IAB, didn't matter to Linda and the work they had left to do. "You cannot ever forget about our victim, Cam. We need to speak for Cassandra. That needs to remain our focus."

The big man looked like he was about to cry.

"One act of stupidity or immaturity or even violence does not define a life," Cam said.

"It does show us who that person is, Cam. Truly who that person is on the inside."

"Cops are not given any type of leeway anymore—the benefit of the doubt. Never used to be like that, or so say the old-timers."

"They're out of touch," Linda said. "This is a new world we police." She tapped her palm on Cam's chest, where his heart beat. She stared into his eyes. "In there, Cam. You are a good cop. Dave," she added, shaking her head, "not a good cop. What he did does not reflect any part of who *you* are, how you police this town—how any one of these great cops around us police this town. He pulled that trigger. Not you, me, or Brad. You have to let this go and believe that Freddie, and whoever stakes claim to his cause from here, will find the justice they search for and deserve. That sounds contrite, maybe even patronizing. But you and I, we believe in the *system*. We are part of it."

Cam held Linda's gaze.

She concluded, "We rely on that system to work and to be fair. There's no place in our world for a racist cop. You've seen that Twitter video, Cam; do you need to see anything more?"

Linda walked away. Then stopped, turned to make sure Cam was okay.

He nodded his head, giving that sign all was good.

The detective went over to the entrance counter, into the squad room, and checked to see if there were any messages from forensics. Linda wanted to know what the DNA proved about the blood on Cassie's jacket. If Freddie's DNA was a match, releasing that info, although it would be met with criticism and scorn from the pundits on cable news as a bash-the-victim type of moment by the po-po, would help quell tensions, Linda knew. The public needed to know she and the boys were serving a warrant on a guy who had potentially murdered a missing teenager and who had broken into a house. It did not, Linda knew full well, excuse what happened to Freddie Banks. But it did give the incident a bit of legal and social context.

Carmen came over. "You all right, kid?"

"Yeah, yeah…Carm. You know how it is. These things happen.

We deal with them. Now, any word from forensics on that jacket? I told them to text me. They have plenty of DNA from Freddie Banks. What's the damn hold up here?"

"Not yet. Any day now, they tell me."

Linda looked up, saw the elevator door *ding* open and Iris Starr walk out.

Shit.

Linda had a scowl on her face as she stared at the woman in three-inch heels, emitting a cloud of perfume Linda swore she could smell from where she stood twenty feet away.

"How the *hell* did you get in here?" Linda snapped at the reporter. Her grimace had turned to raw anger. There was a hard edge in Linda's voice.

Iris smiled.

"Let me rephrase that," Linda added. "Who did you have to bang to get in here?"

That one stopped Iris in her tracks.

Even Carmen was surprised by it.

"You shouldn't talk to me like that, Detective."

"It's the captain," Carmen said. "He likes her show. He didn't want to refuse her access now, what's going on with IAB."

Linda rolled her eyes.

Gutless. Those white shirts. No freakin' balls whatsoever.

"Not in enough trouble already?" Linda said, turning, seeing all eyes in the squad room on the two of them. "You had to come *here*? You send me an e-mail like that again and I will have your office on notice that every cop in this county will never speak to them again. I don't give a shit what the captain likes, I'll make certain of it."

"I need you to see something," Iris said.

"No, no, no," Linda shouted, putting up two hands, closing her eyes. "I do the talking right now." She paused, thinking. Then: "Follow me."

Linda walked Iris into an empty office with no windows along the edge of the squad room. She showed the reporter in and closed the door behind them.

"Okay. Let's hear what the Greek goddess has to say." Linda popped the HOME button on her iPhone and set the timer at two minutes. "You've got one hundred and twenty seconds. As you know, I'm sure, we're up to our ass in problems here, and this better not be about that. I will never, ever, *ever* talk to you or any reporter about what happened out there."

"No, no, no," Iris said, with an almost I'm-on-*your*-side tone. "This is about Miss Ariana Olahu."

Linda found a spot on the desk and parked her right butt cheek, never taking her eyes off Iris.

What a damn day already.

"Okay, Detective," Iris said. She seemed nervous, Linda recognized. For a moment, Linda thought the cliché was complete in that Iris was the bimbo snapping gum on the arm of the gangster, but realized the reporter had this strange tic of moving her lips when not talking. "I need you to listen to me. It's important. We can help each other."

"What. Do. You. Want?"

Iris handed Linda her cell phone. She pointed one of her long, pink-polished fingernails down onto the screen and tapped it, making a terrible clicking noise.

Linda took the phone, looked up at Iris, then down at the small screen. She knew, of course, what Iris was showing her.

Benjie and Scottie: idiots and their photos.

The cop studied the images. After scrolling through several, Linda looked off to her right, sighed, then handed the phone back to Iris.

"Photos of a crime scene before a case is adjudicated, Iris, nice." Linda got up, walked to the door. "I'm sure the DA will love hearing about this. And your sources: One of them is in our jail downstairs. The other one, well, doesn't matter."

"The other one was sleeping with your missing girl, from what I hear."

Linda stared at the TV reporter.

Iris wore about ten—Linda didn't actually count—silver bracelets, each one thin as spaghetti that clanked every time she moved her left arm. Kind of looked like she had put on a Slinky toy before leaving the house. The noise ground on Linda's nerves.

"If you can drop this whole tough-girl, feminist-cop thing you got going on here"—Iris whirled one hand in the air between them in a circular motion, as if she was washing a window—"and give me a chance to explain myself, maybe we can cut the shuck and jive and speak like two adults. Maybe we can help each other."

"Oh, there it is. Great racial reference there, Iris." Linda clapped. "Congratulations." As Linda spoke, Iris reached into her purse, pulled out a tin of mints and popped one into her mouth. "Listen," Linda continued, "not that I need to explain anything to you, but I don't have time for bullshit, Iris Starr. I am a busy cop. Lots of things going on, as you seem to know. And I do not need to get involved with a case that, as of now, the state police are handling. Something else you should already know. As for Cassie Caldwell, you had better stay the fuck out of that. Consider that, my dear, a threat."

Linda turned and stormed out of the office.

Something occurred to the detective as she made her way back to her workstation: That Iris knew about Benjie and Cassie having sex. Without facing Iris, Linda stopped, put a hand on a nearby desk to balance herself, and said: "Carmen will show you out."

As Carmen hustled Iris out of the office, Linda said, "Wait. Let her be another moment, Carm. Iris, I need you to stay the hell out of our business here. You understand me? Whoever your fuck buddy in the department is, stand clear of me and my cases. You tell your source that if he divulges anything else to you, I'll have his job."

Iris did not have a poker face. "Not sure what you mean?" she said. Then brushed off her dress with both hands as if she had fallen.

As Linda walked toward her subject, Cam got up from his desk and followed. He had watched the entire scene play out.

"Are you making erroneous accusations and threats toward me, Detective, for an entire squad room to hear?"

Cam walked over, grabbed the phone out of Iris's hand.

"Hey, hey…give me that back."

Cam tossed it to Linda.

Linda went into Iris's text messages and e-mail. Looked around. Clicked on the texts from Spiked Hair and Shaved Head, then read them. She deleted the photos, knowing that Iris probably had backups for them. But then, she probably didn't—because, Linda Kane knew, in the end Iris Starr was a media whore. She cared nothing for news.

"Here," Linda said, tossing the phone back to Iris. "Now get your ass out of here. Don't come back." Linda put a finger up to her lips. Thought a minute. She called out to a blue nearby. "Listen, before that one there leaves, write her up a summons for trespassing on high school property."

As Linda walked back to her desk, a subtle smile on her face, a blue came over.

"Lin, you got a call. It's that Tiffany Barnes girl you and Cam interviewed—the one from the woods who found the missing girl's jacket."

Cam was nearby. He and Linda looked at each other.

32.

TIFFANY BARNES WAS A victim, Linda had explained to Cam after they released her. "Typical abuse victim."

A blue had followed the girl for a time, realizing she was trying to get back on track, just as she'd promised. She certainly did not know—or have any connection to—Cassie.

So why was she calling? Linda wondered, picking up the phone. "Yes?"

"Ma'am, ma'am," Tiffany said; she was crying, absolutely hysterical. "I… It is Tiffany. Tiffany Barnes."

"Tiffany? You okay?"

"I am not. I did what I said: I stayed with family. I wanted to get back into life. But I decided to go back home. My little sister, you know. I have a little sister. I worried so much about her. The moment I walked in…it wasn't good. I got into it with my father immediately."

"Where are you now?"

"I'm at a pay phone…" Linda could hear that Tiffany was looking around, trying to decipher a landmark of some sort. "It's near the center green, by a restaurant, a diner or something."

"You're back in Royal Oaks?"

"Yes. I had nowhere else to go. I'm sorry."

"I'm here to help," Linda said. "Stay where you are; I'll be there in a few minutes."

A distraction, Linda considered. Just what she needed right about now.

It took Linda five minutes to drive from the PD to the town center, where she found Tiffany Barnes sitting on a curb, smoking a cigarette, shaking in the cold air of late afternoon. She had changed some. Tiffany had her nose ring back in; a gold barbell through the columella, that meaty section between the nostrils. One of her eyebrows had slashes shaved through it like streaks. Her hair had swaths of pink. She wore a hoodie and jeans with pre-ripped sections on the thighs and knees. A winter wool cap. Bags under her eyes, she looked tired.

"You back on the shit?" Linda asked. "Get in." She had the window rolled down and had pulled up next to the teen.

Tiffany stubbed out her cigarette, bounced up and sat next to Linda, closed the door. She put her cold hands up in front of the heating vent, rubbed them together to warm up.

Linda pulled over and positioned the Crown Vic between two white lines in the parking lot of the diner.

"I'm not. Promise."

Tiffany's mascara was running from having cried.

"I need you to press full charges against that sick son of a bitch; my father. I want him gone. Put away. In jail."

"Your sister?"

"How did you know?"

"Tiffany, you put an asshole scumbag on a train in Hoboken and send him to Palm Beach, that same asshole gets off."

Tiffany wasn't sure she understood the analogy, but nodded her head as if she did.

"You think he's not going to touch your little sister—that he was exclusive to you?"

"You mind if I smoke?" Tiffany asked. She pulled out a pack of Marlboro Lights, a white package with gold-and-black lettering.

"Outside the car, please."

Tiffany put the pack away.

"Come down with me to the station and I'll put you with a cop who can take care of this. She'll bring you back to your town. She'll take you into the local police station. Make sure you follow through.

Most don't. You will, though, right?"

"Fuck yeah, I will. My little sister. Damn it all."

"Take care of her." Linda put her hand on Tiffany's forearm, gently squeezed. Stared into her eyes: "Make it your priority, Tiffany. Focus on your sister's well-being. That will help you."

Tiffany nodded her head up and down. Linda felt an odd connection to the girl. They had a shared experience. But Linda was having a hard time finding out where it resided in her.

As they drove back to the PD, Linda had a revelation. She saw a bit of Sherri in Tiffany. The same street toughness. The same edge. That same look of fear, of frustration, of living with a monster.

Shit, Linda recognized, looking at Tiffany's leg bounce a mile a minute as they pulled into the PD parking lot. *How Tiffany's and Sherri's stories were so much alike?*

33.

THE INCIDENT AT ROYAL Oaks PD with Linda Kane had pushed Iris Starr into wanting revenge. She had not planned on getting involved in the riff between law enforcement and the Black Lives Matter movement, but that was yesterday. Today, Iris felt, she was all about reporting topical news, inserting herself into what was one of the more high-profile news stories surrounding the missing girl. Suddenly, it wasn't about Cassandra Caldwell and her whereabouts anymore; the story was a dead black suspect, a white cop holding a smoking gun, three other cops standing around him, one of whom was now on the top of Iris's very short shit list.

Yum, Iris woke up and thought as she did her hair and makeup, prepping for the interview.

The white lights were scorching bright, pointed into the reverend's face. The sweat beaded up on his forehead and he kept having to wipe it away with a folded hanky. He wore a double-breasted gray suit, white shirt, red tie. Very political. Very businesslike. Very media-friendly. His assistant, a woman named Natasha, sat off to his right, a notebook and cell phone on her lap.

"Sorry about those lights," Iris said, sitting down across from Smalls. "I appreciate this—an exclusive interview with me. Just to be clear: You will not be speaking to any other reporters on camera until after this interview airs tonight?"

The clergyman nodded his head in the affirmative.

Natasha, too.

Reverend Smalls and Iris sat face-to-face, about three feet apart, inside a conference room at the local Holiday Inn Express in a town just outside Royal Oaks that Iris and her cameraman, Roger, had been staying at since their arrival. Iris had put in a request to interview Smalls about the recent cop shooting, and he was happy for the opportunity to spread his message.

Iris cleared her throat. "Reverend," she said, "I want to start by thanking you. I know this is a tough time, the wounds raw, but it's important to tell this story."

"Are we rolling?"

"Yes."

"Let me just say up front, this is not about us being anti-police. I just want to make that clear. It's time for the public, especially the white establishment of cops in this country, to change its mind about policing and policy and how each one of them views the black man differently—however big or small—than the white man. Especially on the streets. In that report, this small town of Royal Oaks, as we can clearly see, is no different than, say, Harlem or Baltimore or Chicago."

"In your view, Reverend, where did the police go wrong here? Is this the case of a superior officer not doing her job? Is it a managerial issue? Training? What is it?"

"What it is, Miss Starr, is looking into the tearstained eyes of another black mother and telling her that her son was murdered by a white cop. We are tired of that narrative. Another family is going to bury a man whose life was cut short by those hired to protect and serve the people. As a civil rights leader, I am certainly and profoundly aware that justice and change do not happen overnight. But we need a revolution and we need it now. We need justice and we need it now."

"Or you will not have peace, am I right in saying that?"

He hesitated. Then, wiping his brow again, said: "That is about the gist of it all, yes. Justice comes swift for the black man on the street, being stopped and frisked and tossed against a squad car and busted up because he looks like a hustler or a criminal, or *not* like the white guy walking next to him. This cannot be the norm. It's not about a black man being shot by a white cop. It's about racial inequality on the street; how they all—you included—look at us differently. If you do not have that one basic, fundamental human right being displayed by your civic leaders, your civil servants, how can *you*, I should ask, expect peace?"

"So, the fact that my sources tell me Freddie Banks likely had something to do with the missing girl's disappearance is beside the point, then?"

Iris knew this would stir the clergyman up a bit.

Reverend Smalls shifted in his chair. It squeaked from the weight of his enormous frame. The sweat dripping from his brow was relentless. With him wiping his forehead every so often, Iris knew, it gave the interview a larger context, an immediacy, a ticking-clock feel that Iris knew would play well for ratings. Smalls was in the hot seat and he was, Iris understood, birthing his role in the movement here and now.

"That is just the thing I am referring to," the reverend said. He raised his voice, moved toward the reporter, put one hand up, using it to make his point, "You nailed it. He is *presumed* to be guilty and there is not a *shred* of evidence that has been made public against the man. We call this 'Black Presumption.' He's guilty by association of his race. It must stop."

"I'm told"—and Iris went to her notes and read for show purposes only; she already knew this information—"that Mr. Banks was being taken into custody on B&E charges, kidnapping even, for breaking into his girlfriend's house. Those are serious charges. My source tells me this Linda Kane detective, from Royal Oaks, had been after Freddie Banks from day one of the investigation into the missing girl, Cassandra Caldwell, whose mother Freddie Banks had dated. Kane had been looking to get him into the station for questioning. Let me ask, Reverend Smalls, do you think Linda Kane targeted Mr. Banks because he's black?"

"Linda Kane was one of the four at Mr. Banks's murder scene. She knows what happened there. She knows the truth. She knows where justice lies. She knows what is in her heart. We need to change the policy and the procedure, yes. But apparently, we need to change the thought process of the police. I don't know what else to say. We can get there. It's gonna take time, but we can get there. A person in the position of this Linda Kane can help us get there."

"Did she, again, target Mr. Banks because of his race?"

"I do not know and cannot speak for her, Miss Starr. Next question, please. I know what you are doing here. I'm not ignorant."

"Will there be protests scheduled in the coming days?" Iris asked, ignoring the preacher's rising blood pressure.

"The logistics are being worked out now. These will be *peaceful* protests, Miss Starr, I need to make that *very* clear. My people are God-fearing. They believe in their right to free speech, their right to mount a protest without being tased and gassed and shot at with sandbag guns. This is America, is it not?"

"You cannot control everyone, though, Reverend Smalls. We've seen the rioting and looting. How can you be sure that it will not occur here?"

"Let's not even go there, Miss Starr. We intend to voice our concerns and see that Mr. Banks's family gets the justice they deserve. But here you are, of course, in speaking about a majority of black people mounting a protest and you go right to the looting and rioting, as if, you suggest, it is expected." He pointed his finger at her: "This is the mentality that *needs* to change. You are part of the problem. Not the solution."

Iris did not want to comment on those accusations from the preacher. Instead, she went back to her tone of instigation: "Or you will have no peace, am I right in saying that? I mean, I don't want to put words in your mouth. But no justice equals no peace; that is your core message, right?"

"You said that twice now, Miss Starr. You are part of the problem, as I said, yet you don't even see it. The problem is not guilt or innocence, the accusation whether Freddie Banks broke into a house or not. Or who he dated. Even whether or not he took that girl and he raped and murdered her. Those are not the issues. It is that a white cop saw a black man as guilty of doing something— reaching for a gun—because of the color of his skin alone. Nothing else before or after that moment matters much to us."

"But, let me just say—"

"I think we're done here. I have nothing else to say to you."

"Will you seek the resignation or firing of the other officers that were at the scene of Mr. Banks's murder?"

Reverend Smalls stood. He got all tangled up in the wires from his microphone. "At the least, those other officers should be put on desk duty until this is resolved," he concluded. "Now can you get these wires off of me?"

Smalls then motioned for his assistant, Natasha, and they both walked out of the room.

"Mr. Smalls," Iris said, feeding the flames with a lie, "I will tell you that my sources claim there is a video of the shooting out there somewhere. I have not seen it, but I hear it's very difficult to watch."

"Where have you heard this from?"

"Not at liberty to divulge my sources, sir. But perhaps you should inquire if the Royal Oaks PD has dashboard video."

Before exiting the room, Smalls stopped and turned. "Miss Starr, I need you to understand this. Frederick Douglass said that 'power concedes nothing without a demand; it never did and it never will.' We demand justice for our brother Freddie Banks's family. We will get it. I promise you that. Good day."

Iris looked into the camera at Roger. She did that thing with her hand like she was slicing her own neck. "Cut," she said, a smile on her face.

"You know what you're doing?" Roger asked. He started to break down his camera and the lights. Iris took out her cell phone.

"Roger, I know *exactly* what I am doing. Once I put some voice-over to this interview and we run it, well, let's just say Linda Kane is going to have herself one pissed-off clergyman looking to get his base riled up—hopefully against her."

"She's just doing her job, Iris." Roger seemed to be siding with the PD on this.

"Just doing her job? Huh. You mean, not letting us do *our* job."

Iris dialed into the studio. Told them to warm up the voice-over edit suite. She and Roger were bolting into town with an exclusive interview she was going to edit and narrate that afternoon. "I want it on air tonight."

Roger wound an extension cord around his hand and elbow, watching Iris, shaking his head.

34.

LINDA WALKED INTO WHAT was a vast office space she often referred to as a cubicle farm. With her eyes, she scanned the room. After a few seconds, she saw him through a glass door. He sat behind an old oak desk, one of those lime-green antique desk lamps illuminating a file open in front of him. The man had his arms up on the desk in front of himself, fingers woven together. Kind of hunched over, reading, he had a concerned look on his face.

Patty Doyle was an old friend of Linda's. In his early sixties, white hair and blotchy red skin, Patty was thinking about retirement more than the cases that came before him as the captain of Troop N. Linda had wanted to do a stint in the state police when she first thought about law enforcement as a career, but opted for the local Royal Oaks PD, instead. Patty had become somewhat of a mentor to Linda, someone she could bounce investigatory ideas and internal problems off of. He had shown Linda the ropes. Taught her things she could never learn in the academy or even on the street. Patty was the lead investigator on Sherri's case. One of the reasons why Linda Kane had gone into police work, to begin with. As a child, Linda could recall sitting in a room full of cops, all of them staring at her, as she answered questions. It was Patty who made her feel like a human being. It was Patty who convinced Linda it wasn't her fault. And it was Patty who promised Linda that what happened to her friend that day had been out of her control.

"Lin," Patty said after looking up, hearing a knock on the door. "How are you?"

They hugged like father and daughter.

"Mr. Bean Counter," Linda said.

Patty laughed. "Sit down. Sit down. Good to see you. Jesus, that cop shooting your suspect. Man. Could you *not* have any more problems with that missing-girl case? How are things going over there right now?"

Linda sat with a heavy *thud* into a leather chair with gold buttons. She faced Patty. He put his arms back up on his desk, pushed that lamp to one side, and leaned toward her. She studied the plaque on Patty's desk facing her, designating his name and rank. A gold plate with etched letters. Nearly forty years of law enforcement service: guy deserved more than a piece of redwood and a metal name tag.

"Not good, Patty," Linda said, meeting his gaze. "You guys have Officer Dave Michaelson somewhere, I guess, preparing him for arrest. There's a cavalcade of protestors congregating outside the gate of our building. They're dug in for the long haul. They got the fifty-five-gallon drum burning a fire, you know, like railroad strikers. Tailgates opened, full of food. Lawn chairs. Signs. Lots of coffee. Bullhorns. And that Pastor Rufus Smalls character is getting them all stirred up, from what I hear." She watched as Patty slowly shook his head back and forth.

"Son of a bitch," he said, "you got your hands in the dog crap, kid. A small town is supposed to be quiet and not even be on the radar."

"That shit is for television."

Patty chuckled. "Stay as far out of all that noise surrounding this as you can. Let them do their thing. Focus on your work. It always feels worse in the beginning than it actually is. You been interviewed by IAB yet?"

"They had us give them a statement, but the big sit-down interviews with brass are any day now. They won't tell us when."

"Good. Tell them everything. Let them know you're their friend. The men and women running the investigation are good people. They know your record. It'll be fine. I'll have a talk with their supervisor—I play poker with him." Patty sat back, took a breath. Linda watched Patty's big belly move up and down, in and out. "What about this Cameron cop and the other uniform on scene?"

"Cam's my protégé." Linda knew she did not have to elaborate any more than that. Patty understood. "Brad, the blue, well, I don't know him. But he seems to be a solid human being. He'll tell it like he saw it."

"That look when you said 'Cam.' What was that?" Patty asked. "I've seen that before. What's going on in that head of yours, kiddo?"

Linda squinted. "Come on, Patty."

They smiled.

"You three at the scene will be accused of shirking the blame on the shooter, you know," Patty said, getting more serious. "Not sticking together. That blue-blood-brother bullshit. Be prepared for that."

"Least of my worries."

Linda explained about the photographs she'd just seen. Iris. And how it wasn't the photographs that bothered her about the high school case, Ariana Olahu's murder, the real reason behind her surprise visit. The state guys could drag Benjie and Scottie in and get whatever they knew out of them. Linda told Patty there wasn't much there. None of that was what concerned Linda Kane.

"What is it?" Patty asked. Leaning back, he placed his right hand across that large belly, his white shirt tight as a balloon around his stomach.

"It's this suspect you have on radar. I'm told it's Harry Dean Rollins, that scumbag who's being looked at for all those girls behind the Hartford strip mall."

"Who told you that?" There was admiration in his voice.

Linda smiled. "I learned from you, Patty, come on. I have my connections."

She winked.

They laughed at the same time.

"Yeah. We think he's good for the dead girl, Olahu, in Royal Oaks. Almost certain of it. Preliminary DNA tells us it's him. We're just waiting for absolute confirmation. These state's attorneys today, shit, they want everything stamped and sealed and wrapped up before they'll sign off on a warrant. We also hear he's somewhere in state, not in Florida as we first thought. There's sort of a low-key, under-the-radar manhunt going on for him as we sit. They're getting close, or so I'm told. Why, what's up?"

"I'm thinking he could have grabbed my girl, Cassie Caldwell. I didn't think so at first, but I'm leaning that way now."

"I thought you were square with the restaurant manager, the African-American guy your cop killed?"

Linda made a doubtful face. She wasn't so sure, after all. Despite what Trudi had reported Freddie saying in the bedroom, something nagged at her. Something was missing from the Freddie Banks scenario. Something wasn't adding up in Linda's gut. Like the simple fact that Freddie Banks never left town after breaking into his girlfriend's house. The more she thought about it, the more it spoke volumes about Freddie. And also, that he admitted to Trudi he saw Cassie on that night. Why even tell anyone you saw the girl if you had murdered her?

"I'll pass that information along to the guys. You have DNA in your case, I've heard. Is that right?"

"Yeah, we're kind of waiting on results, too. And one more thing, my guy, Cameron, we call him Cam. He knows the Rollins family and might have some insight into Harry Rollins for your guys if you need it. They go way back in town, I guess. Cam worked on the farm where Rollins was raised."

"Good. I'll tell the boys working the case. They might want to talk to Cameron. But, look, if our guy Rollins did your girl, Caldwell, bet your ass to doughnuts his DNA was left on whatever you have. He's sloppy. He likes to leave bodily fluids behind, you know what I'm saying?"

"Thanks. I'll get a report over as soon we have it." Linda looked down. Then back up: "How's Terri?"

"The missus is, well, she's good, Lin. What can I say? Been married for almost forty-two years now. I thought only old dudes could say that."

Linda stood. "Well, that's about it. Good to see you, Patty. Been too long."

"I'll have my people call your people and we'll do lunch very soon, Lin, okay?" He smiled. Stood. "Come over here, kid."

Linda laughed. Walked over and hugged Patty, feeling the warmth he'd always given her. Then she realized it was the first time in over a week that she had cracked a genuine smile. It felt kind of liberating. *It's okay to feel okay*, Linda thought, as she walked out of Patty's office and made her way out of the building.

35.

AS LINDA DROVE BACK to Royal Oaks PD, thinking she had to stop and see Trudi and Katherine soon, she looked at the clock on her dashboard and hadn't realized how late it was. Past 7:30 p.m.

"Darn," she said out loud. "Time flies when the shit hits the fan."

This made Linda feel good; another quote her dad had told her to live by.

"Lin, you there?"

It was her two-way. Cam's voice startled her.

"Go ahead, Cam, what's up?"

"We got us a situation brewing over by the house where Freddie was killed. Better get over here now."

"What's going on?"

"I know you haven't seen Iris's report because you don't own a TV, but she stoked the fires with the reverend. Fed him some info and got him going. There's a crowd congregating. I'm in my car now, parked out front of the house, trying to keep it at bay with several blues. But I've had a few run-ins with some pissed-off people. It feels like it's gonna get ugly."

"Jesus…what did she report? You know what, forget it. Doesn't matter. I'll deal with that bitch at a later time. Be careful. Watch your back. I'm on my way."

"Ten-four."

"Cam?"

"Yeah, Lin, go ahead."

"I mean it. Watch your back."

Took Linda about fifteen minutes, blue light twirling from the top of her Crown Vic, siren blasting her way toward that house where Freddie Banks was gunned down by a nervous, jittery, racist cop. Linda knew she needed to get this situation under control before they had a full-on riot, windows smashed, people screaming, people getting hurt, cars burning, looting, the national news all over it.

When she came around the corner and saw the crowd, Linda felt a sense of relief that it was small. About twenty-five or thirty people. Reverend Smalls wasn't part of the demonstration. Seemed to be all blacks, young men and women from a neighboring small town. When she got out and spoke to a blue who was trying the best he could to maintain control, he said (over the shouting of the protestors), "Lin, hey…they're pissed off at that report on TCN tonight. They want some sort of response from the department. I don't know what to tell them."

"Where's Cam? He called me. Said he was here."

"Not sure. Haven't seen him in a few. Got my hands full."

Linda got in between the blue and about six protestors. "You need to stand back, now," she yelled. "This is not considered a peaceful protest. This is private property. There's crime scene tape still up. A police investigation in progress. You need to leave this area immediately."

"I live here," shouted one man. He had a rock in his hand. "I give them all permission to protest wherever they want to."

Screams from the crowd roared.

Linda looked over the crowd and saw that Cam was being forced up against the van parked in the driveway, several men around him, pointing in his face, yelling.

She ran.

"Hey! Hey!" Linda said, coming up on the scene. "Let go of him right now."

One man grabbed Cam by the arm, another was in his face, inches away, spewing hateful remarks, spittle spraying from his mouth. "Die, pig. You gonna die tonight, pig."

Linda saw the situation growing out of control real fast. She needed to do something drastic.

The problem was, what?

Cam was about to throw a punch. She could tell he wasn't going to take much more before fighting back. One man had a bat in his hand, and he was walking toward Cam, slapping the meaty portion of the bat against one of his palms. There was a look of absolute disdain and confusion on his face.

Linda stepped back from the crowd, unholstered her Glock, and fired a round into the sky.

Everyone stopped what they were doing.

Silence.

Cam jumped out from where he was and stood by Linda. Took out his weapon.

"Thanks, boss. Shit. A freaking mob here."

Linda walked to her car, popped the trunk open, and took out her bullhorn.

"All of you need to go home or you will be arrested and booked. End of story. I have a bag full of zip ties here and we will begin using them. Your call."

The crowd began to disperse, mumbling things to one another, shouting, "Pigs need to die" and "Cops are killers."

"Everyone," Linda said, her weapon in the other free hand, "needs to go back to their homes right now." There were a few men still standing around. Talking to each other.

The entire crowd then disbanded.

Cam took a deep breath.

"You all right?" Linda asked him.

"Shit, now, yes, thanks to you."

Linda watched the last few people walk down the block and disappear out of sight.

"This won't be the last of it," she said, staring down the road. "They'll regroup and come back. Maybe not here, but…*holy shit*, that thing could have gone another way." She approached Cam. Put her hand on his forearm. "Hey, good work there. Restraint is key to police work when this sort of thing happens. You showed the type of cop you are tonight, Cameron. Proud of you."

"Thanks, Lin." He took another deep breath. "Scared me. That dude with the bat. He had hatred in his eyes. Was coming for me."

"Listen, Cam. I need you in tip-top shape here, psychologically speaking. We gotta find that girl. We cannot lose sight of Cassie. We're already a few steps behind."

"Yes." Cam paused. Looked at her. "Linda…?"

"Yeah?"

"Nothing."

They walked toward Linda's Crown Vic, leaned against the hood. The other blue on scene, as well as six more that arrived as the situation wrapped up, walked over and asked Linda if they were good to go.

"I'd like a few out here patrolling tonight. Station a blue in front of the house. Are we done in there yet? IAB finished with the scene? Find out. If so, get that goddamn yellow tape off the porch—it's just fueling this sort of thing. A constant reminder."

"Right, Lin."

"Come on, Cam, I'll drive you home."

They rode in silence for a few blocks before Cam said, "Hey, Lin, really, thanks for that out there. You knew what to do. How far to take it."

"I'm serious, Cam. I gotta keep an eye on you. Watch out for you. I need you."

They went quiet.

"Listen, I spoke to Patty Doyle. You know him, right?" Cam nodded. "They might ask you about that Rollins character you know. You worked on that farm of theirs, right?"

"I did. Rollins was a sick fuck. Killed the animals without so much as a second thought. I caught him with a lamb once—"

"Nope. Nope," Linda said, interrupting. "TMI, Cam. I'm good. I get it. The main thing here is they like Rollins for the girl behind the school; Olahu. They think he might be good for several more."

"Cassie?"

"No. Well, let's just say the DNA from the jacket will prove that out. But no way. Our Cassie is… That thing has a different feel to me now. We're missing a big piece of it all somewhere."

Linda pulled into the complex parking lot of Cam's building.

She stopped the car. Stared at the dashboard. Leaned over, put her hand on Cam's shoulder. Squeezed. "You did good out there. I cannot say that enough, Cam. That's real police work. Don't ever forget it. I'll see you in the morning. Get the hell out of my car and go get some sleep."

Cam smiled. Closed the door.

Linda watched him walk up the path toward his front door.

36.

LINDA NEEDED TO VISIT Trudi and Katherine and gauge their response to Freddie Banks being shot dead. She got up the next morning and headed right over. It felt like days since she'd even thought about Cassie's case. It was time to forget about protestors and social issues she had little control over and get back on track. She'd also promised Trudi she'd be by days ago and never showed up.

The detective pulled into the neighborhood and parked just down the block from Trudi's raised ranch. This was the corner, Linda and Cam had figured out, where Freddie claimed to have dropped off Cassie on the night she went missing.

Linda got out of her car and did a three-sixty scan of the area.

Her iPhone *dinged*. She looked down.

Cam.

DNA results coming soon. ☺

She tapped back an answer: Busy. Send ASAP to me and also Patty at CSP. Thanks.

A moment later, Linda thought about something, and texted Cam back.

You okay? Last night was scary.

I'm good.

Linda walked toward an empty lot between two houses, a red Cape and a brown ranch, each with kids' toys spread throughout the yards: a Barbie car and a Playskool yellow-and-red plastic slide; a basketball hoop; a jungle gym play set made from pressure-treated lumber; a football, sitting on the grass, covered in leaves.

Middle-class, suburban domesticity.

Where in the hell was Cassie in all of this?

The lot had grown over with weeds and tall, beefy trees. For whatever reason, the builder had not sold the land and let it go. It made a great place for the local kids to hang out, Linda could see. As she walked through the lot, she spied beer bottles and food wrappers, cigarette butts, soda cans and condom wrappers. There were small stones mixed with boulders the size of soccer balls. A large rock several kids could sit on together was positioned toward the back of the lot. It was spray-painted with graffiti. Rap stuff. Nothing Linda recognized.

Linda wondered if Cassie hung out here. She would have, no doubt. When she and Trudi got into it at home, and Cassie took off, did she come here? Did she sit on this rock, hang her head, ask herself why nobody in the entire world understood her feelings?

Making her way back to the vehicle, Linda stopped for a moment and pictured Freddie pulling over by the side of the road next to a red-and-yellow fire hydrant, telephone pole, brown and splintered, a missing person's flyer with information about Cassie tacked to the side at eye level. Linda could picture them arguing. Cassie crying. Holding her forehead. She saw Freddie yelling for her to get out of his truck.

Then a feeling snuck up on Linda. She saw someone else standing where she was, behind a tree that would have camouflaged the person's body. This person watched Freddie and Cassie argue.

Linda saw this person look on as Cassie exited Freddie's truck. The person ducked behind the tree. Watched—no, stalked—Cassie. Maybe called out to her.

Did Cassie know her stalker?

Pulling into Trudi's driveway moments later, Linda got out and walked up to the porch. Rang the doorbell.

Katherine let her in.

"How are you?" Linda asked Trudi's daughter.

The child said nothing. Instead, she hugged Linda's legs, tight, burying her head into Linda's midsection. Then she stepped back and pushed her glasses up the bridge of her nose as she stared at the floor. Her braces looked especially large to Linda, like aluminum foil covering the child's teeth.

"You getting ready for school, Katherine?" Linda said. "Is your mother home?"

Trudi stepped out of the kitchen, keeping her hands warm by holding a cup of tea. She looked like she'd been up most of the night. It was chilly in the house, magnifying the house's smell.

"Trudi, hi. How are you two doing?"

Trudi shrugged. Ever since Linda had met Trudi, her appearance hadn't much changed. Trudi always looked as if she'd just woken up—especially her hair. This morning it was pulled back in a ponytail, as if she didn't care anymore how she looked. She wore baggy sweaters, loose-fitting jeans; filthy sneakers.

Talk about giving up.

Linda followed Trudi into the living room. Katherine sat at the kitchen counter and worked on an adult coloring book. Every once in a while, she'd hold out the picture in front of her, checking it for blemishes and areas she might have missed, slowly tilting her head from side to side like a dog hearing a whistle.

"Can we get you a cup of tea, Linda?" Trudi asked. There was pain in her voice, as if it had taken every ounce of energy to ask this one question. But also a feeling of the end, Linda noticed: Trudi felt the case, with Freddie's death, was solved. The only problem was that her child was still missing.

"No thanks." Linda looked toward the foyer, where she'd walked in. There were several pairs of shoes—Trudi's, Katherine's and, she guessed, Cassie's—lined up on top of an old towel. She paid particular attention to a set of large-sized sneakers with odd-colored mud on them.

"I don't know what to say," Trudi began. "What do we do now?" She put her tea down for the first time since Linda had arrived. She scratched her forehead. "This stuff seems to be happening everywhere—white cop, black man, a death. I know you can't tell me what happened, but, my goodness, Freddie pulled his gun on you guys? That seals the deal for me right there."

Linda looked down. Rubbed her hands together.

"I cannot comment on any of that, Trudi. Sorry. I would ask, though, if a reporter—any reporter, actually, but specifically a woman named Iris Starr—contacts you, or the Black Lives Matter people contact you, I'd appreciate it if you told them you have no comment until your daughter's case is resolved. Our main concern is finding your daughter. That other stuff is noise right now trying to drown out the main reason we were interested in Freddie to begin with."

"I understand."

What was Linda actually doing here? Stopping and checking in on them? She had nothing new to share. Freddie Banks was dead. Trudi had made it clear that her life was beginning to calm with him out of the picture. Finding the jacket meant Cassie was probably dead. This Freddie thing was just a distraction from Trudi's pain, always there, smothering her and Katherine like campfire smoke, choking every bit of life out of them.

"You know," Trudi added after thinking about it, "I might have loved him. He scared me sometimes, but I think I could have loved him. How fooled we are, Linda. How unsettling that bad people have a way of sneaking into our lives, and we don't have a freaking clue as to their actual motives."

Linda believed you couldn't have both in the same human being. It was one or the other.

"He always talked about buying the restaurant," Trudi continued, never looking into the detective's eyes, something Linda picked up on and made note of. "Moving me and the kids into a big house. All of us being together. Everyone happy. Cassie fine with the situation. He really wanted her approval. I never thought Cassie's feelings about him would continue. I assumed she'd get over it. At the end there, or rather, in those days leading up to her disappearance, there was something larger than Freddie bothering the girl—that is for sure." Trudi sipped her tea, walked over to the window, stared out into nothing. "I'll tell you, Linda, we're all just standing around the corner from evil. Only we don't know it."

"Sounds like Freddie had a fantasy he had placed you and the girls into," Linda said, waiting for a reaction out of Trudi that never came. Then: "Kids. We think we know them. We never ask ourselves when parenting, *'Who do you want to be in this situation? What's important to you about this?'* Children feel stronger as they begin to learn that it's not how they feel, but how they respond to the feeling, that counts. I've also learned that evil is as evil does. It is everywhere if we look hard enough. Now, you said something about Cassie having a 'larger' issue to deal with just before you last saw her? Any indication what it might have been?"

Katherine looked in from the kitchen. Then went back to her drawing.

"No. I have no idea. Been through it over and over. Nothing comes to mind."

Linda believed her; then she made a mental note to call her own daughter. It had been some time since they had a long talk. She was going to make it to a volleyball game, too, she decided. *No matter what.*

Jenna.

It was at this moment when Linda felt a tug of discomfort. Something was off within Trudi. Her voice, hampered by weakness and turmoil, had a trace of disconnect. Linda had a tough time putting her finger on it, but Trudi's entire demeanor gave the cop pause.

Despair?

No.

Anger?

Nope.

Frustration?

Unlikely.

Doubt and deception?

There it is.

Linda could pick those two traits off of anyone the moment they entered a room. It was one of her specialties. Same as her memory. She had an internal radar tuned in to such physiological changes in people. An inner polygraph.

Deception detector.

Linda now recognized that Trudi Caldwell was lying to her—if only by omission—about something that had maybe died with Freddie, or walked out the door with Cassie that night. There was much more to the relationship between Trudi and Cassie than Trudi was willing to share. And now she was quick to write off Freddie Banks as the one behind her daughter's vanishing act.

As Linda was leaving, saying her good-byes, she looked at Trudi and a horrible, sinking feeling struck her. One of those kick-in-the-chest realizations cops sometimes get: *Trudi knows what happened to her daughter*. And Linda realized for maybe the first time since she'd met Trudi that it wasn't black or white with the mother—there was now this gray area, where anything was possible. Anything could be true. Anything could fill in the colors of the past.

37·

"**I NEED YOU TO** do something for me," Linda Kane said. She sat in her car staring at the Caldwell house.

Moments before, Linda had walked out of Trudi's with a deteriorating sense of trust. Something about the mother bothered the detective. Now was not the time to press Trudi about this, Linda knew. Let her accept the death of her, well, who was Freddie Banks to Trudi Caldwell? Her boss? Wait a few days, then ratchet up the pressure. Trudi had hidden things before and she was doing it again.

"Follow Trudi," Linda said. "Get a sense of what she's doing for a few days. Then bump into her and spark up a conversation. You know what I mean? Bait her so she starts talking to *you*."

"What's going on, Lin?"

"I have this feeling, Cam." Linda stared at a child's Razor Scooter leaning against the garage door. "There's more to Trudi than we think here. Being in that house just now, I was struck by something."

"You think maybe Freddie and Trudi knew something about Cassie's whereabouts?"

Until that moment, Linda hadn't thought of Freddie and Trudi conspiring together. But she liked the way Cam's mind was working this morning. Outside that box, there were always answers.

"I'm not sure, Cam, about anything anymore. Trudi needs to be watched, though."

"You got it." He paused. "Hey, listen, that DNA…nada."

"What?" The comment snapped Linda out of her train of thought.

"Nothing on the DNA. Definitely not Freddie Banks's DNA anywhere near that jacket. It's kind of inconclusive, the scientist said, because the blood is, although being mostly Cassie's for certain, mixed with another donor."

"Male or female?"

"He's not one hundred percent certain because of the cross contamination of the two donors, so he's a bit apprehensive about locking in."

There was silence between them.

"So if he had to guess, then?"

"Again, he said he's—"

"Cam. Come on, here."

"Female, *if* he was pressed to answer. But, listen, he's not sure. It's not pure science because of the—"

"I know, I know, cross contam. Shit's sake, these scientists kill me sometimes. We're looking for a girl here."

Linda started her car. Bells and various electronic sounds went off. Her two-way radio chirped on. The seat belt's alarm began *dinging*, annoying her.

"Tell him to check it again."

"Lin, I don't—"

"Cam. Tell. Him. To. Run. The. DNA. Again."

"Got it."

"Don't forget. We've got those interviews with IAB today—I got the call last night. You got my text, right?"

"I did."

"I don't want you thinking too much about what you're going to say. I want you to say it as it comes." Linda backed out of Trudi's driveway and stopped at the edge of the road. She looked in both directions and did before a backward half K-turn. Then she hit the gas pedal and took off. "It's going to be fine. We're truth tellers, you and I. They know that."

Except when it pertains to the two of us.

"Thanks. I have a few things to do here, some paperwork to finish. You wanna meet me somewhere for lunch?"

That was tempting. Linda had other plans, however. "I can't. Don't talk to anyone about IAB, Cam. *Nobody*."

"Yup."

Linda waited at a light just down the block from Trudi's. A woman in the vehicle next to her was applying makeup using the sun visor mirror. She was singing to the radio.

"All right. See you soon."

She stared at the light.

Vinnie.

Where was the now–ex-boyfriend in all of this?

Suddenly Vinnie Costello had disappeared from Trudi's life, too. And Linda Kane was curious as to why.

38.

CAM AND LINDA RETURNED to the office after three hours of IAB interviews that afternoon. They'd been informed that the case was likely going in front of a grand jury by month's end and everyone involved on the prosecutorial side expected an indictment. Cam and Linda were told they'd need to make themselves available for a full hearing at a later date, and also to give testimony in front of the grand jury.

On the way back to the station, Linda explained to Cam her concerns about Vinnie. She said she was going to go over a few things at home that night. She'd want his opinion after that.

"No problem. Got a few of my own investigatory secrets brewing at home, too," Cam said in a jocular, chummy way.

"Can't wait to hear, Cameron."

As Linda thought about how the Freddie Banks situation was going to affect police work in general for Royal Oaks, she was forced to stop the car about fifty feet before the Royal Oaks PD entrance.

"Shit," she said.

"Great," Cam added, looking up from his iPhone. "Here we go."

Protestors were a hundred strong this time, at least. Not your neighborhood rabble rousers, looking to cause a little uproar and break some heads—this was orchestrated. Pastor Rufus Smalls, wearing a shiny purple suit, orange shirt, black tie, was leading them in a chant, a bullhorn for a mouthpiece, pumping his balled-up fist in the air.

"No justice, no peace."

Oh, boy.

The crowd waited for his lead and then came back with the same, pumping their fists in unison.

"Show us the video."

"No justice, no peace."

"Show us the video."

"No justice, no peace."

The chant continued as Linda tried to force her vehicle toward the entrance. Louder. Then softer. Smoke billowed from that fifty-five-gallon drum, flames spitting out the top, wood inside the barrel cracking and popping. It had started to drizzle, a cold, damp murkiness to the air, the weather not hampering their efforts one bit.

Linda was forced to stop the Crown Vic as a crowd of about thirty stepped in front, not about to let her through. Several banged their fists on the hood of the car, slapped the windshield with their palms.

"You know, I kind of side with them in some respects," Cam said. "If they weren't so fucking vicious-looking and seeming to want revenge, I could understand that."

Linda glared at her man.

Please.

"I mean it."

"Cam, I get it. But this here, this is ridiculous. The other night, shit, you were almost beaten by some dude with a bat. They shouldn't be messing with us. Trying to stop us from doing our job. They should leave us out of it. Their fight is with the system."

"We are part of that system, though," Cam said.

Among the crowd, a white hipster stood out; his hair coiled in a bun, sporting a scraggy goatee tied off with a rubber band, wearing a BLACK LIVES MATTER t-shirt. His sign read: *KOPS BELONG IN KUFFS*. Linda knew with that sort of mentality—an unreachable antagonism—there would be no common ground to stand on for anyone. At least, not on this day.

"They need to have their voices heard," Cam said. "This is far different from the other night." He opened his door. The chants and screaming became louder, overpowering.

"They need to get the *hell* out of my way," Linda cracked.

Two black men came up to Linda's window, repeating what the pastor was shouting through the bullhorn. Their faces butted up against the glass. Tiny droplets of rain bubbled up around their cheeks. Their exhaled breath fogged up the window.

Linda did not make eye contact.

Cam kept one foot in the car, one on the ground. He used the door as a shield and to push several protestors away from the vehicle. He was clipped by the shoulders of protestors bumping into him and shouting in his face. He stood behind the door, using it as a barrier between him and the main group, his arms hanging over. "Please move away from the vehicle. You are violating the law. We need to get through."

"Show us the video. No justice, no peace."

"Show us the video. No justice, no peace."

The chant was in harmony. They had practiced, for sure.

Pastor Smalls walked over to Cam, the bullhorn a foot away from Cam's right ear.

"Show us the video! No justice, no peace!"

"What fucking video?" Linda said to herself. "My goodness."

Cam held his hands over his ears, no doubt experiencing a piercing ring. Linda watched, her right palm firm on the grip of her Glock, her eyes scanning the perimeter of the vehicle.

"Get back in the car, Cam!" Linda shouted. "Where are the blues keeping this thing in check out here?" She looked around. It was difficult seeing through a crowd that had now entirely surrounded the car. She grabbed the two-way.

"Get someone out here, now."

It was a blessing that not one of the protestors had recognized that Cam and Linda were two of the four that had been there when Freddie Banks was shot and killed. If they had, that would mean absolute mayhem. Even Smalls, who must have seen Linda's photo in the newspaper, did not seem to recognize her. Mainly because, by department design, the newspaper had printed an old photo from when she had just graduated from the academy.

Cam did as he was told. Sat down. Closed the door. Rolled

down his window.

"Pastor," Cam said, "come on here. This ain't right. We gotta get through. You're not allowing us to get through."

Smalls walked over, dropped the bullhorn to his side. He held a hand up in the air for the chanting to stop. He seemed to want to hear what Cam had to say.

"I need you to step up here and get these people away from our vehicle," Cam added. "You know this is not the proper way for you and your people to be heard."

"'*You people*'?" Smalls said, hearing Cam differently. His eyes bulged. "Is that so, Officer?"

"Come on, man, you know I didn't say that. That's unfair."

"Where's the video?" Smalls yelled.

"Video? What?"

"Miss Starr told us about the video."

Linda leaned down, looked over Cam, out the window. "Reverend Smalls, this is not the way to have your voices heard. We need to get into the parking lot. You're not allowing us to do that." Linda could feel the vehicle beginning to rock back and forth. The crowd around the Crown Vic was working itself into a frenzy. "There is no video. That is a lie."

Smalls leaned down, looked into the car, stared at Linda. Then at Cam.

It was clicking for him.

"Hey, you two are… Are you two the cops who were there when Banks was gunned down?"

Linda pressed the gas pedal slightly.

Two blues, who had been stationed inside the main entrance of the PD to keep an eye on the protest, walked over. Managing their way through the crowd—"Come on, move it, get out of the way"–one bent over and stuck his head into the car through Cam's open window, kind of nudging Smalls out of the way.

"What do you want us to do, Detective Kane?"

Smalls was putting the bullhorn up to his mouth. Cam leaned back so Linda could address the officer.

She thought about it. An image pierced her train of thought. She saw arrests being made. Chaos ensuing. Fighting. Screaming.

Protestors with zip-tied hands behind their backs lined up, sitting along the curb, their heads bowed. The news crews parked along the road showing the video that night. The protest getting out of hand the next day. The rioting. Looting. Activists from all over the country parading into town.

A circus, they would call it.

A public and political mess, Linda knew.

"Just see if you can get them to move so we can sneak by. No force, Officer."

Smalls was beginning to speak: "Listen to me…everyone, please, listen to me. In this car right here, we have…"

Linda figured out what Smalls was preparing to say and laid on the horn. She started to creep the car ahead.

The crowd, banging harder on the hood as it passed, not really listening to Smalls, shouted: "Show us the video! No justice, no peace!"

Linda snaked past the crowd, well on her way into the parking lot. "There *is* no goddamn video," Linda said. "What the hell? They think some backwoods PD has budgets for body cams! That damn Iris Starr, stirring up all this with her lies."

"Doesn't even matter if there's a video anymore," Cam said, looking back at the crowd. "It's out there. That reporter fucked us."

Linda parked. They got out. Walked up to the squad room without saying anything more to each other.

39.

INSIDE HER APARTMENT THAT night, after Linda, Cam, and anyone else who wanted to leave the PD had gone out a back way, Linda tossed her car keys on the counter to a loud jingle-jangle. She opened the fridge, closed the fridge. Stared at the white door. Then opened it again. This time, she grabbed an already-opened bottle of chardonnay sitting inside the door rack.

On the fridge, Linda kept an age-progressed computer mock-up image of Sherri she had one of the forensic artists construct for her years ago. It was her way of maintaining a sense of hope in a hopeless situation.

Below that, a square wallet-sized photo of Jenna was pinned to the fridge door with a colorful bottle opener/magnet in the shape of New Hampshire. It was Jenna's senior photo. She smiled. A phony kid smile—"say cheese." Her arms strategically placed along a fake fence rail, her shoulders straight. A country setting background: hay, tall grass, a red barn in the distance. Jenna's hair was pushed to one side, a part to the left, a long, thick, corkscrew bang running over the right side of her cheek and neck.

Linda shook her head, disappointed in herself.

Next, Linda grabbed a glass from the cupboard, an old jelly jar, filled it halfway with wine, and then placed the bottle on the counter.

She turned on her Bose stereo system next to the toaster and hit the BLUETOOTH button. Embracing her feeling of solitude, Linda called up the Jeff Buckley song "Just Like a Woman" on her iPhone. Hit the right arrow button to get it playing. Buckley was Linda's favorite. By far. Always had been. Always will be. The grace. The raw emotion. The sheer haunting power of his vocals. The clean guitar. The lyrics expressing sadness and loneliness. Not to mention, Buckley jumped into the Wolf River Harbor in Memphis for a swim one night while recording an album in town and never came back up. His body was found days later. No drugs. No booze. Just a freak accident.

That was Linda's life sometimes: a freak accident.

Buckley spoke to Linda's proneness to melancholy. She saw her own life somewhere in the free-floating silence of drowning.

Whispering along to the song, she sat down on the couch.

Linda decided to go back and look at that first ring around the center of the bull's eye: family and friends of the victim. Patty had always told her: *"That's where you'll find your killer nine out of ten times. I mean, Lin, how many people are murdered by someone they* don't *know?"*

After the DNA certified to Linda that Freddie Banks had nothing to do with Cassie's disappearance, she needed a different tact if she was going to find the girl. Vinnie moving out was a major red flag. Why had he left? Trudi had insisted he was a card-carrying racist. If true, it meant he had a certain cold, hard hatred within. Had he influenced Cassie to hate on Freddie? After all, Vinnie knew Freddie was banging his girlfriend.

Linda took a sip of wine. It was bitter and cold. Sour. Dry, but smooth. Then opened a file she'd brought home from the office, studied Vinnie's comings and goings throughout the period in question. Cam had locked it all down, written a solid report, backed up with supporting documentation.

What stood out was how Vinnie, on most nights, stopped at that bar and drank for a few hours—or until last call—before heading home. He also habitually never went to the bar on Mondays. On those nights, he visited his mother in a nearby convalescent home.

A check in the good-guy column.

Cassie had gone missing on a Tuesday.

Another check; opposing box.

Linda continued studying.

Vinnie lived a boring life. He worked, drank, worked, drank. Visited his mom.

Linda had her feet up on the coffee table. She took another pull from her wine, and held the glass against her temple as she read through a timeline for Vinnie on the night in question. His time card from work told a story. Vinnie had clocked out at 9:30 p.m., clocked back in at 11:05, working a double shift. Odd time for a lunch break, Linda concluded. She looked up at the ceiling.

Putting the wineglass down, the file next to it, she picked up her phone.

"Yeah…?" Cam said. He was out of breath.

"Treadmill?"

"Yup."

Linda could hear grunting in the background. People talking. The treadmill Cam was running on motoring—*thud-thud-thud*—away.

"Vinnie; his work shift that night. You ever wonder why he clocked out and back in an hour and a half later, *after* what was a company-policy normal eight p.m. lunch hour for second shift? Doesn't seem right. You look at all of his time cards you grabbed copies of? When he worked second shift, he always took his lunch between seven-thirty and eight, same as everyone else. Not once, in what was two months, did he choose nine-thirty—except the night his girlfriend's kid goes missing."

Cam stopped running. He took in a deep breath of air. Linda pictured Cam with his elbows on his knees catching his breath. His chest heaving in and out. White earbud wires hanging down. His phone strapped to his arm like a blood pressure test.

"I looked into that, I think," Cam began, catching his breath. "I…don't have the report…in front of me, but I…I thought he said he went to see his mother at the home that night. That she called or something and demanded he come, like, right then. He generally went on Monday nights, I think. But she asked for him to come on that night, too. She's a bit of a paranoid old lady, and Vin is her only source of social interaction. He's a mama's boy. He does what she says. Everyone at his work and the bar confirmed that.”

Linda took in the info. Ran it through her deception detector. Took another pull from her wine.

“You okay, Cam? You haven't said much about the other night and then the protest today? Stay strong for me, okay?”

“I'm solid, Lin. Just tired. All this bullshit going on, wearing me down.”

“Okay, good. Sorry to bother you, Cam.”

“Lin, come on. No bother.”

“I'll see you in the morning.”

Linda picked up the file again and paged through it. There was an interview with Vinnie backing up what Cam had said. But nobody had checked with the home.

Needs follow up, Cam had written along the margin of the transcript.

Problem was, nobody had followed up.

Damn.

Linda looked at the time on her iPhone.

She picked up the glass of wine and killed it. Then she put her shoes back on, grabbed her jacket, and hit the door.

A minute after leaving, Linda Kane walked back in. Inside her one messy kitchen drawer, among the odd-sized rubber bands and paper clips, matches, thumbtacks, pens, a collection of those bread tie twisty things, various Chinese food sauce packets, a fortune cookie, pencils, she dug away, looking for something.

After being stabbed by a tack in the thumb, Linda found the Visine and squirted two droplets in each eye. Then took two mints from an aluminum tin on the counter.

Off she went.

Daisy Sunshine Comfortable Living Center was the only old folks' home in town. It had one of those sliding doors like in a *Star Trek* episode when you walked in, a fish-eyed lens following your every move from the moment you entered the building until you reached your desired destination.

Linda found a supervisor.

Nurse Camille was behind the counter. She wore a red-and-white, candy-striped uniform. She was doing paperwork. This time of night, it was quiet in the facility.

The nurse said she knew where they kept the video-monitoring equipment and the recordings.

"But maybe I should call my boss to find out if it's okay to share it with the police."

Linda had her elbows on the counter. She dropped her head in her hands.

This one here is going to play hardball with me?

"I just want to see if you've taped over the night in question already or you keep an inventory of days. Can we just start there first?"

The nurse thought about it.

"Tell you what. My nephew wants to become a cop. You put in a word for him?" She walked up to the counter.

"Hell yeah," Linda said.

Not a chance.

"Okay, follow me."

That was easy.

Nurse Camille walked in front of Linda, fast, stopping every so often to check in on a patient, ask how they were. Linda followed just behind. She felt rushed.

The place smelled of diarrhea and industrial-cooked foods. It was choking. Almost as if a stomach bug had gone around.

"You know a guy by the name of Vinnie Costello, by any chance?" Linda asked, catching up.

"Vin, sure. I work second shift. But I am here sometimes well into third shift, sometimes into first shift also, because our staff is—"

"Ma'am, Vinnie Costello?" Linda said.

"Oh, geez, sorry. Vinnie? Well, Vinnie is a nice guy. Looks after his mom. He comes on schedule. 'Clockwork Vinnie,' all the nurses call him."

There was no sense in asking if she recalled a week ago, a time frame on that certain night, because Linda wanted to see it for herself on camera.

"It's that girlfriend of his," Camille offered as they walked toward the destination, having passed what was a fake, man-made forest in the middle of the building: plastic trees and rocks, a calming Zen waterfall, a taped loop of birds chirping. "What a piece of work she is."

"What do you mean?"

They walked by a room. A woman was moaning. She sat in a wheelchair; her hair thin, like a coconut's. She wore a bathrobe. Slippers. She stared into an abyss only she could see. Drool hung from her mouth. Linda locked eyes on her as they passed.

"I mean that…and look," Camille said, and stopped walking. She turned to Linda, used her hands to articulate, but to the detective it felt like a scolding. "I don't want to come across as talking about someone who is, I can empathize, going through hell with a kid missing. I read the papers. But she is too much. She'd come here with Vinnie—and this was months ago. Not recently. And we all knew when she walked in, watch out! Here comes the drama. She always had something to say about how we were treating Vin's mother. Like she needed to have control over every single part of Vin and his mother's life."

"What do you mean by 'drama'?" This observation interested Linda. This was a side of Trudi she would never have guessed.

Camille was walking and talking again. "I mean that she picked these fights with Vinnie. Over nothing. I'd be going to give Mrs. Costello her meds and that woman"—she snapped her fingers, thinking—"Tracy—"

"Trudi," Linda corrected.

"Right, Trudi. She'd be wagging a finger in Vin's face. Admonishing him about whatever. Bills. The upkeep on their house. Never being around. And especially her kids. Oh, geez, those kids. Here was a guy who had taken care of a mother and this woman's two kids and she treated him like a piece of garbage. Same as that one who is missing, Cathy."

"Name's Cassie. Actually, Cassandra."

"Right, sorry. So many names and granddaughters and people coming and going. But let me tell you, I know two nurses here who, trust me, would not treat Vinnie like garbage." The nurse laughed through her nose.

Linda thought how this picture of Vinnie was in stark contrast to the characterization Trudi had given.

"Strange question, but any African-American nurses here that Vinnie would interact with?"

"Oh, of course. We're an equal-opportunity employer and we pride ourselves on—"

"Ma'am?"

"Again, sorry. Um, Nurse LaTonya. Nurse Jacqueline. Both black. They love Vin. He makes them laugh."

Interesting.

Linda was beginning to think that perhaps Trudi had been lying about Vinnie. But, why?

Camille came to a dark-gray metal door with a serious industrial lock. She took out a set of keys and flipped through, stopping at one painted red.

She unlocked the door.

Linda stepped into the room. Here was the computer brain behind the entire operation of the building. She could hear those little fans on the back of computer towers spinning, blowing out air and dust. Small circular lights, red and green, blinked on and off all around her. Wires, like backstage at a concert, snaked everywhere. There were at least ten monitors lined up alongside one wall, Linda counted. All had black-and-white images on them. All showed some part, some section of the building, inside and out.

Perfect.

On a desk, inside a file box, Linda found a stack of DVDs. Each was dated.

Man, did Linda Kane love it when things worked out in her favor.

As Linda approached the box, there came a shrieking scream. Then Camille's hip buzzed. She called a colleague.

"I need to run. There's an Alzheimer's patient loose in Unit C."

Not a problem, Linda thought.

"I'll be right back," Camille concluded as she took off down the hallway. "You can look through there and see if what you need is inside, but we'll need some sort of paperwork for you to view anything."

"Of course, ma'am," Linda said.

40.

THE NIGHT CASSIE WENT missing, Linda realized as she sat and watched the video, was busy inside the Daisy Sunshine Comfortable Living Center. People walked in and out most of the early evening. She'd taken the DVD marked with the date she was looking for; there was no sense in messing around with Camille. After Camille had returned, she explained how she had found the patient wandering in the parking lot and had gotten to him just before he would have fallen down an embankment. So Camille was feeling that high of doing a great job, patting herself on the back. Linda seized on the feeling and explained to Camille that what she was looking for was not inside the file box. And she wasn't lying, because by the time Camille had returned, that disc Linda needed was inside her coat pocket.

If it came down to where she needed to have the disc back inside the file box and they needed it for court, well…slipping it back into the same box she'd found it would not be a problem. Camille was an easy mark to manipulate. And for the greater cause of finding a missing child, dead or alive, Linda felt it was a chance she'd take any day of the week.

LINDA HAD HER LAPTOP opened on her coffee table. The disc was spinning and humming. The entire screen focused on one camera: the entrance to the facility. There was no other way for Vin to walk in or out. If he had gone into the facility on this night, as he had said during a police interview, he was going to walk right into Linda's view.

The detective poured a glass of chardonnay, sat back, hit PLAY.

Hour after hour, Linda watched, just to get a feel for the ebb and flow of the place. She would speed up the video, then slow it down. With her memory firing on all cylinders, Linda knew that each person who walked into the facility also walked out of the facility through that same set of doors.

There were young and old visitors. Men and women. Some even brought the family pets along. Each sauntered in and under that fish-eyed lens on top of the doorway. A few even looked into the lens, made funny faces, smiled, waved at the camera.

When the time stamp readout came near the moment Vin would have walked in, Linda paid close attention. The videos from his work had shown Vin walking out of the factory at 9:37 p.m. He had a bag in his left hand. He hurried. On no other night that week had Vin Costello ever walked as fast as he did on the night Cassie went missing. He also had an odd look about him. It was hard to make out facial expressions, of course, because of the grainy quality, but Vinnie was turning and looking in all directions as he rushed toward his car.

As if somebody was watching him.

Back to the Daisy Sunshine Comfortable Living Center video, about 9:46 p.m., the elapsed time it had taken Linda to drive from the factory to Daisy Sunshine, no one walked in or out. In fact, as Linda noted, between nine p.m. and midnight, only four people crossed the threshold of the home's front entrance: two custodians from a cleaning crew, a young man of about thirty, who Linda learned was the boyfriend of a nurse, and finally a doctor, called to the home to look after a potential diabetic seizure case, according to the log.

Vinnie Costello was nowhere in sight.

He'd lied during his interview.

41.

A PUFF OF AIR from the spring shock absorber on the glass door into the squad room *swooshed* behind them. Carmen met Cam and Linda at the squad room entrance counter.

"He's in the box."

"How long?" Linda asked, walking into the office space, heading over to the board on the wall, placing the marker by her name from OUT to IN. Doing the same for Cam.

"Oh, maybe three hours."

"Perfect."

The previous night, Linda had phoned Cam and discussed her strategy regarding how to question Vinnie.

"I'll have a few blues pick him up middle of the night to rattle him a bit," Cam said.

"Yes."

Linda was going to drive the interview. Cam would act as the calm and collected cop, the cop who could appreciate the perp's point of view. Linda would be her all-business self. No good cop/ bad cop here. Linda never played that game.

Linda stopped for a cup of water on the way into the box where Vinnie Costello waited. Her mouth always went dry during these interviews. It was the adrenaline.

"What the hell is going on here?" Vinnie said, standing up as soon as they entered the room. His face darkened.

"Whoa, whoa, big guy. Sit down, sit down, please," Cam said, walking over, showing Vinnie by his mere presence who was in control here.

The room smelled of chemicals: fresh industrial paint.

Linda's mind flashed to something: Vinnie, with Cassie, losing his patience. The wrath in his voice just then. How he'd jumped up and went right at them. She recalled how one coworker had said, "You do *not* want to piss Vin off. He's calm and cool and seems okay one minute. Then that Italian temper flares—and watch the fuck out." Had Cassie met up with that same temper? What type of relationship did the two of them have? Had Vinnie been sneaking into Cassie's room at night? But then she got older, stronger, and said enough was enough?

"We good now?" Cam asked, putting his enormous bear claw of a hand on Vin's shoulder, squeezing, making sure the man felt his strength.

Linda took a sip of water. Smacked her lips a few times. Opened a file for show.

"Mr. Costello, we're going through some information we've recently received and we wanted to re-interview you about that night your girlfriend's daughter went missing."

Vin ran his hand across his mouth. Breathed in through his nose. Stood again, turned his back to them. Walked toward the wall, his head down, a hand on his chin.

"Mr. Costello," Cam said, standing. "Sit. Back. Down."

Vin turned quickly, did as he was told.

"Nervous, Mr. Costello?" Linda queried.

"Yeah, I'm fucking nervous. You people pull me out of my house in the middle of the night, bring me here, make me wait three or four hours in a white room, three fucking chairs, a metal desk, and that stupid TV-cop-show, two-way mirrored glass staring at me. Like I'm some fucking monkey. What the hell is going on?"

"Well, for starters, no one pulled you out of *your* house. You're living with a friend now, I'm told. Second, you were asked to come down under the assumption that we needed to question you. You've been read your rights, I assume?"

"Yes. They told me I'd be arrested, anyway—what fucking choice *did* I have? Do I need a lawyer, or what?"

"Up to you. I'm going to ask that you control your mouth. That language here will not get you anywhere with us. This would be easier without a lawyer. You want to bring a lawyer into this, then I'll be up your ass so far, your entire life will be turned inside out. You want to answer a few questions, we might get you into work on time later this afternoon."

Vin put both hands on his head, leaned down, elbows on the table, and mulled that over for a time. Then, coming back up, he said: "Or maybe you shoot me as I reach for my wallet, eh?"

Linda ignored the dig. She wrote something down. Meaningless doodle.

"What is it, then?" Vin said. He looked at Cam, then at Linda. He tapped two fingers on the table in a rhythmic drumroll.

"Here," Cam said. He handed Vin a napkin. "Wipe your brow, dude. You're sweating. We just need to ask you a few simple questions, Vin. Come on. This is easy stuff. Help me and the lady out. We want to find this girl."

Vin took the napkin. Looked Cam in the eyes.

"You told us, when we interviewed you last," Linda said, "that you went to see your mother on the night Cassandra went missing."

"Yes, so what?" He stared back and forth at the two of them.

"Well, we have information that leads us to believe you did *not* go to the home to see your mother." *That's because you killed the girl*, Linda wanted to follow up with as a mere intimidation tactic, not so much a statement, but resisted.

Vin went silent. Looked off to his left. Blinked several times.

"Maybe I might need that lawyer after all."

"You're screwed then," Cam added into the conversation. "Just saying." He put his hands up, palms facing Vin.

"How so?" Vin asked, looking at Cam.

"Then we cannot help you. Look, Vin. There's a solid explanation for what we need, I know you have it. Just tell us what's going on here and we're off your ass. No harm, no foul. We've got two very different versions of Vin Costello. We want the true version."

Vinnie began to think about this; Linda could tell. Cam was learning. He had picked up on her sense of questioning a suspect.

What a great cop, Linda thought. *He's getting it.*

"Look, I need to explain," Vin said. Then he paused.

Here we go.

Vin stared down at his hands. He picked at a scratch in the table with his index fingernail. It made a clicking sound.

Linda looked at Cam.

He's nearly there.

"We're all ears here," Linda said. She noticed, though, that Vin's shoulders had not dropped. Whenever a suspect was ready to give it up, his shoulders went limp. Not the case for Vincent Costello.

Weird.

Just then, a blue popped the door into the box open, startling them all.

"Officer," Cam said, standing up, "we're conducting an important interview here. Please—"

"This cannot wait. I need to talk to you both."

All three went out into the hallway. There was some commotion they could hear coming from inside the squad room office. People were talking over one another. Shuffling around. Lots of voices.

"Sit tight, Vin, be right back," Cam said.

42.

IRIS STARR AND HER cameraman, Roger, had made it back into town. They spent the night at that local Holiday Inn Express in Vernon, a good-sized town of about thirty thousand just outside Royal Oaks. Iris had taken an early-morning call from her source, who explained there was a red barn, old and run-down, ready to fall over with the right gust of wind, on the edge of Royal Oaks. It was located on Chapel Hill Road, to be exact, near a sawmill.

"You cannot miss it. Some big-time shit is about to go down. But you stay back, Iris. This is dangerous. I'm telling you only because I want you to have the exclusive, once it's all over."

Iris was on a roll, coming off the broadcast of the Rufus Smalls interview. Here, again, she saw the word *exclusive* flash before her eyes. And that was all she needed to hear.

Roger and Iris grabbed coffee in the lobby from one of those pump coffee thermoses with a picture of coffee beans and COLOMBIAN ROAST scrawled across the front. They sat inside the van, rubbing their hands together, trying to get warm as the van heated up. The temperature had come up some, but had started out that morning close to freezing.

"Let's freakin' go, Roger," Iris snapped. "Time is not on our side right now." She popped the HOME button of her iPhone and realized how late it was: 12:47 p.m.

Giving herself a pat on the back for hanging around all that

morning, Iris felt her instincts were about to pay off.
Roger hit the gas, looked both ways, and took off.

43.

THE TOWN OF ROYAL Oaks was home to a certain number of what townies referred to, in an uncharacteristically jealous, hostile and derogatory manner, as "the Germs." German immigrants who followed the Mennonite way of life for the most part. Their earliest ancestors had migrated into Royal Oaks almost one hundred years ago, so reported the historical society. The women wore no makeup, kept their hair in buns or long, ropey braids, and sewed their own denim dresses, which ran down past their ankles. All the wives dropped their kids off at soccer and lacrosse practice and school in the same navy blue minivans. The children, regardless of age, were not allowed piercings or tattoos. The homes had no televisions or radios. The men all wore collared, button-down, short-sleeved work shirts, plaid-patterned with one breast pocket, brown khakis, and black leather work shoes. They went off every day to work trade jobs—carpentry, farming, electrical, plumbing—while the women cared for the home. The Germs owned all the farms in town, a furniture store that people from all over came to buy over-priced dining-room sets, hutches, premade sheds and garages, and children's playscapes. They also operated an apple farm offering hayrides, and a local roadside stand that sold apple strudel and all sorts of homemade jams.

They kept to themselves. They did not associate with anyone else in town besides their own. Though the kids did have playdates and participate in school sports with all the other children, they were forbidden to participate in certain after-school activities that did not jibe with their ultraconservative Christian values. Linda guessed there were probably three thousand Germs altogether. They ran the town, politically. They gave out all the building permits and did most of the construction work; they easily controlled town elections with their votes. They were kind, gentle, God-fearing people, who wanted to be left alone. Unlike their counterpart, the Amish in Pennsylvania, the Germs spoke to townies and interacted with locals at PTA and school events. They just wanted to live their lives according to their own plan.

The way the world was today, who could blame them?

Every once in a while, however, a rogue Germ had broken from the pack and totally went off the rails.

Harry Dean Rollins was probably the worst the Germs ever produced. He'd been expelled from the community as an eighteen-year-old kid, after being accused of sexually assaulting a fellow Germ girl, age eleven. After that, he took up with a prostitute in Hartford. Rollins smoked a crack pipe for years and then graduated to meth. He never associated with any of the Germs after his excommunication. Harry Rollins, in fact, had murdered that prostitute he lived with, who was later found behind a strip mall as one of four he'd killed and dumped in the same general wooded area. Rollins had been on the run for six years; no one had been able to pin him down.

Until today.

Like a wounded animal, Harry Dean Rollins returned to his place of birth, Royal Oaks. It was reported that he was holed up inside a Germ barn with enough firepower to hold everyone off for at least a few days, so said the Germ who had called the information in to the Royal Oaks PD. This info caused the stir inside the squad room, interrupting Linda and Cam's interrogation of Vinnie Costello.

Now Iris and Roger were heading out to that farm to get video of what was going down. As were Cam, Linda, and several blues Linda had handpicked.

The state police had things under control, or so they claimed, but needed Royal Oaks on scene because of jurisdictional issues with a potential prosecution later on down the road. Not to mention the rapport Royal Oaks, especially Linda Kane, had with the Germ community. Add to it that Cam had worked on the Rollins family farm, knew them well, and could maybe help out with talking to Rollins, a team effort might produce the outcome everyone desired.

Linda and Cam, along with four additional Royal Oaks blues, were almost on scene.

Roger found a spot along a riverbank about a mile back from the barn, where Iris had been told Rollins was hiding. Apparently, on his way back into town, Rollins had picked up another girl, a twentysomething hitchhiker, told her he'd killed before, and was going to kill again—if she didn't do "exactly" what he said. The girl made the peace sign with two fingers and gouged the son of a bitch in the eyes. He lost control of his van. Ran the rust trap into a ditch. The girl took off. Called police.

"Harry Dean Rollins's van was recovered by the first state police trooper on scene," Linda and Cam were told by a trooper who had come into the Royal Oaks PD with the news. "But he was nowhere in sight. It's about two football fields away from the barn he's said to be holed up in now. That first cop on scene followed a muddy path just beyond the van that led down into a cornfield, across a small stream. Footsteps imprinted in the dirt from the van to the stream were a good indication as to the direction Rollins had taken. The cop put two and two together and snuck up on the barn. Rollins came out as soon as the cop got close. He had a Germ girl, maybe ten, underneath one arm; a .357 Magnum, the barrel on the thing a small cannon, in the other arm; a jagged hunting knife between his teeth. After spitting the knife onto the ground, he pointed the Magnum at the cop, who stood about forty feet away, his Glock aimed at Rollins's head. Still holding the girl, Rollins said, 'You come near me, I blow her fucking head off.'"

The cop had retreated back up to where the Rollins van had crashed and was now waiting for backup.

Cam and Linda said they were all in.

Inside Rollins's van, police recovered a note. In part, it read: *I know in my heart I am evil. If I cannot make heads or tails of this life, I will not be long for this world. And so it's on to the next.*

He signed it with the name the newspapers had given him: *Sick Ripper.*

Suicide by cop was what everyone had been told was Rollins's plan.

As cops arrived and searched the van, they uncovered a shovel, some clear plastic that was bunched up and wet, zip ties, rags that smelled of kerosene, a machete, two bottles of Benadryl, handcuffs, a syringe, a crusty, black, cakey substance (dried blood, they guessed) that was all over one portion of the van, and….

You get the picture.

The dude was a serial killer.

What interested Linda and Cam as they met those first blues on scene at Rollins's van was a pair of pants. No doubt dried blood on the crotch area and the backside, the jeans could easily fit a girl Cassie's age.

"THAT NEWS VAN ON the edge of the road, marked TCN on its side, parked about a mile back, Officer," Linda said to the blue. "You go and tell that news lady, if she comes anywhere near this scene, she's going to be locked up. In fact, I don't even want to see her on this road. Block the road off by the farm stand, there, where they're parked, keep everyone back beyond that point. No one gets through. Then double-back and do the same a mile in that direction"—Linda pointed down the road the opposite way—"and have a few others set up a perimeter across the street and on the other side of that barn."

"Got it, Lin. On my way."

Linda stepped toward Cam, who was looking inside the back of Rollins's van.

Just then, a line of state police cruisers arrived, followed by a SWAT truck full of cops in ready-for-anything gear: goggles, Kevlar vests, gloves, helmets, automatic weapons.

They filed out of the vehicle and lined up along the road in unison, facing the direction of the barn. They'd been trained right—a side effect all cops appreciated from 9/11 and the rash of school shootings across the country.

These boys were ready for war.

Linda felt a rush of adrenaline pass through her spine. "Come with me," she said to Cam. She had a bottle of water in her back pocket. Hoisted it up to her mouth, took a pull.

A captain stepped out of the trooper vehicle closest to Cam and Linda and walked up to them. He had a radio in his hand. His cop-issued, gray-and-blue Stetson, with the CSP logo on the front, was tilted down along his brow. Its small, black strap wrapped around the back of his gray-haired crew cut. He held an intimidating gaze. He wore a heavy blue jacket, with a thick fur collar; gold tassels on the shoulders, patches on the sleeves.

Mr. Law Enforcement.

"Detectives," he said, looking at Cam and Linda. "Captain Dennis Moody." He grabbed the front of his Stetson like a cowboy, tipped it. He was no doubt, at some point in his life, a marine, Linda figured.

"Sir," Linda said.

Cam nodded.

Moody explained what was going to happen. As he spoke, six of the cruisers behind him took off down into a clearing leading toward the barn. The SWAT truck slowly followed behind; all those dudes decked out for combat marched behind it in an orderly fashion.

North Korea.

"This is what will happen," the captain said. He looked toward the barn. "We have solid information that Mr. Rollins has an AK-47 with several clips, in addition to the .357 the first cop reported. He had a knife, plus the hostage. Not good numbers if you add it all up. He's dug in for the long haul. If we can develop contact with him and begin a dialogue, I might ask Cameron here—I understand you know the Rollins family—to step in and say something to Mr. Rollins. Our hostage negotiator will be by Cameron's side, of course."

A trooper walked up: "Excuse the interruption, sir. We've got the barn sealed off, Captain. Cruisers all around, the SWAT guys parked in front of the window where we've seen Mr. Rollins sitting on a bale of hay. The girl is balled up in a fetal position by his feet, shaking."

"She's still alive, Trooper. Let's keep it that way. Don't make a move until we're"—he looked toward Cam and Linda—"down there."

Linda expected the trooper to salute the captain before walking away, but he didn't.

Moody addressed Linda and Cam again. "I need you two positioned behind the SWAT truck. Let us take care of this. It's going to be okay. I'm going to get your hostage out of there alive."

"Yes, sir," Linda said.

Cam nodded.

Moody added: "Let's file down there now. My guys are the best at what they do, so let's allow them that space of hostage negotiation and rescue. We want to take the girl, obviously, knowing that he is likely not going to give her up." They followed as the captain walked toward a clearing along the side of the road. The position of the barn, and where Rollins was situated inside, made it impossible for Rollins to take a shot at any of them as they walked in that direction. If he tried, the SWATs would be all over him, anyway. "So my best sharpshooter is positioned right now inside the SWAT truck, his weapon sticking out a small hole. He's been ordered to take a shot once he has Mr. Rollins in his sights. But that's plan B. I'll explain plan A down there."

Before they left, the blue came back and approached Linda. "That reporter was gone. Couldn't find her."

"Shit. Keep an eye out for her, okay?"

"Yes."

As they made it through the trees lining the road and into the clearing, a massive cornfield, the sun hit all of them in the face. It felt warm and comforting, like walking by a window in winter, with the rays of the sun beaming in.

Linda looked at Cam. There was no other cop she'd rather be in this situation with.

Captain Moody got a little up ahead of them.

Certain the captain was out of earshot, Linda turned to Cam: "Have you ever wanted to take a moment, a snapshot of your life, and just freeze it there? Go back to that moment and stay?" She was thinking about a time before Sherri went missing. How life was, as a child, uncomplicated and routine. How much she appreciated being a kid, sitting down to a home-cooked meal, her parents around, her friends doing the same. A game of kick-the-can maybe that night under a streetlight after everyone ate. So simple and uncontaminated.

"You're old, remember, Lin." Cam laughed. Nine years separated the two, but there was no time limit of life experience, and Linda had him by twenty years there. "I'm just a puppy."

Linda stared at Cam, a half-smile on her face. "Just trying to break up the stiffness here that the captain is perpetuating. *Yikes.* I thought *I* was all business."

Cam smiled. "Hey," he said. "You know why Scots wear kilts, Lin?"

"What?" Linda said, then realized Cam was being Cam. She rolled her eyes. "Another one of your Internet jokes?" She knew he was trying to lighten the mood as well.

Cam's eyes were locked on the barn as he spoke.

"Enlighten me," Linda said.

"Well," Cam continued, looking back at Linda, "the sound of a zipper scares the sheep away."

Linda tilted her head to one side. She could tell Cam was nervous. This was his way of cutting through that anxiety.

"We're going to be all right here, Cam," Linda said. "Just follow what you've been trained to do. I got your back. Let them handle this. We're here because of politics. You get that, right?"

"We need to get that Germ child back, Lin. We can't lose another kid."

Linda shook her head in agreement.

The captain stopped walking, turned. "I just got a call. Rollins is getting antsy. He's moving around inside the barn."

They were about fifty yards away. As they approached, Linda noticed how each trooper was parked around the barn, weapon in hand. He bent down on one knee, the barrel of the weapon rested on the hood of the vehicle; the red laser trained on the barn. If Rollins made a move beyond that barn, he'd be peppered with bullets from every angle.

Still, Linda Kane resisted the urge to feel that all would go as planned.

Hell, she knew better.

44.

TWO ROYAL OAKS POLICE officers met Cam and Linda in back of the SWAT vehicle. One had brown hair, with a well-groomed stubble of trendy peach fuzz on his face. Linda guessed he was in his late twenties. The other was blond, clean-shaven, and smelled of Axe body spray.

"You boys stand back from this," Linda instructed. "I think these guys here have the situ under control. I need you to be eyes-on only. You'll be writing the reports of what happens." Both cops looked at each other. Great. "Let them take care of this. It's their show. If you're called on, of course, respond accordingly. But I get the picture we're here only because the state's attorney's office made them call us in."

Spectators.

The afternoon sun beat down hard on everyone. It was hot now, with all the equipment on. Linda felt the urge to take off her vest.

There was an old tractor, rusty, with weeds growing up, around and inside it, half its engine missing, parked to the left of the barn. Bales of rolled hay, waist-high, were lined along the right side of a gravel and dirt road leading up to the barn's entrance. The rolls of hay reminded Linda—as they always did when she drove around town—of cinnamon buns. Coils of dried grass, ready for the winter months. The work a farmer did to earn a meager living.

There was a smashing sound. Glass breaking.

Linda, Cam, and the two blues turned toward it.

"I'm going to put a bullet into this little girl's head if you don't back off," Rollins said. It was the first they had heard from him. "I'm not playing here." His voice was raw. He stuck the barrel of his AK out the same window, his head just a bit, and fixed his eyes on Linda and Cam.

Showtime.

A row of troopers had parked in front of the window, maybe fifty feet back. Cam, Linda, and the SWAT truck were to the right of those vehicles, about twenty yards.

The negotiator got on his bullhorn: "Mr. Rollins. There is no way out of this for you. Can we end this without any violence, sir?"

No response.

Moody made a rolling-circle motion with one finger, beckoning the negotiator to give it another try, as if they had a prearranged script of what to say.

"Mr. Rollins, we are here for the duration. We will starve you out of the barn. Hurting the child will do nothing for you. It will only make matters worse."

"I want to speak with a cop—a real cop," Rollins said. He studied the faces of Cam, Linda, and the cops standing near them. They could see he was manhandling the girl, holding her by the hair. "Not a fucking politician who's been told what to say."

There was a tense beat of silence. Moody looked at Cam. "I need you to tread very carefully here with him. Make him talk to us more than you're talking to him. That's the key."

"I'm waiting," Rollins said. After another tense moment, Rollins fired, and everyone scooched farther down than they already were, tucking their heads into their Kevlar vests like turtles.

The shot hit the front tire of the vehicle the negotiator—and now Cam—stood behind, a loud hissing sound made everyone aware that Rollins could fire a weapon and hit a target of his choosing.

"That's your one warning shot," Rollins said. He had the girl by the neck now with his one free hand. He pulled her up to the window so they could see her struggling to breathe. He then forced her neck onto shards of broken glass sticking up in the window frame. "The next round goes into her head. Or, better—I slit her throat in this window and you *all* watch her bleed out."

Linda looked on. She watched as the negotiator and the captain got together and talked. She couldn't hear them. She then stared at Cam, who positioned himself behind the armored SWAT vehicle. Safe and protected. The captain walked over to Linda after the short conversation and stood by Linda's left side. He hunched over. For a brief moment, Linda's head was just above the armored vehicle's hood.

"How long will this go on, sir?" Linda asked. "I need to have a promise that the child will not be put in the middle of an ambush. My detective, also, Cameron, he is part of this now."

"The child is our first priority, Detective Kane. We've got someone around back of the barn as we speak. Plan B. He's working his way stealthily inside now. Hopefully, your guy can keep Mr. Rollins's attention focused this way as our guy sneaks in and puts a bullet into the back of Mr. Rollins's head, and the child walks away physically unharmed."

Sounded like it could work. Linda did not have a problem with it. She trusted these cops knew what they were doing. They had done this sort of thing many times before. Still, a modicum of anxiety boiled inside her nervous system. Linda grew worried.

Contingencies.

She'd seen too many play out on disastrous levels.

Cam peeked his head up above the hood of the armored vehicle. He glanced at the window that Rollins had his weapon drawn out of. Then he quickly dropped his head back below the firing line.

Linda met Cam's eyes and frowned, as if to say, *Don't do that again.* She let loose a deep breath.

"Mr. Rollins. Name is Cameron. Cameron Van Zandt. I worked for your family on their farm as a teen. I know them well."

"Not interested in walking down nostalgia boulevard— Cameron! Come on, this the best you fuckers can produce? I'm counting the minutes here until I kill this child. Blood on your hands."

The girl screamed. They could hear Rollins say, "Shut your fucking mouth, you little whore, or I'll slice your fucking throat like a pig." He had that special tone to his voice reserved only for psychopaths.

"Mr. Rollins, look," Cam said. "You can't win. There's no way out of this for you."

"Who the fuck says I want to win, Cameron? I can take a few of you with me, though. That is for fucking sure, cop. If I go, this little bitch goes, and a few of you, too."

"Mr. Rollins, your family is worried. I spoke with them. Don't you care about their standing in the Germ community?"

Rollins fired another round at the ground in front of the armored truck.

Cam looked at the captain.

"I'm told through my earpiece," the captain explained, Linda refocusing her attention on him, "that our man is inside the barn. He's got Mr. Rollins in his sights. He's waiting for word to take the shot."

Linda held a hand to her head, then looked at the sweat she'd wiped on her glove, giving the leather a shine. Cam stuck his head over the hood of the armored truck, just past the bridge of his nose, and stared at the window where Rollins had since disappeared from. Linda knew Cam was thinking about his next move.

Cam turned to look at Linda, and the two of them met eyes.

"It won't be long now," Moody added. "I'm going to give the word in five, four, three, two…"

Cam stood about a foot above the hood of the vehicle now, the microphone from the bullhorn in his hand. He keyed it and spoke: "Mr. Rollins, please. Let's end this. We can give you anything you might want here—a car, a helicopter, whatever you need to get us the girl back in one piece."

Linda looked toward the window where Rollins had reappeared; the barrel of his weapon was now trained on Cameron.

Then she looked at Cam.

Back at Rollins.

Linda could feel the impact before it happened.

"Let me think about that, Cameron…" Rollins said, trailing off.

Linda watched Rollins position his left eye into the sight and squint.

Finger on the trigger.

Cam turned to the captain.

Rollins spoke again: "While I put a bullet through your fucking head, cop."

Rollins squeezed the trigger, taking one shot.

Linda heard two blasts.

Before she could run for her man, before she could scream at him a warning, Linda reached Cam in time to feel the energy created from the bullet hitting its target.

The echo of both shots cracked across the field.

A squirt of blood streaked across Linda's face like a slash.

It all happened in an instant. The snap of two guns: one round hitting Cam in the head, the other from the back of the barn entering Rollins's brain.

Cam locked on Linda; his eyes glassy and lifeless. There had been a spray of his skull behind his head, a burst of bone and tissue, like a firework as Cam fell to the ground.

It felt as if it all had happened in slow motion.

Linda screamed.

No...Cam. Please. No. No. No...

He was on his back now, on the ground, eyes open. Blood gushed from the back of his head, soaked into the dry dirt underneath his skull. His body convulsed. His right arm twitched.

Two blues ran over.

"Shit," one of them said. "Cam's been hit."

Linda cradled Cam in her arms, her rifle on the ground beside her. Moody gave the signal. The girl was out of the back of the barn, in the arms of a trooper.

Rollins was dead, shot in the back of the head by that cop inside the barn, half his body falling out of the window, a good portion of his head missing.

The Germ girl was crying. She smelled of horse manure and gasoline.

"No...no...no..." Linda repeated. It felt as if she was crying, but no tears came. She was too focused on not allowing Cam to slip away. "You are not going to die on me here. Stay with me. Get some help, now," Linda screamed. "Right now! Help me. Help us here."

Linda, nor anyone else, had any idea the two of them were there, but Iris Starr and her cameraman were about a hundred yards away, burrowed in the woods behind some brush. Roger had gotten the entire shooting on video.

Cam's eyes were turning gray, clouding over. His lower lip trembled. His body limp. Deadweight. His skin clammy and pasty. Linda started CPR. Pumping and blowing. Pumping and blowing. Crying.

She could almost smell death approaching.

An ambulance was on the way.

45.

IT WAS A PART of herself Linda Kane had always been unwilling to share with anyone. If only because it did not matter, in the grand scope of her life. But what Linda missed most about summer was the smell of fresh-cut grass. That distinctive seasonal odor, whenever she stepped out of her Crown Vic and the men were buzzing around the PD building on tractors, spraying fresh clippings into the country air. It always brought her back to her childhood. Before *that* day. Before the world caved in around Linda Kane. Before her youth got sucked into a vacuum of despair, shame, and guilt, and she became the *other* girl, the one who didn't go missing.

The one left behind.

Now this; Cameron was fighting for his life in intensive care. Tubes down his throat. IVs stuck into his arms. Wires connected to little suction cups stuck to shaved patches of his muscular chest—an unconscious man taking a lie detector test.

One side of Cam's head had been shaved. The sound of machines beeped and breathed for him. An up-and-down valve-like apparatus on the wall pumped air into his lungs, organs which had trouble functioning on their own. All of this after a tennis-ball-sized portion of his skull had been blasted off by one .357 Magnum round from the weapon of a twisted psychopath whom Linda could not even take revenge on. The shooter was lying in the morgue; lots of answers to other crimes there beside him…bodies buried no one would ever find.

Linda sat in a chair by Cam's side. The room was not completely dark, but felt gray and ominous. She was hollow. Not any sort of emotion the detective could register. Not anger. Or guilt. Not sadness. Or that childhood desolation she had been so accustomed to. Maybe it was emptiness? A deep hole. Dark and bottomless. The only comparable situation she could measure was the day after Sherri Lafontaine went missing and Linda sat inside the precinct in a room with a female cop, staring at a bag of potato chips and a can of Coke she was never going to consume. How more cops came in and sat down and she thought everyone was staring at her, wondering if she'd done something to her friend.

The other girl.

A nurse walked in and pulled the sheets up and over Cam's chest, as if he had any idea he was chilly. She checked his numbers on the machines keeping him alive, tapped several of them into an iPad chart in her hand.

They'd called it "an induced coma to see if the swelling in his brain would go down."

Linda inferred only one word.

Zombie.

Inside her front pocket, Linda's phone buzzed. She took it out, stared at the screen.

Jenna.

Linda turned. Jenna stood outside the room, her hands on the glass as if someone held a gun to her back. She had a look of concern about her. *Let's forget about everything and start over* was written on her face.

The idea of death did that to people. Brought them together.

The cop stood up from the chair she'd spent the past eighteen hours sitting in. She stared at her protégé after walking over, looking into Cam's closed eyes. She shook her head slowly back and forth—*How could I let this happen?*—and then turned, walked out of the room.

She and Jenna said nothing to each other at first. Jenna hugged her mother. Tight. Like they were old friends at an airport. Linda had her eyes closed. She rubbed a circular pattern on Jenna's back.

Took in a solid whiff of her daughter's hair. She'd always loved the smell of her child.

Purity.

"I'm so sorry, Mother," Jenna said in a near whisper. "I brought you some Chinese food. Your favorite. General Tso's chicken. I know you haven't eaten and you definitely need to eat something."

They walked over to the ICU's family lounge area. A TV was on in the corner of the room. Some sort of Spanish soap opera.

"I can never tell if they are arguing or talking."

"You should have taken Spanish, like I said. French is for girlie-girls." Linda took the bag of food. She did not have an appetite. "I'll eat this later, okay? Thank you for bringing it and thinking of me."

They sat.

Jenna stared at her mother, held her hands on her knees. The chairs were the type you'd find in any doctor's office: Stiff, fake leather, puke yellow, oak arm rails. An imitation fern plant stood in the corner of the carpeted area. In front of the TV were building blocks for a child to keep himself occupied while adults discussed the unfolding tragedy happening around him. Magazines were spread across the coffee table in front of them. A poster-sized ad promoting flu shots tacked to the wall.

"They don't know yet, of course, if he'll live, walk, talk, anything," Linda explained. "Ten percent chance, I'm told by his doctor."

"Cam is strong, Mother. Young and strong. He'll come out of this."

"Yeah, but…I don't know." Linda looked toward Cam's room. "This is not good, Jenna. He's in bad shape." Linda had tears in her eyes.

They both stared at the television.

"Hope, Mother," Jenna said, staring into her mother's eyes again. "Please believe he's going to come back. And when he does, tell him."

Linda looked up. Was it that obvious?

Heartbreak—the great reconciliatory thread. How families bonded over the misfortune of others. How the truth came out.

Linda had told her boss she'd be taking some time off from the Cassandra Caldwell investigation—actually, from most everything.

However long it took to get a good read on Cam's status was how long Linda Kane said she was going to hang at the hospital and her apartment. Once she knew for certain, she'd be back in the office. Yet, Linda Kane also understood that living another day of what she had gone through over the past thirty-six hours and she'd be knocking on doors once again, following up with Vinnie Costello, losing herself in the hardship of the Caldwell family. Other people's pain was a drug that numbed your own, Linda knew. She'd need a fix sooner or later.

The DNA had come in, on the pants found inside the Rollins van, Linda's boss had said during this same conversation. Was not a match to Cassie. Come to find out, it was from an old girlfriend of Rollins's he'd raped with some sort of metal object. Learning that, Linda had said, "Well, it's a damn good thing he is no longer with us to hurt another human being. Piece of shit. Hope he burns wherever it is he went off to."

As Jenna and Linda spoke, a blue walked over. He said he needed a minute of Linda's time. He was sorry, but this could not wait.

"I was just gonna leave, anyway," Jenna said. "Call me, Mother, when you know something. I'm…Listen, I am…" Jenna started to say something, but then stopped herself and kissed her mother on the cheek.

Linda watched as Jenna walked down the hallway and out of sight.

"Vinnie Costello," the blue said. "We did what you asked. He gave it up."

"Gave *what* up?"

"The night the girl went missing."

"Please enlighten me, Officer." They walked toward Cam's room. Stood outside the door, a glass wall allowing them to see in.

"Vinnie left work and drove to the bar. He wanted to see if Freddie Banks and his lady were doing what he had suspected for some time. Said he wanted to be sure, because he was thinking of moving out of the house."

"Wait," Linda said, staring at the cop, "he was at the bar during that window of time?"

A nurse talking to a doctor walked by. She held a clipboard in her hand and seemed to be reprimanding the nurse for something. Linda and the blue waited until they passed before continuing.

"Exactly. He waited in the parking lot. He'd been told by a patron in the bar"—the blue referred to his notes to be certain—"named Toby Liston that Trudi and the manager there, Mr. Banks, were shacking up. So he wanted to prove it to himself."

"Anyone backing this up *besides* Vinnie?"

"Video from the bar. Shows him arriving in the parking lot, parking in the back, sitting in his car, eating his lunch. Then leaving to make it back to work about ten minutes later."

Linda rubbed the back of her hand over her lips. Then bit her bottom lip.

There was no way Vinnie could have had anything to do with Cassie's disappearance.

Back to square one.

How far Linda's instincts had been off with Freddie and now Vinnie. Was she losing her touch?

"Thanks. Appreciate you coming here to tell me."

"How's Cam?"

"Not so good," Linda said, looking toward Cam's bed, feeling those words get caught in her throat. A doctor was at the nurses' station in back of where they stood. He had his head tilted to one side, signing some paperwork. Linda turned to watch him. "Thank you for asking. If you learn anything more, text me, okay?"

"We're going to get up a collection for Cam. Fundraiser. We believe he'll pull through, Lin. He's a fighter."

Linda nodded, but did not speak.

The blue sighed and walked away, hat in his hands.

Linda opened the door to Cam's room to the smell of rubbing alcohol. The sounds of the machines were like daggers. Each beep, each puff of the ventilator, counting down the moments Cam had left. There was no way around it. The guy was not going to make it. Linda was certain of this.

Walking out of the room an hour later, after sitting and thinking about it, Linda knew there was only one way for her to relieve the ball of stress tightening inside her system. She felt as if every muscle was cramped up. Her legs ached. Her arms felt like stone. Her stomach a constant knot. She could not eat.

"You'll call me," Linda said to the head nurse at the station, "if anything changes?"

"I will, Detective. Right away."

"Anything, understand?"

"I do, ma'am."

Linda checked the time on her iPhone. She said thanks. Turned. Walked down the hallway. Drove home.

46.

WHEN HER MOTHER WAS alive, Lucy Kane would tell her daughter that she reminded her—in attitude—of a 1966 Berkeley, California hippie, who would've, had she not chosen to become a cop, likely gone to work for some sort of women's group.

"So you think I'm a feminist?" Linda had asked her mother that day. They were having tea. Linda was in her late twenties. Sitting outside her mother's home by the garden. Linda's father had passed of a heart attack the previous year. Lucy would soon die of a stroke. This had been one of the last serious conversations Linda had with her mother. A woman she loved more than anyone else in the world.

Her mother laughed at the feminist comment. "Something like that."

Linda never saw it. She viewed herself as a woman who believed in the same things any female who cared about her rights did. She was tough, sure. But she'd never go topless, paint slogans on her breasts, and join a march in a park over breast-feeding in public or picket outside the building of a company using whale oil to make cosmetics. Just wasn't part of Linda's character to share with anyone what her guarded personal beliefs were.

That all said, Linda did sympathize with the feminist movement, like her mother had preached in the household as Linda grew up. Still, one of her absolute fundamental principles in life was that you got out of your life whatever you put into it. Nothing more, nothing less. Some bigoted asshole showed you who he was, you stayed away. You put yourself in a position to be around people you admired. Men and women with integrity.

Linda had gone to UConn for two semesters but quickly realized she didn't need a state university education degree to become a cop, so she enrolled at a local community college and worked security at night for extra money. College was for careerists. Being a cop wasn't a career, Linda felt; it was a calling. Kids who joined clubs, fraternities, and spoke out about apartheid and world hunger were not ever going to see the real world they interacted with. Linda was shy, passive, in that manner. She believed in action. Absolutely. She was not one to sit in a dorm and study subjects she had no interest in. Getting out and being a service to the community was her way of activism.

Marrying Ted, even getting pregnant, though she'd never admit it, had been her great mistake. She'd never loved Ted. She felt comfortable with him at the time they'd met. Thought he'd make a great addition to the white-picket-fence life she wanted to show Lucy Kane she could have, shunning that feminist moniker Lucy had mentioned, perhaps just out of spite. Jenna came along and the script was being written without any input from Linda. So she went with it. Only Ted was a demanding, by-the-book, suburban-husband wannabe. Dinner. Dry the dishes. Walk the dog. Sitcom television. Cut the lawn. Straight-up, get-on-top, pump-a-few-times, and then-cum sex. Pick the kid up at day care. Come home at six and do it all over again the next day.

"No, Linda, I do not want you working. I need you home with my children."

Ted.

Mr. Suburban.

My *children.*

What an asshole.

Linda wanted depth. She wanted resolution for past mistakes.

She wanted answers.

She wanted to find her fucking friend.

Sherri.

Now add Cam sleeping forever into the mix.

It was the type of thing to drive a woman batshit crazy; enough to put the barrel of her Glock into her mouth and say good night.

LINDA POURED HERSELF A scotch. The chardonnay would not suffice for what she had planned. She needed liquid guts. Scotch grew those balls mighty quick.

Inside her bedroom, between sips of that dry, oaky, hot liquid, Linda filed through the dresses in her closet. She needed the perfect one. Something she'd only wear on this particular occasion.

Scotch in one hand, she used the other to pass the dresses on coat hangers to the right.

Nope. Nope. Nope.

Maybe?

Never.

Black was what she desired tonight. Black sequins, short, cut halfway between her crotch and knees. She needed her legs to be seen.

Locating the chosen one, Linda laid the dress out on the bed. Took a step back and stared at it.

This was the secret—maybe too strong a word—she'd questioned whether to share with Cam. Problem was, she thought he might think less of her if she had. Then she'd never have a chance with him. Or, Linda knew, sharing it was a way to sabotage herself and any chance of the two of them getting together. Maybe that was the goal: make it so that he couldn't be with her. She would denigrate herself in his eyes. He admired her as a cop, as his mentor. He liked her, too, in that way. She knew. Still, she would be sure to make it her decision not to consummate the relationship. If she let him in on this, she would be the cause of their non-hookup. It was that energy between them. Undeniable.

Her wish now was that she'd said something. Perhaps not about her one flaw, but at least about how she truly felt.

After a long, hot shower and a heavy slathering of makeup, which she detested but understood was part of the fantasy, Linda put the dress on and twirled around in the wall mirror, a solid buzz guiding the way. She then found the perfect purse and black pumps to match, took one last pull from her drink, felt that powerful glow, and headed out the door.

An Uber waited by the curb. She never took the town-issued Crown Vic when she went on these—what was it she began calling them last time?—*excursions*. These nights out.

HARTFORD WAS A THIRTY-five minute drive from her Royal Oaks apartment. The Uber dropped Linda off in front of Zylon, a club where the average age fell far below Linda's forty-plus crowd. It was dark inside, the music loud, thumping, very bass-centered. Lights strobed. For a Thursday night, it was busy. The entire place was awash in soft blue light. The metal bar had a darker blue tint all around the edge, same as those plastic tube lights kids crack in half and wear around their necks at an ecstasy rave. The bartender wore a skintight white t-shirt. Dark slacks. He had a hipster mustache, curled up on both ends, like a barbershop quartet singer wore.

Linda ordered a Maker's Mark, straight up. No ice.

"Make it a double."

Who is it going to be tonight?

Linda sipped the liquor, which went down hot and slow, burning her throat (in a good way). She scanned the bar with her eyes. He had to be exactly what she desired. No deviation from the plan. Not too muscular. Not chubby, either. Not too much like an insurance salesman. Not too coplike. *Definitely* not coplike. No. He had to be a man whose only ambition tonight was the same as hers: to go somewhere, pick someone, and fuck their brains out, with the least amount of talk possible.

It took a few minutes. But there he was. Just a smile taller than Linda. Black hair. Slicked back like a Wall Street dude—the only setback, Linda considered. But he'd do. He wore a button-down collared shirt, she couldn't tell what color because of the lighting in the club. Fancy designer jeans she knew cost him over a hundred bucks, which meant he had somewhat of a decent job. He wasn't a loser.

As she walked closer, the smell of expensive cologne hit her. She could tell right away, the moment he opened his mouth, he would do just fine.

"Ingrid," she said. "Nice to meet you." It was difficult, but Linda forced a smile.

"I cannot really hear you," he said over the music. He stuck out his hand. "Brian."

Ah, yes. She should have guessed.

Brian.

How perfect.

"I love your red hair. My, my, my," Brian said. "Fiery. You're freakin' beautiful, Ingrid."

"Aw, thanks, Brian." Linda leaned in and spoke in his ear: "You want to get out of here?" Linda never minced words when she decided—and she did this about three times a year—to meet a man and give him the night of his life.

"Yeah, sure," Brian said. He smiled. Took a pull from a private batch, IPA fall pumpkin-spiced beer, with hints of barley and oatmeal—or whatever piss he was drinking—and followed Linda out of the bar.

Inside the Uber on the way to Brian's condo, Linda told him not to ask questions. She was in total control of the rest of the night. As the car drove by a towering stone building downtown, Linda considered how in seeking out a man for a one-night stand, many would have a problem with it. Yet it was okay, her argument went, for a man to do the same? Not a woman? Double-fucking-standard. She could not have cared less what other people thought. Or at least Linda told herself this.

"It's kind of like, well, Patty, you know me," she said one day years ago, just after her divorce, when they got to talking. *"I…don't deserve to be loved. That I am always 'the other girl.' The one who lost. The one who doesn't get to love."*

Was this just one more way for Linda to prove to herself she didn't deserve the love of a good man?

Linda leaned over, grabbed Brian by the cock. Kissed him all over his neck.

Brian grew hard.

They got out of the car near a row of elms, a grated, tic-tac-toe sewer drain below their feet along the curb. Brian led the way up into his condo. A third-floor studio overlooking the Connecticut River, just beyond downtown Hartford, in a village called Rocky

Hill.

Walking in, Linda felt confident she'd chosen the right man. The condo was immaculate. Clean and tidy as a model room that assholes selling time-shares used to trick potential buyers. If the guy was this obsessive about his living space, Linda knew, he was clean all over.

For the next three hours, Linda Kane gave Brian a sexual experience he would be telling his friends about for the remainder of his life. Brian came four times. Linda once. That was all she needed. All she wanted. The only conversation between them was of a sexual nature: "Don't touch me there. Yes, there. Move your legs. Bend me over." Brian didn't care. When they were finished, Linda hit the Uber app on her iPhone, ordered a car, told Brian thanks, and went back home.

Done deal.

Linda Kane could now refocus on what was important.

47.

SOMETHING WAS MISSING. BESIDES, of course, two teenagers.

Linda sat by herself in the bleachers halfway up. She could hear Cam whispering in her ear: *"Just go to a volleyball game, for shit's sake. Make her happy. Sit through it. Forget about work."*

So here she was.

Cam had been right, of course. She wished she could tell him as much.

Sitting, watching her daughter's varsity team roll over their rival, a neighboring town called Coventry, Linda got lost in the grace her daughter displayed on the court. Amid the squeaking of sneakers on the wet-looking gymnasium floor, the piercing blowing of whistles, the shouts from coaches and players, moms and dads, there was Linda Kane, watching her daughter, who moved around the court like a dancer. A proud moment. Made her feel as though she'd done something right within a life of chasing ghosts.

Sitting and watching the match made Linda think of something. It was interesting to her, when she used to go to Jenna's tournaments on weekends, all those volleyball parents squawking around with their tripods and video cameras and false hopes of their babies being recruited by some Division I school. What a freakin' joke. Fools. Their kids were mediocre, at best, same as Jenna, only Linda and Ted and Jenna weren't afraid to face facts in that respect.

Volleyball was for fun. It built character. The tournaments they used to frequent together, something to do during the doldrums of winter, were difficult for any number of reasons, Linda had tried explaining to Jenna. Standing courtside all day, the smell of sweat and ass, all those male referees with beer belly stomachs and females with the butch haircuts checking out the girls' thick bodies, ballooned legs. Linda feared she'd say something. Somebody would piss her off and she'd lash out. But more than that excuse, it *was* Ted and his wife. Linda couldn't suck it up. She couldn't play the role of the amiable ex-wife. Wasn't in her. Being there, watching the three of them, reminded Linda that she'd come out the loser in it all. Ted had beaten her. Sure, there was no way Linda could have taken Jenna in after the divorce, but it didn't mean she would not have tried.

Yet, here she was at a game. Looking on. Forgetting all that. Taking Cam's advice. Cheering Jenna on in her own way. Ted and his fucking trophy wife were sitting in back of the players' bench. Ted up on his feet, clapping, pacing, yelling, his hands cupped around his mouth. The wife reading her Kindle. Probably some sappy, stupid-ass Nicholas Sparks love story.

What a freakin' joke.

Something was missing.

Linda was lost in thought when she spied Katherine sitting across court, on the opposite side of the gym, about ten rows up. Katherine didn't see the detective. She had her face buried in a book, or whatever was on her lap. She wore those damn garish glasses, windshield-thick. Why hadn't Trudi taken her in to get some trendy glasses? One less form of ridicule for a child likely prone to it.

Linda really liked this kid. Felt sorry for her.

Katherine wore a turtleneck sweater and baggy jeans, probably handed down from Cassie. Her braces flashed every once in a while when she moved and a beam of light hit her face. Linda saw herself in Katherine, the idea of being viewed as the girl spared. On the outside looking in. Katherine had burdened the brunt of everything that had happened inside the Caldwell household all these years. A casualty no one paid attention to. She was going to suffer the most, in the end. Trudi knew this. Yet, Trudi was too wrapped up in her own pain to pay the slightest bit of attention to her youngest child. She was so focused on mourning one daughter and managing her shitty life, maybe even stifling secrets of her own, that the other child was slipping away.

Katherine Caldwell was turning into Cassie—the girl was *already* missing, and had been for some time.

Linda walked around the court and stepped up into the bleachers where Katherine, she could now see, was busy working on some type of drawing.

"Hey, Katherine, how are you?" Linda said, sitting next to the child. The Asperger's syndrome, Linda knew from the small amount of Googling she'd done after meeting the family, kept Katherine from realizing her full potential as a social creature—a symptom of the condition. Linda recalled a cop she'd once worked with who had a son born the same way and he'd talk about the boy's symptoms when they were on stakeout and riding the beat as partners. The social cues Katherine had missed in those people around her. There had been times when Linda was talking to Trudi about everyday things—times and places and routines—and Katherine acted as though she did not understand what they were discussing. The way she spoke in a flat monotone cadence that never changed, regardless of what she said. All of it was part of the disorder.

All of it, too, making her a special child; Linda could now see.

Katherine looked up, didn't respond to Linda's hello. Then she went back to what she was doing.

"You don't go to this school?" Linda said.

Katherine shook her head no without looking at the cop. The middle school, Linda realized, was just up the road.

"How's your mother? I've been meaning to get over there and see her." Linda guessed the high school, about a five-minute walk from Trudi's, was a good place for Katherine to hang out. A safe zone for a girl like her—somewhere close where she could fold into a crowd and take flight from when she felt the need for isolation. It wasn't as if she was on the corner with four friends, and Katherine had to be somebody she wasn't. In here, the gym, she was another face in the crowd. She could come and go any time she wanted, without any questions, without those stares and people wondering what was up with her.

"But your friend was shot in the head and he bled and he's dying, isn't he?" Katherine said, never looking up from her work. "The brain is not a place you want to be shot."

"Something like that," Linda said. She watched the game some. Jenna had made an incredible play by jumping above the net, spiking the ball down into the face of a girl. The crowd went crazy. The bleachers rattled. She could feel the energy of the crowd pulsing.

Katherine never flinched.

Linda gazed over at what Katherine was working on: an incredibly elaborate drawing of a house. Something a graduate school architect student might hand in. She had a compass and straight edge and was making designs on one particular room. She'd draw a line. Stop. Lean back. Hold the picture out in front of herself. Size it up. Lean back in. Continue. Totally focused, she drew, with her tongue curled up around her lip.

"Mother works too much," Katherine said. She did not make eye contact with Linda.

"Yeah. I kind of get that," Linda said. "Does it bother you?"

"Mother works all the time."

"She does, huh?"

"Mother doesn't have time for me. I know. It's okay, though. I understand."

"She loves you, Katherine. I can tell. What's that you're working on?"

"Mother was tired of Cassie's 'games.' Her word choice. Not one I would use. This is a house. A big house. Like the Kim Kardashian house."

Linda felt as though this was going somewhere. They'd never been able to get Katherine alone and have any sort of extended conversation with her. Trudi was always around, always wanted to be there when Katherine spoke. Linda assumed Trudi was being an overprotective mother of a child with issues.

Until now.

"*Mother was tired of Cassie's games,*" Linda repeated to herself. "What do you mean by that, Katherine? What games?"

"I'm done," Katherine said. "Talking, I mean. You will not

beckon me to talk more. I need to finish my work on this house."

Linda patted the child on the back of her shoulders. "That house is awesome, Katherine. Best house I have ever seen."

Katherine did not respond.

Linda walked down the bleachers. She stood courtside and waved good-bye to Jenna, who was sitting on the bench.

Jenna smiled. Waved back.

Mending fences.

On HER WAY INTO the station, Linda took a detour to see Cam.

There was no change. Cam was being kept alive by machines, and doctors weren't sure, even if he ever woke up, if his brain would function at all. So far, his toes were not responding to pricks with a pin. The machines with the digital readouts of brain waves didn't show much in the form of cognitive thinking or stimulation. But that didn't mean it wasn't there. "The drugs," the doctor explained. "We're heavily sedating him."

Awful. Just awful.

Linda got up to leave, turned, and in walked Iris Starr.

The look Linda gave the reporter should have told Iris to walk the fuck back out immediately.

But she didn't.

"I come here in total peace," Iris said, her hands up.

"Out of the room."

They stood in the hallway.

"Hear me out, please, Detective."

"I'm not sure why I don't have you arrested. How dare you incite that crowd by telling the reverend there was video. If this shit here with my partner didn't happen, I was coming after you."

"I am sorry. Truly, I am. I have something I want to give you. That's why I came here today."

Iris had a look about her that was nothing like the TV personality she was. Linda, if she was being honest with herself, would have said Iris was showing a bit of humility.

The reporter reached into her Gucci handbag and took out a large manila envelope. There was a video disc inside.

"That's the original," Iris said. "To spite you, I was going to air it as an exclusive. But with your friend here, Mr. Van Zandt, and his condition, I thought better. It's yours to destroy. Again, I am sorry."

Linda took the package.

"You recorded the shooting?"

"We did."

"Get out of here. Do not ever come back here."

Iris turned and walked away.

Linda walked over to the garbage can. She took out the video disc, broke it into pieces. As she finished and looked up, Cam's family walked toward her. His mother and father, younger sister. Linda wanted to avoid any of that conversation. So she said hello, walked back into the room, grabbed Cam's cold, clammy hand, kissed three of her fingers, stamped that kiss on his forehead, said her good-byes, and left.

48.

WEEKS WENT BY. THE protestors had all disappeared in the days after Rollins shot Cam. Reverend Smalls held a press conference and talked about forgiveness. About how God would want him and his supporters to focus on love. About how black lives do, of course, matter; yes, they do. But, Smalls concluded, they could have their voices heard some other way.

The cop who killed Freddie Banks was indicted. He was going to plead guilty, according to his attorney. He asked and hoped for leniency. His hand, however, had been forced. Someone had leaked an iPhone video of the cop yelling and screaming the *n*-word at a local rally for a senate candidate. Then the Facebook video of him in line at 7-Eleven went viral.

So there had been not one, but two videos, after all—and now there was at least *some* peace, too.

The cop had shot Freddie not out of hatred for blacks or some sort of white cop's planned insurgence to rid the streets of black people. It was, as one psychologist pointed out on Anderson Cooper's CNN show, an inherent racism so deeply embedded into this kid's psyche that sooner or later it was going to emerge, and so it did. The analyst asked Cooper how many more cops were out there with that same type of hidden hatred they themselves might not even know existed within their souls. Cooper responded by saying it might be about more training and better psychological testing for all cops—which sent the argument back to where it had begun.

There was still a black man dead at the hand of a white cop, and nothing, really, had changed.

The bottom line, Linda had explained during a meeting with her team after the indictment, was that when Dave watched Freddie Banks reach around for his wallet: "All he saw was a black person reaching for a weapon. And that sort of bigoted way of thinking is not going to be tolerated within the ranks of the Royal Oaks PD."

Linda stood at a lectern in front of a room full of cops. She didn't like to, but she wore reading glasses because she read from legal notes given to her by the town attorney. Her glasses were down on the tip of her nose, like Mother Goose. She stared at the team over the top of the frames. The entire moment made her feel old.

"Are we all understanding what I am saying here?" Linda asked.

A collective reply of "yes" filled the room.

"Good."

Linda held vigil at Cam's side for as long as she could. It had started out as every other night, fell off to two days a week, then one—all day Sunday. Cam came out of the coma—or, rather, the induced coma. He was still unresponsive. He was a body in a bed being sponge-bathed by nurses and fed through a clear tube connected to an apparatus that beeped and blinked red and green.

Cam was dead, his body still alive.

Linda would sometimes sit by his side and play Daniel Barenboim's piano concerto classics through her iPhone and a set of earbuds placed in Cam's ears, having read that music helps people in a state of unconsciousness by exciting the receptors in the brain. She didn't believe it, but it gave her something to do besides obsess over trying to resurrect yet another ghost in her life.

For weeks, Linda followed Trudi when time permitted. She found her to be predictable. Here was a woman trying to cope with the loss of her daughter, while everyone was now resigned to believe and maybe accept she was dead. Cassie had fallen into that bottomless pit that Sherri had slipped and fallen into long ago: the place where the ghosts hover. Her spirit, like Sherri's, was roaming the planet, in search of a place to settle.

One Friday, Linda stopped by Trudi's to say hello, check in, and update the mother on the progress they'd made with her daughter's disappearance.

Which was zero.

Trudi was planning on suing the company that owned the restaurant where she'd worked for the past ten years. Her boss had taken advantage of her, she was now claiming. Linda knew this to be the work of some ambulance chaser. But there you go: American capitalism at work.

Linda learned that Trudi had since gotten a job at a local credit union as a clerk. Quite a change from delivering food to tables and catering to the local drunk crowd, but she liked the routineness of the new job, she told Linda. The nine-to-five hours suited her well.

"I can focus on Katherine."

"I have nothing for you," Linda said. "I wish I did, but we know nothing more than we knew six weeks ago. I'm very sorry."

Trudi bowed her head.

"How's Katherine? Do you two have plans for Christmas?"

"Coping well," Trudi said, looking up. They sat at the breakfast bar. "We're going to stay here. Nothing big. I'll cook a roast."

"What about Vinnie?"

"No chance we're getting back on. He's done. I asked him to forgive, but Vinnie is, well, let's just say Vinnie has his own issues. Like we all do, I guess. Just as well. Look, I need to be here for Katherine. She's heading into high school next year."

"Trudi, I find no evidence that Vinnie is racist. Why did you make me think that about him? You lied to me."

Trudi dropped her head. "Linda," she said, "I am sorry. I don't know why I did that. I wanted you to focus on Freddie and Vinnie. I thought they were two good suspects. I do not know what I was thinking."

Linda had thought about her next set of questions for some time. She decided to let the Vinnie lie go for now.

"Trudi, is there anything I have missed? Anything at all that maybe you think I should have done that I didn't do? Anybody I missed speaking to?"

Trudi stood up from her stool. She walked over to the sink,

rinsed out her teacup. Linda spun around on her swivel stool and stared at Trudi's back, her hands folded over her thighs. She felt something between them that gave her pause. She couldn't so much put a finger on it, but there was a strong pull, nonetheless. Linda's gut was again speaking to her. She felt like this wasn't over. There was more. Something she *had* missed.

Trudi turned and leaned against the sink. Crossed her feet. Her head down. She stared at a damp dishrag she fidgeted with in her hand.

"I failed. I failed my daughter. Both, actually. If I would have been a better mother, Cassie would not be gone."

"Trudi, please…" Linda began to say. She stood. Walked over and stood in front of Trudi about three feet away. Two mothers. Each suffering in her own way.

"No, let me finish." Trudi tossed the dishrag into the sink. She propped both hands on the counter. "If only I would have listened to my daughter. She was trying to tell me something." She then turned and looked Linda in the eyes. "A mother should *never* give up on her child."

"What was it, exactly, Trudi, that the two of you were fighting about in those days before? I know we've gone over this, every which way we can, but now that you've had some time, is there *anything* you can think of that we might have overlooked?"

"I've been through it a hundred times in my head. I told you and your detective… How is he, by the way? My goodness, I apologize for not sending flowers to the hospital, but we're on a budget and I am just making it."

Linda wanted to keep her focused. "Thanks, he's stable. But, listen, what was it you and Cassie fought about? Tell me again."

Trudi crossed her arms. Held herself as if she felt a chill. She explained that Cassie had been with friends the night before Halloween. A girl and two boys.

Linda nodded. She had interviewed the three of them. They knew nothing.

They'd crossed the border into Massachusetts, Trudi continued, and decided to get drunk, smoke some weed. It was Cabbage Night, that day before Halloween when kids feel the need to let loose and cause mischief and mayhem. It was routine teenage nonsense, Linda had found out. Lots of teens get into trouble on this night. Toilet paper on trees. Smashed pumpkins. A few demolished mailboxes. That sort of thing.

So what.

"Cassie had come home and passed out in the basement. She thought she was hiding it all," Trudi continued. "When I found her down there, like I told you before, I was pissed. She stank of booze. I know that smell. Believe me. I worked around it. I woke her. I screamed at her. I said something about the example she was setting for Katherine. I said other things in a fit of anger I don't recall. Cassie stood up. She lashed out at me. Pointed in my face. Yelled about me not knowing who she was, what she wanted—she blamed me for her father's death. That was where Cassie claimed her rage was rooted—in Jeremy's sudden death when she was really young. A man, Linda, Cassie never even knew. She was only two when he died. Still, she made up this fantasy of the two of them—"

Linda interrupted her. "He fell or something, right? From a crane? A terrible accident, I think I read in one of the reports. You told us the story."

"Yes, when we lived on Long Island. He was working in Manhattan on one of those skyscrapers. Cassie adored the man, I'll give her that. She was attached to him like a two-year-old would be. But as she grew, she developed this image of herself with him that never existed. She was too young to even really know him on any level, but that was my daughter: forever looking for a way to explain her heartache in life and blame it on someone else." Trudi walked over to the stove. "I gave Cassie—and I still give Katherine—the best life I can. Anyhow, there was no way I could've prevented her father from dying. She knew that. But she wanted to blame me for it later, after she found out the circumstances. I was an easy target. Not the best mother, Linda. The stories she told her friends about him were beyond lies—she'd made all of it up."

"Why was it, do you think, she said all of that? Why would she say all those things, Trudi?"

Cassie's mother poured a box of dry macaroni elbows into a pot of boiling water. She took a wooden spoon, stared at it, sighed, and then stirred.

"I don't know. For sympathy, maybe? To get people to feel sorry for her? I do not know. As she grew, she learned from me that we had been talking about moving from Long Island to Connecticut and I had talked her father out of it. I wanted to stay on Long Island because I liked it there. I had friends. I had screwed up my life, but it was changing for the better. He died about two months after we decided to stay."

"She blamed you for not moving?"

"She did."

"But she called the guy in Texas her father, why?" Linda asked.

"Habit. He adopted her. Gave her his name. She disliked him. He reminded her of what she'd never had, I guess. She never said that, but I always got the feeling. She felt I robbed her of a normal life by changing the course of events and staying on Long Island. Ridiculous, I know how it sounds. But kids, they view the world inside a box of their own selfishness. Everything becomes about them."

Linda did not need to have this explained to her.

Steam from the pot billowed up in ribbons and disappeared above the stove burners. A fan buzzed and rattled the overhanging metal hood.

"Confused kid, eh? She sounds angry, too. Is Cassie what you might consider an angry child?"

"Freddie brought out that anger in her again. But she hadn't been that angry for quite some time. She'd gotten help for it. Freddie and the idea of the two of us together truly hit some kind of nerve inside her. Listen, Linda, I need to get dinner ready for Katherine. She'll be home soon. I think we've been all over this before, anyway."

Damn. Linda was onto something. She could feel it. She could tell Trudi was heading somewhere with what she was talking about. Maybe it was just too painful for her to revisit?

"Can we talk again, Trudi, soon?" Linda didn't want to push her. Everything came out in time. Secrets were for keeping, which, in a sense, kind of gave them a meaning. But in due time, all of that ugliness emerged.

"Yes, of course."

"How 'bout I come back tomorrow?"

"Maybe. Can I call you?" Trudi took an elbow macaroni out of the water and tasted it for doneness.

"Yes. Text me. We'll set it up."

49.

BACK AT THE OFFICE, Linda sat at her desk. This was where she spent the least amount of time lately. That vacant space in front of her was too much to bear. How Cam's chair just stood there, empty. The Peanuts calendar he tore the pages off each day after reading the short comic he kept near his stapler still had the day of the shooting. Linda could not bring herself to keep it up to date.

She was sick about not telling Cam she had a thing for him—whatever it was. He deserved to know there was more between them than work colleagues. Hell, Linda even disliked the idea that she was, in some capacity, his superior. She never saw it that way.

Hindsight, the great reality check.

"Lin, you got a minute?" a vice detective came by and asked. The guy was short and stocky. He wore a ball cap, Red Sox. Torn-up jean jacket. Long hair, in a ponytail. A concert shirt, Aerosmith. Greasy blue jeans. A wallet connected to a long chain.

"Yeah, what's up?"

"I have something you might want to take a look at before it gets filed away into the Caldwell box. I think…I mean, did you know that the girl was going to be wealthy when she turned eighteen?"

"Cassie?"

"Yeah. This report"—he handed over a quarter-inch-thick batch of white paper—"was in a pile of papers we found inside Cam's apartment, spread out on a table in his living room. His family called to tell us that we might want to come by and grab everything he was working on at home." The cop explained that it was part of an insurance report Cam appeared to be immersed in studying. "I think he just obtained the report in the days before… It was on top of a FedEx package dated three days before he was, well, um, you know. The shooting. Anyway, the guy had all sorts of files and reports he was reading at home. But this one here, it was the only one of the bunch he highlighted in several places."

Cam, Linda thought. *Good man. Taught him right.*

"Thanks, appreciate this."

"Knew you would."

"Hey, why wasn't I called about this when you guys went over to collect it?"

"The lieutenant didn't think it was a good idea for you to go into Cam's apartment, you know. Because of everything."

"Oh, I see." Linda closed her eyes and shook her head. "Listen, I love the lieutenant as much as everyone else"—they both smiled—"but next time, please send old Linda Kane here a text and let her know what's going down so she, as an adult, can make up her own mind as to what she wants to do."

"Ten-four, Lin. Sorry. I should have done that."

"No worries. I understand." Linda held up a hand, palm side out. "I get it, Detective. And listen"—Linda held up the report and shook it—"thanks for this report."

Linda opened the file, put on her glasses, and read.

The short end to a long story was that Cassandra Caldwell, on the day she turned eighteen, was set to inherit a shitload of money. Something in the neighborhood of one million, tax-free American dollars. She was the sole beneficiary of her biological father's insurance policy. The money had been put into a trust for Cassie. Katherine had come along later on, Linda found out, and was Cassie's half-sister. A daughter from another father, that dude in Texas who'd adopted Cassie. Katherine, it seemed, didn't know it, Linda realized after reading statements from Trudi given to the insurance company in form of a deposition. Trudi and Mr. Texas were under oath—it was part of a law suit they tried filing to get their hands on that money. Reading into the file further, Linda found a copy of the will Cassie's father had left as part of the trust. Jeremy Riser, Cassie's biological father, had stipulated just in the months before his death that he wanted Cassie to have control of the money if anything should happen because he didn't trust that Trudi could handle it, the way her life was beginning to take shape at the time. He never elaborated.

Linda wondered what that meant, exactly.

As she read on, it was clear that on the day she turned eighteen, Cassie was going to receive a lump sum payment and there was nothing anyone could do to stop it. Save for her untimely death, Cassie was going to be rich. In the event that she died, Trudi had been able to set forth into the trust after her law suit was tossed out of court that the money would go to Cassie, her guardian at the time, or any children she had.

Linda tossed the report down. Sat back. Looked up at the ceiling.

Son of a bitch.

Here were several new facts Trudi had felt the need to leave out of the cop–missing person's mother dialogue all along. The question Linda asked herself was, why?

Motive?

The oldest in the book.

Money. Greed. Whatever you wanted to call it.

Linda stood from her desk, took off her glasses, put on her jacket, and walked out of the squad room into the elevator.

SHE DROVE TO THE local rep's office for the insurance company, a major provider, the one with the deer as the company mascot. She walked in and asked to speak to, and here she took out the report and found his name, "Louis Castellassi."

A very hard name for Linda to pronounce, "Mr. Cast-ell-assi," she said, extending her hand, after reception led her into a small maze of desks. "Linda Kane, Royal Oaks PD. You have a minute and somewhere private"—Linda scanned the room, all the ladies in the office with their probing eyes were checking her out—"we can chat?"

"Over here, Detective," Louis said, taking the card Linda handed him and reading it along the way.

"I got your name from this report here," Linda explained as they walked into a small prepackaged boardroom: glass table, eight chairs, four on each side; a second table along the wall with an empty pitcher of water, eight matching glasses; plus a painting of a meadow on the wall.

IKEA. From top to bottom.

Linda tossed the report on the table. Louis closed the door. They sat across from each other.

"Can you give me a read on that and tell me what the gibberish part of the fine print actually means? I've highlighted it in green. Don't pay any mind to the yellow highlighted sections."

Louis picked it up and read.

Linda walked over to the window as he studied the document. She stared out at the town she'd called home for the past four and a half decades. Trucks drove by. Cars following behind. Delivery vehicles and even tractors with blinking lights and red triangle warning signs on the back clogged up traffic. People milled in and out of a cleaners across the street that advertised shirts for $1.99 EACH, so said the bright orange sign in the picture window. Everything had a coating of Christmas on it: tinsel, green and red lights, lots of snowmen and elves.

The holidays.

Merry Fucking Christmas, Royal Oaks.

"This here," Louis said, taking off his glasses, holding them. As Linda turned and sat back down, Louis used his glasses to point out what he was referring to on the page. "This here, well, it is a standard union policy, issued by us through the construction company. Every employee gets one. Dangerous jobs specify as much. Here, though, this man, Jeremy Riser, right? That's his name"—he looked for it on the page—"he modified the policy, it appears, just before he died. That's not unheard of, though not common, either. He went to a lawyer and had it drawn up, and our policy is that you'd need to add a will to the policy—which he did."

"And what does it mean, in the scope of his chosen beneficiary, if said person dies before he or she can collect?"

"Let me see." He put his glasses back on, never taking his right hand off the frame. He read to himself. His lips whispered the words.

"Means that if the beneficiary dies, in this case a minor, before she can collect, her mother—or grandmother even, if said mother is dead, or even her closet blood relative beyond that or her guardian at the time—receives the money. If she has a child, that child could claim the money. That's kind of standard policy language. Nothing special there. Trickle-down insurance premiums is what we call it around the office."

Cute.

Still, Linda couldn't believe it. How had she missed such a fact within her investigation?

"There are stipulations, however. We would not pay this policy if, for example, the person committed suicide. We'd only pay a small stipend. Very small, actually. That's a prerequisite of signing with us. A standard policy for us across the board, simply because we cannot allow for personal demons to intrude upon what should be the fairness of the danger these men and women face on these types of jobs."

"What about murder?"

"*Murder*?" He was stunned by the word. "*That's* why you're here?"

"I'll need your complete discretion about this meeting, sir. No one can know about this conversation we're having right now."

"I understand, Detective. But murder, my goodness. I assume so, yes."

"What stipulations exist there, if any?"

"Not many. The murder would have to be proven, is all. Or, I should note, the person making the claim would have to have a certificate of death with homicide listed as the cause."

"What about a body?"

"You mean with no body? Well, let me see." He thought about it, chewing on the end of the glass frame a minute. "Not necessarily. I've seen this in a case when I worked in California. You need only for the city or town to issue a certificate of death. A good lawyer can get that done with some maneuvering and, I'm sure, a third of the payout."

"How long would you have to wait after said person was, let's just say for the sake of argument, missing, for that person to be declared dead, by murder or otherwise?"

"Ah, okay…Ms. Caldwell, if that is to whom you are referring"—he put his glasses down on the table—"would have to be gone, I believe, about one year. We don't just hand out one million dollars without an investigation of our own into the life of the beneficiary. It's a complicated process."

"Can you tell me if Trudi Caldwell has indicated if she plans to seek her daughter's fortune?"

He stuck the end of his glasses into his mouth again and thought about it. Then Louis stood. "Be right back."

Linda watched from the room through the glass door as he went to a nearby desk and pecked away at a keyboard, looking up at the computer monitor every so often, then back down at the keyboard. After a few moments of this, Louis leaned in really close to the monitor, put his finger on the screen, and ran it across, stopping on a piece of information.

Walking back into the room, Louis said, "It appears as though she has not applied for the beneficiary dollars as of yet."

Insurance companies, Linda thought. How they complicate matters of such simplicity.

There was one other thing bothering Linda.

"And how," Linda asked, "well, more importantly, why did it take my partner so long to obtain this document? He got hold of it eight days after the Caldwell girl went missing."

"A subpoena. He filed a subpoena, that's what it said in the file when I looked at the computer. Somebody, I am assuming your partner, wrote an affidavit and filed it. We complied, no problem, and generally do with police. But it takes time. Eight days is actually pretty darn quick."

"Okay, I'm gonna have you call my office. Set up an appointment with Carmen, our go-to and scheduler, and have you come in and give us a complete statement of facts regarding this report. Are you okay with that?"

"I do not think that would be a problem." He cleared his throat.

"And again, you cannot talk about this with anybody. Not your wife, kids, employees, clerks, no one. This is between the two of us." Linda used her finger to point at him, then back at herself as she said it.

"I understand."

Linda had Louis Castellassi make a copy for himself after he asked if he could study the documents on his own. She then walked out to her car and sat down.

50.

TRUDI WAS AT HOME. In her bedroom. Enjoying another Xanax buzz. She stared at the television set on her dresser without paying much attention to the *Seinfeld* episode depicting Jerry discovering the best soup in the city, before explaining there were certain conditions in getting your hands on a bowl of the stuff from a man he called the "Soup Nazi."

Yawn.

Trudi lay on her right side, her hands folded underneath her head as a comforting way to kill some time before Katherine got home and they had dinner. Her eyes soon focused on a picture of her, Katherine, and Cassie, just the three of them. They'd had the family photo done at Sears during one of those advertised specials. It was her favorite photo. Katherine was in grammar school, and Cassie was just entering middle school. The smiles were genuine. They were happy then. So long ago that seemed now. So far away from where her life had ended up.

As much as it would hurt, Trudi knew she needed to go through Cassie's closet, drawers, and dig into her life—or, rather, what was left of it here at the house after Linda and her team had rifled through everything. A lot of Cassie's belongings had been returned. Some had not. Trudi needed to decide what to do with everything. Six weeks was long enough.

She got up. Made a cup of tea and went into Cassie's room. She began to look through her closet. The fact that she could still smell her firstborn child, but couldn't hold her in her arms, gutted Trudi. Tore her apart.

Inside one of Cassie's drawers, Trudi found a trinket box. An old cookie tin container Trudi had tossed in the garbage and Cassie must have fished out. Cassie had redesigned the thing with different colored Sharpies, drawing hearts and crosses and other shapes all over it.

Trudi popped the lid.

Inside the tin were rings and necklaces, a pencil with Cassie's name along one side, her teeth marks still indented into the yellow wood. There was some toy jewelry Cassie had won at the state fair. A few plastic toys she'd gotten out of the gumball machines for a quarter near the registers at Kmart. Several letters from her girlfriends. Postcards from aunts and uncles and friends. A report card. Lots of bracelets, Cassie's favorite; leather bands and those knotty things made out of yarn that tighten once they get wet. A few pink rubber bands she'd bought in support of the local "think pink" cancer movement.

Trudi grabbed the stack of letters. Sat on the edge of Cassie's bed and ran her hand across the bedspread, a blue-and-white quilted pattern; her school colors. The child could not leave her room in the morning without making sure the bed was made.

Cassie.

The first letter Trudi read had a heart drawn on the front. Cassie's handwriting, for sure; she'd drawn something on each of the letters sent to her, personalizing them. Trudi tilted her head, stared at the heart, traced the outline with a finger. The letter was folded into the shape of a square. Opening it, Trudi saw that it was from Winona, a girl Cassie had met in kindergarten and stayed in touch with. Winona still lived on Long Island. Her father was a pilot. Mother a banker. They'd lived down the block. Trudi and Cassie had stayed on Long Island for a few years after Cassie's father was killed. Winona and Cassie remained pen pals and friends after they'd moved to Connecticut. Trudi would even send Cassie out to visit Winona for weeks at a time after they'd relocated. Before that, though, there had been lots of sleepovers and birthday parties at

Chuck E. Cheese or Build-A-Bear Workshop together. Trudi could picture Winona sound asleep next to her little Cassie, both of them cuddled up with their favorite stuffed animals. *Two peas in a pod*, Trudi would think, making sure they were warm enough, tucking the blankets in over them.

Cassie had written to Winona as recently as three weeks before she went missing. This was Winona's response to that letter. They e-mailed and texted, of course, but Cassie had always encouraged friends that hand writing letters was her way of showing just a few close BFFs how much she loved them. It was personal—and certainly more private—and emotional to put pen to paper and send it in the mail.

Trudi crossed her legs, cradled one hand under her chin, unfolded the one-page letter onto her lap, and read.

Winona said she missed her old friend and was wondering when Cassie was going to visit again. She talked about how the two of them could go down to the wharf and see that boy Winona liked. *Fun in the sun*, Winona wrote, a heart drawn crudely next to the word *sun*.

From there, it was your typical teenage banter: homework, her mom taking her phone away for slacking grades, her dad never around, always flying into some city *with a plane full of hot flight attendants*. Winona even mentioned how she couldn't wait to graduate and get the hell out of Long Island.

Kids, Trudi thought. *They always think the grass is greener.*

The last few lines of the letter got Trudi's full attention.

I'd tell her if I were you. Don't worry, everything is going to be okay. I can help.

What the hell does that mean? In the scope of a normal life, those two sentences meant very little, Trudi knew. But now, with everything that happened…

She stood. Walked to the window. Stared out into the street. The rain-slicked tar had a sheen to it. Trudi pictured earthworms collected in the gutters, leaves clogging up that sewer drain out in front of the house. How the girls, when they were little, would love the smell after a rainstorm in summer, the steam permeating hazily off the road. How they would, unafraid, pick up the worms and toss them at each other, running into the puddles with their red boots and yellow rain jackets.

As she got lost in what Winona had written, a familiar car drove by the house and snapped Trudi from her train of thought.

Linda?

It was Linda's blue Crown Vic. Trudi followed the car with her eyes as it drove by the house and pulled over down the block by a fire hydrant and telephone pole.

She put the letter down. Walked downstairs. Looked out the east-facing window in the kitchen. Stretching, craning her neck, she could just see through the lilac tree outside the window. Any other time of the year, the leaves on the tree would have blocked her view.

Linda parked by that telephone pole. Trudi watched her get out of the vehicle and stand by the fire hydrant.

What in the world is she doing?

Trudi put on her jacket and walked out of the house.

51.

LINDA HAD INDEED PARKED down the block near that telephone pole and empty lot where she and Cam believed Freddie Banks had argued with Cassie. She walked about halfway into the lot, turned around, stared at the road. She had always felt there were eyes on Cassie that night. Somebody watching her. Waiting. Stalking. Linda could not shake this feeling.

In back of where she stood, maybe fifty yards or so, was a chain-link fence about six feet high; barbed wire ran along the top of it. Linda could see a small section of the fence cut out and curled back so the neighborhood kids could get into the forest on the opposite side of the fence. Posted signs were everywhere back there, warning anyone thinking of trespassing that it was not only private property, but hunting grounds. You entered this area not only breaking the law, but at your own risk. Linda knew from talking to several blues patrolling the area over the years that the kids generally stayed away. The acreage itself was so vast, the terrain so rough, they hadn't gone into the woods to search. There was a steep mountainside just after you slipped through the fence. A trip and fall down that mountain and you were not getting back up. Plus, the owner of the property wasn't too keen on cops searching his land. He demanded a warrant.

No probable cause, no evidence, no warrant.

As Linda took it all in, out of the corner of her eye, she saw Trudi walking up the sidewalk.

"Hey, Linda, I saw you drive by the house," Trudi said. Linda had walked out of the lot and met Trudi by the pole on the sidewalk. "What are you doing here?"

Trudi seemed like a woman on a mission, focused on checking in with the detective to see what she was up to.

As Linda studied the mother, a neighbor's dog, a little thing that looked a bit like a gremlin, barked. Or yelped, rather. He was confined by an electric fence, those little white flags stuck into the ground designating where he could and could not meander.

"I'm trying to figure out where your daughter went after she got out of Freddie's truck that night," Linda explained. She gave Trudi a pained look.

"If he even let her out, you mean? Were they really ever here?" Trudi offered. "I think he put her in the lake, if you want my opinion. Why are we back to that now?"

"Maybe. But we searched as much of that lake as we could with divers. Then again, there's nothing to tell us Freddie was lying and didn't drop her off here."

"So you're sort of role-playing, trying to get a physical sense of what might have happened?"

"Something like that."

Linda walked to her vehicle. She opened the door, the bell *dinged* for her to close the door or insert a key. She reached in and grabbed a manila folder on the front seat.

"Glad I caught you," Linda said. "I was going to stop by once I had a look around here. But, listen, why is it you never told me that Katherine and Cassie are *half*-sisters?"

Trudi winced. A look of total shock. She grabbed her jacket collar and pulled it tight around her neck. She stared at an old scar on her right wrist.

"I, I… How did you know that? Well, actually, it doesn't matter how you found out. I don't see how that would have changed anything in your investigation. You checked out Katherine's father, so you said. Cassie's father, as you know, is dead. End of story."

"Does Katherine know who her father is?"

"Linda, please. I need you to find my daughter, not expose family secrets. That stuff there, it's my business." Trudi never looked

Linda in the eyes.

Linda was doing the math. "Let me ask: Were you pregnant with Katherine when you left Long Island?"

Linda considered how she might view Trudi differently now.

Like a suspect.

She was keeping a secret. Katherine believed she and Cassie had the same father. Why would she not tell her? Why keep that from her?

Trudi turned and walked over to Linda's Crown Vic and leaned against the front fender wall. She looked down at the ground, at the small stone by her foot and kicked it, following its path with her eyes.

"Trudi, in order for me to be of any service to you—"

Trudi interrupted: "I know, I know, I know. You need *everything* or you cannot find the truth. We've been down this road before, Linda. It's gotten us nowhere. My daughter is still missing. Presumed dead now, I would expect." Trudi stared down the road. Two small children were chasing each other, yelling, having a blast. "Is that what all of you think at this point?"

Linda placed her right hand on her Glock. Then let go. Trudi had deflected and changed the subject. Pivoted.

Why?

"We are looking at all angles, Trudi. We have to."

"All angles? That means you're still working on this? Huh. I know you spend maybe a few hours a week now on the case. You can't tell me different. My daughter has been forgotten."

They had come to a wall. Neither said anything more. Linda decided against bringing up the insurance policy. There was one more stop she had to make first. Something that needed checking before she came at Trudi with that information.

"How is Katherine? I saw her the other day at the gym."

"She told me. She's coping. Very consumed with a project she's been working on for a college-level course she wants to take next year. That type of focus for her is essential. She loses herself in all of that and forgets about the world. Which is a shit place, as you and I both know."

Linda didn't respond.

Trudi pushed herself off the fender wall, dropped her arms to her sides, and walked closer to Linda. They both looked at the missing person's flyer tacked to the telephone pole. Someone had put plastic wrap over it to protect it from the elements, though it was still tattered and torn.

Trudi ran her finger over Cassie's photo.

"Any leads or calls from these flyers, Linda?"

"Several, nothing of consequence."

"This flyer on the pole," Trudi said, still staring at her daughter's image, "it looks so American, doesn't it? How many times have we seen this on TV? In the movies? Now it's my life. It can't happen to you. That's what we think. Then it does and your entire life is on hold. Cassie is among the missing. That picture of her on that flyer—nothing more than a paper ghost now, one of several from this town. She's among the children of the night who never came home." Trudi turned to Linda, paused, and then stared at her. "Much like your friend, huh, Linda?"

It was the first time Sherri had come up between them.

Linda wanted off this subject. She took a step and put her arm around Trudi's shoulder. They both stared at the photo.

"Let's get you home," Linda said. It had started to drizzle. She looked up into the sky. "It's going to pour soon."

"Where are you?" Trudi whispered at the photo.

"Come on, Trudi," Linda said, pulling her along.

She said it again: "A mother doesn't ever give up on her child. I did. I have to live with that."

Linda walked Trudi back to the house. Promised to stop by soon. She understood Trudi's emotional state was raw and vulnerable. Maybe it was time to take a poke at getting some information.

"Listen, is there something you can tell me that might take this another way? I am running out of options, Trudi."

Trudi hugged herself tighter. She looked at Linda.

"Cassie has—shit, had, rather—a friend on Long Island named Winona. You should head out there and talk to her—they were tight. Cassie spent summers out there even after we moved. They remained close friends."

"Anything else?"

Trudi did not mention the letter.

Back at her Crown Vic fifteen minutes later, Linda turned, one hand on top of the open door, one hand on the roof of the vehicle, her right foot in the car. She had stopped herself before sitting down. Stared toward the Caldwell house. Rain soaked into her jacket and she could smell the fabric cleaner.

Secrets.

Driving away from the empty lot toward Trudi's house, Linda got Carmen on speakerphone.

"Yes, Lin?"

"Can you book me an early-morning ride to Long Island on the New London Ferry?"

"Long Island?" Carmen double-checked.

"Yes."

"Also, Carm, those woods behind the Caldwell house, the fenced-in property down that mountainside where the Germs hunt, have we thought about talking to the judge again about attaining a warrant?"

"The Pine Barren Woods?"

"Yeah."

"The state boys spoke to them on our behalf. They really want a warrant to go in there. It's standard Germ policy. The judge is a bit apprehensive unless you have something solid."

"I'll stop by there when I get a chance. Speak to Mr. Baylor about us going in, maybe he'll come around."

"Why, Lin, you onto something over there?"

"Just wanted to cross that off the list, is all."

"Gotcha."

Just then, Linda passed Trudi's house. Trudi was looking out the front picture window, her arms folded, waiting for Linda to drive by.

Their eyes met and stayed locked, until Linda was too far down the road to see the mother.

52.

THE NEXT MORNING, LINDA had a half-hour before she needed to drive to New London, ninety minutes south of town, and catch the ferry across the Sound to Long Island. Her plan there was to chat with Winona. Weeks back, Cam had phoned Winona after seeing those letters from her in Cassie's room. But she didn't seem to have much to share. Linda knew, however, that a detective showing up in person was more unsettling. People sometimes remembered things when the law was in their face.

Leaving her apartment, Linda drove to the bar. She had called the night before and told the new manager, Marc Josephson, to meet her there around eight A.M. She needed to look at something.

Linda had a hunch.

Marc showed Linda into the office Freddie Banks had once occupied. There was no one else inside the bar at this hour. It smelled of bleach from the night cleaning crew.

"I made some coffee, if you'd like a cup," Marc said.

"That's kind of you, sir, but no thanks."

"All of our records are here, in these filing cabinets," Marc explained. "You're welcome to them." He seemed like he wanted to say something more, but was waiting for Linda to extend the offer.

"Is there something else, Mr. Josephson?"

"There is, actually." He held up a finger, beckoning Linda to hold on just a second before digging in. "If I may speak frankly."

"Please do."

"That woman, that Trudi woman you're interested in—call me biased because of the lawsuit she's threatened to file against my company, but she is terrible. Just terrible, ma'am."

"What do you mean by that? And please, call me Linda." Linda was after the time cards from the night Cassie disappeared. That and any other paperwork explaining Trudi's time at work. She had copies of the stuff in the file back at the office, but there was nothing, Linda knew, like studying the actual evidence. They had missed a clue here. She was certain of it.

"What I mean is, she loses one daughter; yet, when she was here for those weeks after the incident, all she did was call and scuffle with her other daughter."

"'Scuffle,' sir?"

"Yes, I'm a bit of a writer on my own time, so I thought about this word carefully. *Scuffle* is accurate. Trudi would, and I in no way was eavesdropping, you have to understand, but if she chooses to use her cell phone on company time and I am nearby, around the corner, well…" He flipped his hands out. Rolled his eyes. "Anyway, I could tell the mother, Trudi, she was being firm with her daughter. Making sure the child understood something whenever they got on the phone."

"Tell me what you think she might have said? 'Something'? What does that mean?"

"Nothing *too* pejorative."

Linda made a mental note to look that word up later.

"Explain."

"Well, for example, Trudi would say, 'I told you to stay in the house, not talk to anyone, not to go anywhere, not to text anyone.' But she said it coldly, like the child had not only failed to listen, but actually disobeyed an order that would have grave ramifications if not followed."

"Not following the 'ramifications' part of your memory, Mr. Josephson."

"It's Marc, by the way, Linda. What I mean is, they had made some deal not to talk about a particular subject and there was a chance the child might have breached their oral contract in some way."

"Got it." Linda wanted to get into those cabinets without seeming annoyed or uninterested in what Marc had to say. She felt he was overreacting to a conversation that took place a month ago. So she looked at the time on her iPhone. "I need to make an appointment in, like, forty-five minutes, so I don't have much time here."

"Just this feeling I had."

"I understand. What I'll do is send an officer here and have her take a statement from you—sound good?"

"That would suffice."

Linda noticed a slight smile on the man's face. She'd made him feel as if what he had to say was being taken seriously. Which was what most people wanted, in the end. Linda then took a file out and sat down with it at Josephson's desk. She picked through several time cards. Got to Trudi's for the night in question. She had no idea what she was looking for.

"So you had this feeling about the way in which Trudi spoke to her daughter over the phone. That right?" Linda said, looking at the time cards, deciding to keep Marc talking. The man had gray hair, tinted with a coating of black, George Clooney, businessman-like. He wore a bow tie.

"Yes. I am never wrong. My external instinct for troublemakers is, bar none, the better of anyone I know."

"You mean *internal*, right?"

"No, no, no. Allow me to explain."

Marc Josephson then broke into a long diatribe about how great he was at reading people.

Linda stopped looking through the cards. As she finished, the detective looked up from her seat at Marc, and said: "Let me have it straight then. It's just the two of us here talking off the record. What is your general feeling of Ms. Caldwell?"

Marc rubbed his chin. "It's like this, Detective. Trudi is mean and belligerent to her child. Controlling and manipulative. I heard evidence of it several times before she quit."

"What is it that convinced you? Pretty bold claim there, Marc?"

"I heard Ms. Caldwell telling her daughter one day something about Cassandra being wrong about their father."

"That's good information, sir. I appreciate it. Do you think her tone had anything to do with Trudi being under a tremendous amount of stress based on her situation, though?" Linda picked up two time cards. Both Trudi's. She handed them to Marc. Then changed the subject: "Why the different colored ink on the time cards? Why not all the same type of ink?"

"Different clocks to punch in and out of. And I don't think this was nerves or stress, Detective." He straightened his tie, a tight knot the size of an acorn. "Employees can use the one time clock in front of the building. Or here, come with me." He turned and walked out the office door across the kitchen. Linda got up and followed. "This one." Marc Josephson pointed to one of those old-school time clocks that attaches to the wall at hip level. You stick the card underneath the time. Hit the red lever on the side. It made a popping noise.

"Can you get me a blank card?" Linda asked.

Josephson walked away and came back with a manila-colored card with printed columns along one side. Days of the week along the other. NAME/DATE was at the top.

Linda set it inside the clock and pushed the lever down, stamping the time of day on the card. 8:16 A.M. Black ink. The font was distinctive, something she had never seen before.

Linda then held it up to Trudi's card for the night her daughter went missing.

"These font styles don't match."

"She probably used the other clock."

"Show that to me, please."

They walked to the front of the restaurant, down a set of stairs, and wound up underneath the foyer entrance to the dining portion of the building. At the bottom of the stairs was another time clock. This one was more old-school, but the same general idea.

Linda punched the time: 8:22 A.M.

"Not the same," she said, holding them up.

"Isn't that strange," Marc said.

"Can I take these cards?"

Marc thought about it. He had an index finger on his pursed lips. After tapping several times, he dropped his hand and said, "Sure."

Just then, a kitchen worker came down the stairs and, after punching in, grabbed a box of bell peppers stored near the clock. He'd just arrived.

"Morning, Curtis," Marc said.

He nodded.

Linda followed Curtis up the stairs. She stood by the door. Her Crown Vic was parked just outside between two white lines. She stared at the car while thinking.

"I'll be in touch," Linda said to Josephson.

"I will be here, ma'am."

53.

THE RIDE FROM ROYAL Oaks to New London, the oldest seaport town in Connecticut, a place Linda had enjoyed visiting as a child with her family, was back country driving.

Ocean Beach, the touristy section of town, was one of those places Linda held close to her vest of childhood memories. Every time she visited her mother near the end, and Lucy was feeling nostalgic, the old woman took out a family photo album and pointed out how Linda loved the miniature golf course at Ocean Beach State Park. There was one photo that always teared Linda up for some reason: her, standing on the top of a whale's head, putter in hand, smiling for the camera. The photo spoke to all of that childhood innocence lost in the years after. Even Lucy, her own mother, had looked at Linda differently after Sherri went missing. She'd catch Lucy staring at her as she did homework or folded laundry. "What's wrong, Mom?"

"Nothing, honey," Lucy would say.

But Linda felt the look. Lucy was asking herself if she'd raised a child who could have done something bad to another child. And there was nothing that was ever going to change the feeling, Linda accepted. A mother was supposed to protect her child, at all costs, Linda understood. But once there was any type of surreptitious air thrust between them, that loyalty disappeared. And you could never get it back.

Parked in a line of vehicles waiting to drive onto the ferry taking them across the Sound to Long Island, Linda watched a seagull squawk and fly around the port, shitting white chalky liquid on everything.

She thought about Cam. *He comes out of the coma, I'm telling him*, Linda decided. She went through all that life-is-too-short nonsense and we-should-tell-people-how-we-feel rhetoric saved for these circumstances and fell into it. Not only did Cam deserve the chance to hear how she felt and react, but so did she. Happiness was for everyone, Linda knew. Even the little girl who'd grown up and spent her life searching for a friend she was never going to find.

She went over it: "*Cam, listen, I need to tell you that you mean more to me than…*" She stopped herself. That was not Linda Kane. It sounded so weak and impersonal.

Her iPhone was in the cup holder below the dash. As Linda lost herself in the bird's flight and thoughts about Cam, it buzzed, vibrating the plastic, startling her.

She picked it up.

All caps. A long text, too.

It was from Carmen.

Linda let loose a deep breath, found her glasses. Put them on.

Not halfway through reading, she tossed the phone on the seat to her right, turned on the vehicle, grabbed her blue light, reached out the open window, slapped it on the roof, hit her siren, and beckoned any cars near her to get the fuck out of the way.

Now.

Then she made an abrupt U-turn, screeching the tires on the concrete, blasting out of the line and back toward Royal Oaks.

54.

COUNTRY COPS DREAD THE start of hunting season. As soon as the first bell of the new season tolls, and hunters go out into the forest in search of the elusive buck, guess what? Reports trickle in of men and women tromping through the forests and running across all sorts of objects kept hidden by the dense foliage of summer. Stolen bicycles. Lost—and dead—dogs and cats. Household items people toss into the woods (dryers and washing machines and old microwave ovens) instead of bringing them to the junkyard. Ripped-out trees and shrubs. Old decking. Busted-up concrete.

And, yes, once in a while, a body.

That call from Carmen: A hunter had found Cassandra Caldwell.

She was not holed up in some bunker, scared to come home, living off the land, drugged out of her mind. Nor was she the victim of some random psychopath who'd decided to snatch her and hold her hostage in some crude, prefabricated cage, so he could do all those perverted sexual things parents can't help to think about when their kid goes missing.

Beyond that empty lot, down the street from the Caldwell house was the Pine Barren Woods, of which Linda had wanted to search. If you kept walking from the road into the back of the empty lot, through that cutout section of fence Linda had discovered last time she was out there, about ten feet ahead, was a steep drop—a mountainside running down a slope of about one hundred feet.

If you weren't careful and did not know the terrain, especially at night, you'd fall down this slope and surely hit your head on rocks and trees along the way, tumbling to certain death.

At the base of that mountain was one of the only places in town to hunt legally. If you were on good terms with the Germs and they allowed you, that is. Hundreds upon hundreds of acres of woods spread out from this space. There was one dirt access road in, gated at a farm entrance on the opposite end of the forest. The entire woods was home to a deer population that hunters from all over New England had heard stories about.

Just so happened that today was the first day of the new season. A hunter had entered the forest from the other side of town, four miles in the opposite direction of that empty lot and Trudi's neighborhood, and trekked all the way back to the mountain base in his truck along the dirt access road. He'd parked. With his dog, he started walking, rifle tucked underneath the crook of his right arm. "My dog here tracked a deer," he explained to the two blues who met him there after he'd called in. The scent had led his pooch to an area at the base of the mountainside, which that empty lot above overlooked.

"Looks like she might have fallen from the mountaintop," the hunter told the blues. He flipped his camouflage cap with the earflaps off, put it back on. He wore an orange vest, blue jeans. Rubber boots up to his hips. "Poor thing. Startled me. Kloter, my Lab here, he's the one who discovered her." The dog stood next to him, his tail wagging, his entire backside moving with it. The hunter rubbed the dog's head.

The first two blues on scene took the hunter's statement. Seemed legit. They both stood at Cassie's feet, looking down at her, up at the mountainside cliff.

"Maybe," one of them said. "Seems logical."

It did, indeed.

Perhaps Cassie had scooted underneath the cutout section of the fence in the dark and, not realizing where she was, tripped and fell off the cliff. Her face was bloodied and bruised, though hard to tell because of the decomposition. Any blood had now dried and turned black. Much of her skin was peeling off or had rotted. Leaves stuck to what was left of her jowls. Small branches and other debris were gummed up in her knotty, gnarled hair.

"I found that blanket over there on top of her," the hunter told the blues. He pointed to his left.

"Why'd you take it off?" one asked.

Shrugging, he said, "Wanted to make sure it was a person."

The two blues looked at each other.

"Fuck you think it was?" one asked.

The other blue put a hand on his partner, "That's not important, sir. Thank you for calling this in. We'll need a formal statement."

Cassie's skull appeared to be caved in from the back side, a large pushed-in region of the parietal bone (that section of the skull a Jewish yarmulke would cover) about the size of a grapefruit. The skin was gone there. The white bone of her skull kind of looked like a smashed-in hard-boiled egg. Her legs were straight; her arms folded over her stomach. She'd been here, the medical examiner would soon estimate, about six weeks—give or take a few days. Cassie's body was in bad shape, but there was no doubt in anyone's mind it was her.

"Nobody touches anything," the blue said as additional uniformed cops, CSUs, and Dr. Bernard Valentine M.E. arrived. "We need to wait for Linda."

They hustled the hunter out of the area and had him give a more complete statement to a female officer directing traffic at what became a staging area for the scene about fifty yards away.

The blues then did what television cops do: blocked off the entire area with yellow tape and instructed everyone not to touch anything, including the medical examiner and the CSU team. Another hour in the scope of how long the girl had been missing was not going to matter.

"Funny thing about the dead," Linda had always told first responders, "they won't get up and walk away."

Linda arrived and, ducking under the tape, walked out to the scene by herself. Everyone else stayed behind at the staging area. Linda had parked on the dirt road, about one hundred yards away from Cassie's body.

Within a few minutes of studying Cassie and the way her body was positioned, looking back up the mountainside behind where she had been found, then back down at the body, it didn't seem to Linda—although she wasn't prepared yet to rule it out—that the girl had fallen down the side of the mountain to her death.

Obviously, Linda told herself, Cassie knew the layout of that empty lot. She had to. Plus, the way her body was positioned, it didn't seem as though it could have fallen all that way down the mountainside and landed where it had, with her arms folded over her stomach, her legs straight as boards.

Man, did Linda miss Cam now.

Linda squatted on bended knees, latex gloves on, and studied Cassie's head. She got on her radio and asked for Archer; Officer Treat Archer. She'd seen him along the service road, acting as one of the blues there to secure and hold the scene.

"CSU and the medical examiner are getting antsy to get out there, Lin, over," a blue said back, after telling Linda he'd send Archer right out.

She keyed the button. "Well, they're going to have to wait."

It was that simple.

"Have Archer bring a large plastic evidence bag."

"Ten-four."

She'd found something.

Linda would note that Cassie's body was in a state of extreme decomposition—butyric fermentation. Basically, this was a body found between twenty and fifty days after death. The skin was various colors of brown, black and gray. The fatty portions and tissue of the body were, as the term implied, in the process of fermenting.

"What's up, Lin?" Archer said. Treat was a big guy. Not quite in the neighborhood of Cam, but a close second. A former collegiate basketball star for the UConn Huskies, he'd hurt his arm his senior year and missed out on being selected in the first round of the NBA draft. How life could change in an instant. One day, the kid was preparing to sign with the Los Angeles Lakers, buy a home in Hollywood, cars, women, the whole shebang. The next, he was applying for the Royal Oaks PD.

"Hey, Treat. You got that bag?"

"Here, here," he said, handing Linda a large Ziploc baggie with a white stripe of space to write the date, item number, and any notes. "What's going on? What have you got?"

"See that," Linda said, pointing about ten feet behind Cassie's bashed-in skull.

"Oh, shit. Yeah."

Linda photographed where it was with her iPhone, then picked it up and placed it into the baggie. It was a rock about the size of a shoe, pointed at one end. It had what seemed to be dried blood on the front of it, some hairs sticking to the blood.

"That's our murder weapon," Linda said.

"Hell yeah, it is."

She stepped back for a moment from the immediate scene and looked around. Then, up the mountain; there seemed to be someone up top. A shadow. Linda could not make out who it was. As soon as she pointed and asked Treat if there was a blue up there, the person backed away from the cliff.

"Get someone up there now and see who that is," she told Treat.

He reached over to his left shoulder, where the mic was clipped to his collar. "We have anyone up top, near that fence, over?"

"No, Treat. We were told to keep it low-profile up there—they didn't want the neighborhoods all riled up. The vic's family lives up there."

"Send Smitty and a few others up there to have a look around, over. Keep it discrete."

"You got it."

Linda was focused on the task at hand, tuned into the scene like a jeweler working a diamond under one of those glass magnifiers connected to his desk by a long steel arm. Now it was Cassie's turn to speak—a dead girl who was going to finally tell Linda what happened and by whose hand.

"Must have been pretty strong," Treat said, "to pick up that rock and bash in that girl's head. All I'm saying. Shit."

Linda glanced at Treat. Back down at Cassie's head. Her eyes were gone, a meal for the maggots. In fact, maggots had eaten most of any area where Cassie had bled. Her skin was peeling off like the paper on garlic. Any fatty tissue exposed had been consumed by bugs or, again, maggots.

Treat asked Linda, "You know about the blanket, right?"

"*Blanket*?" Linda said. She turned to stare at the cop.

Treat keyed his mic again. "Somebody bring that bag with the blanket down here, over." Treat filled her in. When the hunter found the body, there was a pink blanket, sort of like baby's first blanket, puffy and cotton-filled with tiny hearts and bonnets sewed into it, placed over the upper part of the girl's body.

"Continue, Treat?" Linda said.

"The hunter removed it. He wanted to see what was underneath."

People, God Almighty.

"I need to see that blanket now." Linda knew the blanket was significant. It personalized the murder.

Treat keyed his radio mic again: "Let's go with that blanket, get it out here now."

After Linda took a moment and pictured the killer placing the blanket over Cassie's body, she radioed in for the team to come out and get to work. As she walked back to her car, it hit the detective.

Trudi.

Katherine.

Shit.

She was going to have to break the horrible news that Cassie had been located down a steep mountainside, dead, the entire time.

Right in their backyard.

After a few hours, and a good look at the blanket, Linda had seen all she needed. The medical examiner was the next person she wanted to speak to when he was finished. Already on her mind was the fact that it appeared as though Cassie was not sexually assaulted. She had been found fully clothed. Of course, that psycho Rollins had sexually brutalized the other girl and put her pants back on, but that was an anomaly.

Still, there was something else about the scene that bothered Linda as she approached her vehicle. She turned, stared back into the woods. Cassie had worn trendy jeans, now ripped and torn apart by a fall or whatever struggle had ensued, and a flannel button-down collared shirt, with a crisscross pattern of gold and orange and yellow. But the fact remained that her shirt had been tucked in and straightened. It was as if her killer had made certain her attire was in the best possible shape it could be.

Linda put a hand on the car door handle. She looked at her reflection in the window.

That blanket.

<h1 style="text-align:center">55.</h1>

A FAMILY'S REACTION TO the untimely and shocking death—in this case a murder—of a loved one can vary, Linda Kane knew from experience. There was no set response to hearing a cop tell you your sister, daughter, mother, father, son, whoever, had been murdered and wasn't missing, after all, but was now lying on a slab of metal in the morgue, being dissected like a frog in biology class. Reactions ran the gamut: from complete denial to adult men and women being so consumed by grief, they were unable to speak. Then there was absolute stoicism—or that dreaded openmouthed look. Others were so taken aback by the news, they fainted or passed out.

Advice Linda had been given long ago by Patty Doyle was what she had routinely followed: "Expect the unexpected. But also gauge the reaction—it can be telling in respect to your investigation."

Trudi invited Linda in.

"I'm sorry about acting so weird the other day," Trudi said. She seemed restless and not herself. "I'm losing my mind here, Linda."

Great.

"Is Katherine home, Trudi?"

"That sounds serious."

There was no way for Trudi to know that a half-mile from where they stood inside her kitchen, down a cliff, into the woods at the bottom, a team of CSUs was going through a murder scene where her daughter's body had been found. Most every cop and first responder had gone in from the back side of the forest, through the farm's gated entrance. Not one cruiser or first responder had passed through Trudi's neighborhood.

Still, there was something in the air, and Trudi sensed it. "No… Katherine is at the library. Why?"

"There is no easy way for me," Linda began to say, but didn't even get the rest of her words out, when Trudi fell into a La-Z-Boy in the living room and cuddled herself into a fetal ball, hugging her knees to her chest.

"No…Linda. No, no, no," was all the mother said, not looking at the detective.

"We found her about four hours ago," Linda explained, looking up for a moment toward the ceiling. "I'm sorry. I'm so sorry, Trudi. I wanted this to turn out differently, as you know, but it did not, and I am so, *so* sorry for your loss."

Linda had taken photos of a section of Cassie's shirt on her iPhone, a bracelet the teen wore, a necklace, and her sneakers. If Trudi could identify her through those channels, she would not have to endure the horror of seeing her daughter in the state she was now in.

All Trudi did was shake her head and, with the knuckle of her right hand balled up in her mouth like an infant, nod in the affirmative over and over as Linda swiped through the images.

"I bought her that shirt at Kohl's just the week before she went missing. I…it…it was going to be something for us to begin a dialogue about again…My God, Linda. My baby."

Linda had wanted to see Katherine's reaction. Then again, a girl with Asperger's would have no reaction to tragedy, and Linda would be left guessing how the death was going to affect the poor child. Katherine was, Linda concluded, the other victim in all of this. Maybe the most important victim from it all. She was going to bear the brunt of her mother's anguish and pain until she had a chance to strike off on her own and leave the house behind.

There was a basket of folded laundry on the floor between them. Trudi had been folding clothes when Linda knocked. Such a common, casual domestic chore allowing us to think and ponder what's going on in our lives, now forever marred by the moment the cop walked in and told the mother her daughter had been murdered. Was it ever going to be possible for Trudi to fold laundry again and not think of Cassie dead in those woods behind the house?

"I need to be alone," Trudi said. She stood up suddenly. She soaked up the tears with the collar of her sweater. Then picked up the laundry basket.

"Let me take that," Linda said, grabbing the basket. "Where do you want it?"

"I can do it."

"I insist."

Trudi dropped her head, pointed down the long hallway.

Linda walked. Trudi followed.

As she passed an open door, Linda saw a desk. A computer. A couch. A sewing machine. Rolls of yarn. A magazine rack overflowing. Books all over the place. The room was a mess.

"In here?" Linda asked.

"No, that room is my daughter's." Trudi could barely get the words out. "Her 'messy room,' she calls it. She allows herself one space in the house to be 'un-neat.' That is it."

Linda saw an old-school typewriter sitting on the desk. It was a Royal or Underwood, she couldn't tell because she'd walked by so fast, feeling Trudi almost pushing her from behind. New England was famous for both of the factories, Royal and Underwood, and her father had taken an interest in the machines as a collector after retirement. It became his passion. Linda got involved so she could spend time with him. Seeing the typewriter brought her right back to her father's smiling face whenever he came across one of the machines as they were out digging through people's junk at tag sales and antique shops. She was fascinated by how simple objects in our lives dredged up certain moments.

Not all of them, of course, pleasant.

"Just put the laundry there by that door," Trudi instructed. She pointed to a room at the end of the hall.

Both were clogged up at the end of the narrow hallway. They turned and this time Trudi led the way back to the living room. As

Linda passed the open door again, she saw that it was a Royal. And she heard him: *"The Royals are for the noir detective writers, Lindy… classic, classic look, big keys, lots of noise when they strike the page."*

Certain Trudi could not see her, Linda smiled at the memory.

"How do you think Katherine is going to take this?" Linda asked when they returned to the living room. "Would you prefer I be here when you tell her, in case she has any questions I can answer in a nonthreatening-cop sort of way?"

"I'm going to have to get the school involved. The social worker. She'll know what to do. How to approach it."

"Right now, there's no media involved, but that will change in about, oh"—she peeked her head around the corner and looked at the rooster clock on the wall in the kitchen—"about an hour. I would get Katherine from the library and head to the school as soon as you can. You sure you don't want me to help with that? I can drive you."

Trudi coughed into the crook of her arm. Tears came. She bowed her head.

"Allow me, please, Linda. I need to do this."

Linda was at the door. "I told you I'd bring your daughter home." She upped the vigor in her voice for the next bit: "I'm telling you now, Trudi, as I stand here, I will bring her killer to justice. I give you my promise. This will be my entire focus from here out."

Trudi shook her head without looking at Linda. She had the back of her wrist over her mouth. The impression Linda took away at first was that Trudi Caldwell was going to collapse once she shut the door.

But then, stepping out onto the concrete porch steps, Linda paused, turned, and looked back at the house.

Something's off.

Linda walked to her car, stopping for a moment to look back at the Christmas wreath hanging in the center of Trudi's closed front door, bells and a red ribbon attached at six o'clock.

Sitting in her car, hesitating before turning the key in the ignition, a thought struck Linda Kane. Turning the key, staring at the windshield, it occurred to the detective that Trudi had never asked how, where, or what they knew about her daughter's murder.

56.

AT THE MEDICAL EXAMINER'S office, Linda Kane got the news she'd expected. Cassie had died of blunt-force trauma to the head. It was that one crack of her skull by that rock Linda had bagged at the scene.

"Homicide, certain of it," Dr. Valentine said.

"That one injury to the skull?"

"Yes."

"Drugs in her system? Alcohol?"

"In prelim tests, no. It'll take some time before the blood comes back, but I suspect nothing will be found."

"Could that injury have been from a fall?"

"There's no way she fell *before* death. She did fall, but all of those injuries—besides the one that killed her—took place postmortem."

This made Linda sit up straight.

A man and woman walked by the medical examiner's office, both wore head-to-toe turquoise-colored scrubs. The smell down here, Linda had always noted, was akin to that moment you opened the shed in spring and found a few dead raccoons inside. Atrocious and potent. Some of the older cops Linda knew said they'd gotten used to it after years on the job, but Linda couldn't fathom how one ever got comfortable with death on any level. If you did, there was something wrong with you.

The medical examiner pulled several X-rays up on his computer monitor and spun the screen around so Linda could see. They sat across from each other in comfortable leather chairs. A library of books—technical, boring stuff with gold lettering on the spines—lined the wall in back of the doctor. "Let me explain. You see those right there?" He pointed with a pen to several fractures—left femur, right anklebone, both forearms—and made a point to add, "Those took place *after* death. We don't see any blood secretion from the muscle tissue or the nerves themselves or the marrow at the time of the fractures. Means that blood was not flowing—or pumping, actually—when the injuries occurred. It's simple science, really."

Linda saw a picture of Cassie's death emerging, but she kept it to herself.

"So, wait a minute. You're saying that she was killed and *then* her bones were broken."

"*I'm* not," the doctor said, "but the scientific evidence we have is suggesting it one hundred percent."

If she ever needed Cam to bounce theories off of, boy, now was the time.

"Okay, so she's murdered by blunt-force trauma?"

"Yes. It's the only answer. This injury to her skull here"—he circled it with his pen—"would have killed her in about five minutes; seven, tops. She was knocked unconscious immediately by the blow, for sure. That point on the rock went deep into her brain. But death took some time. The brain swells, blood and brain fluid begin to mix together, the frontal lobe pushes back the cerebellum, as the right and left hemispheres begin to tighten. The brain basically suffocates itself as if in a vise. The heart and lungs fail. The computer telling them to function has, essentially, shut down."

Linda sat back in her chair. Horrible way to die. That kid suffered.

Son of a bitch.

A student came into the room carrying a sandwich he'd gotten from one of the chain sub shops nearby. There was one large bite missing from the top of it. He was chewing. An aroma of raw onions filled the room.

"We're busy here, Marvin," the medical examiner said. "Is there something I can help you with?"

"Several reporters… Excuse me." He finished chomping, swallowed. "Several reporters, Doctor, are calling. They all want to speak with you."

Linda took over the conversation: "He won't be speaking to any media about this case right now, son. Now go and enjoy that sandwich, please."

"Marvin, allow us some privacy here. Come on."

They waited until the boy was gone.

"Sorry about that, Detective Kane. Anyway, I was out at the scene, as you know," Dr. Valentine continued, lacing his fingers, putting his arms behind his head, sitting back in his chair, looking at Linda. "My best guess, Detective, is that she was killed up top of the mountainside and then, after death, dragged. We found scratch marks, best we could tell with the decomp on her back, all along the back side of her legs and buttocks, and her clothing was somewhat torn in those actions. We figure she was physically tossed down the side of the mountain." He sat up straight. Looked at his notes, the doctor flipped a page over and read for a moment. "It's the only plausible theory that makes sense. There's no way that her killer broke her bones any other way. You getting all of this?"

Linda went to the image of how Cassie had been found. It didn't add up.

"So then someone would have had to go down the mountainside and position her? You saw her? Do you agree?"

"I might."

"Because she *was* posed, somewhat. I'm not sure I would buy that she tumbled down the cliff and landed that way. And that blanket?"

"I'd heard about the blanket. So that's a fact as of now I'd have to wait on to see what results come back."

Linda knew he meant DNA. She said, "Far as we can tell, CSU is processing the blanket now, just to make sure it was over her at one time. But we have the witness, the hunter who found her, backing it up." She took a moment. Then: "You think she was surprised by the blow?"

"Absolutely," Valentine agreed, referring to the blanket. "She was no doubt positioned. I'll agree to that. Surprised? Um"—he tapped his pen against a corner on the desk and stared at it—"I would assume, yes, she was. A blow like that, the direction and angle of it, I'd even have to say she would have likely been sitting or kneeling down and definitely, yes, facing away from her attacker."

Linda got up. She seemed to be considering an alternative theory, but didn't mention it.

"When you finish with your report, e-mail it to me, okay?"

"Yeah, sure, Detective."

"And thanks for putting a rush on this."

"Ah, Detective, I never said I was…but, yup, no problem." Linda got up to leave. "There is something else," the doctor said. "Again, the blood work will solidify it for me."

"What's that?"

"Look, Detective, I believe your victim"—he looked down again at his notes—"Cassandra Caldwell…she was pregnant."

Linda put her hands on her hips. Her eyes popped open. She'd had a feeling there was a much larger secret here in the mix somewhere, and pregnancy with missing teens had to be considered. But she'd let go of that thought weeks back.

She looked down at the industrial carpeting under her feet.

"When you confirm it, please text me right away."

"I will."

LINDA DROVE STRAIGHT OUT to see Patty. She needed some advice and a bit of insight from her mentor about the crime scene. She had a thought, but Linda wanted to confirm it with Patty Doyle.

"He's in the back break room," a trooper told Linda when she walked into the building.

Patty sat at a round table, drinking a cup of coffee out of a white Styrofoam cup, and eating a cheese pastry. When he saw Linda, he stood, wiped his mouth. He knew she needed to talk about the case.

They found an empty office nearby.

Linda went right to the blanket.

Patty mentioned several cases throughout the years in which babies and young kids (five, eight, ten years old) were murdered by their mothers and, in each case, "I noticed a similar connection, Linda. Mothers who killed their children always placed some sort of personal item with the body. Blanket. Stuffed animal. Necklace."

Linda had felt the same, but had never investigated such a case, only read about them.

"I even saw a school drawing once," Patty added. He took a sip of his coffee. Tossed the empty cup in a trash bin nearby. "It's their way of personalizing the crime. It makes them feel closer to the child in death and takes away—as strange as this might sound—part of the guilt they feel from having murdered their own kid. They minimize their guilt. They believe the murder is justified for some reason."

"You only get this information," Linda said, as Patty chimed in and mimicked what she was about to say: "When you treat your suspect like a human being."

"Yes," Patty said. "I've questioned many of these mothers— telling them it's okay, I understood what they did and that they had no other choice."

"Trudi Caldwell? That's gotta be my focus now, Patty."

"You've learned from the best," Patty said, slapping his belly, smiling. "Go bring the mother of the missing girl in and get to it, Linda. Be her friend. Get her talking. It'll take hours, but she'll give it up."

Linda said thanks. Hugged Patty.

Walked to her car.

57.

LINDA KANE NEEDED TIME to process all of this new information. Where better than bedside, in Cam's room. A recent diagnosis by his doctors was somewhat inspiring in the sense that there had been no change in his status. In fact, all indications were that Cam was going to live. What that life would consist of was still up in the air, but his doctors were hopeful that Cam, because of his size and physical shape, might regain some function and be a candidate for rehab.

Linda sat and stared at a stiff body, still breathing through a tube, machines buzzing and beeping around her, and felt that Cam was never going to be right again. She saw her man sitting in a wheelchair, drooling all over himself, a vacant look on his face. People feeding him baby food, wiping his mouth. Changing his diaper.

Some fucking life that is.

Cam… She teared up. She wanted to tell him everything. About the case. About her life. About how she felt.

A bullet to the head? No doubt from a .357 Magnum! How many were walking the planet and able to articulate that story to friends and coworkers?

Zero.

As she changed her focus and thought about the case, it occurred to Linda that if Trudi had kept the insurance policy and Cassie's potential windfall from her, she had known about Cassie being pregnant and that was perhaps the basis for the falling-out between them. All the other stuff she'd mentioned—Freddie and Cabbage Night—were deflections.

But who was the unborn child's father? That person would have to be placed on the top of Linda's suspect list. If it was Vinnie, an older boy, or even some random dude Cassie met online, maybe he was getting rid of a problem by smashing Cassie over the head with a rock and then flipping her body off the side of a mountain.

Was this the reason why Cassie had broken up with Benjie, only she didn't tell him? Or, had she told Benjie and he killed her?

Linda stood, put one hand to her mouth, and paced. She felt an urgency. Time was on her side now, but her anxiety kicked up and she felt rushed, pressured to uncover the truth.

Freddie Banks? That argument. Had Cassie told Freddie she was pregnant? Or were the argument and the pregnancy separate issues?

She heard a knock on the glass door behind her.

It was Treat.

Linda waved him in.

"Ma'am," he said, hat in his hands. Treat came across passive and stiff. This room of Cam's had turned into sacred ground. Cops walked in and acted different than they would outside the doors, as if Cam was watching, listening. Everyone was on his or her best behavior when inside the room. Linda thought it particularly strange.

"Treat, enough with the 'ma'am' thing, okay? Linda is fine. What's up?"

"Yes, course. Sorry. You got a minute?"

"Yeah, yeah, shoot. *What* do you have?"

Treat walked over. He had a piece of paper in his hand. He handed it to Linda, then stood by Cam for a moment, as if paying his respects at a wake.

Linda read.

"So the blanket was definitely on top of Cassie at some point, CSU is ready to stand behind that with science?"

Treat nodded.

"But we knew that," Linda said.

"Keep reading." Treat crossed himself and then stepped back into Linda's space. "The end of the report." He pointed. "Right there."

Unknown Female DNA.

That was all Linda had to see. They'd uncovered another donor on the blanket. A female.

Patty. Guy knew his shit.

"We have to get Trudi in and talk to her," Linda told Treat. "I don't care what type of warrant you need to dredge up. I need her in the box."

"The judge will be more open-minded now, since we have a body."

"Right."

"You want us to pick her up?"

"No, no." Linda tapped her lips with an index finger, her other hand inside her pocket. She stared at the floor. "Let me stop by and feel her out, see what's going on over there. But I want to wait until tomorrow. Give her the night with Katherine and the weight of what's happening. Have a blue watch the house. Do not let her out of your sight, understand me?" Things seemed to be falling into place for Linda, making more sense now. "Those time cards—that different font—I gave you, Treat, have you found anything?"

"Not yet. Working on that."

"Trudi had left work and fudged her time cards to make it look like she was at the job all night, that's the assumption we're working under."

"I got it. But none of the video—I went back and watched it all, like you asked—shows her leaving or coming back that night." Treat was reading from notes on his iPhone.

"There's a way out of the restaurant without being seen by the cameras. Cam figured that one out. Look, if she makes a move, I want to know. Wake me up, even if it's the middle of the night."

"Got it."

Treat held his phone and pointed it toward Linda. "Text," he said. "Coming in as we speak. My contact in CSU." He read the text. Then addressed Linda: "Apparently, they put a rush on that unknown DNA and it came back. Remember, we have Trudi's DNA—she gave it up. They've sent it all out for more thorough testing, but prelim results show she is likely the unknown donor on the blanket. Not one hundred percent, but the science says Trudi cannot be excluded at this point."

Linda walked over to Cam and stared down at him. It felt good to have some sort of result. An answer. She wished she could share it with him.

Leaving the hospital, Linda drove to the park. Yes, that park. The one with the pool. The baseball fields. The jungle gym and monkey bars. The tennis court. The stone monument up at the top of the meadow where the town fireworks were held, overlooking all the fields and the community pool. The same place where she and Sherri had been on that day.

The day her life changed.

The day Linda Kane became the other girl.

She parked in a spot facing the pool. There were two other cars in the lot. A kid and his girl fooling around, smoking cigarettes, listening to music. And a cable-TV dude in a van, doing some paperwork, drinking a coffee, eating a pastry. The pool was, of course, closed, covered with a dark green tarp; wet leaves spread out everywhere; puddles of water collected in swirls, weighing the thing down in sections. All the patio chairs and tables had been put away for the winter months. The oversized lifeguard chair, painted fluorescent orange, still stood at one end of the pool. The ball fields around the pool were barren, the puffy white base bags stored in the maintenance shed. The grass all over the park was a straw color, a result of the first frost.

Linda needed to clear her mind of this Cassie-Trudi thing. She needed some distance from that. She knew that within an empty space new answers came. She would stop here from time to time and try to see that day again. What she might have missed? The background noise of the afternoon, she knew, was where the truth to Sherri's disappearance would be eventually found.

IT WAS A BUSY day. Summer. Kids and lifeguards and parents and townies all walking around enjoying the hot weather. There was a guy selling lemon ice in flimsy wax paper cups. He drove a tricycle with a large cooler on the back, a small door that looked like the holding tanks for bodies along the wall inside the morgue. Linda saw ground crews. Even several teachers from Linda and Sherri's school were there. It was July 23rd. The warmth, Linda recalled, rising up from the hot tar in waves. She remembered the breeze. Sultry, hot air; soft, like summer should be. Walking around with her best friend, it felt as if the world was theirs. Everything about that afternoon was perfect.

Until it wasn't.

Linda and Sherri wore flip-flops and bikini bathing suits. They had been swimming. After getting out of the water, they took a walk up to the monument and sat, talking about boys and how they wanted to maybe start to take a dance class together. "Tap," Linda said.

"Jazz," Sherri said.

When they were finished chatting, agreeing on taking both classes, Sherri told Linda she wanted to go swimming again. They were both sweaty and hot.

"But our ride is coming," Linda had said.

"We have another forty-five minutes until my dad comes," Sherri said, and jumped up. She grabbed Linda by the hand. Started toward the pool, skipping down the hill, singing some silly song.

As they passed the baseball field, several boys from class were kicking a soccer ball around. They waved. Linda and Sherri, as they always did, held hands, giggled, and continued toward the pool, ignoring the boys.

There was a crowd gathered over by the pool house and it seemed something was going on that neither could quite see.

"Let's check it out," Sherri said.

"No. Let's not, Sherri. I want to go for a quick swim."

LINDA HEARD A CAR beep and, on instinct, looked that way, stepping out of the memory for a brief beat. She'd been over this a hundred times. Nothing ever that much different came from reliving it.

BACK INSIDE THE MOMENT, it was this part of the afternoon that always went a bit fuzzy. The large crowd talking over one another. Maybe forty kids of all ages, even adults all bunched up together in a large circle. There was a fight. Two boys. High schoolers. They were circling each other like boxers, fists in front of themselves. Some in the crowd were egging them on to throw the first punch. Linda and Sherri were about twenty feet behind the crowd, tiptoeing, trying to see over everyone. Sherri pulled Linda closer toward the fight, trying to maneuver them in between the swelling crowd.

"Let's watch, Lindy."

"Let's not, Sherri."

"Please?"

And as they got mixed into the crowd, it was here that Linda heard her name. Someone had called out to her from behind, two times in quick succession.

"Linda."

She looked.

"Linda."

Linda recognized the voice, but then didn't. She immediately turned away from Sherri. And that was when her and her best friend's hands unclasped.

As she went back to the moment, it felt as if it had all happened in flashes. When she felt Sherri's hand slip away, Linda turned back around to look for her. She expected Sherri to be right there, mixing in with the crowd, heading toward the first ring of people around the fight.

But Sherri was gone. Nowhere in sight. Linda could not see her.

Everything sped up. All the faces. The different people. The yelling. It turned chaotic.

"Sherri?"

This was the moment when Linda Kane became the girl left behind.

At first, Linda thought Sherri had been swallowed up by the swelling crowd, gotten lost among them all, and when everyone dispersed, her friend would pop her head out. But as the fight cleared and the adults broke everyone apart, and Sherri's father showed up about fifteen minutes later to pick them up, Linda had still not found her best friend.

"What do you mean, *gone*?" Sherri's father had said. "That's impossible."

Then the police arrived. Sherri's dad had rushed home to see if Sherri's mother had come by and picked her up, or Sherri had gotten a ride home some other way. But he soon came back and said no. The father was frantic. In a panic. Then the dogs were brought in. New crowds gathered. Grid searches around town were set up, front-page reports in the local newspapers reported it all. Days, weeks, months, years, passed.

No sign of Sherri.

As Linda sat, staring at the pool all these years later, for the first time since it happened, she felt she knew who had called out to her. She could see an image of the person. Clear as if she was watching a film play out in front of her.

Had she figured it out finally?

Finally.

After all these years.

Linda started her car.

She took off quickly from the parking lot, drove to her apartment.

58.

LINDA KANE WANTED TO not only speak with a few of Cassie's friends on Long Island, but she wanted clear-cut forensic and DNA results. She spent most of the next day on Long Island, talking to Winona, Cassie's best friend from childhood, where she had been headed the moment Carmen called and she took off from the ferry line.

While she was in New York, the DNA had come in and backed up all her earlier assumptions. The DNA on the blanket was an almost perfect match to Trudi's profile. At some point, Trudi Caldwell had touched the blanket that had covered her daughter's dead body.

"Don't bring her in," was all Linda had said over the phone to Treat. "I'll be back later today. I'll take care of it. But continue to watch her."

Cassie's best friend on Long Island provided an interview indicating that she believed she knew who the father of Cassie's child was.

"I know that she was about to tell her mother," Winona explained. Winona was unlike what Linda had expected. She was a straight-laced kid, excellent grades, a volunteer in town at the homeless shelter, a mentor to the younger girls at her church.

"Did she?"

"I'm not sure." Winona was crying. Linda had explained that

the pregnancy scare was true, Cassie's body had been found. The news of both deaths devastated the child.

"She's certain the father was Benjie?"

"He was the only boy she'd ever had sex with."

"Is there anything else you two discussed that might help us, Winona? I know this is hard under these circumstances, but it's really important."

"She talked about having a major issue at home. Something that was growing out of her control and she couldn't handle it anymore. The pressure was driving her crazy. I assumed she meant with her mother. Ms. Caldwell was never home. Cassie hated that. Cassie became the mother to Katherine, and it was very difficult, the older Katherine got."

Linda handed her a tissue. Put her hand on Winona's shoulder. Squeezed. "I'm so sorry. I know this is awful. But you're doing fine here and really helping."

There was not going to be any sort of eleventh-hour revelation from Winona, Linda guessed. It was all good context. Solid information. It felt as though a narrative was developing. She could shine it all up a little on an arrest warrant with Trudi's name at the top. But she'd hoped for some sort of final nail. Even the DNA was no smoking gun. There had to be something she missed.

Winona's mother stood behind her daughter, rubbing gentle circles on her back. Looking at Linda, she said, "Is that going to be it, Detective? This is terrible news for my daughter to hear."

Linda took the hint.

"Winona," Linda said, now she was on bended knee as Winona sat on a couch in front of her. They held hands. "If you think of anything else, your mother has my personal cell number. Call me anytime. And listen, I am going to find the person who killed your friend. Okay?"

Winona nodded her head, wiped her nose with a crumpled tissue.

Linda had once read somewhere that "murder retains in real life its primitive power to shock." She believed this. Violence, in any form, was a reaction. It generally, Linda knew, was rooted in some form of failure.

As a mother, Trudi had said numerous times, she had failed her daughter.

Had Linda also failed Cassie?

HOURS AFTER INTERVIEWING WINONA, Linda pulled into Trudi's driveway and spied Trudi out in back of her house. Trudi did not see Linda right away. It was late afternoon, almost evening. The sky was dark, a cloudy week that persisted, with the chance of rain every day, adding yet another layer of gloom to the discovery of Cassie's body. Trudi wore a blue sweater, black sweatpants. She was putting a bag of garbage in the bin.

Linda walked up and startled her.

"Oh, hey, Linda. It's you."

Trudi Caldwell's hands were shaking, Linda noticed. She looked like she had not slept one wink since hearing the news of her daughter's murder.

"You have a few minutes to chat, Trudi?"

"I suppose. Haven't heard from you in a day or so. Any progress yet in finding my daughter's killer?" They walked toward the back door into Trudi's house. Trudi stopped just before the steps and turned to Linda. "When will you release my daughter's body so we can bury her?"

"We're looking at everything as a whole, and things are coming together, Trudi. Just not comfortable right now sharing what we're working on. In due time. I'm sorry. I know you and Katherine are wondering, and I need to thank you both for your patience." Linda paused, looked toward the left of the door. There was a black garbage bag of what appeared to be clothes sitting in the flower bed. "Cassie's body will be released, I'm told, in two days."

Trudi put her hand on the door and held it open for Linda to go in first.

Linda said thanks, walked up the three stairs. She stepped in through the back part of the house, which led into the rec room, up four flights of stairs and into the kitchen. By the front door, Linda passed that section in every house where the shoes and jackets collect.

They stood in the kitchen, both leaning against the countertop, facing each other. A familiar setting. A familiar scene. Now with an unfamiliar tone.

"You want some tea?" Trudi asked, turning on the pot. She ripped open a tea bag and placed it in a mug.

"No, thank you. Listen, I need to ask you a few questions and they might feel a bit harsh under these circumstances, yet I'm obligated to ask, okay? This is all standard-procedure business I have to get out of the way. I am actively involved in a murder investigation now, as you know—it's no longer a missing person. So some things have changed on our end."

"Oh."

"Where's Katherine, by the way?"

Trudi looked at the clock. "Probably on her way home from the library about now. That's where my daughter goes every single day after school. God bless her. I think sometimes her disability is a gift. It allows her to focus on life instead of grief."

"Did you know your daughter was pregnant?" Linda had decided to just come out with it.

Trudi dropped her head in her hands.

"I had a feeling. I could never be certain, you know. But a mother knows. I found a few letters. One of them alluded to it."

"Setting aside the fact that you did not share any of this with me, would you have any idea who the father was?"

"No. I suspect, though, it is, or was, that Benjie kid she was dating. I've never met him. Katherine admitted she'd caught them once or twice in Cassie's room…together."

Another little fact left unspoken. Jesus, woman.

The conversation wasn't going as Linda had envisioned: coarse and accusatory on Trudi's part. Why wasn't Trudi jumping on her?

Trudi walked toward the living room and Linda followed. The two ladies had been here before: one following the other, asking questions; secrets then rising to the surface.

"I'm going to have to ask you to come into the station, Trudi. I have an officer down the block. She's going to wait for Katherine and bring her in, once she's back. Do you understand what I'm asking here? Is all of this okay with you?"

Trudi sipped her tea. She dunked and re-dunked the tea bag,

trying to darken the liquid. Then, calmly, looking up at Linda, she said: "You think I killed my daughter? That what you're saying, Linda? That why you came here today?"

"Right now, Trudi, I just need you to understand that we have some questions we have to answer and we generally wouldn't do that—in the context we're speaking of—in a suspect's living room."

It was by design Linda dropped that word into the conversation.

Trudi had been sitting. She stood and stepped into Linda's personal space, into her face.

"Suspect? You saying I killed my daughter, Linda?"

"Trudi, compose yourself and back off, please." Linda could feel the mother's anger. There was an energy around Trudi that Linda had not experienced.

"What about Freddie? Freddie killed my daughter, Linda. What, is he off-limits now because of the race card? Because your cop killed him?"

"If you push someone too far into rage, they can feel murderous, yet not act on it," Linda said. "I'm certain that was Freddie Banks. Yet, sometimes they do act on it. And that is the person I am after right now, Trudi."

Trudi turned and started to cry. She sat down, bowed her head in her hands; her shoulders bounced up and down. When she finished, she stood again, and looked into Linda's eyes. "I fucked up, Linda. I really screwed up here. I know that. I am reminded of it every single day. But you're wrong. You're fucking wrong about me." She took a breath. "How *dare* you?"

"I need you to come with me, Trudi. I'm sorry. Don't make this difficult. It's not about me."

Linda walked Trudi out of the house. She did not handcuff the mother. She helped Trudi—"Watch your head"—get comfortable in the backseat of her Crown Vic and drove to the Royal Oaks PD.

59.

BY THE TIME LINDA pulled into the precinct parking lot, with Treat Archer waiting by the back door into the booking area, the clouds had given way to a bright half-moon. The air was sharp and biting.

Linda escorted Trudi from the car in through the back door, where the ten cells Royal Oaks PD had in the bowels of the building were lined along both sides of the corridor. It smelled of urine and cleaning fluids. Four of the cells held perps: two dopers, a shoplifter, a teenager who'd been starting fires. Spike-haired Scottie Mathers— spiked hair no longer after not having access to hair gel—was in the county lockup now after pleading out his case to a year.

Trudi hunched over and stared at the floor as they walked past the cells toward the fingerprinting and mugshot station.

After reading Trudi her rights, Linda excused herself and walked upstairs.

"The warrant," she told the cop processing Trudi, "should be filed already." Treat had completed it while Linda was on Long Island. The judge had signed off because of the DNA on the blanket.

Upstairs, Linda told Carmen she wanted Trudi put in the box after processing. "I don't want her in a cell."

Linda collected herself. Freshened up. Had a cup of coffee and a Reese's from the vending machine.

"You want me to go pick you up some solid food or something?"

Treat asked, sneaking up on Linda in the kitchen.

"No thanks. Some Tylenol would be great, though." Linda rubbed her temples. "I have this nagging headache."

"Lin, listen, Katherine hasn't come home yet."

"Check the library."

"We did."

"And?" Linda sat down at a round table. She looked up at Treat as he spoke.

"Yeah, well, they didn't know who we were talking about."

"What do you mean?"

Two blues, discussing a basketball game, walked in and stared at the vending machine.

"We showed them a photo of Katherine. They said she was not a familiar kid they'd seen before hanging around the library."

"The high school have a volleyball game going on?" Linda realized after she'd said it that she should know herself, with her daughter being on the team.

Treat Googled it.

"Matter of fact, yeah. Varsity."

"That's where you'll find Katherine."

"I'll get someone over there now. You all right, Lin? You don't look so good."

"Just tired. Beaten down. I'm okay. Just need a break, some caffeine and sugar."

Before stepping into the box, Linda stared at Trudi, who sat with her head bowed, her arms folded on her lap. She appeared overwhelmed. Maybe ready, Linda felt, to give it up and end this.

"You want some water, Trudi?" Linda asked as she walked in, closing the door behind her.

Trudi shook her head no, without looking up.

Linda sat. Put the file in front of her. Cup of coffee next to it.

"Trudi, why would you lie about Vinnie being racist? Let's start there. All the evidence we find, he's no bigot—"

"I want a lawyer," Trudi said, lifting her head, not allowing Linda to finish. The detective had not heard this tone from the mother before.

"You sure about that?"

"Linda, listen to me. I want to speak with a lawyer. I'm done talking to you."

As Linda walked out, Trudi stopped her. "Wait."

"Yes?"

"Katherine? Did your officer meet my daughter? Is she here, too? Where is my daughter?"

"I'm told that situation is under control, Trudi. I cannot let you see her, though."

Trudi turned. Looked down at the table.

Linda left the box and sat at her desk. Trudi had kept so much from her.

As Linda went to call Carmen so she could get Trudi that attorney, a thought struck the detective. Linda got up. Walked back toward the box.

A blue was just then escorting Trudi down the hallway. They were going to put her in a room downstairs, not a cell, until they could find a public defender. They'd use the kid-glove treatment as a bargaining chip with the lawyer.

"Wait up," Linda yelled.

Trudi and the blue turned around.

"Answer me one question, Trudi?"

Trudi shrugged. Arched a brow.

"Those shoes, along the edge of your stairs, where you hang jackets, are they yours?"

The question startled Trudi. She turned and walked away.

Linda ran down the hallway in the opposite direction. She found Treat.

"You get that search warrant approved, too?"

"Yeah, we are going in tomorrow."

"Meet me at the house with everyone as soon as you can."

"Hey, Lin. Katherine wasn't at the game."

But Linda knew that already. She ran outside, got into her Crown Vic, and drove back to Trudi's.

She felt a chill.

Slapping on latex gloves, Linda walked into the house through the back, using a key Trudi had once told her she kept underneath the stone by the door for the kids.

She ran up the stairs and stopped at the shoes. Picking up a pair of boots, Linda noticed the size.

Katherine's.

She studied the mud. She'd seen it before. In only one place in town.

As Linda left the house, she spied Royal Oaks troops burning up the block, preparing to dig in and search the Caldwell home.

Linda parked down the street by the empty lot. She called Treat and told him where she was. They'd see her vehicle. She didn't want anyone coming down unless she called.

It was pitch dark. Linda had her city-issued flashlight in hand as she made her way through the lot toward the cutout section of fence in the back.

Linda crawled through the kid-sized cutout, shone her light to her right.

Nothing.

Then to her left.

There it was: that same mud. It was runoff from a company drilling a water well on the property—the same sediment, a mixture of ground up gray stone and red rock pulverized from the drill and forced out of the well—that was on Katherine's shoes back at the house.

Farther down the trail, Linda saw a faint light. She started toward it. But as she hurried, Linda lost her footing and slipped, *holy shit*…along the edge of the mountainside.

On her butt, a one-hundred-foot drop in front of her, Linda Kane weighed her options. One wrong move and she was going for a ride.

She grabbed a branch, hoping like hell it held, and pulled herself back up.

The branch cracked.

She slipped.

Fell about five feet down the cliff, stopping herself by digging a foot into the mountainside. Rocks and pebbles and debris falling in silence down the cliff.

Carefully, Linda pushed her way back up the cliff, using bushes for leverage to hoist herself over the top.

She was on flat ground again.

Damn close.

Brushing herself off, Linda followed the light.

As she approached Katherine, who was sitting cross-legged, staring at that house project in her lap, not once looking up to see who was coming toward her, a small lantern illuminated the area around the child so she could see.

Linda stopped in front of Katherine. Pointed the flashlight on her face.

"Hey, Katherine, what are you doing out here?"

"This is the only place I can make sense of this."

"You come here every day after school?"

The girl nodded yes.

"So you don't go to the library?"

"My mother does not check. I only tell her that."

Linda scooched down on bended knee. She and Katherine were at eye level now.

"Katherine, hey, I need you to focus on me here. Put that down."

Katherine looked up. "But this is our house—mine and Cassie's. This is where we were going to live. Until she ruined everything."

Linda stared at the drawing of the house Katherine had been working on.

"It's all over, Katherine," Linda said. "I know. I know about it. You want to tell me what happened? Can you explain to me what happened out here? Do you understand what I am asking of you?"

Katherine had a look of confusion. Not that she didn't understand. But more of how long it had taken Linda to put it all together. The shoes, for Linda, became the latch locking into place, the key turning, the door opening. From there, it was easy to see that Katherine had been the one to wait for Cassie that night in the empty lot. Get her down by the mountainside, have her sit down, then walk up from behind and smash her sister in the back of the head with a pointed rock she'd chosen in the light of day from the field. Linda could picture Katherine, her meticulous mind working hard, stripping that jacket from her sister, putting it in a bag, tying the bag, and walking down to the lake after school, tossing it over the edge. Katherine was a puzzle solver. Her mind worked kinetically. She saw only the gears when she looked at a bike. The inside guts of a watch spinning and keeping time. Placing that blanket over her sister was Katherine's way of saying she was sorry, but she did what needed to be done. Another line connected to a beam in the structure she had been designing.

"She was going to ruin everything," Katherine said. Her voice sounded no different than when she described her work. "She always did. She always took all of the attention. The baby destroyed our plans. Did you know that she was not my full sister? Did you know that they kept that from me? I had to read about it in Cassie's letters."

Linda dropped her head.

"Katherine, I'm going to have to ask you to come with me, okay? Do you understand what I am telling you?"

"Do you know that the money Cassie was going to get, she told me she was going to share it with the baby! She said there would be no house for us. We made plans for our own house. That money was for our house."

Katherine held up the drawing.

Linda began to say something.

The child started crying. Her body shook. She screamed. It came from a deep place, Linda knew. Where the rage lived, all that pent-up anger fueling such a malicious, wicked act lived—though Linda realized in that moment the child, herself, was not evil.

"Please, Katherine, please try to calm yourself if you can," Linda said. She had no other words.

Katherine curled into a fetal ball, fell to her side, and trembled. She was mumbling words Linda could not interpret.

Linda called Treat and explained.

"On our way," he said.

Then Linda reached down and held the child. Held her close. Told her it was going to be okay. She kissed her on the top of her head. Brushed her hair back, away from her eyes.

"Everything will be fine, Katherine," Linda kept repeating. "It's over now. *Shh*…quiet now…it's going to be okay. I promise you."

60.

ON HER WAY TO his house, Linda took a call.

"Nurse Comstock here."

Linda Kane pulled over.

It was about Cam.

"Yes, what is it?" Linda's heart raced. Her pulse throbbed in her ears. A car, which had been following close behind, veered out of the way and beeped as it went by. Linda gave him a fuck-off stare and continued listening.

"I think you better come here. His family has gathered. They're discussing the situation. Decisions are being made."

Linda had worried all along that they'd pull the plug, for lack of a better way to consider it. Allow destiny to decide on the remainder of Cam's life. She'd once heard them talking about Cam not wanting to ever be a vegetable in a bed, sucking up taxpayer dollars, deteriorating like some corpse with a manufactured pulse. Cam had integrity, his sister had told Linda one day, in tears, and he would never want to end up like this.

Linda stayed away from that conversation. She'd live with whatever the family decided. Understand and learn to accept it. Still, she had always told the nurse she wanted a moment to say good-bye. This call was shocking because a little voice inside her head had convinced Linda that Cam was coming back around, that he could hear her when she said hello and good-bye to him. How she felt she could, after all, love him. She'd even seen his hand move one day. The doctor said it could "be nerves or the brain firing up," but who knew?

Linda ran from her car to Cam's room.

There were ten people, it seemed, hovered around his bed. She could not see Cam.

Too fucking late.

Rushing up, shoving two white coats out of the way, Linda was stunned by what she saw next.

Cam's eyes were open. He was staring at everyone. He couldn't talk, but he was blinking his eyes. His lips were parched. His skin pale.

Linda teared up. Grabbed his hand.

Cam lightly squeezed back.

Life had a way of balancing itself out, Linda thought in the hours that passed. Doctors explained how the road ahead was long, but Cam was probably going to come back.

He'd made it.

As she left the hospital, Linda knew Trudi and Katherine would make it, too—in their own ways. Last she heard, the DA was going to charge Katherine as a juvenile, which would probably get her around fifteen years. Trudi had broken down in front of Linda when she was told, explaining how she would support her daughter all the way through the process. That it was her fault for not getting Katherine the help she deserved. "I played a direct role in Cassandra's murder, Linda," Trudi had said. "It's as if I was there, too."

Linda never bothered to ask Trudi if she had known Katherine committed the murder all along and failed to tell them. She decided that the woman had been through enough already and she was going to allow Katherine and Trudi to disappear into the system.

61.

IT WAS A TASK she needed to complete within her own time frame. Linda had told herself that once the Cassie situation was resolved, she'd face it. She'd been on her way to his house when the nurse called about Cam. But now, she was back on track. Finish this part of her life. Pull the white sheet off the ghost who'd been following her around for thirty years, expose him, and be done with it all, for good.

It had been seeing Tiffany Barnes again, hearing about the sister, the father with his sights on the little girl, setting it all in motion for Linda. It'd taken some time to mature in her mind, but it was the only solution that made sense.

Leaving the hospital, Linda pulled up to his house, parked on the road by the curb. As she stepped out of the car by the pathway leading up to the front door, there was a stumble, some vertigo, blurred vision. A few seconds later, Linda got her bearings back and felt okay.

The headaches. Feeling strange. Now this.

Gotta get that checked out.

She took a look at the yard where she'd spent so many years of her childhood playing. As she walked toward the front door, she stopped a moment, took it all in. How many years had it been since that blowup with Sherri's father? Already eight.

How time flies.

She hadn't been back here since.

This house—the secrets it held.

Walking by the old light post, Linda stopped, grabbed hold of it. Staring at the door, she knew the inside of this house as well as her own childhood home. Through the foyer, past the stairs, was that chipped wooden door leading down into the basement. On the far wall after descending the fourteen stairs, etched on a wooden post beam holding the weight of the house, were her and Sherri's heights from third to fifth grade notched in the wood. They'd done it on the same day every year: Halloween, just before they went out in their plastic masks with the rubber band that pulled and pinched your hair, carrying the pillowcases for treat bags. The fire-retardant costumes of whatever comic book or Disney character they'd fallen in love with that year. *"Our tradition,"* Linda could hear Sherri say. *"Step right up… Man, Linny, you grew a whole inch taller than me this past year."*

Linda approached the door. She hesitated. Then knocked. Turning around, looking out into the yard, she saw herself and Sherri running in circles, chuckling and out of breath. They were chasing each other, Sherri holding a long red streamer, its tail end fluttering in the wind like a radio wave. They both had lollipops in their mouths.

Cherry for Sherri.

Sherri's mother opening the door and yelling: *"Don't you be running with those pops in your mouths. If you fall, you'll choke."*

Her back to the door, Linda heard it open.

She spun around.

"Yes…yes," the old man said. "What is it?"

Sherri's family had never left town. They'd lived in the same ranch for sixty years. Her father, Jack, was frail and weak now. He'd had two bypasses. Sherri's mother had died fifteen years after Sherri went missing. The longest suicide, Linda had maintained, on record. After Sherri disappeared, the woman picked up the bottle and never put it down.

Sherri's father, Jack, stood at the door behind the screen. He had one of those clear oxygen tubes snaked over both ears and below his nostrils. In back of him was what looked to be a scuba tank on wheels, which the tube was connected to. He wore a dark green sweater, misbuttoned over a white shirt stained with what looked to be phlegm or puke, dark blue pajama bottoms with the New England Patriots football logo stamped all over. Moccasin-type, with the fur inside, slippers. The white stubble indicated he hadn't shaved in what was likely days. His long nose hairs, black and gray, curled up and over his nostrils.

"Don't slam the door. This is more of an official visit," Linda said when she realized he'd recognized her. She opened the storm door and put her foot in the doorway to make sure he heard what she needed to say.

"What are you talking about? I told you *never* to come around here." The resentment the man had on his face was intense. But the answer was in his eyes, Linda thought: guilt.

Jack started coughing.

"You called my name," Linda said. She stared at him. "You showed up early to pick Sherri and me up. When we were all looking for her, you left and came back. You said you wanted to go home and check to see if she had gone back, or someone else brought her home."

Sherri's father stared at the detective. She could hear him struggle for breath through the tube. His eyes were yellow, a thick, gelled film of cataracts.

"I know," Linda said, pointing a finger in his face. "I know what you did, Jack."

ABOUT THE AUTHOR

True-crime analyst, creator/executive producer and former host of Investigation Discovery's *DARK MINDS* (2011–2014), M. William Phelps is the *New York Times* best-selling author of 42 nonfiction books and winner of the Excellence in (Investigative) Journalism Award from the Society of Professional Journalists. ***THE GIRL LEFT BEHIND*** is his first thriller—a book based on a career's worth of missing person cases he's investigated. Following loosely to his iHeartRadio podcast, "Paper Ghosts," this first novel in a series unites his 20 years of experience working in true-crime, having consulted on the popular Showtime series "Dexter," along with his eight years interviewing serial murderer Keith "Happy Face Killer" Jesperson.

Phelps has made over 300 hours' worth of appearances on television: *KILLER COUPLES, WICKED ATTRACTION, ICE COLD KILLERS, EVIL STEP MOMS, TWISTED, DEADLY WOMEN, SNAPPED*, and many more.

TV Rage says, "M. William Phelps dares to tread where few others will…"